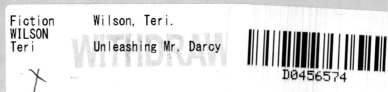

Dear Reader,

Thank you for choosing to read *Unleashing Mr. Darcy,* my debut book for Harlequin HQN. This is a book I wanted to write for a solid year before I actually put the words to the page. I was busy working on other projects, and I wasn't sure if anyone would want to read a story about Mr. Darcy set against the nutty backdrop of the dog show world.

But I couldn't let go of the idea. Sometimes I would catch myself dreaming up conversations between Darcy and Elizabeth. This happened often enough that I finally had no choice but to write the book. I had a ball. I hope it shows in the writing. And I hope you enjoy reading it as much as I did creating the story.

One of the fun challenges of writing a modern-day novel based on a classic is finding opportunities to weave in words, phrases and situations from the original text. There are many such little gems from the original *Pride & Prejudice* sprinkled throughout *Unleashing Mr. Darcy.* And for fans of the BBC film production of *Pride & Prejudice,* I threw in a special moment for you as well.

This book is the first in a three-book series of retellings of classic romances. Be sure to look for my next adventure, *Unmasking Juliet,* coming this summer.

Happy reading!

Teri Wilson

TERI WILSON

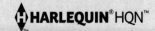

Recycling programs
for this product may
not exist in your area.

ISBN-13: 978-0-373-77835-5

UNLEASHING MR. DARCY

Printed in U.S.A.

www.Harlequin.com

For Mr. Darcy lovers everywhere.

With special thanks to my family,
Elizabeth Winick Rubinstein, super-agent,
Rachel Burkot, Tara Parsons and Susan Swinwood at Harlequin,
fellow writers Beckie Ugolini, Meg Benjamin, and Rachel Brimble,
Sue Baxter and the Baxter Borders,
the very real Bliss and Finn,
and the illustrious Jane Austen, to whom I owe a debt of gratitude.

1

It is a truth universally acknowledged that a single woman teetering on the verge of thirty is in want of a husband. Miss Elizabeth Scott, age twenty-nine years and three hundred sixty-four days, was a notable exception to this rule. Pressure from her mother notwithstanding, Elizabeth was quite content with her single status. More so in recent weeks, perhaps, than ever before. There was something about capturing the unwanted attention of a very powerful, very *married* man who couldn't take no for an answer that made her appreciate the unconditional love of her dog in an entirely new way.

Dogs were loyal.

Dogs didn't get people fired.

Dogs understood the word *no*.

Which was why spending her birthday weekend at a dog show off the Jersey Turnpike seemed like a little slice of heaven. Was there a better way to forget that her life was virtually falling apart at the seams than to spend two pleasurable days grooming her Cavalier King Charles spaniel to perfection and winning a handful of shiny satin ribbons?

No.

Elizabeth would consider it the perfect weekend, even without the ribbons. She smiled at Bliss, who blinked up at her with wide, melting eyes from her position on the grooming table. Bliss stood on her hind legs, craned her neck and swiped Elizabeth's cheek with a puppy kiss. She loved the dog, almost too much. Definitely too much, according to her sister Jenna.

"Do you know what this reminds me of?" Jenna nodded toward Bliss and smirked. "That big Barbie head you got for Christmas when you were nine. Remember? She had the hair that you could set in rollers and that gaudy blue eye shadow."

"Of course I remember." Elizabeth spritzed Bliss's ears with volumizing spray. "LuLu."

"Oh, good grief. I forgot you named it that." Jenna took a giant swig of her Starbucks and shook her head. "Who renames Barbie?"

"I do." Elizabeth eyed the latte with envy. Starbucks was exactly the type of guilty pleasure unemployed teachers— even *temporarily* unemployed ones like herself—couldn't afford. So were dog-show entry fees, for that matter. She planned on making this one count.

"Seriously. It's basically the same thing. The brushing, the blow-drying." Jenna picked up a pair of thinning shears and examined them until Elizabeth plucked them from her fingers. Those thinning shears had cost her two full days' pay.

Back when she was employed.

You're still employed. It's only a one-week suspension. Think of it as a vacation, albeit a forced vacation that you can in no way afford.

Elizabeth took a deep breath, wielded the shears over the top of Bliss's head and snipped away a few wisps of downy puppy fuzz. She drew back to take a final look. "Perfect."

Bliss yipped in agreement, and Jenna rolled her eyes. "You should have been a hairdresser, sis, instead of a teacher. I'm afraid you chose the wrong profession."

No sooner had the words left her mouth than she bit her lip to silence herself. "I'm so sorry. Poor choice of words."

Elizabeth pasted on a smile. "Forget it."

A look of chagrin crossed Jenna's features. At least Elizabeth hoped it was chagrin and not pity. "I'm an idiot. Don't pay any attention to me. You're a great teacher. The best. This whole 'administrative leave' thing is temporary. You'll have your job back before you know it. I'm an idiot, and that Grant Markham is a dog."

"Don't say that." Elizabeth pulled the grooming smock over her head and smoothed down the front of her dress. "It's an insult to dogs."

"Right." Jenna winced. "I want to make it up to you. How about a latte? My treat, birthday girl."

Elizabeth slid Bliss's show lead around her neck. If Jenna left now for Starbucks, she'd miss seeing Bliss in the ring. Not that Jenna would really mind. She didn't much care for dog shows. Elizabeth knew she'd only come because she was worried about her sister spending her birthday weekend alone. Trying to explain that she wasn't alone—she had Bliss, after all—had only made her more determined.

Sweet Jenna. Always the protective older sister.

"That would be great." Elizabeth tucked Bliss under her arm. "Pumpkin Spice. Skinny."

"I'm ordering it with whip. It's your birthday. Live a little." Jenna slung her purse over her shoulder and grinned as she disappeared through the maze of camping chairs and portable tables in the crowded grooming area of the dog show.

Elizabeth gave Bliss a little squeeze. "Just you and me, girl. Are you ready? It's showtime."

The area ringside was abuzz with nervous energy, even more so than usual. Bliss was Elizabeth's first show dog and, at nine months old, very much a puppy. They were perfectly matched in their inexperience, so butterflies were still an unquestionable fact of life. Ordinarily, the other handlers seemed to take everything in stride. Today, however, everyone was wide-eyed with concern and clustered in groups of two or three.

An eerie silence had fallen over the area around ring 5. Even the dogs had stopped barking.

Elizabeth tightened her grip on Bliss and sidled up next to one of the small groups of exhibitors who were busy whispering and furrowing their brows. "What's going on?"

"There's been a judging change." A round-faced woman with a mass of blond curls wound the length of her tricolor Cavalier's show lead around her fingers until her fingertips turned white.

"A judging change?" Elizabeth's gaze darted to the ring, but it was empty.

"Yes. Some visiting judge we've never heard of before."

Another of the exhibitors nodded and murmured behind her hand. "Rumor has it he's from England."

Elizabeth couldn't help but smile. Why were they whispering? The judge, whoever he was, wasn't even there yet. For once she was relieved to be the new kid on the block. She wasn't familiar enough with the judges to care one way or another if there was a judging change.

Simple curiosity propelled her to the giant white clipboard posted at the steward's table beside the entrance to the ring. She glanced at the top of the board, where the scheduled judge's name had been marked through with a bold, black line. Directly beneath it, simple block letters spelled out the name of the replacement.

Mr. Donovan Darcy.

Elizabeth lifted a brow.

Donovan Darcy. What kind of name is that?

A rich one, by the sound of it.

Plumbers and auto mechanics didn't name their kids Donovan. Elizabeth had worked at one of the most prestigious private schools in Manhattan long enough to learn a thing or two about blue bloods. Thus she knew good and well that a man named Donovan Darcy wouldn't have dirt under his fingernails.

She scrunched her face in disgust. Grant Markham had finely manicured hands, but that didn't make him any less dirty.

"Donovan Darcy" came a clipped British whisper over her shoulder. "Aren't we lucky?"

Elizabeth turned around to find the voice belonged to an older woman decked out in a matching tweed skirt and jacket. Rather than leading a dog around on a leash, she pushed a stack of four crates on wheels. Scruffy terrier faces peered out from the wire doors. The kind smile that reached all the way to the woman's eyes told Elizabeth her comment was sincere.

She smiled back. "Lucky? How so?"

"He's a breeder judge. His dogs are legendary. Haven't you heard of Chadwicke Kennels? The big country estate out in Derbyshire?" She didn't wait for an answer, just shook her head and made a few clucking noises before continuing. "What am I thinking? Of course you haven't. This is America. I keep forgetting."

Elizabeth could only laugh. "You keep forgetting?"

"Yes." She waved a hand toward a red-faced man organizing a stack of armbands at a grooming table. "My husband's company expanded last year. For fourteen months now we've been flitting back and forth between home and America. I'm afraid it's beginning to wear me down. Sometimes I forget where I am entirely."

"I hate to break it to you, but you're in New Jersey." Elizabeth offered her hand. "I'm Elizabeth."

"Sue. Sue Barrow." She nodded toward her husband, still at the grooming table, huffing and puffing while struggling with a wad of rubber bands. "And that's my dear Alan. Poor thing. He's not terribly fond of dog shows."

Elizabeth nodded her understanding. Alan looked about as thrilled to be there as Jenna had before she'd made her escape to Starbucks.

She swiveled her gaze back to the posted judging schedule. "So, what were you saying about this mysterious Mr. Darcy?"

"Oh, yes." A faint flush rose to Sue's cheeks. "He's wonderful. His kennel has excellent bloodlines."

For some reason, Elizabeth doubted that rosy glow had much to do with his kennel's bloodlines. "What kind of dogs does he breed? Terriers?"

Sue's flush intensified. She fanned herself with a copy of the show catalog. "He's here."

A tall gentleman with a ramrod-straight spine strode past them and into the ring. His presence brought with it a flutter to Elizabeth's heart. She tightened her grip on Bliss's leash and tried to tell herself it was a simple case of preshow jitters. Bliss looked up at her with a crease in her furry brow. Even the dog seemed to know Elizabeth was kidding herself.

Mr. Darcy was handsome. Sweaty-palms, forget-how-to-breathe handsome. Apparently, his dogs weren't the only genetic-lottery winners.

Elizabeth made an attempt to take a deep, calming breath and willed herself not to look at his intense, dark eyes or his broad shoulders, shown off to perfection with the tailored cut of his suit jacket. It wasn't easy. Everything about the man was captivating. Noble, even. Which, when she thought about it, really should have disgusted her. She'd been right, after all. Mr. Darcy was clearly wealthy. What kind of person jetted all over the globe to judge dog shows?

Good grief. He was rich, imposing and handsome enough to cause heart palpitations. Next to Elizabeth, Sue's fanning arm had gone into overdrive.

Life just wasn't fair.

Of course, Elizabeth had learned that lesson long ago. And, just in case it slipped her mind, the recent Markham incident had served as a painful reminder.

"You're up," Sue whispered.

The comment barely registered in Elizabeth's consciousness. She blinked. Somehow she was once again staring at Mr. Darcy. She must have also been hallucinating because he seemed to be staring back at her. All the breath whooshed out of her lungs. His intensity was almost crippling when it was aimed directly toward her, even though it was only in her imagination.

"Elizabeth," Sue hissed. "You're up."

The older woman gave her a shove, and she stumbled forward. Bliss let out a little yip as Elizabeth tripped over her and slammed into Mr. Darcy's impressive chest. It seemed he'd not only actually been staring at her, but he'd also taken several steps in her direction.

Horrified, Elizabeth backed up. "I'm so sorry, Your Honor.

I mean, sir…um, Mr. Darcy." Too mortified to look him in the eye, she aimed the words at his tie. It was royal-blue, by all appearances silk, and likely cost more than Elizabeth's entire ensemble. Shoes included.

The tie rose and fell with his irritated sigh. "Cavalier King Charles spaniel puppy number eight?"

"Yes, that's us."

"The steward has been calling you for two full minutes. Is something preventing you from entering the ring?"

Your exquisite bone structure? "No. I'm sorry. I was a bit… distracted."

"Would you care to enter the ring now, or do you require an engraved invitation?" His smooth voice and the beauty of his British accent did little to soften the blow of his sarcasm.

Once she got over the initial shock, Elizabeth was almost grateful for his rudeness. At least he was no longer perfect. He was a man, just like any other.

She squared her shoulders and lifted her chin. Even then she almost had to crane her neck to look him in the eye. A wasted effort, since he appeared to look right through her.

"That won't be necessary," she whispered.

"Then by all means…" He waved her through the white lattice ring gates with a flourish.

Elizabeth's cheeks burned. The other judges she'd encountered since she'd begun showing Bliss had all been friendly. Or civil, at the very least. With only three strides of his long legs, Mr. Darcy was halfway across the ring. Even at that distance, Elizabeth could still feel the frosty chill emanating from his every pore.

What is his problem?

All she could reason was that, unlike Sue, Mr. Darcy was fully cognizant that he was in New Jersey rather than his posh country estate in England. And he appeared none too pleased with this realization.

"Number eight?" From his place in the center of the ring, Mr. Darcy tapped his foot. Bliss watched it with rapt attention. "If it's not a bother…that is, if you aren't too *distracted,* could you take your dog around the ring?"

Elizabeth wasn't sure what happened in the next instant, other than that she'd finally reached her breaking point. After all she'd been through, she couldn't tolerate breathing the same air as another arrogant, wealthy man. Even one who looked more like a god than a mere mortal.

The words flew out of her mouth, as if of their own volition. "I have a name, you know."

A hush fell on the crowd of onlookers standing ringside.

Mr. Darcy crossed his arms, revealing the tips of his French cuffs and a discreet pair of gold cuff links. "I beg your pardon?"

"I have a name." Elizabeth's voice was shakier than she would have liked. She cleared her throat. "And it's not number eight."

Mr. Darcy's eyebrows rose. "Do enlighten me."

"It's Elizabeth. Elizabeth Scott."

Electric sparks of tension ricocheted around the ring, bouncing off the white lattice separating the two of them from everyone else. The only one who appeared oblivious to what was going on was Bliss. She inhaled a wide, squeaky dog yawn and curled into a ball at Elizabeth's feet.

Elizabeth poked the dog with the toe of her ballerina flat. "Bliss, get up, baby."

The Cavalier rose to her feet and glanced back and forth with her wide, round eyes from her mistress to the judge.

"Very well, then," Mr. Darcy said evenly. "Miss Scott, please take your dog around and then place her on the table."

Elizabeth gathered the end of Bliss's show lead in her left hand. Her palm was damp with perspiration, as was the back of her neck and the area between her breasts. She could only hope no one else noticed.

"Come on, Bliss. Let's go." She tried to infuse her tone with as much enthusiasm as possible.

It wasn't the loveliest lap Bliss had ever made, but Elizabeth could hardly blame the poor dog. She cooed and cajoled and, in general, made a fool of herself in an effort to get the Cavalier to perk up a bit. It felt like the longest trot around the ring in dog-show history.

When it was finally over and they reached the table, Bliss's little doggy eyebrows looked as though they were scrunched in concern. Elizabeth couldn't resist planting a tiny kiss on her head as she scooped her up and placed her on the grooming table.

In Elizabeth's experience—limited as it was—most judges gave the handler time to get the dog stacked, or posed, on the table in order to show off its beauty to its best advantage. Then there were the judges who loomed impatiently over the table, reducing the more timid dogs to quivering masses of fur with their tails stuck between their legs. For obvious reasons, Elizabeth fully expected Donovan Darcy to fall into the second category. So she was more than a little surprised when he stood back and watched from a safe distance of about five feet.

Elizabeth's hands shook as she gently picked up each of Bliss's feet and placed them an equal distance apart. Then she smoothed down the fur on Bliss's back in order to draw attention to her perfect topline. All the while, she felt Mr. Darcy's gaze on her. It burned with the force of a white-hot poker.

Despite her desperate prayers to the contrary, her fingers refused to still themselves as he approached. Elizabeth fixed her gaze on her dog. She didn't want to see the self-satisfied smirk that was sure to appear on Mr. Darcy's face when he realized he'd succeeded in rattling her nerves.

He offered his hand, palm up, to Bliss for a sniff. The Cavalier wagged her entire back end with delight. Elizabeth wished she could tell the dog to show a little self-respect.

"Miss Scott?"

She looked up at him, finally. "Yes?"

"Could you show me your dog's bite, please?" He gave her a cool smile, showcasing a charming set of dimples next to his well-formed lips.

Shame coursed through Elizabeth when she realized that if she had a tail, it would indeed be wagging. "Of course."

She peeled back Bliss's lips to display her teeth. Mr. Darcy inspected them and gave a cursory nod, and she returned her hands to Bliss's leash. Once again, she was taken aback by his gentleness as he stroked Bliss's coat and inspected her withers, rib spring and the set of her hips.

Then he stood back and crossed his arms. The smile, and accompanying dimples, vanished. "Miss Scott?"

"Yes?" Elizabeth gulped. She really wished he would stop saying her name like that. It was beginning to unnerve her. Then again, she'd asked for it.

"Take your dog down and back, please."

She scooped Bliss off the table and set her back down on the carpeted floor. As she righted herself, Elizabeth realized—a tad too late—that the V-neck of her raspberry silk wrap dress gaped open when she bent over. Horrified at the thought of flashing the very proper, and equally irritable, Mr. Darcy, her hand flew to her neckline. She sneaked a sideways glance at the judge and wished the ground would open up and swallow her whole when she noticed the amused gleam in his auburn eyes.

Oh, good God. Will this ever end?

She made a mess of the down-and-back, rushing through it to such an extent that Bliss could hardly keep up. Elizabeth no longer cared what color ribbon they took home. She just wanted to get the whole ordeal over with.

This weekend was supposed to be carefree, a time to finally escape the doubts and worries that kept her awake at night while Bliss snored peacefully in the crook of her elbow. It was her *birthday,* for goodness' sake. Her *thirtieth.* How had her troubles followed her to New Jersey?

As she crossed the ring back toward Mr. Darcy, a lump formed in her throat. Rebellious tears stung the backs of her eyes, threatening to spill over and make her humiliation complete.

She brought Bliss to a halt about an arm's distance away from him and waited for some sort of dismissal. He appraised her with one slightly arched brow in a way that made Elizabeth wonder if he was evaluating the dog's appearance or her own.

"Miss Scott."

Again with the name. The lump in Elizabeth's throat prevented her from speaking, so this time she simply nodded.

"Nice expression. Exceptionally fine eyes." He frowned, and a whole new wave of derision followed the downturn of his mouth. "It's a shame about the freckles, though."

Stunned, Elizabeth's hand fluttered to her cheek, where a tear dampened her fingertips. She hadn't even realized she'd begun to cry.

2

Donovan Darcy watched in horror as the lovely, yet clearly fragile, exhibitor's lower lip quivered. He'd seen that kind of quiver before and recognized it as the precursor to something that horrified him even more—womanly tears.

He hadn't pegged the enigmatic Miss Scott as a crier. Unpredictable, yes. Wildly attractive, most definitely.

But a crier?

Donovan wasn't a betting man, but if he were, he would have bet against it. The woman had rocked him on his heels with her whole *I have a name* outburst. And now she was standing in front of him with a tear—yes, an actual tear—making a trail down her cheek.

Donovan waited for the inevitable disdain to settle in his gut. Or, at the very least, indifference. In his experience, feminine tears served as weapons more often than displays of heartfelt emotion. That had certainly been the case with Helena Robson each of the half-dozen times he'd refused her admittance to his bed. She'd proved as much that first time, when his genuine attempt to console her had ended with a slap to his face and the insinuation that he must be gay. He'd learned his lesson. From then on, when she'd tried to turn one of his country-house parties into some kind of romantic rendezvous, a clipped *no* had been his only response, followed by the slam of his bedroom door.

Even his aunt Constance, a self-assured woman if there ever was one, had been known to shed a manipulative tear or two.

As cold as it sounded, Donovan had become immune. Which was why he was caught completely off guard by the very sudden, very real, desire to wipe away Miss Scott's tear with a brush of his thumb.

He clenched his fists in case he lost his head and reached for her. "Miss Scott, are you crying?"

"No." She blinked furiously, but not fast enough to prevent a few more tears from spilling over.

Donovan crossed his arms, even though they itched to wrap themselves around Miss Scott's slender shoulders. It was as if those arms belonged to another man entirely. "Miss Scott, I recognize tears when I see them. I urge you to get ahold of yourself. There are people everywhere."

"I don't care." She lifted her chin. It wobbled with emotion.

Donovan averted his gaze before that wobble became his undoing.

He heaved a frustrated sigh. What in God's name had convinced him coming all the way to America to judge this show was a good idea? He had more than enough on his plate back in England. Between acting as his sister's guardian and running the family foundation with his aunt Constance, he barely had time to think. Not to mention that his favorite dog, his pride and joy, was about to have puppies any day.

Poor Figgy was bursting at the seams. He'd been distracted beyond reason worrying about her.

Donovan inhaled a deep breath and directed his attention back to Miss Scott. Only then did he notice the fine sprinkling of freckles the exact color of cinnamon across her pert nose. Realization dawned, a little too late. Miss Scott obviously thought he'd been insulting her complexion, not critiquing her dog.

He let his gaze linger on her porcelain skin. The freckles only added to her charm, giving her the same sort of inviting quality as a pastry dusted with sugar and spice.

Get ahold of yourself. She's a woman, not a dessert.

Donovan moved as slowly as he could, as if approaching a spooked polo pony, and took a step closer to her. "Miss Scott..."

The careful approach was useless. She sniffed—rather loudly—and then rolled her eyes. "For God's sake, would you stop saying *Miss Scott?*"

He held up his hands in surrender. "Miss Scott is your name, is it not?"

Another sniffle. "Yes, but you make it sound so formal. It can be rather intimidating."

He lifted his brows. "Perhaps we should go back to number eight, then?"

He'd meant it as a joke, but the angry flush crawling up Miss Scott's lovely face, threatening to all but obscure those delightful freckles, told him his attempt at humor had missed its mark.

Some sort of action was most definitely in order. He'd somehow managed to lose control of his own ring in less than ten minutes.

"Miss Scott, when I expressed my disappointment in the

freckles, you do know I was referring to your dog?" He waved a hand toward her little Blenheim pup.

She looked at the dog, and her forehead crumpled in apparent confusion. Then she ran her fingertips over her cheekbones with a featherlight touch. "Oh. Of course. I knew that."

Right. Donovan couldn't resist playing with her a bit. "Did you, now?"

"Look, can you just give us our ribbon and let us go?" There was nothing remotely playful about her tone.

Donovan bristled. "Miss Scott," he began.

Her eyes flashed, switching from warm brown to fiery copper in an instant.

"Miss Scott." He enunciated with exaggerated slowness. She may have grown weary of hearing him say her name, but he wasn't about to go back to calling her number eight. "You do realize that I'm the judge and you're the exhibitor."

She gave an almost imperceptible nod. "I do."

I do.

She sounds like a bride.

The nonsensical thought blindsided Donovan. He railed against it, injecting more irritation into his tone than he intended. "And as a judge, I have the power to withhold a ribbon from your dog. Or, if I so choose, I could have you excused altogether."

She narrowed her gaze, staring daggers at him. Her slender fingers tightened around her show lead. Donovan was left with the impression of a mother bear defending her cub.

An unexpected wave of tenderness washed over him. Miss Scott clearly loved her dog. It was a condition with which he readily identified.

Donovan said nothing. After fixing his gaze on hers for a prolonged moment, he looked back down at her Cavalier.

The little dog blinked up at him with wide, expressive eyes. She really was a nice puppy, more so upon second inspection. Freckles notwithstanding.

Donovan turned and strode back to the judge's table, making the proper notation in the official book. He could feel Miss Scott's presence behind him as he surveyed the arrangement of neatly stacked ribbons at his disposal. He selected a smooth royal-blue one and offered it to her.

A smile tipped her rosy lips.

At last.

Donovan had to force himself to look away from her mouth. He cleared his throat. "I'll see you again for the Winner's Bitch competition." He couldn't resist adding, "Miss Scott."

"Thank you." The warmth returned to her eyes, changing them back to the pleasing shade of warm chocolate. "Mr. Darcy."

She smiled again, and Donovan felt his worries slowly slipping away. For the first time since he'd boarded the plane at Heathrow, all the stresses of home seemed every bit as far away as they actually were. A kind look from Miss Scott, coupled with the sound of his name coming from her sweet honey lips, was a startling balm to his troubled soul.

"Pardon me for asking—" Sue greeted Elizabeth with a wry smile as she exited the ring "—but what the hell was that?"

Elizabeth made an attempt at nonchalance and shrugged. Not an easy task when every pair of eyes ringside was trained on her. The other exhibitors were openly staring at her, slack-jawed. She wanted to crawl under the bright blue carpeting and disappear, like Bliss did under the covers whenever there was a thunderstorm. "What do you mean?"

"What do I mean? Are you seriously asking me that? After what just happened?" Sue gestured toward Mr. Darcy, waving the next group of dogs into the ring.

Elizabeth had no idea if he was watching her or not. She couldn't bear to venture a glance in his direction. She looked at Sue instead. The older woman appraised her with a look that was a peculiar combination of curiosity and sympathy. It hadn't escaped her notice that the other exhibitors were slinking away as though she had the plague or something. Only Sue Barrow remained at her side.

At that moment, Elizabeth decided she liked Sue. She liked her very much.

"Was it that bad?" Her stomach plummeted, indicating that, yes, what had transpired in the ring had indeed been *that* bad.

"I'm not sure if I would call it *bad,* per se." Sue grimaced. "Although at times it looked as though you were about to slap Mr. Darcy."

How would she ever show her face at another dog show? "Oh, my God. What have I done? I can't believe he didn't excuse me after the things I said."

"Probably because it also looked like you wanted him to kiss you."

"You must have been hallucinating."

Sue wagged a finger at her. "You can't fool me. I've been around the block a few times, dear. You don't know whether to slap that man or kiss him silly."

"Ha. As if. Never in a million years." A phrase from college English Lit ran through Elizabeth's consciousness. *"The lady doth protest too much."* Shakespeare. What a smarty-pants.

"Okay, then. Slapping it is." Sue nodded resolutely, but behind her glasses her eyes twinkled with humor. "Personally, I would have gone with the kiss, but to each her own."

"Just who are you planning on kissing?" Alan, Sue's husband, sidled up next to them. He'd obviously given up on his war with the rubber bands. At least a half dozen of them, knotted together in a spaghetti-like mess, held his armband in place.

"Only you, dear." Sue gave his cheek a fond pat. "Only you."

Elizabeth couldn't help but smile at their easy affection. It was a welcome diversion from the great slapping-versus-kissing debate. She extended her hand and introduced herself to Alan. "Hi, I'm Elizabeth."

"Cheers, Elizabeth." Like Sue, he spoke with a British accent.

For a fleeting moment, Elizabeth let her mind wander back to Mr. Darcy's similar manner of speaking. When he'd first said her name, she'd loved the way it had sounded. *Miss Scott.* So poetic. Lyrical. Alluring, even.

Then he'd gone and ruined it by insisting on saying it over and over again, until she'd wanted to strangle him with Bliss's show lead.

"Elizabeth!" Sue waved a hand in front of Elizabeth's face. "Helloooo?"

She snapped back to attention. "Yes?"

"Distracted again, are we?" Sue exchanged a knowing glance with Alan. "Thinking about Mr. Darcy, no doubt? Which was it this time? Kissing or slapping?"

"Strangulation," Elizabeth deadpanned.

Alan snorted with laughter.

"Well, here's your chance. You're up again." Sue wrapped

an arm around Elizabeth's shoulders and steered her once more to the gap in the white lattice fencing that indicated the entrance to the ring.

Somehow Elizabeth resisted the urge to turn tail and run all the way back to Manhattan. Perhaps it was the thought of all the cardboard boxes that awaited her there, ready to be filled with her personal belongings, that gave her the resilience to walk back into Mr. Darcy's ring. She had barely been able to afford her rent back when she'd had a paycheck. As much as it grieved her to admit it, her days in the fourth-floor walk-up were numbered.

Facing Mr. Darcy again didn't seem so painful when compared to the prospect of moving back home with her parents. The mere thought of it made her shudder with dread. Literally.

So she relaxed her shoulders under the pressure of Sue's grip, gave Bliss's leash a gentle tug and crossed the threshold back into Mr. Darcy's territory.

She lined up behind the winners of the other classes of the Winner's Bitch competition. Since Bliss was only a puppy, her chances of winning against the more mature dogs would have been slim under any judge. Given Mr. Darcy's apparent prejudice against freckles, Elizabeth knew they didn't have a prayer. Bliss had a few chestnut spots, which Elizabeth had always found adorable, right next to her little black nose. Of course, hers wasn't exactly an unbiased opinion. She had her own smattering of freckles across her cheekbones.

She scrunched her face and tried to pretend they weren't there. She knew Mr. Darcy was judging Bliss's appearance, not her own. He'd cleared up that humiliating misunderstanding.

But something about the way he looked at her just did

her in. Every time he turned his penetrating gaze in her direction, it was all she could do to remember her own name.

"Miss Scott."

Oh, God. Here we go again.

Well, one thing was certain. She'd never forget her name so long as Mr. Darcy kept repeating it like that.

She steeled herself and looked away from Bliss, straight into his eyes. "Mr. Darcy."

He smiled when she said his name. As infuriating as she'd found him before, she still wouldn't have believed he could become more handsome. But the smile took his breathtaking good looks to a whole new level.

She swallowed and said a little prayer of thanks that he couldn't read her thoughts.

She fully expected him to walk away, for his long legs to carry him to the other side of the ring so he could view the dogs as a group.

He didn't. He stayed right where he was, unnervingly close. "It's nice to see you again."

His voice took her by surprise in both its mere presence and its sincerity. Judges rarely spoke to individual exhibitors in a crowded ring, and certainly not about anything unrelated to the show. Part of her wondered if he was simply mocking her. Her earlier appearance in the ring could hardly be described as nice. But the haughty air about him had somehow seemed to dissipate, leaving her in a fog of confusion.

Will the real Mr. Darcy please stand up?

"Um, thank you." She kept her response brief. To the point.

What was she supposed to say? *Lovely to see you again, Mr. Darcy. The last time was such a pleasure. Let's see...I can't seem to recall which moment I enjoyed the most. Could it have been when*

I accidentally flashed you, and you looked down my dress? Or perhaps when you insulted my dog? Or maybe when I started to cry? Yes, that's it! A moment to cherish, for certain.

He paused, as if waiting for her to continue. When she didn't, thunderclouds gathered in his eyes before he finally turned away.

The exhibitor beside Elizabeth groaned under her breath. "Thanks a lot."

Elizabeth glanced at her, more out of curiosity than anything else. She was taken aback to find the woman glaring at her with hostility. "Excuse me?"

"I said thanks a lot," she hissed without moving her lips, "for putting the judge in such a foul mood. I don't know why he didn't excuse you or why he's even talking to you, for that matter."

"For your information, I'm not responsible for his mood." Elizabeth cast a fleeting look at Bliss in search of support. A nod would have been nice. A low growl perhaps?

Nothing.

The woman rolled her eyes. "We all saw the way you acted," she muttered, once again without the slightest movement of her lips.

Elizabeth was beginning to wonder if she was a ventriloquist. Probably not, she decided. How could someone who worked with puppets be so bitchy?

Elizabeth started to explain that Mr. Darcy was undoubtedly born in a bad mood, but thankfully, she caught him watching her before she opened her mouth. She turned her back on the woman and made every effort to focus solely on Bliss.

I will not screw this up. I will not make a scene. I will not flash the judge, and I most definitely will not cry.

She inhaled a deep breath. All she had to do was go through the motions and wait for the winners to be awarded their ribbons. Bliss didn't have a chance. So getting out of the ring without losing it again would be her only victory.

Mr. Darcy made a circular motion with his right hand, and everyone obediently led their dogs in a loop around the ring. The exhibitor at the front of the line paused once the lap was complete, obviously expecting Mr. Darcy to request to see each dog trot across the diagonal of the ring individually, as was customary.

Instead, he pointed at the second dog in line, a very nice little black-and-tan girl. "This is our Winner."

His announcement was met with squeals of delight from the winning exhibitor and several people standing outside the ring. Despite herself, Elizabeth felt a stab of envy. To see a judge point to Bliss like that, even once, would go a long way in helping her forget all about everything that had happened back home. It might even make nasty Grant Markham nothing but a distant memory.

Before she could give herself any kind of mental pep talk, or even quell her disappointment the slightest bit, Mr. Darcy pointed his elegant finger once more. And this time, he aimed it directly at Bliss. "And this is our Reserve Winner."

Elizabeth looked at Bliss, expecting to see a different dog on the end of her lead, as if Bliss had traded places with another Cavalier when she wasn't looking. A Cavalier with a creamy-white, freckle-less muzzle. But to her complete and utter astonishment, she found her own dog still there.

Bliss reared up and pawed at the air with her tiny fringed feet, reveling in the joy of her victory as runner-up. Her happiness caused a knot to wedge in Elizabeth's throat, and it quickly became clear that she would soon break her pledge not to cry.

She gathered Bliss into her arms and headed toward Mr. Darcy to collect her Reserve Winner's ribbon. Somewhere behind him, Elizabeth could see Sue Barrow jumping up and down and clapping like mad, but Sue was little more than a fuzzy, dreamlike vision. She was focused on one thing and one thing only—Mr. Darcy's magnetic gaze, drawing her to him. No longer stormy, his molten amber eyes pulled her in, held her spellbound, until all else disappeared.

"Miss Scott." His gaze turned questioning when she reached him. "Those are happy tears this time, are they not?"

"Yes. Very much so." She nodded and swallowed around the lump in her throat.

She had the very sudden desire for him to say it again…her name, in that debonair accent of his. *Miss Scott.* How could she have tired of hearing him say it before? It was like poetry.

He presented her with a satin ribbon. The left half was white and the right half purple, and it was printed with shiny gold letters that spelled out Reserve Winner.

She ran her thumb over the words. Seasoned dog-show exhibitors might have accepted such an honor with a tinge of disappointment. Reserve Winner was, after all, simply a fancy term for runner-up. The reserve dog didn't earn any Championship points.

But it was the highest honor ever bestowed on Bliss. Elizabeth couldn't have been happier, even if it did come from Mr. Darcy. Or perhaps *because* it came from him.

"Thank you," she breathed and tugged on the ribbon, ever so gently.

He held on to it, playfully refusing to let it go, until he gave her a liquid-gold wink. "You're welcome, Miss Scott."

As Elizabeth gripped her ribbon and floated out of the ring toward the grinning faces of Sue and Alan Barrow and Jenna, fresh from her Starbucks run, toting a venti-size paper cup in each hand, she was left with the distinct impression that Mr. Darcy, of all people, was flirting with her.

3

Elizabeth watched Jenna pick a piece of confetti out of her wineglass. Black confetti, to match the black streamers and oh-so-charming balloons tied to Elizabeth's chair that screamed to the world she was now Over-the-Hill.

"One more time…" Jenna buried the confetti in her napkin. "What does Reserve Winner mean again?"

Sue and Elizabeth exchanged an exasperated look. Hadn't they already explained this several times since arriving at the restaurant next to the show site for Elizabeth's intimate birthday gathering? *Intimate* meaning it consisted only of Elizabeth, Jenna and the Barrows.

Alan chimed in. "First runner-up."

At least he paid attention. Elizabeth doubted if any of her family members would ever know what Reserve meant, no matter how many times it was explained to them.

"Like in the Miss America pageant. I get it now." Jenna sipped her wine, likely ingesting a tiny paper coffin or two. She'd been a little heavy-handed with the decorations. "So if the winner ends up being a former stripper or if there are naked photos of her somewhere on the internet, then Bliss takes her place?"

Alan's face split into a wide grin, and he motioned toward Jenna. "I like this one."

Elizabeth laughed and took a sip of her own drink, which she'd let Sue order for her—something British called a Pimm's, which was surprisingly delicious. "Let's not forget to congratulate Sue here. You won Best of Breed today, didn't you?"

"Well, my dog did, if you want to be technical about it. And under Mr. Darcy, no less. Quite an honor. He's positively renowned back home in Britain. And all my other terriers won their classes, as well. I don't know what I would have done today without your help, Elizabeth. You're a good handler. I wished you lived in England. I could put you to work in a heartbeat. I can't very well show four dogs at once."

"Wait a minute." Jenna made a time-out motion. "The judge's name is Darcy? And he's from England? Is this a joke?"

"No. He's very much real," Elizabeth said.

If anything, he was *too* real.

"Real as can be. The English never joke about men named Darcy." Sue pushed her empty glass toward Alan. "Alan, dear, I'd love another."

"Your wish is my command." He gave Elizabeth and Jenna a questioning glance. "Anyone else need a refill?"

Much to her irritation, Elizabeth's thoughts wanted to snag on the mention of Mr. Darcy, and she had to fight to keep up with the conversation. "No, thank you."

"Have another. It's your birthday." Sue lifted her gaze to the shiny black balloons, as if Elizabeth could forget she was turning thirty. "I'm off to the loo."

Once Sue was a safe ten feet away from the table, Alan winked and then whispered to Elizabeth and Jenna, "You would never know that I own my own company and am actually the boss of about fifty people, would you? She says jump, and I ask how high."

From her spot halfway to the ladies' room, Sue waved a dismissive hand and shouted, "Whatever he's telling you, it's not true. Don't pay any attention to him."

Elizabeth laughed. "How did you know?"

Sue scurried back over to them. "Oh, please. We've been married for over forty years. I know what he's thinking even before he does."

Jenna's eyes grew misty. She'd always been a hopeless romantic. "Forty years. Wow."

"We met when we were twelve years old." Alan winked again. Only this time, he aimed it at his wife. "I've loved her ever since."

Jenna held her glass of wine toward them, as if giving a toast at a wedding. "Cutest. Couple. Ever."

Elizabeth could only agree. And for a split second, she wondered if she was wrong about marriage, after all. Maybe there were good men out there, as Jenna and her mother so often insisted. Maybe there was a man somewhere who would look at her like Alan looked at Sue, even after forty years together. They couldn't all be Grant Markhams. Could they?

As Sue and Alan went off on their respective errands and Jenna checked her phone for text messages, Elizabeth sipped her Pimm's and gave herself permission to think about Donovan Darcy. Only for a minute, she decided. She'd been doing her best to forget him ever since they'd left the show site, but that had been before the black balloons.

And the alcohol.

Like Grant Markham, he was certainly rich. And powerful. Those two qualities alone would have been enough to make most women swoon. Elizabeth was not, however, most women. She knew firsthand how dangerous such a combination could be. And, to top it off, Donovan Darcy had already proved that his words weren't always as pretty as his face.

The man was a mystery, equal parts beautiful and maddening. Sue had been right. Elizabeth had wanted to slap him, right across his gorgeous face. Then he'd gone and switched gears on her, awarding Bliss Reserve and turning on his British charm. Elizabeth wondered if he had any idea how overpoweringly appealing he could be when he wasn't scowling.

Oh, yes, he knows, she decided. *He can probably turn it on and off on command. They probably teach it over there in some kind of James Bond charm school.*

Feeling a little shaken, and more than a little stirred, she aimed her attention back at Jenna. "Thank you, big sis."

Jenna looked up from her phone. "What for?"

"For coming this weekend." Elizabeth smiled. "And for this little party. It's perfect." *Aside from the morbid decorations, but let's not get picky.*

"I'm afraid you might not think so after..." Jenna's voice drifted off, and her eyes grew wide as she focused on something in the distance. "Who is *that?*"

Elizabeth knew without even turning around in her chair that her sister was looking at none other than Donovan Darcy. In the flesh. Her cheeks grew hot with embarrassment, as if she'd conjured him simply by indulging in a little harmless daydreaming.

She glanced over her shoulder. Sure enough, there he stood, at the hostess stand. Glowering, as usual.

Elizabeth glowered right back, until he aimed his gaze directly toward her.

Damn.

He'd caught her openly staring at him. She tried to tell herself otherwise, that he hadn't even noticed. The slow grin that came to his lips told a story all its own, however. He most definitely had noticed. And it appeared to please him.

She looked away, took a deep breath and tried to calm the frantic beating of her heart.

If ever there was a man who embodied the word *dangerous,* it was him. Elizabeth would sleep better at night when he went back to England and there was a vast, fathomless ocean between them.

Jenna cleared her throat. "I said, *who* is *that?*"

"Who?" Elizabeth feigned innocence to buy herself more time to regain her composure.

"You know who." Jenna lifted a brow in Mr. Darcy's direction.

Great. Now he knows we're talking about him. She wished she could shrink small enough to crawl into the tiny plastic coffin that sat atop her birthday cake in the center of the table.

"Oh, him." Elizabeth doubted she was fooling anyone with her attempt at nonchalance, least of all Jenna. "That's the judge from this afternoon. Our very own Mr. Darcy."

Jenna's gaze grew even more appreciative, if such a thing were possible. "That explains why he looks like he just climbed down from a polo pony."

"Didn't you see him earlier today at the show?"

Jenna shook her head. "No. Definitely not. I was actually looking at the dogs."

That was a first. "Well, don't let those good looks fool you. He's an ass."

"He looks like Daniel Craig's younger, hotter brother. And besides, he almost crowned Bliss Miss America. How big of an ass can he be?"

Where to start? "You have no idea."

"Let me guess." Jenna returned her glass to the table with a little too much force. Wine sloshed to the rim, threatening to spill over onto the crisp white tablecloth. "He's rich."

"Of course he is." Elizabeth plucked a piece of tombstone-shaped confetti from her lap and rolled it between her fingers.

Jenna leaned forward, her gaze probing. "And that automatically makes him an ass?"

"It doesn't help his case." Elizabeth squirmed. Jenna looked as though she was on the verge of a full-on lecture. Where was Alan with her refill? She could use a sip of Pimm's—or wine, or anything with alcohol, really—right about now.

"Not all rich men are like you-know-who. There are a few decent wealthy people in the world." Jenna crossed her arms and gave her a look somewhere between smug and sympathetic.

"Name one." Elizabeth sat back and waited, sure she'd found just the words to silence her sister.

She was wrong.

"I'll name two." Jenna's voice softened. "Alan and Sue."

Elizabeth glanced at the bar, where Alan Barrow stood chatting up the bartender, his face split into an endearing grin. "Alan and Sue?"

"Surely you've realized they're rich. They divide their time between London and New York. She raises Champion dogs and shows them all over the world. Did you think they were poor?"

Elizabeth slumped a little lower in her chair. "I hadn't given it any thought, actually."

"Well, maybe you should." Jenna reached over and gave her hand a squeeze. "And maybe you shouldn't be so quick to label that hot judge an ass."

Elizabeth stole another quick glance in his direction.

He appeared to be studying a menu, but everything about his countenance said he was fully aware the two sisters were talking about him. His lingering wry smile, the subtle gleam of satisfaction in his eyes...the casual way he crossed his feet at the ankles and leaned against the doorjamb of the entryway—all a deliberate, and successful, attempt at looking carelessly sexy.

Or maybe he just really was that sexy without even trying.

It was infuriating.

Elizabeth turned back to Jenna, full of fresh indignation. "Jenna, you never see a fault in anybody. But I assure you, Mr. Darcy thinks awfully highly of himself. You weren't there. You didn't see how he treated me in the ring today."

"Well, here's my chance." Jenna took a larger-than-usual gulp of her wine. "Don't look now, but he's coming over here."

Elizabeth stiffened. "He is not."

"Yes, he is." Jenna muttered a countdown under her breath. "In four, three, two, one."

She sounded like Mission Control.

Elizabeth's stomach churned with each passing second. *Houston, we have a problem...*

"Miss Scott."

She opened her eyes and found him looking down at her with a gracious smile. Gracious, but somehow still sexy.

She returned his greeting in a neutral tone. "Good evening, Mr. Darcy."

"Are birthday wishes in order?" He motioned toward the balloons tied to her chair, which she'd conveniently forgotten about, and the cake with its black plastic coffin topper.

The decorations looked even tackier next to him. Elizabeth wanted to die. Since that wasn't an option, she opened her mouth to affirm that, yes, she was indeed the one who'd become over-the-hill. But before she could utter a word, a very pretty, very *young* woman joined him at his side.

"Zara." Mr. Darcy turned and gave her a kiss on the cheek.

As she watched him welcome his lady friend, Elizabeth couldn't help but notice two things. First, this Zara woman was nowhere near over-the-hill. With her slim hips and luminescent skin, she looked as though she'd never even seen the hill, much less crossed over it. And second, when he looked at her, Mr. Darcy didn't show an ounce of the coldness he'd had on full display since Elizabeth had first laid eyes on him. In fact, he practically oozed warmth and charm.

Well, looky here. Mr. Darcy is all politeness.

Elizabeth couldn't stand to watch. For reasons she doubted she would ever understand, her insides twisted into a jealous knot. Such intense feelings only irritated her even more because the entire scene was so ridiculous—so cliché—that any attraction she'd ever felt toward Mr. Darcy should have evaporated on the spot. He was rich, handsome, arrogant and, apparently, some young girl's sugar daddy.

Elizabeth glared at Jenna, sending her unspoken I-told-you-so's with her eyes. Jenna didn't seem to notice. She was too busy studying Zara's handbag. Louis Vuitton, by all appearances. Elizabeth doubted it came from a van in a fishy-smelling back alley in Chinatown, like the one where Jenna had purchased her Vuitton last year on a trip to the city.

Jenna had a thing for handbags. Elizabeth really should consider giving her the Prada bag she'd recently acquired—a Christmas gift from one of her students. It was only one of a number of ridiculously extravagant gifts that had turned up on her desk during the holidays. The parents at the Barclay School weren't above trying to buy special attention for their children.

Or other things.

"I'm sorry." Mr. Darcy swiveled his admiring gaze away from Zara and back toward Elizabeth. "This is…"

Elizabeth cut him off. "Zara. Yes, we heard."

"Elizabeth!" Jenna's sharp reprimand was accompanied by a swift kick to the shin underneath the table.

Elizabeth, shin throbbing, lifted her chin with as much dignity as someone sitting in front of a death-themed cake could muster. "And yes, it's my birthday."

She turned away, not only so she wouldn't have to look at him with his beautiful, young companion but also so he wouldn't see the wounded expression that was surely written all over her face. A wounded expression for which she had no reasonable explanation. Jealous? Over Mr. Darcy?

Not only was she over-the-hill, but apparently she'd been hit with early-onset dementia.

"Happy birthday, then." His words bounced off her back, hollow as they were. Every cutting syllable told her he knew he'd been dismissed. "I'll let you get back to your celebration."

And then, right when Elizabeth thought the worst of the evening was over, an unmistakable, shrill "Happy Birthday" pierced the air.

No. This is not happening. This can't *be happening.*

Elizabeth prayed that she was mistaken and that perhaps Pimm's contained some sort of hallucinogen.

But when she heard them burst into song, Elizabeth cringed and turned around. Sure enough, right over Mr. Darcy's left shoulder, she saw the top of her mother's favorite outrageous flowered hat.

"I'm sorry," Jenna whispered. "I started to tell you…"

A frozen smile found its way to Mr. Darcy's lips. He slipped his arm around Zara and looked as though he wanted to sling her over his shoulder, caveman-style, and run for the nearest exit. If Elizabeth hadn't been so mortified, she would have found it at least somewhat humorous.

"Mom," she said. "What a surprise."

"Oh, it's not just me. Gracie, Laura and Heather are here. And your father, too, of course." Her mother waved a hand toward the entrance, where Elizabeth's younger sisters were bickering over something as they made their way to the table.

Behind them, with his head bent over his BlackBerry, her father pulled up the rear. He smiled at her, almost apologetically. "We've all come to surprise you for your birthday. Are you surprised?"

"Very." Panic had begun to edge its way into Elizabeth's voice. If she didn't somehow get rid of Mr. Darcy soon, he would be wedged in on all sides by her family members. "I told you I'd be fine celebrating my birthday at the dog show. Alone. You didn't need to make the trip out here."

"Alone." Her mother shook her head. "It's a pity none of you girls have found a nice husband to keep you company on such occasions."

Oh, no. Oh, God, no.

Elizabeth wanted to leap across the wineglasses, the cake, the mortifying decorations and clamp her hand across her mother's mouth. If she thought for a moment she could actually hurdle the table with its crisp white cloth—the better to show off the glittery black confetti—she would have done it in a heartbeat. But she'd never been terribly athletic. Now that she was over-the-hill, especially, she doubted any move she could make would be fast enough to compete with her mother's quick tongue.

Sure enough, before Elizabeth could move a muscle, her mother was at it again.

"It's such a pity about your job, too. I mean, that was the perfect opportunity for you to cross paths with rich men." Mrs. Scott shook her head, the feathers on her hat waving with her every move. "Don't you worry about a thing, dear. You'll just move back home and work for the family business. Scott Bridal needs someone to model the wedding gowns, and you're the perfect size. We'll get you in a white veil one way or another."

Elizabeth's mother laughed, seemingly oblivious to the awkward glances being exchanged around the table. Elizabeth felt someone reach for her hand and give it a squeeze. Jenna.

"I'm sorry," Jenna whispered. "When I invited them, I thought it would only be us."

The frantic urge to leap across the dishware left Elizabeth as quickly as it came. It was too late now. The humiliation train had already left the station. She stared down at her lap and her hand in Jenna's, oblivious to whatever else was going on around her, save for Mr. Darcy and his beautiful companion making a quiet escape.

"I would ask who your friend is, but the dirty look she gave you made it clear that you two aren't exactly close." Zara looked past Donovan, in the direction of Elizabeth's table.

Once seated, Donovan had turned his back on the train wreck that was apparently Elizabeth Scott's birthday dinner. He couldn't bear to watch another second of it. Although, as with any other gruesome oddity, he felt inexplicably drawn to the scene. Fortunately—or not, depending on how he looked at it—Zara possessed the same penchant for gossip as most other eighteen-year-old girls and insisted on giving him a play-by-play of the goings-on.

"Oh, my God. You should see the mother now. She's chewing with her mouth so wide open I can see her molars. I think one of them is gold." The look on Zara's face teetered between one of horror and fascination.

"Zara, stop staring. It's rude." Donovan tapped his index finger on the drinks menu, hoping the waitress would notice and hurry over to take his order. God, he needed a drink. Or three.

"I'm not staring." She dragged her gaze away from the Scotts' table, clearly marked for all the world to see with those horrid balloons.

At the memory of the Over-the-Hill balloons bobbing about Elizabeth Scott's beautiful face, Donovan's finger tapping went into overdrive. He didn't know how much longer he'd be able to sit there without the distraction of a martini. Or a Pimm's. Anything, really. If Donovan were the knight-in-shining-armor type, which he most definitely was not, he would march right over there, snatch Elizabeth Scott from her seat and take her somewhere far, far away. Precisely where, he had no idea. Somewhere quiet. Somewhere intimate. And, most definitely, somewhere without balloons.

Not that Elizabeth Scott would welcome a rescue, at least not by his hand.

"Why are you scowling?"

Donovan was forced to tear his thoughts away from Miss Scott, *again,* and focus instead on Zara. "I'm not scowling."

"Yes, you are." Zara knit her brows and gave him her best grimace. She'd always enjoyed imitating him. "I know you like a brother, remember?"

"I *am* your brother." Donovan felt himself relax ever so slightly.

"The best." She aimed her sweetest grin at him.

"You can stop kissing up. We're here, aren't we? America. Just like you wanted." If Donovan had a soft spot, Zara was it. She'd been not only his responsibility but the entirety of his immediate family since the death of their parents. She was certainly the only person who could tear him away from Figgy and the impending arrival of the puppies. Her burning desire to finally see the Big Apple was the deciding factor in his acceptance of the judging assignment.

Not that suburban New Jersey felt anywhere close to New York City.

But they would remedy that tomorrow. After a day or two of taking Zara sightseeing and shopping, he would be on his way back home. Surely Figgy would hold off until then. And if not…well, that was why he had full-time kennel staff.

Donovan hoped it wouldn't come to that. Figgy was special. He wanted to be there himself for her first litter.

The waitress finally arrived, and Donovan relaxed even further knowing he was within minutes of a cocktail. Anything to dull the memory of Miss Scott's family. More specifically, her mother. Even now, he could hear her shrill laugh from across the room. And if he had a penny for every time he heard her bellow something about rich men, he could add a new wing onto his country house.

Once again, Zara's gaze drifted over his shoulder. "So, what's the story over there?"

"I've no idea." Donovan shook his napkin and arranged it across his lap. "A birthday celebration, I gather."

Although it looked more like an exercise in humiliation.

He couldn't help thinking Miss Scott deserved better. Few didn't.

"No. I mean, what's with you and the pretty one? What did you say her name was?"

"Elizabeth." Donovan lowered his voice, not that anyone would hear him over the mother. "Elizabeth Scott."

"So you *do* think she's pretty, then?" Zara grinned, obviously pleased with herself.

"Calm down, Zara. There's nothing going on between Miss Scott and me." Donovan wasn't sure why, but this admission brought a pang to his temple.

"Why? Because of her crazy family?" Zara shook her head. "Poor thing."

"No." Donovan accepted his drink from the waitress and took a long sip. Somehow, it didn't put any distance between him and the spectacle at the Scotts' table. In fact, the urge to go over there and rescue her grew even stronger.

Maybe it's the jet lag, he reasoned.

Donovan pushed his drink away. Perhaps lowering his inhibitions wasn't the best idea.

Zara, in all her trademark tenacity, wasn't about to abandon her line of questioning. "So, why haven't you made a move?"

"Because I'm here to judge a dog show. And to take you on a little sightseeing trip." Donovan massaged his temples.

And because she despises the very sight of me.

Zara leaned forward and lowered her voice to a conspiratorial whisper. "Ask her for a drink or something. I'll get an in-room movie back at the hotel. Now's your chance...."

Donovan cut her off, ready to put an end to the conversation. His undeniable attraction to Miss Scott was unsettling enough, given that the feeling was most definitely not mutual. The last thing he needed was to be on the receiving end of this relentless badgering from his sister. "Zara, enough. I find Miss Scott tolerable. Nothing more, nothing less. If you think you can convince me otherwise, you're wasting your time."

"Um." The color drained from Zara's face.

Donovan sighed. He'd been abrupt, no doubt. But he hadn't meant to hurt her feelings. He opened his mouth to apologize, but before he could get a word out, Miss Scott slipped past him.

Donovan felt her presence before he actually saw her. It was the same stirring sensation that had come over him in the ring—an odd combination of tranquillity and awareness. Miss Scott was like the final, still moment of dusk that held the promise of a fiery sunset.

He lifted his gaze to hers, hoping for the impossible, that she hadn't heard his frustrated diatribe meant solely for Zara's ears.

But the smallest glance was enough to know.

Elizabeth Scott had heard every word.

4

Monday morning, Elizabeth opened her eyes, and for a split second, panic set in. She glanced at the clock on her nightstand, heart pounding, convinced she'd overslept and the students in her first-period class were sitting at their desks pondering the whereabouts of their teacher.

It didn't take long for reality to set in.

Get real. They're teenagers. That's the last thing they'd be pondering, even if I were late.

She wasn't late.

It wasn't possible to be late when she wasn't even expected at school. Elizabeth closed her eyes, imagined the fresh-faced substitute teacher who was sitting at her desk right that very second and opened them again. Reality, as bleak as it was, was better than thinking about what should have been.

On the pillow beside her, Bliss yawned with abandon and stretched into a downward-dog position. Clearly the Cavalier wasn't experiencing any difficulty adjusting to their new routine. Or nonroutine. Whichever.

At least the sight of her dog brought a smile to Elizabeth's face. Until she remembered, with excruciating clarity, the events of the weekend. How had the dog-show getaway she'd been anticipating for so long gone so horribly wrong?

She would have liked to blame it on her mother. With her garish hat and unfiltered approach to conversation—and life in general—she was hardly innocent. As were the other members of the Scott family. Save for Jenna, of course. For once, though, Elizabeth couldn't hold her family 100 percent responsible for her mortification. True, she'd been embarrassed beyond belief when they'd shown up at dinner. Her mother had managed to make reference to both Elizabeth's career crisis and single status in the first three seconds. Impressive, even for her mother.

In all honesty, things had started going south earlier in the day. More precisely, the minute Elizabeth had first laid eyes on Donovan Darcy. Okay, maybe five minutes or so *after* first laying eyes on him. Those initial moments she'd been too busy ogling him to notice the downward spiral she was about to fall into.

Mr. Darcy.

The thought of his name brought with it a tumble of emotions. First and foremost on the list was humiliation.

Tolerable.

He'd called her tolerable. It was almost worse than being called hideous. Having never been called tolerable, or hideous for that matter, Elizabeth couldn't be sure.

Forget him. Who calls someone tolerable? A conceited ass, that's who. The whole thing is ridiculous. He's ridiculous.

Elizabeth hopped out of bed. She wasn't about to spend the day lounging around thinking about Mr. Darcy. Not even if those thoughts included slow and painful ways to kill him. There was plenty of time for that later. She needed to

stop by the school and pick up her personal effects. And—
fingers crossed—have a little chat with the headmaster while
she was there.

"Wish me luck, Bliss," Elizabeth muttered, after she'd
showered and changed.

She and Bliss were not moving to New Jersey. Elizabeth
would not, *could* not, do it. She would never survive working
at Scott Bridal. She didn't know how Jenna did it, day in and
day out. Then again, Jenna was a saint. Elizabeth had never
met anyone nearly as patient as her elder sister. Maybe that
was her secret to surviving the family business. Elizabeth, on
the other hand, didn't have the stomach for it. She couldn't
show her face in the state of New Jersey without her mother
sticking a veil on her head. Since she'd moved to Manhattan,
she and Bliss had settled into a nice, peaceful routine. Entire
days passed where no one around her uttered the name Vera
Wang. It was like heaven.

She held on to the fragile certainty that everything would
work out as she headed uptown to the Barclay School. Situated in the posh Upper West Side, the private school had
been responsible for educating the offspring of New York's
elite for over a century. When Elizabeth had first walked
through the enormous carved doors into the lobby, which
boasted a gilded replica of the school's seal on the marble tile
floor, she'd felt as though she could conquer the world, or at
least the part that resided close to Central Park West. Now,
as she walked through those same doors, her emotions were
decidedly different.

Gone was the happy optimism she'd come to associate
with the school. *Her* school, as she'd taken to calling it. Despite the fact that the students' average weekly allowance was

likely quadruple her monthly take-home pay, she'd always felt at home here.

Until the day she'd dared to give Grant Markham's son a failing grade.

Since then, all hell had broken loose. And with the ensuing scandal came the unshakable feeling that Elizabeth was somehow less than adequate.

Subpar.

Tolerable.

The word echoed in her subconscious.

Damn you, Donovan Darcy.

"Elizabeth." Mrs. Whitestone, the school secretary, greeted her with a stiff smile.

"Hi, Mrs. Whitestone. I'm here to pick up my things and perhaps have a word with Dr. Thurston." Dr. Thurston. Just last week, Elizabeth had called the headmaster by his first name, Ed. "Is he in?"

"Yes, he is. Go on in. I believe he wants to have a word with you, as well."

The tiniest amount of relief coursed through Elizabeth. The headmaster wanted a word with her. That sounded promising. Maybe, just maybe, her administrative leave would be cut short and she'd be back in the classroom before the day was over.

Ed's door opened. "Elizabeth," the headmaster boomed. "Please, come in."

Any relief she felt vanished when he escorted her inside the office and took his place behind his desk. He looked rather red. And very, very serious. "I'm glad you stopped by. There are some new circumstances surrounding your suspension that we need to discuss."

Elizabeth's hands began to shake. She clasped them together so Ed wouldn't notice. "I'm sorry?"

"I'm afraid this…situation…has grown complicated."

Nothing like a little bribery to turn something as simple as a failing report card into a *situation*.

Although it wasn't technically bribery. More like *attempted* bribery. She hadn't for a moment considered accepting the five-figure check that Grant Markham had tossed at her during their parent-teacher conference.

Correction: checks. Plural.

The more she'd refused him, the more insistent he'd become. He'd written one check after another, as if the problem had been the amount of the bribe, rather than its inherent wrongness.

"How much?" he'd finally asked, leaning close, his breath hot against her skin. "Women like you—the ones who come from nothing—always have a price. Why don't you save us both some time and tell me what it is?"

Those words had reached inside her, touching on her deepest insecurities. It was hard to grow up around the tulle and lace at Scott Bridal without sometimes feeling like an impoverished Cinderella among a whole world of entitled stepsisters. Their clientele were the sort who believed that a fat wallet could buy them anything. Truth be told, it usually did.

Women like you…the ones who come from nothing.

Stunned into silence, she'd been unable to do little more than watch in horror as Grant Markham had casually touched the inside of her wrist. His fingertips had crept upward, and his gaze had flicked ever so briefly to her breasts.

He hadn't made an outright pass at her, but the implication had been clear. He could buy her silence. And he could buy *her*. The only thing standing in his way was the matter of compensation.

In retrospect, she probably shouldn't have slapped him. Perhaps if she'd just walked away right there and then, she wouldn't be in this mess. Maybe Grant Markham wouldn't have gone to the headmaster. Maybe he wouldn't have disputed his son's grade and insisted Elizabeth be placed on administrative leave for a week while an independent auditor looked at her grade book.

Or maybe it wouldn't have made a difference at all. Slap or no slap, he still hadn't gotten his way.

Yet.

"I suppose things have become rather ugly." Elizabeth nodded her agreement. "But as I told you before, Grant Markham wouldn't take no for an answer. His behavior was most inappropriate. I hope..."

The headmaster held up a hand to stop her, just as Mr. Darcy had done in the show ring on Saturday. In this context, it wasn't quite as infuriating. In fact, it was daunting.

Elizabeth obediently shut her mouth.

"There's more to this than Joe Markham's grade. Much more."

Joe was a nickname. His full name was Grant Markham III. Why did rich people insist on using the same names over and over again?

Elizabeth wondered if Donovan Darcy came from a long line of Donovans. Then she gave her thigh a good, solid pinch. A punishment. Because really, what was she doing thinking about Mr. Darcy at a time like this? It was absurd.

She cleared her throat. "You don't need to explain. I know Joe is the captain of the rugby team. His failing grade made him ineligible for the play-offs. People were upset. I realize that. But Grant Markham cannot expect me to change his son's grade in exchange for money."

Ed clasped his hands together on his desk and shook his head. "I've spoken with Mr. Markham. He's aware of your accusations, and he disputes them. Quite vehemently."

Of course he does. "I can't say I'm surprised. I didn't think he would admit that he tried to bribe me."

Or that he'd hinted at an affair. She still hoped she'd only imagined that part.

"Actually, he says the money was your idea." Ed's voice was low. So low Elizabeth almost didn't hear it.

"My idea?" It was a slap to the face, every bit as real as the one she'd given Grant Markham.

"Yes. Mr. Markham says you attempted to extort money from him in exchange for giving his son a passing grade." He leveled his gaze at her. Worry lines creased his forehead, which appeared to be growing redder by the second. "He also mentioned a designer handbag."

The Prada. Elizabeth was overcome with a sudden numbness. "That was a Christmas gift. You know how the parents around here are. The head of the athletic department was given season tickets to the Yankees for Christmas."

Elizabeth hated the way her voice shook. She would have rather sounded confident, offended even, in the face of such an accusation.

She was neither of these things. At the moment, she was terrified.

"Elizabeth." Ed, no, Dr. Thurston—Elizabeth was certain she would never again address this man by his common name—exhaled another sigh and looked back down at his clasped hands. The top of his head glowed redder than ever. As Elizabeth stared at it, she prayed he didn't keel over while she was sitting in his office, lest she become not only the teacher who'd tried to extort money from parents, but also the one who'd killed the headmaster.

He looked back up, still alive. Thank God. "There will be an investigation, of course."

"An investigation?" This should have been good news, of course. What could an investigation turn up when she'd done nothing wrong? For some reason, it failed to put Elizabeth at ease.

"The investigation will be handled internally." Dr. Thurston tugged at his shirt collar, causing the knot in his tie to tilt crookedly.

Elizabeth fought the urge to straighten it, a quirk she'd acquired during all those years she'd spent at Scott Bridal while she was growing up. She could recognize a perfectly crafted Windsor knot from a mile away. Dr. Thurston's was far from perfect. "Internally? What does that mean, exactly?"

"The board of directors will be looking into the matter."

The board of directors.

A sinking feeling settled in Elizabeth's stomach. Grant Markham's wife was on the board of directors. So were nine other people the Markhams had likely had over to dinner, probably on their yacht or something, throughout the years. Elizabeth's fate was in the hands of the alleged victim's wife and her high-society friends.

It was over. She was finished.

Elizabeth sat quietly, trying to absorb it all. "So what happens now? Do I need to get a lawyer?"

"No. A lawyer wouldn't be able to help you, anyway. As your contract states, your position here can be withdrawn at any time, for any reason. But let's not get ahead of ourselves. In a few weeks, perhaps this will blow over. For now, your suspension stands until the conclusion of the investigation. At that time, the board will determine a permanent outcome." He released a heavy sigh. "Elizabeth, you're a wonderful teacher. I'm not saying I don't believe you. I'm not saying that at all, but the financial stability of this school hinges on how we handle this situation. The Barclay School is a private institution, and it depends on tuition payments to keep the doors open."

So it all boiled down to money. Didn't everything? "How long should the investigation take?"

"According to the bylaws, four weeks."

Four weeks. Approximately three weeks longer than she could afford her Manhattan apartment without the benefit of a regular paycheck.

Perhaps it was a good thing Elizabeth still possessed the skills she would need at Scott Bridal. Because, come next Monday morning, she'd probably be clocking in bright and early. Her head was already itching for a veil.

Dr. Thurston urged her to take advantage of her time off—to go on a vacation, enjoy some downtime. Elizabeth barely heard a word he said. She was too distraught to concentrate. Before she knew what was happening, he was finished with his speech and had steered her by the elbow out of his office, across the marble floor with the fancy school seal, directly to the big carved double doors.

She glanced up at her boss before walking through those doors for what she fully expected was the last time. At some point he'd straightened his tie.

"Goodbye, Dr. Thurston," she whispered.

And then she was out the door, standing on the busy Manhattan sidewalk, as though the school had purged itself of her.

The sounds of honking horns and sirens wailing in the

distance, ordinarily so familiar and comforting to Elizabeth, were a shock to her system after the stillness of the headmaster's office. She stood motionless, trying to get her bearings as New Yorkers, clothed in standard black, wove around her as if she were a statue. She found it odd that no one stopped to stare at her, the teacher who'd been accused of extortion. Surely such a damning accusation was somehow visible, even to strangers. A scarlet letter of sorts, only shaped like a big fat dollar sign.

Elizabeth turned in the direction of her apartment. It took all her concentration to put one foot in front of the other. She felt faint, as if she were about to disappear. She focused on her shoes—sensible black ballet flats—and each step they took, making sure they made contact with the asphalt.

She narrowly collided with a pair of black, square-toed boots and teetered perilously close to the curb. No sooner had she managed to get back on track than she found herself toe to toe with a pair of men's loafers—black, of course. Beside the loafers was a pair of ballet flats not unlike her own. Only these were quilted, with interlocking C's on the toes. Elizabeth had seen those same flats on the girls at the Barclay School. Chanel.

Elizabeth paused and waited for Loafers and Chanel to sidestep so she could pass. They didn't.

"Excuse me." Elizabeth looked up and in a heart-stopping moment discovered that her day, which had been far from stellar thus far, had just taken a turn for the worse.

The loafers didn't belong to some nameless, faceless New Yorker. They belonged to none other than Mr. Donovan Darcy.

He knit his perfect brows and said her name as though it were a question. "Miss Scott?"

Elizabeth panicked for a moment, as if she didn't know the answer. She looked over at the woman standing beside him, the owner of the Chanel flats, and recognized her as his companion from the restaurant in New Jersey. Zara.

Good grief, she looks even younger than I remember.

"Hi," Zara said and gave a little wave.

Elizabeth was struck with the nauseating thought that she didn't look a day older than Joe Markham.

This realization brought with it a fresh wave of annoyance. How was she the one in trouble when Donovan Darcy was dating a girl barely out of high school?

"Mr. Darcy," she spat. She turned to Zara and pasted on a smile. "Zara."

"What are you doing here?" To Mr. Darcy's credit, he didn't come off as rude when he asked her this. He sounded befuddled, in an oh-so-charming-Hugh-Grant sort of way.

Elizabeth wasn't fooled. She remembered the Hugh Grant scandal of the nineties with perfect clarity. Not pretty. "I live here."

"In New York City? Alone?" He looked at the empty space around her own non-Chanel ballerina flats, as if he expected someone to materialize.

Alone? Who did he think he was? Her mother? "Yes, alone. Not that it's any of your business."

"I didn't mean to pry." He crossed his arms, and Elizabeth caught a glimpse of his cuff links. Silver this time, like the ones that were always on display in the windows at Tiffany's.

As at the dog show, everything about Mr. Darcy's appearance was resplendent. From the polished sheen of his loafers to the narrow cut of his suit. And Elizabeth couldn't help but notice his tie was folded into the most perfect Windsor she'd ever laid eyes on. Of course.

Given the many bridegrooms Elizabeth had seen at Scott Bridal who didn't know the top end of a cummerbund from the bottom, she'd always found men who dressed well particularly sexy.

Damn.

"Miss Scott, I think you misunderstood me. I was only wondering about your charming little dog, the Blenheim Cavalier. Bliss, right?"

Despite the warning bells going off in her head reminding her that this was Mr. Darcy of all people, she found herself softening toward him. Just a little.

How many dogs did a dog-show judge see in a weekend? Hundreds, at least. Maybe even a thousand.

And he'd remembered Bliss's name.

She relaxed ever so slightly and gave herself permission to smile at Mr. Darcy. "She's at home. I had to, um, run an errand."

He smiled back. "I hope she's doing well."

"She is. Thank you."

Elizabeth wasn't sure what else to say. Her gaze flitted to Zara, who stood quietly watching their exchange. If it bothered her that Mr. Darcy had stopped dead in his tracks to carry on a conversation with another woman, she gave no indication of it. Then again, why would it bother her? She'd heard him call her tolerable. She knew Elizabeth was no threat.

At the very least, Elizabeth figured Zara would be ready to move on and away from the pedestrians who jostled their way around their little threesome. Oddly enough, she didn't seem to care a whit about any of it.

Elizabeth glanced back at Mr. Darcy. His dark eyes were trained on her, watching her with his trademark intensity.

Her first instinct was to look away, but the unexpected earnestness in those brooding eyes made her fix her gaze on his.

He looked at her for a long, silent moment before he finally spoke. "I'm afraid you've misunderstood a few things I've said."

Something about his gaze was so tender, Elizabeth could feel it down to her toes. And she couldn't quite put her finger on it, but somehow she knew he was referring to the *tolerable* comment. If it were possible for a person to make amends with just a look, Donovan Darcy was giving it a go.

Elizabeth was captivated. She felt as though they were the only two people on the busy sidewalk. Impossible, of course. People swarmed all around them, not to mention the very-present Zara.

Then Elizabeth's handbag barked, breaking the magic spell.

Zara's baby-smooth forehead creased in apparent confusion. "Was that a bark?"

Mr. Darcy tilted his head and lifted an amused brow. "Are you sure Bliss is at home? It sounds as though she hitched a ride in your purse."

"It's my ringtone." Elizabeth fished around in her bag for her barking phone. "I should probably answer this. It could be important."

In fact, the likelihood of the call being important was slim at best. It was just something to say, a way to extricate herself from what was beginning to feel oddly like some sort of love triangle.

Love triangle. As if.

Elizabeth wanted to kick herself.

Instead, she answered the phone. "Hello?"

Mr. Darcy stood right where he was, rooted to the spot. Why wasn't he leaving? What was he doing here, anyway? Although the collection of shopping bags dangling from Zara's slender arms hinted at the purpose of their trip. Chanel. Gucci. And especially nauseating, Prada.

Elizabeth averted her gaze before she spotted a bag from Tiffany's. She didn't think she'd be able to stomach such a thing.

"Elizabeth, dear, is that you? It's Sue. Sue Barrow."

"Oh, Sue. How wonderful to hear from you."

As she spoke, Elizabeth was aware of Mr. Darcy watching her mouth. She was sure it was because she was talking. What else did he have to look at? Still, it unnerved her in a way she was ashamed to admit wasn't altogether unpleasant.

"Sue, could you hold on for a second?"

"Certainly."

With Sue safely on hold, Elizabeth clutched her phone to her chest. Clearly a dismissal was in order. Mr. Darcy didn't appear to be in a hurry to get anywhere, and Elizabeth was ready for him to go. As pleasant as he was to look at, she had no desire to hang out with him and Zara.

"Well, it was nice seeing you both." Elizabeth smiled. "But I really need to take this. Enjoy your stay in the city."

Something flickered in Mr. Darcy's dark eyes. Frustration? Elizabeth couldn't be sure.

"Miss Scott." He bent at the waist slightly.

A bow. He'd bowed at her. Who did that? What was she supposed to do now? Curtsy?

She settled on a wave. "Bye."

Elizabeth walked away, letting the swarm of people on the sidewalk swallow her up. She picked up her pace as she picked up the phone. "Sue, hi. I'm so sorry."

"No worries. Alan and I are sitting at the airport, waiting

for our flight home. No hurry." Elizabeth could hear a smile in Sue's voice at the mention of her husband.

"You're on your way back to London?"

"Yes. Alan has business meetings this week. Actually, that's why I'm calling. Alan and I have a proposition for you, Elizabeth. One I hope will sound appealing."

Elizabeth's steps slowed. "A proposition?"

"The other night at dinner, we couldn't help but overhear your mother mention that you were out of work at the moment."

Overhear. Sue was being polite. Elizabeth's mother had roared on and on about it, as was her custom.

"Yes, I am." She struggled for an explanation. The Barrows seemed like nice, accepting people, but admitting she'd been accused of extortion would threaten the limits of anyone's understanding. "Temporary layoff."

"I'll get right to the point, then. We have a job offer for you. You were such a help at the dog show in New Jersey. I could use an extra pair of hands for the shows across the pond. It's so difficult finding help back home, and my dogs respond so well to you."

Elizabeth clutched her phone with both hands, desperate to make sure she'd heard Sue correctly. Someone bumped her from behind, and she almost fell to her knees on a manhole cover but she didn't even care. "You have a job for me?"

"Yes, dear." Her words had the effect of a welcome breeze, strong enough to lift a wedding veil straight off Elizabeth's head and send it sailing away into the distance. "In London."

5

Donovan was exhausted. He hadn't slept a wink on the flight to Heathrow, a fact he chalked up to his preoccupation with Elizabeth Scott. She'd tormented his thoughts all the way across the Atlantic.

Donovan wasn't accustomed to chasing women. In fact, the opposite was a far more regular occurrence. Case in point: Helena Robson, who'd called him at least once a day during his trip, leaving syrupy voice mails and several times even sending him texts that bordered on sexting.

It was pathetic.

And now here he was, among the infatuated. He was mortified at himself. He was, in short, a mess.

To make matters worse, the puppies had come. Donovan knew it as soon as his butler opened the front door. His anxious expression said it all.

"Sir," Lawrence started.

"Don't tell me." Donovan held up his hand to stop him from saying the words aloud. He didn't think he could bear it. "I'm late, aren't I? Figgy had the puppies."

"I'm afraid so, sir. Yes." Lawrence's shoulders sagged. "But everything went smoothly. Figgy is doing marvelously, as are the puppies. Four in all."

Four puppies. And he'd missed the entire event.

"Puppies!" Zara dropped her carry-on bag on the threshold. It landed with the heavy thud of three shoe boxes from the Chanel store. "Oh, let's go see."

She maneuvered past Lawrence, just as Finneus, the sire of Figgy's litter, danced and wiggled his way toward Donovan.

"Come along, little man. Time for you to pass out cigars and such." Donovan scooted Finneus inside with a nudge of his foot and shut the door behind him.

"Um, sir, there's something else I should tell you." Lawrence shot a nervous glance toward the drawing room, where Donovan had set up Figgy's whelping box before he'd left for the States.

Donovan exhaled a weary sigh. "Honestly, so long as the little mother and the puppies are happy and healthy, nothing else matters. Is everyone okay?"

"Absolutely." The butler nodded. "But…"

Donovan shook his head. "No buts. I'm going to go take a peek for myself."

He was doing his best to look on the bright side. It wasn't as if he could turn back time and get home to watch over the birth. He only wanted to check on the litter and sit quietly with Figgy for a bit before dealing with the multitude of other things on his plate. He'd be willing to bet whatever Lawrence needed to tell him had something to do with Aunt Constance. Or the family foundation. Or any number of other ulcer-causing things that could wait until later.

He turned and headed toward the drawing room. Situated on the ground level of the row house, it was at the end of the hallway to the right of the foyer. Donovan spent the majority of his time there when he was at his London home—his desk was there, and it was his favorite spot for taking tea. So he'd chosen the room, with its peaceful, willowy hues, as the place for Figgy's whelping box.

But as Donovan strolled into the room, the aforementioned weight crashed back down on him with full force. There, leaning over the whelping pen with her designer denim-clad bottom pointed directly at him, stood Helena Robson.

Oh, good God. Why now?

A little warning would have been nice. Then Donovan remembered Lawrence's worried glances toward the drawing room. Why hadn't he listened to the butler? Butlers were all-knowing, all-seeing. When would Donovan ever learn?

Zara glanced up at him. She looked at Helena beside her and shot him an exaggerated eye roll. She'd never been a fan of his friend Henry Robson's sister.

Helena glanced over her shoulder, still pointing her back end at him as if he had a target painted on his forehead, and cooed, "Welcome home."

Subtlety had never been the woman's strong suit.

"We have company. Super," Zara deadpanned.

Donovan averted his gaze. He looked at his desk, then the floor. Anywhere but Helena's bum. "Helena."

In his periphery, Donovan saw her right herself. "You don't sound at all happy to see me. Aren't you surprised?"

"Oh, I'm surprised." He strolled past her to get a clear view of the puppies.

"Aren't they cute?" Zara whispered, not wanting to disturb the little family, Donovan supposed. "I just love puppies."

Figgy let out a whine of delight. Her tail beat against the blankets in a happy rhythm, but she remained on her side so her four wiggly puppies could continue nursing. They were gorgeous, every bit as lovely as Donovan could have wished. Four fat, healthy little Blenheim bundles. And Figgy was clearly reveling in her role as mummy.

He could have wept with relief. He might have, if Helena hadn't been there attempting to press herself against his side.

He took a step backward, away from the whelping pen, and leaned against his desk.

Helena's expression never wavered. She smiled sweetly at him. "How was your trip to America? Was the Big Apple everything Zara hoped it was?"

Zara glared at Helena. The fact that Helena spoke about her as if she wasn't in the room had always been one of Zara's chief complaints.

Donovan didn't care for it much, either. He assumed Helena did it deliberately, so Zara would leave the room in a huff and they would be alone together. The allure of the new puppies proved more potent than Helena's condescension, however. Zara stayed put.

Thank God.

The last thing Donovan wanted was to be alone with Helena.

"We had a very nice trip." Donovan gave her a tight smile. He yawned, ready to use exhaustion as an excuse to get rid of her. But before he could say a word about jet lag, Zara slipped between them.

She held one of the puppies close to her chest, and her lips curved into a Cheshire-cat grin. Donovan frowned. His little sister was clearly up to something. It pained him to even guess what it might be.

"Did Donovan tell you that he met someone while we were there?" Zara's smile grew even wider.

He watched as the blood drained from Helena's face. "Why, no. No, he didn't."

She lifted a perfectly groomed brow at him. "Is this true, Donovan?"

Zara answered for him. "Of course it's true. He met a woman named Elizabeth Scott. An American. They only had eyes for each other."

"Zara." Donovan shot her a warning glance.

He had no intention of letting her use Elizabeth to make Helena jealous. Not only was she stretching the truth considerably—his eyes might have been drawn toward Elizabeth, but her eyes had seemed to have plenty of places to look other than his direction—but he didn't want Elizabeth's name batted about so casually.

He preferred to leave the memory of her intact, a sweet place filled with a thousand tender recollections he could visit now and again. Privately.

"I'm all astonishment. An American. How quaint." Helena attempted a smile, but it came off as more of a sneer. Donovan could see panic gathering behind her eyes. "Well, it's getting late. I really should be going."

She slithered past Donovan, leaving him choking on a cloud of her perfume. She paused when she reached the doorway, then added, as an apparent afterthought, "Nice puppies."

"Thank you," he answered, but she was already gone.

He turned toward Zara. "That was uncalled for."

"You should be thanking me. She's always throwing herself at you." Zara stepped into the whelping pen in her stocking feet and placed the puppy back beside Figgy's belly. "Anyway, she deserves it."

"Helena may deserve it, but Miss Scott most certainly doesn't deserve to be in Helena Robson's crosshairs." The throb in his temples intensified into full-on jackhammer-ing. "For one thing, she's not quite as besotted with me as you indicated."

"Oh, relax," Zara groaned. "What difference does it make? It's not as if Helena will ever actually meet her. You'll prob-ably never see her again yourself."

Her words, although true, were an arrow straight to his heart. He felt himself caving in beneath their weight.

He straightened. Why should he care if he ever saw Miss Scott again? There were plenty of beautiful women right here in England, none of whom made a habit of looking at him with obvious disdain in their eyes. Still, it was a struggle to clear his throat and speak with any sort of composure. "True."

Zara laughed. "And it's a good thing. Can you imagine if she were here? Helena would eat her alive."

Donovan shuddered.

Eat her alive indeed.

Elizabeth's first impression of London was that it was rather like looking at New York through rose-colored glasses. The people were far more fashionable. There wasn't a pair of white athletic shoes in sight, and you couldn't swing a stick with-out hitting someone with a fashionable Burberry scarf wound around their neck. Everything seemed cleaner, too, as if the city had recently had a good scrubbing. Then again, she was gathering her first impression of London from behind the privacy windows of a fancy black Jaguar.

The driver and his luxurious car had been the Barrows' doing. A kind gesture, but one that made Elizabeth a tad ner-vous nonetheless. As she'd slid into the supple leather back-seat with Bliss curled in her lap, she couldn't help but wonder what exactly she'd gotten herself into. Jenna had insisted the

Barrows were rich. Elizabeth had no argument there. They'd just hired a dog nanny, for crying out loud.

Oh, God, had she lost her mind? She'd just moved halfway across the world to become a dog nanny.

Calm down. It's only temporary. Four weeks. The duration of the investigation.

Even if things didn't get straightened out at the Barclay School, it wasn't as if she could move to England forever.

Could she?

Her mother had reacted with predictable horror to the news. "Elizabeth, you can't be serious. You're a teacher, not a babysitter. These people you've only just met want you to be their nanny, for goodness' sake. And not even for children. For *dogs*. What are they thinking? What are *you* thinking? You have a perfectly good job waiting for you at Scott Bridal."

Elizabeth had refrained from pointing out that working at the bridal shop hardly constituted a teaching position, either. There was little point in rocking the boat any more than necessary. She'd made up her mind. "I won't just be their nanny. I'm going to show the dogs for the Barrows at the autumn shows. I helped them out at the show in New Jersey and did quite well. Better than I've ever done with my own dog, actually. This is my chance to see England, all expenses paid. And the timing is perfect, since I'm on hiatus from school."

It had been almost frightening the way the words *on hiatus* had fallen right off her tongue. Elizabeth wasn't about to tell her family about the accusations Grant Markham had leveled against her. With the exception of Jenna, she hadn't breathed a word about it to another soul. In the meantime, words like *hiatus* and *temporary layoff* had a much better ring than *extortion* and *investigation*. Her mother had pressed for more information, naturally. But Elizabeth had managed to satisfy her maternal curiosity by blaming the bad economy and skyrocketing unemployment.

At least Jenna had been supportive.

"Of course you're going," she'd said. "This is perfect for you."

Elizabeth had wished, not for the first time, that Jenna was accompanying her. She'd felt awful leaving her behind at Scott Bridal. "You promised to visit. Remember?"

"Of course. As soon as you get settled, I'll be on the first plane across the pond. Don't tell me you're worried about being lonely? Bliss is going with you. And the Barrows seem like sweethearts." Then Jenna's eyes had sparkled with mischief. "Hey, I just thought of something. You know someone else over there. Besides the Barrows, I mean."

"What are you talking about?" Elizabeth had asked, but she'd had the uneasy feeling she knew precisely who Jenna meant.

"That hot judge from the dog show. What was his name again? Daniel?"

"Darcy," Elizabeth had corrected, hating the way her stomach had flipped when she'd said his name.

"Are you sure it wasn't Daniel?" Jenna had sounded wistful.

"You seriously need to get over your Daniel Craig fixation. I'm sure. It's Darcy. Donovan Darcy."

"Well, there you go. Donovan Darcy. Someone to keep you company in jolly old England."

"Don't be ridiculous," Elizabeth had protested, but her cheeks had grown warm all the same.

"Why is it ridiculous? I think it sounds marvelous. He's gorgeous. And remember his accent? Oh, my God."

Elizabeth had remembered his accent. All too well.

"Have you forgotten the woman he was with? The one

who looked half my age?" Zara of the smooth forehead and designer shoes. "Besides, I'll never run into him over there. He doesn't even live in London. He lives in the country somewhere on a giant estate. At least that's what Sue told me. It even has a name. Can you imagine?"

"A house with a name? Donovan Darcy is sounding better by the minute," Jenna had teased.

Elizabeth had laughed along, but not once had she mentioned her chance meeting with Mr. Darcy on the street in Manhattan. She'd told herself it was because Jenna didn't need any more ammunition, but she wasn't altogether sure that was the whole truth.

In the backseat of the fancy Jaguar, guilt pricked her conscience. She rarely kept secrets from Jenna.

Quit overthinking things. It's not a secret. It was nothing. Just a coincidence. It didn't mean anything.

It meant nothing.

Nothing at all.

She fixed her gaze on the scenery out the window and wondered how soon she'd arrive at the Barrows' townhome in South Kensington. She couldn't help but notice the neighborhoods had grown exponentially more exclusive the farther the car carried her away from Heathrow.

Sue and Alan had seemed so down-to-earth and genuine at the show in New Jersey. Nothing at all like the proper, stuffy Mr. Darcy. Bowing to her and all. He might be attractive enough to make her weak in the knees, but he was more than a little intimidating.

"Here we are," the driver called out as he maneuvered the elegant car onto a charming street called Sumner Place.

Elizabeth experienced a moment of relief at the sight of the graceful white row houses, with their low black wrought-iron fencing and meticulously shaped topiaries. Somehow the neighborhood managed to look both affluent and welcoming at the same time. At one end of the street was a quaint stone church with a steeple rising high up to the sky, and at the other, a cupcake bakery with lace curtains fluttering in the windows.

Elizabeth gave Bliss a squeeze. "We're going to love it here. I can tell already."

The driver pulled alongside the curb—the one on the left-hand side of the street, Elizabeth noted—and opened the door for her.

"Elizabeth, you made it, dear." Sue appeared on the porch and held her arms open wide, putting to rest any stereotypes about the British being reserved.

Elizabeth grinned and led Bliss up the three small steps to the porch. She stepped into Sue's embrace and was somewhat surprised when a lump lodged in her throat. She supposed it wasn't until she was standing on British soil, wrapped in a pair of maternal arms, that the full impact of what the Barrows had done for her really hit her full force. In their eyes it might have been a job, but to Elizabeth it felt more like a lifeline.

"Let's get you inside. Alan's at work, of course. I'll show you and Bliss to your room, and then I'll get you reacquainted with the girls." Sue's eyes sparkled as she spoke about her "girls," the pack of Border terriers that would be Elizabeth's charges.

"That sounds wonderful." She turned, prepared to go back to the car for her luggage, but the driver had already carried both her big bags in. They sat at the foot of the very narrow staircase, just inside the door.

Sue pressed a few colorful bills into his hand, and he was

off. The Jaguar barely made a sound as it pulled away from the curb.

"Thank you for sending the car, by the way. You're spoiling me. I could have taken a cab." Elizabeth gathered Bliss into her arms and followed Sue across the threshold. The foyer of the row house was painted with bold black and white stripes. An umbrella stand filled with cherry-red umbrellas stood next to a shiny full-length mirror. Bliss caught a glimpse of her reflection and growled.

Elizabeth could tell at once that the house suited the Barrows. It was casually elegant and welcoming, just like Sue and Alan. She was ashamed of herself for worrying that she would feel uncomfortable here.

"Just leave the bags there. We'll get to those later. I'm anxious for you to see your room. We've just had it redone. I'm afraid it's on the second floor. That's the downside." Sue began climbing the slender staircase.

Elizabeth followed. Bliss planted her head on Elizabeth's shoulder and kept her eyes trained on her reflection until it was out of view. "We're accustomed to stairs. My apartment in New York is on the fourth floor."

Was on the fourth floor. She had to keep reminding herself that she was no longer a New Yorker. All of her things were currently stashed away in a storage unit in Queens. Even with a temporary job, she couldn't afford to pay rent on a Manhattan apartment when she wasn't even there.

Perhaps she could call herself a Londoner for the time being. That had an awfully nice ring to it.

The climb was longer than she expected, but still not as strenuous as the trek up to her New York apartment. Sue explained that in Europe, what Americans referred to as the first floor was called the ground floor. What Elizabeth knew as the second floor was subsequently the first floor in England, and so on. So her bedroom was situated on the top floor of the home, up three flights of stairs.

Sue led her through a set of white double doors at the top of the staircase.

"What do you think?" Sue waved her hand with a little flourish. "I do hope you like blue."

Elizabeth was at a loss for words. It was the most beautiful bedroom she'd ever laid eyes on. The walls were covered in pale blue toile wallpaper that featured scenes of French women in ball gowns and large powdered wigs. Tiny dogs danced around their feet. The duvet cover on the four-poster bed was fashioned from matching fabric, as were a pile of over-stuffed throw pillows.

Elizabeth ran her fingertips along the smooth white wood of one of the posts at the foot of the bed. "Oh, Sue. This can't possibly be your guest room. It's gorgeous."

"It is most definitely the guest room. I could never convince Alan to sleep anywhere so girlie. Or froufrou, as he calls it." She shrugged.

Elizabeth shook her head, struggling to take it all in. "This room is fit for a princess. Not a dog nanny."

"Oh, don't be silly. What's the use of having such a pretty room if no one's enjoying it?" Sue grinned. "So, you like it, then?"

"Are you kidding? I love it." Elizabeth gave Bliss a squeeze and released her to explore their new home. Much to Sue's delight, she shuffled straight to a sweet little dog bed with a toile cushion that matched the duvet cover. "Correction— we love it."

Elizabeth gave Bliss a little pat and noticed the large window on the far wall, framed with a generously proportioned window seat. More throw pillows, toile and pale blue crushed velvet, made the bench a cozy-looking refuge. She felt drawn to the area at once, captivated by the view of Sue's charming neighborhood.

"This is fantastic. Look, I can see everything from up here."

"Yes, it's an excellent spot for spying on the neighbors." Sue clapped her hands. "Success, then. I want you to feel at home here. There's a tiny kitchenette at the end of the hall, right next to the water closet."

"Water closet?" Elizabeth turned away from the window and searched Sue's face for a clue. All she saw was a hint of amusement.

"The powder room, dear." She laughed. "Don't worry. We'll make a Brit of you before you know it."

Elizabeth had known she coddled Bliss, but she hadn't realized to what extent until she'd been introduced once again to Sue's Border terriers. They were the most perfectly trained dogs she'd ever seen. It was remarkable. They moved in flawless unison. If Elizabeth told one of them to sit, they all planted their rumps on the ground at the same exact moment. A *down* command elicited a similar uniform response. After only an hour of looking after them, Elizabeth had begun thinking of them not as a pack of dogs but rather a military unit. A scruffy, wirehaired infantry.

The jet lag hit Elizabeth full force, and by nine o'clock she could barely keep her eyes open. She slipped into her nightgown and situated herself on the window seat. As she gazed out at the darkened London street and reflected on her first day in the Barrows' household, Elizabeth wondered why they'd hired her. Other than to help out at the shows, of course.

Those dogs—Violet, Hyacinth, Daisy and Rose—could run the house themselves. They hardly needed a nanny. Although she supposed they were smart enough to get in serious trouble if left to their own devices. They had a television in their room. Or the telly, as Sue had called it. When the house was empty, Sue left it on to keep them company. Elizabeth wouldn't have been surprised if the Border terriers tuned in to the home-shopping channel, dialed the phone with their little paws and ran up thousands of dollars in credit-card bills for crazy things like the ShamWow or a blanket with sleeves. That was the kind of intelligence they possessed. These were not normal dogs she was dealing with.

Bliss danced around on her hind legs, peeking over the edge of the seat until Elizabeth scooped her up. Not that the Cavalier wasn't fully capable of jumping up there on her own. She was spoiled, plain and simple.

"Yep, you're spoiled," Elizabeth murmured as she surrendered and ran her fingers over the Cavalier's silky chestnut ears. "But I love you just the way you are."

Bliss let out a little snuffling sound and wedged her way between one of Elizabeth's legs and the neat row of velvet pillows. Behind her, the window glowed with the soft yellow light of the streetlamps that lined the sidewalk below. Elizabeth smiled at the bright red telephone booth she could make out, even in the dark, right next to the cupcake bakery on the corner.

London was charming.

Elizabeth had been in the country for all of fifteen hours, and she was smitten with the place. The street was quiet now. The cupcake bakery's windows were darkened. Some of the quaint row houses had lights on, but only in one or two windows. Even the church down the street had stopped ringing its bells every hour, on the hour. South Kensington was packing it in for the night.

But as Elizabeth scooped all sixteen pounds of Bliss's dead weight into her arms, ready to head for bed, she spotted something out the window that gave her pause.

Another Cavalier!

She planted Bliss back among the pillows and leaned toward the windowpane for a closer look.

Her bedroom was three floors up, but she could spot a fluffy, wagging Cavalier tail from any distance. The dog prancing around on the threshold of the house across the street was most definitely a Cavalier King Charles spaniel. She squinted and tried to make out the dog's owner.

It was a man. But from so high up, and in the dark, she couldn't tell much else. He appeared to be wearing jeans and a sweater, but there was something about the way he moved that carried an air of formality.

They meandered down the street and, once they'd reached the church, turned back toward home. The man kept a watchful eye on his Cavalier until they'd made it about halfway down the block. Then he suddenly turned his face toward her window.

Elizabeth couldn't make out his expression in the darkness, or his features, for that matter. But her face flushed with heat as she watched him watching her. He stood on the sidewalk with moonlight caressing his broad shoulders for a long while. Longer than seemed appropriate. Not that anything about spying on the neighbors was necessarily appropriate.

Elizabeth knew she should back away from the window and head for bed. She couldn't seem to make herself do it. For some inexplicable reason, she felt drawn toward the pair outside. She told herself it was because of the dog, of course.

Another Cavalier. Why wouldn't she be curious? But the way her heart pounded told her there was a bit more to it than that.

He waved. It was just a slight movement of his free hand, but the stir it caused inside Elizabeth was sizable. She returned the gesture.

The man tilted his head, as though studying her. She was struck with the sudden worry that he could see her face. Could he tell who she was?

Surely not.

What did it matter, anyway? She didn't know a soul here, besides the Barrows. She was anonymous. Invisible.

She swallowed, but a flutter rose up from her belly and settled in her chest. Sitting there, in silent communion with this stranger on a London street, she didn't feel invisible at all. In fact, she felt anything but. She felt alive.

Disappointment tugged at her consciousness when he looked back down at his dog. They headed toward home. Elizabeth kept watching as he opened the door and the pair slipped inside.

"Come on, sweetheart," she murmured to Bliss. "Time for bed."

She crawled under the covers of the impressive four-poster bed, with Bliss curled by her side. Even though she'd traveled clear across the Atlantic Ocean that day and was exhausted beyond comprehension, Elizabeth lay awake for quite a while before she fell asleep. She tingled all over, from head to toe.

At last her eyes fluttered shut. And for the first time in a week, she wasn't awakened by nightmares of Grant Markham.

6

Donovan stared into his tea and wondered if there was enough caffeine in the world to get him going the next morning.

"Lawrence, I won't be going to work today," he muttered.

"Yes, sir." Lawrence just stood there, gaping at him in stunned silence until he vanished back down the hall.

Donovan never missed work. Not that "work" was an actual location. It was more of a metaphorical place. At Chadwicke, he conducted business in the library, surrounded by books that had been on the shelves for generations but were hardly ever touched. Sometimes he stared at the spine of the first-edition Dickens as he listened to Aunt Constance ramble on and on about some minute detail of the family trust while silently wishing he could tune her out and flip through its pages instead.

In London, he worked from the drawing room. But the only thing in the pale green room that interested him now was the whelping pen and its contents—Figgy's tiny, wriggling pups.

He decided to give in and spend the day looking after his

dogs. He wouldn't be of any use to the Darcy Family Trust today anyhow. After his sleepless night, he'd probably give away half the family fortune without even realizing what he'd done.

And what was more, he couldn't have cared less. How could anyone expect him to get any sleep after what he'd seen? That *vision,* for lack of a better term.

He'd taken Finneus out for a final walk up and down the block when he'd looked up and spotted *her.*

It wasn't really Elizabeth Scott, of course. He still possessed enough sanity to know he'd only been imagining things. Or the dim light had been playing tricks on him. Whichever, it didn't really matter. He'd seen her again, if only in his imagination. And she was as lovely as ever.

He'd debated leaving for Chadwicke in an attempt to get his wits about him. He couldn't go on like this forever. His behavior was beginning to worry him, to some extent.

Why her? Of all the women in the world, why was he so preoccupied with thoughts of Elizabeth Scott? She may have had a naturally beautiful, captivating quality about her, but that sharp tongue of hers was less than wholesome. In the improbable event he ever did see her again, she'd be more likely to use that sensual mouth to hurl a string of insults at him than what he had in mind.

That prospect brought with it a surge of arousal that confounded him even further. What he needed was rest. Some relaxation, time with the dogs, a good night's sleep. Then he'd be good as new.

He nodded to no one but himself. Donovan Darcy was going to skive off, and he intended to do a right good job of it.

He took a final spot of tea, pushed himself out of his leather chair and stepped over the wire walls of Figgy's whelping pen. She scrambled into his lap when he sank down cross-legged on the floor, leaving her pups confused and searching for their mum as best they could with their eyes not yet open. They stood on wobbly legs, stumbling here and there until they began mewing like kittens.

"Your babies are looking for you," Donovan whispered in Figgy's ear.

Her eyes grew wide, even wider than usual, which was significant considering Cavaliers had such big, round eyes to begin with. Her furry brow creased with worry as she eyed her pups.

"Go tend to them. I'll be here all day." He picked her up and set her back down on the fresh, clean bed in the center of the pen.

She kept her gaze fixed on him as all the puppies, save one, found their way back to her. The wayward pup squealed her displeasure as she nudged her little pink nose against the bumper of the dog bed.

"Don't worry. I'll give you a hand, love." With great care, Donovan plucked the puppy off the ground and gathered her into his palms.

He turned her so she faced him. Her muzzle and nose were bald and pink as bubble gum. It would take a week or so for her nose to begin the transition to black. She had a perfectly proportioned white blaze down the center of her face, framed on either side by rich chestnut. Best of all, she had a much-coveted Blenheim spot square in the center of her little head. Donovan ran his thumb gently over the spot and, as he did so, noticed something unusual.

He narrowed his gaze at the pup's face and turned her toward the light, just to be sure. "Well, would you look at that?"

Beneath her right eye, halfway to her nose, there they

were…a tiny cluster of peach-colored specks. He wiped at them to make sure they wouldn't disappear. They didn't, naturally.

"Would you look at that?" Donovan repeated and laughed in wonder. "I've bred a puppy with freckles."

It was a rarity, both in his breeding lines as well as in puppies of such a young age. That he could see the spots at all when she was only a few days old guaranteed they would be most visible later on.

Oh, the irony.

If this had happened weeks ago, he would have made arrangements to place the puppy in a pet home as soon as she was old enough to leave her mum. Chadwicke Cavaliers were in high demand, whether pet or show quality. Donovan had a waiting list of pet homes as long as his arm.

Things were somehow different now. He couldn't say why, but this was the puppy he would keep even though the rest of them were picture-perfect. All he saw when he looked at those faint hints of freckles were Miss Scott and the little dog she loved so much. For some nonsensical reason, Donovan wanted to hold on to that memory. What was it he had compared her complexion to?

A pastry dusted with sugar and spice.

A dessert.

He brought the pup closer and tucked her against his cheek. "I think I'll call you Pudding."

Pudding squirmed against his face, her coat soft as down feathers. Donovan set her back down beside her mum, and the worry lines on Figgy's brow instantly smoothed away.

Donovan took in a deep breath as he watched the dogs. He felt better already. He climbed out of the whelping pen and went off in search of Finneus. A walk was in order.

After he secured Finneus in his harness and gave Lawrence strict instructions to tell any and all callers—especially
Aunt Constance and, God forbid, Helena Robson—he was
out for the day, Donovan headed outside. He glanced across
the way at the window where he could have sworn he'd seen
Miss Scott the night before. The drapes were open, revealing
nothing but an empty room. No winsome beauty gazing out
at him like a princess in a tower.

He shook his head and cursed at himself for even bother-
ing to check.

Finneus jerked on the end of his lead, bringing Donovan
back to the present. For that, Donovan was grateful. He let
the dog lead the way and followed him toward the bakery
on the corner, since that was where he seemed to be headed.

They'd only taken a few steps when Finneus strained harder
in his harness. The leash grew taut, and Donovan was forced
to tighten his grip. "Settle down, boy."

Donovan looked up and saw a pack of dogs heading in
their direction. Finneus was doing his best to get to them,
as if they were his long-lost family. One of the dogs was a
Cavalier, but the others were Border terriers. Four of them.
Donovan followed the tangle of their leashes up toward the
woman at the other end, and his heart stopped.

Elizabeth Scott.

So he hadn't gone mad, after all. She was here. In London.
On his very street.

He brought Finneus to a halt and waited for her to meet
his gaze. She didn't so much as glance at him but stayed focused on her quintet of dogs, untangling the multitude of
leashes as she went.

The instant she spotted Finneus, Elizabeth's face lit up.
Her cheeks glowed with the warmth of exercise and her ob-

vious excitement at spotting another Cavalier. She picked up her pace and, to Donovan's great pleasure, headed straight toward him.

A wry smile came to his lips as she dropped to her knees at his feet. He couldn't help it. Elizabeth Scott...on her knees in front of him.

Finneus planted his paws on her shoulders and licked her cheek. Joy was written all over Elizabeth's face. Donovan dreaded the moment she realized it was him, for surely her delighted expression would turn to one of revulsion.

He cleared his throat. There was no sense in postponing the inevitable. "Miss Scott, what a pleasure."

She flew to her feet in an instant. Her mouth formed a round O of surprise, drawing Donovan's attention to her perfect pink lips.

They stood there eyeing one another as they had the night before. It had been real, not a fantasy. Donovan smiled in remembrance and watched as Elizabeth's cheeks filled with color. He waited for those exquisite lips to turn down in a frown.

They didn't.

Instead, Elizabeth Scott narrowed her gaze, as if looking at him for the first time.

She said one simple word. "You."

"Yes, me." Mr. Darcy's smile was all warmth and charm.

Elizabeth knew at once he was the man she'd watched through her window the night before. Same dog at the end of the leash, same broad shoulders, same man.

Same flutter in her belly.

The way he was looking at her, with a twinkle in his eye

that could only be described as wicked, told her he'd figured it out, as well.

"Nice dog." She nodded at the cute little Cavalier at his feet. "Is he yours?"

"Thank you. And yes, he's mine. His name is Finneus." He sidestepped a group of women carrying covered casserole dishes who looked as though they were headed toward the little stone church on the corner, then steered Elizabeth and her pack of dogs inside the short wrought-iron fence of one of the townhomes.

Safely out of the way of passersby, Elizabeth gave the dogs a little more slack on their leashes. Bliss went to work sniffing Finneus from head to toe while the Border terriers arranged themselves in a neat row. Rose and Hyacinth—in bookend positions—sat, while Violet and Daisy sank into Sphinx-like downs, with their shaggy legs stretched out straight in front of them.

Mr. Darcy raised his brows. "This is an impressive group you've got here. The Borders belong to Sue and Alan Barrow, I presume?"

"Yes." Elizabeth eyed the terriers with suspicion, as though they were responsible for this surreal situation. "How do you know that?"

"The Barrows are my neighbors." He bent to give Bliss a pat, and she flipped on her back at once, eager for his attention. Elizabeth glared at her. The traitor. "I know your opinion of me could stand some improvement, but believe it or not, I'm not all bad. At the very least, I know my neighbors' names."

"Your neighbors? But that's not possible. You don't live here." Elizabeth glanced at the sleek black door behind him with confusion. Granted, she'd watched him emerge from it last night, take his dog for a stroll and return to it. And here he was again, standing in front of it, as if it did indeed belong to him.

But it couldn't.

Could it?

A trickle of suspicion made its way up her spine.

She looked around, as if some sort of explanation would materialize from thin air. A sleek sports car was parked at the curb, directly in front of Mr. Darcy's alleged house. It was gunmetal gray. An Aston Martin. Just the sort of car a filthy-rich man like him would own.

"I'm afraid it's entirely possible. My dog, my door, my house." Mr. Darcy stood.

She'd forgotten how tall he was. If she took a step or two closer, her head would have tucked neatly under his chin.

Where did that thought come from?

She took a preventative step backward until she bumped into the decorative iron fence with her calves.

"But I thought you lived in a grand country house somewhere." *A house with a name,* she almost added. Thankfully, running into him hadn't rattled her to such an extent that she lost complete control.

Yet.

"Chadwicke." He nodded. Violet, Hyacinth, Daisy and Rose mirrored his nod while the Cavaliers, oblivious to all but one another, tumbled at Mr. Darcy's feet. "You've heard of it?"

Great. Now he probably thought she'd been asking about him. And thinking about him. Which she had not.

Much.

"Sue mentioned it to me."

"And yet she didn't mention my London home, which happens to be directly across the road from hers." The wicked gleam returned to his eyes with unprecedented intensity. "That's odd, don't you think?"

Suddenly everything made sense. Sue practically swooning over Mr. Darcy at the dog show. The job offer, seemingly out of nowhere. The fancy blue room at the top of the stairs that seemed wholly extravagant for an employee.

Oh, my God. Sue didn't bring me all the way here just to be her dog nanny. She's playing matchmaker.

Being the target of such a plan was a tad bit embarrassing. England was halfway around the world. Apparently, she couldn't be trusted to find a man within a thousand miles or so of her own home.

Not that she wanted a man. Men were nothing but trouble. Particularly rich men. They were spoiled, arrogant and thought they could take whatever they wanted without any consideration for the consequences.

Elizabeth prayed that the smug look on Mr. Darcy's face didn't mean that he, too, knew what Sue was up to. The facts were humiliating enough without him being privy to them. He winked, dashing her hopes in an instant.

And damned if the wink didn't send a zing straight through her.

Elizabeth straightened her spine and did her best to ignore the zing. It was a tall order. "I'm working for the Barrows. Just for a month. I'm a dog nanny, of sorts."

"Are you?" He gave the Border terriers an appreciative glance. "It looks as though you've made quick work of whipping your charges into shape."

"I can't take credit for this. They're Superdogs. As you can see by Bliss's behavior, it's nothing I've done." Elizabeth laughed as Bliss tackled Finneus and the two dogs rolled onto Mr. Darcy's feet.

"She's perfect." He bent down, scooped Bliss into his arms and aimed his gaze at Elizabeth over the top of Bliss's head. "Then again, I've always been one to appreciate a feisty streak."

His tone made it abundantly clear he wasn't referring to the dog.

Elizabeth gulped. She had the sudden urge to flee before she did something really stupid. Like flirt back. Or, God forbid, kiss him right on the lips.

Maybe it was the jet lag. Or the fact that she was a world away from home. Seeing him in the moonlight must have done something to her because Mr. Darcy had somehow crossed the line from being pleasingly attractive to bone-meltingly desirable.

She tightened her grip on the leashes and looked around to get her bearings. Her attention was drawn to the red phone booth near the corner and remembered it led to the park where she'd been headed when she left the house. "I should be going. The Barrows aren't paying me to stand around chatting. I'm headed toward Hyde Park."

He kept Bliss firmly wrapped in his arms, successfully aborting Elizabeth's escape plan. "Why don't Finneus and I come along? You look as though you've got your hands full. I can help you out."

"No." She shook her head so hard, she wondered if she was in danger of giving herself whiplash. "That's really not necessary. I'm the nanny. I'm being paid to walk them. It's my job."

"Then I'll walk Finneus and Bliss." He plopped Bliss down onto the sidewalk and slipped his fingers around her leash.

"Surely the Barrows wouldn't object to such an arrangement?"

He had her there. The Barrows—Sue, in particular—wouldn't mind in the slightest. Mr. Darcy could have carried all five dogs on his back, and she would have been pleased as punch. Still, Elizabeth refused to give up her grip on Bliss's leash.

"They wouldn't mind, I'm sure. But…" She trailed off, hoping he wouldn't make her say it.

"But?" He gave her an odd look, as if he hadn't a clue where the conversation was headed.

Elizabeth didn't buy it for a minute. She exhaled a sigh of frustration, hating that he was forcing her to spell it out. "What about Zara?"

"Zara?" He sent a backward glance over his shoulder, toward his house, as if she was somewhere behind that sleek black door.

So she lives here, too. Super.

"Yes. Zara," Elizabeth huffed. "Come on, girls, time to go. Violet, Hyacinth, Rose…"

She gave up on commands once she realized she'd called Hyacinth by Violet's name and Daisy by Rose's. Or was that one Violet?

It didn't matter. She gathered their leashes together as they rose—in unison, naturally—and began trying to get Bliss's attention away from Finneus. She hadn't really thought through the notion that making a hasty exit wasn't possible with five dogs.

"Zara," Mr. Darcy repeated, his voice sounding oddly cold all of a sudden. "You mean my sister, Zara?"

His *sister?*

His *sister!*

Elizabeth came to a halt just as the Border terriers decided to break into a trot. The jerk of their leashes lifted her clear off her feet and sent her careening toward one of the two leafy green topiaries that flanked Mr. Darcy's door. He stepped in her path and caught her firmly by the shoulders.

"Thanks." Elizabeth allowed herself to exhale a sigh of relief.

Once she saw the look on Mr. Darcy's face, however, any remaining relief faded. He glared down at her, his dark eyes stony. "Zara is my sister. Would you like to explain why she would mind if you and I went to the park together?"

Elizabeth opened her mouth, but nothing came out. She stood there with it gaping open like a baby bird as a bike messenger whizzed past them on the sidewalk. The Cavaliers barked at him and scrambled at the ends of their leashes. The Border terriers, of course, remained stoic.

"You thought she was my lover." He spat the word *lover,* as if it made him physically ill.

Elizabeth was mortified to her core.

So mortified that she didn't give a moment's thought to the fact that this misunderstanding, shameful as it was, meant that perhaps he was single. Okay, so maybe she thought about it for a second. Or two. But definitely no more than three.

"No, I didn't. Of course I didn't." She shook her head. Maybe if she shook it hard enough, she could rattle the memories of how horribly she'd treated him and Zara at her birthday dinner. She'd jumped to conclusions. She'd been so awful.

"You did." He narrowed his gaze at her.

She cracked under his scrutiny. "I did. I'm sorry."

He stared at her for a full minute, not saying a word. Finally, one corner of his mouth lifted into a smirk. "You thought she was my lover."

This time he didn't sound so angry. In fact, he sounded amused.

Elizabeth glanced around, hoping no one was within earshot, particularly the church ladies. The only person in close proximity was a young man making his way down the sidewalk in a hoodie, with white headphones plugged in his ears. Thank goodness.

Donovan's eyes sparked with mischief. "Just so you know, I have a butler. You may see him entering and exiting my town house. He's not my lover, either."

A butler. Fabulous. What kind of person had a butler? Elizabeth thought they only existed in old black-and-white movies.

"Must you tease me? I've already confessed. I made a mistake. You have to admit—it's unusual for a teenage girl to live with her brother." She cleared her throat. His newfound amusement over her assumption did nothing to lessen her embarrassment. If anything, her humiliation multiplied. Tenfold. "Besides, we can't all be perfect."

"Surely you're not implying that I think I'm perfect." He laughed. "I assure you I'm not. I have plenty of faults."

Elizabeth thought of Chadwicke, the fancy car parked in front of Mr. Darcy's fashionable London townhome and, last but not least—not by a long shot—his well-formed physique, visible even beneath the thick cable knit of his sweater. "Name one."

She expected him to struggle or, at the very least, take a minute or two to think about his response. So she was surprised when he chimed in immediately.

"I can be bad-tempered at times, and I rarely give people a second chance. My good opinion once lost is lost forever." He crossed his arms. "Everyone has faults."

"I see. So are you telling me that yours is a propensity to hate everybody?" She couldn't help but wonder if she were included in this generalization. They had hardly gotten off on the right foot, after all.

"As yours is to willfully misjudge them?"

Touché.

Heat settled in the vicinity of her cheeks. "I'm sorry, Mr. Darcy. Again. I'd love to forget it ever happened. Could we do that, please?"

He sat down on one of the front-porch steps and let Finneus and Bliss crawl into his lap. The peal of bells rang out from the church's bell tower, bringing a sudden stillness to the neighborhood. Birds chirped faintly overhead. Elizabeth could even hear the soft pants of the dogs. But still Mr. Darcy said nothing.

Violet, Hyacinth, Daisy and Rose all swiveled their gazes back and forth between the two of them, finally aiming their shaggy, inquisitive brows at Mr. Darcy.

Elizabeth had to wonder if he was prolonging her agony intentionally.

Probably. Not that she could blame him, really.

At last he spoke. "Under one condition."

A condition. Marvelous. "What sort of condition?"

"No more Mr. Darcy," he said, his voice softening. "Call me Donovan."

"Donovan," Elizabeth repeated, very much liking the way it felt rolling off her tongue. "I think I can agree to that, so long as you call me Elizabeth instead of Miss Scott."

"Agreed, Elizabeth." He nodded and a slow, sultry smile came to his lips. "And as a further condition, I thought you might like to meet my new litter of puppies tomorrow afternoon."

"You have puppies? Cavaliers?"

"I do."

"Wait a minute. You said one condition. That makes two."

"Then I suppose that makes it an invitation rather than a condition." He looked up at her from the porch step, a thunderstorm gathering in his eyes.

A cool breeze came up the sidewalk, causing the dogs to sniff the air for its source. Donovan's hair ruffled in the wind, and for an instant he looked so uncharacteristically untidy Elizabeth had trouble resisting the urge to smooth it down with her fingertips.

A chill ran up her spine. Clearly, she'd ventured into dangerous territory.

If she had any sense at all, she would retreat. What would possess her to even consider an invitation from Donovan Darcy? He looked as though he'd be more pleased to take a walk to the gallows than to spend another minute with her.

Curiosity got the best of her. Either that or the sight of the sooty-black lashes that framed his glowering eyes. Men weren't supposed to have such nice eyelashes. Or such nice eyes, for that matter.

"An invitation, hmm?" She pretended to mull it over, as though she hadn't yet made up her mind. Just when Donovan looked as though his frustration was approaching its boiling point, she aimed an innocent smile at him. "In that case, I accept."

7

"A Border terrier's coat should be crunchy." Sue peered over the top of her glasses at Hyacinth, standing calmly on the grooming table.

"Crunchy," Elizabeth repeated, reminding herself they were talking about dogs and not cereal.

Cap'n Crunch.

Sue gently gathered a fistful of Hyacinth's coat and squeezed. "See?"

Cinnamon Toast Crunch.

Elizabeth ran her fingertips over the dog's fur. "Yes."

Honey Nut Crunch.

Stop it!

While Sue demonstrated the proper way to hand-pluck the terrier's coat, Elizabeth forced herself to focus. In the two days since she'd run into Mr. Darcy—ahem, *Donovan*—on the sidewalk, she'd found her mind wandering more than ever. At least now she was thinking about cereal rather than him. That could only be an improvement.

"Always strip in the coat in the direction the hair grows," Sue said.

"Got it." Elizabeth nodded and tugged a tuft of loose hair from Hyacinth's hindquarters. "It's rather like plucking a giant eyebrow."

Sue blinked for a beat, then laughed. "Yes, dear. I suppose it is."

"Is there a certain dog you'd like me to concentrate most on?"

"Why, yes—Rose. I'm really hoping to get her Championship this season. That's one of the reasons why I was so keen to bring you here. Your job at the shows is to devote all your attention to Rose." Sue grinned. "And Bliss, too, of course. I suppose you're trying for her Championship, as well."

Elizabeth shook her head. "I don't know. It can take years to earn a Championship. Rose already has Championship points piled up. Bliss doesn't have any."

"Yet." Sue held up her hand. "We'll change that. Don't be afraid to dream big, dear."

"Well, if I'm dreaming big, I'd have to say the ultimate fantasy would be to win Best in Show. It's silly, I know. People show dogs their whole lives and never have a Best in Show win. But that's what I dream of most, even more than a Championship."

Winning the top prize was almost inconceivable to Elizabeth. She'd never even won Best of Breed, for goodness' sake. But Sue had said to dream big, hadn't she?

"That's not a silly dream at all, dear. Lofty perhaps, but not silly." Sue gave a resolute nod. "It's settled, then. While you're here, Rose will become a Champion and Bliss will win Best in Show."

The doorbell rang, punctuating the declaration, and Sue bustled her way down the hall.

Elizabeth leaned toward Hyacinth and whispered in the dog's ear, "See, normal people don't have butlers. Normal people answer their own doors."

Hyacinth's ear twitched.

"Yes, I knew you'd agree." Elizabeth zeroed in on another clump of dead hair near the dog's tail and pulled.

Sue had entered all four terriers, plus Bliss, in a dog show that was being held the following day. So the way Elizabeth saw it, she had four giant eyebrows to pluck and very little time in which to do it. Not to mention the always time-consuming task of making sure Bliss's feathering looked soft, silky and white as snow.

Elizabeth didn't mind the workload a bit. Rather, she was grateful for it. It would take her mind off Donovan Darcy, for one thing.

She'd almost chickened out on going to see his puppies the day before. But then she decided avoiding him would be attaching too much importance to him. She told herself she was being silly, so she'd marched across the street and knocked on his perfectly polished door.

Lawrence, the butler, had answered it and informed her Donovan was away but had left instructions for him to show her Figgy's litter. So Elizabeth had spent an hour cuddling the adorable little puppies with Donovan's butler.

To think she'd almost convinced herself he'd meant the invitation as a date.

It was preposterous.

She'd tried not to wonder where Donovan had gone or why he wasn't home after he'd invited her to come see the puppies. She shouldn't care. What Donovan Darcy did was of no concern to her. He was uptight and full of himself.

And he'd already told her that his good opinion once lost was lost forever. She'd hardly made a good first impression. Or second, for that matter.

But there was just something about him…

She rolled her eyes. *Pathetic. Really, Lizzy. Get ahold of yourself.*

Elizabeth inhaled a deep breath. "Focus. Eyebrows. Plucking. No daydreaming, and *absolutely* no thinking about Donovan Darcy." She zeroed her gaze on Hyacinth. "Time to make you good and crunchy."

"Crunchy? Is she a dog or a bowl of cereal?"

Elizabeth recognized the voice in an instant. Of course she did. She'd known it her entire life. It was the same voice she'd shared whispers with, lying side by side in the dark on nights when her biggest worries had been broken crayons and lost toys. The same voice that had called out encouragement when she'd first learned to ride a bike. What she couldn't figure out was why that voice was in London.

"Jenna?"

Elizabeth turned, half expecting to discover she was only hearing things. But instead she found her sister standing in the doorway, grinning from ear to ear.

"Surprise," she said.

"I don't believe it." Tears stung Elizabeth's eyes. God, she was a bigger mess than she'd thought. "Jenna, you're here. In England."

"Those are happy tears, I hope?" Sue appeared next to Jenna, but didn't wait for an answer. She simply nodded her satisfaction. "Brilliant. I knew you'd be delighted. I'll go make you girls some tea. It will give an old woman something to do. Keep working, Elizabeth. Remember…crunchy eyebrows!"

Jenna jerked her head in Sue's direction as she vanished in the general vicinity of the kitchen. "What on earth is she talking about?"

"Don't ask." Elizabeth folded her sister in a tight embrace. "Jenna, what are you doing here? I'm so happy to see you."

Jenna shrugged. "I told you I'd get out here the first chance I could. The Temperley London Bridal Market starts tomorrow. I figured I'd never find a better excuse, so here I am."

"And Sue knew you were coming?" Elizabeth walked back to the grooming table, lest Hyacinth decide to make a getaway.

She didn't, of course, since she was one of Sue's Border terriers and not the mischievous Miss Bliss. The dog hadn't so much as moved a toenail.

"Yes. I called yesterday, but you were out. Sue answered your cell. We decided to make it a surprise. I assured Sue that Scott Bridal would book me a hotel, but she insisted I stay here with you." She sank onto the plush red leather sofa opposite the grooming table and glanced around at the dog beds lining the walls, where Violet, Daisy and Rose lounged with their shaggy legs stretched straight out in front of them. "This is a bedroom for dogs, isn't it? Wait. Forget I asked. I don't need to know these dogs live better than I do. Where were you yesterday, anyway? Sue made it sound like you were on a date. Obviously, I need to get caught up on things."

"It was *not* a date." Hyacinth winced as Elizabeth apparently plucked with a tad too much enthusiasm.

Oops.

Jenna narrowed her gaze. "You seem awfully adamant. What gives?"

Elizabeth glanced out the sash window toward Donovan's home. His downstairs lights glowed orange and shimmery through the afternoon rain. "Remember Donovan Darcy?"

"Of course I do. Don't tell me that's who you were with." Jenna's eyes grew wide. "It was him, wasn't it?"

Elizabeth gave her a brief rundown of bumping into Donovan on the street, learning that Zara was his sister and ending with her visit with his puppies. And his *butler*.

"So let me get this straight. He lives right across the street?" Jenna twirled a strand of her blond hair around her fingers.

"Yes." Elizabeth pointed to the window. "Right over there."

"And now you're dating?" She exhaled a dreamy sigh. "I knew something wonderful like this would happen while you were over here. It was meant to be."

"We're not dating." Despite her protest, a flutter rose in Elizabeth's belly.

"Mark my words. It's only a matter of time. What's the problem? Do you still think he's an ass?" Jenna frowned. "Never mind. Don't even answer that. If he's an ass, he's an ass who's hotter than Daniel Craig. I repeat—what's the problem?"

"The problem is that Donovan Darcy and I are a world apart from one another. May I remind you I spent yesterday afternoon with the man's butler?" Lawrence had certainly been nice to her when she'd gone to see the puppies. He hadn't been as formal as she'd expected, but he was still a *butler,* for heaven's sake. "Donovan invited me over to see his puppies, and I spent the afternoon with his butler. As far as I'm concerned, he's still an ass. Only now, I know he's an ass who's so wealthy he has more in common with Grant Markham than he does with me."

"Lizzy." Jenna's gaze turned tender. "Just because Donovan is wealthy doesn't mean he's a thing like Grant Markham. That man has stolen so much from you already. Don't let him take this away from you, too."

Was that was she was doing—letting Markham continue to wreak havoc with her life?

No, of course it wasn't. She was more than anxious to rid herself of the memory of Markham touching her, the smell of his breath as he'd leaned close, dragged his fingertips along her wrist as he'd insisted women like her were merely commodities to be bought or sold.

She shuddered. Some memories were hard to erase. And the bruises they left behind—the invisible ones that left marks only on the soul—were even harder.

"I'm not letting him steal a thing. There's nothing going on between me and Donovan Darcy. He was just being nice, that's all." *Nice?* Did she just say that? It didn't make a lick of sense. Somehow she was certain being *nice* wasn't exactly Donovan's style.

"If you say so." A playful gleam came to Jenna's eyes. Clearly she didn't believe a word of Elizabeth's protestations.

The trouble was…Elizabeth wasn't altogether sure she believed them herself.

Donovan stared at his computer monitor, the black letters swimming before his eyes. He blinked a few times in an effort to refocus his attention back to business. He'd begun to feel as though he were under some sort of spell.

Bewitched.

By Elizabeth Scott, of all women.

They had nothing in common. She reviled him, and he

found her obstinate, difficult and far too quick to leap to improper conclusions.

He also found her beautiful, witty and utterly bewitching.

It was a problem, to say the least.

He'd thought the problem could be resolved by simply avoiding her, even going so far as leaving the house for an entire afternoon the day before when he knew good and well Elizabeth would be dropping by to see Figgy's puppies. At his invitation, no less. He'd all but fled, leaving Lawrence to deal with her.

The escape plan had backfired in his face.

Unlike Helena Robson, out of sight didn't mean out of mind where Elizabeth Scott was concerned. To both Donovan's surprise and displeasure, she still consumed a good part of his waking thoughts…not to mention where his mind wandered when he slept. Elizabeth had been the subject of a rather erotic dream or two.

"Mr. Darcy." Lawrence bustled into the office.

"Lawrence." Donovan glanced up, and he found himself wondering what Elizabeth had thought of what he suspected was her first encounter with a butler.

Catching himself thinking about her again, he frowned. *What does her opinion matter? It's of no consequence.* "Yes, Lawrence. What is it?"

"You have a phone call, sir. It's your aunt Constance," Lawrence said.

"Thank you." Donovan picked up the phone and injected a note of enthusiasm into his voice. If Helena was a thorn in his side, his aunt was nearly as sharp. "Aunt Constance. Hello."

"You're home." The voice on the other end came through flatly. "I would have thought I'd hear about your arrival first-hand, rather than reading about it in the newspaper."

Donovan frowned. "The newspaper?"

"My dear nephew, it seems as though the *Daily Mail* is taking a keen interest in your activities of late. That's what comes with being London's most eligible bachelor, you know."

Bloody perfect.

Donovan had enough on his mind without having to worry about a tabloid following his every move.

He sighed. "For once you can believe what you read in the paper. I'm back. I took the day off yesterday."

"I see." She paused, refraining from commenting on his atypical day out of the office. Donovan was sure she had an opinion on the matter, but as an equal partner in the Darcy Family Trust—not his boss, thank God—his aunt wasn't in a proper position to complain.

"Zara and I had a nice trip to the States. And Figgy had her litter while we were gone."

"That's good to hear. Any show prospects?"

"I've got my eye on one of the pups." He smiled down at Pudding. Already her freckles had grown a shade or two deeper. "I hate to cut you off, but Henry Robson will be here soon with some papers for my signature."

"Then I'll make this quick. I'm calling about the party at Chadwicke."

Donovan took a look at his diary. Guy Fawkes Night and its accompanying annual house-party weekend at Chadwicke were fast approaching. He'd completely forgotten. Then again, he'd had his fair share of things on his mind. For once, the thought of going to his country house for a weekend pained him. He was possessed with a sudden, and entirely inappropriate, urge to invite Elizabeth to come along.

He knew at once it was an insane idea.

But he allowed himself a brief moment to indulge in the

fantasy of her there…her thick hair whipping in the country wind, her porcelain complexion growing pink in the autumn sunshine, stealing a kiss from her in the bedroom where he'd grown up.

His chest seized.

"The house party," he repeated to his aunt. "What about it?"

"I've invited your friend Helena Robson." She said it with an air of finality that turned Donovan's stomach.

He clamped his teeth together in an effort to not scream in frustration. "Why?"

"She stopped by yesterday for tea."

Of course she did. He should have known she'd resort to desperate measures after Zara's comment about him meeting someone in America. This was lower than he'd expected, however. Even from Helena.

"Such a delightful girl. And she comes from a wonderful family. You and her brother are dear friends, after all," his aunt said.

He sank into his chair. "I wish you would have spoken to me first, Aunt Constance. I can't disinvite her without offending Henry, but Helena is the last woman I want to spend the weekend with."

"What's the problem? Her brother is coming, isn't he?"

"Yes, but that's different," Donovan ground out. "Henry isn't dead set on marrying me."

She laughed a bit too loudly for Donovan's taste. "Donovan Darcy, you could do worse than Helena Robson."

Not much worse.

Donovan gripped the edge of his desk until his knuckles turned white with anger. "It's never going to happen. That I can promise you."

"There's one thing I've learned in my old age, Donovan."
She cleared her throat, prolonging the moment as if she were
about to impart the greatest of all wisdom to her nephew.
"And that's to never say *never*."

Donovan rubbed the dull ache that had taken up residence
in his temples the moment he learned Helena would be at
Chadwicke, and got off the phone as quickly as he could
manage.

He was still sitting nursing his headache when Lawrence
appeared once again in the doorway. "Mr. Robson is here
for you, sir."

Donovan rose to his feet and came around the front of his
desk. "Send him in. And thank you, Lawrence."

"Of course, sir."

Donovan rested against the edge of his desk with his feet
crossed at the ankles and waited for Henry to enter. As he
stood there, he realized the window opposite his desk likely
afforded him a clear view of the Barrows' house across the
way. He crossed the room and peeled back the edge of the
sheer curtain with the tip of his finger.

Nothing.

No Border terriers. No Bliss. And most important, no
Elizabeth.

A stab of disappointment pierced his chest. It felt oddly
like heartburn.

"Donovan, mate." Henry's voice boomed as he entered
the room. "What on earth are you doing? Spying on the
neighbors?"

Donovan took a giant step back from the window. "Of
course not."

Oh, good God, I am. His horror at this self-discovery was

tempered only by the fact that Henry had no real idea what he was doing or who he was looking for.

"What's so interesting out there?" Henry trod directly to the window and threw the sheers wide open.

Donovan did his best not to wince.

Henry shrugged, unimpressed, and sank into one of the chairs opposite Donovan's desk. "Looks like the usual to me. London. Blah. How long until your house party at Chadwicke? I'm ready to get out of the city."

"Three weeks." A mere twenty-one days before he left for the countryside.

The idea of inviting Elizabeth once again invaded his thoughts. He dismissed it at once, but it refused to go quietly. Visions of her at Chadwicke danced in his imagination. When he tried to seize upon them, they vanished like smoke, elusive as Miss Scott herself.

Forget it. He just needed to stick with the avoidance plan.

He ordered all thoughts of Elizabeth Scott to vacate his head at once, and concentrated on Henry. "Aren't you supposed to be in court this morning?"

Henry laughed. "Good one. You know I never go to court."

It was a running joke between them. For as long as Henry had been a prominent London barrister, Donovan could count the number of times he'd been to court on one hand. He chalked it up to Henry's good-natured demeanor. With his boyish flop of blond hair and his easygoing smile, Henry often charmed his opposing counsel into whatever he wanted for his client without ever darkening the door of a courtroom.

Donovan probably would have found it baffling had he not known Henry since he was a young boy. For someone born into old money, Henry Robson was remarkably down-to-earth. He was also deceptively brilliant, possessing a keen legal mind that belied his happy-go-lucky exterior. It was a lethal combination that served him well as a barrister. He'd been handling all legal matters pertaining to the Darcy Family Trust for years, as well as Donovan's personal affairs.

"Donovan?" Henry leaned his head against the brandy-colored leather and leveled a knowing gaze in Donovan's direction. "You've been keeping something from me."

"Ah…" Donovan struggled to come up with a reasonable explanation. He hadn't intended Elizabeth to be a secret, necessarily. But he'd gone about *not* thinking about her with such a single-minded focus that he'd forgotten almost everything else. Between her and Figgy's litter, he'd been consumed.

"Here I haven't seen you in weeks, my best mate. And now I discover you have a secret." Henry shook his head as he rose to his feet. He frowned for a second, maybe two—a long time for someone with Henry's good-humored nature. Then his face split into a wide grin, and he clasped Donovan on the shoulder. "You've got puppies. I had no idea."

"The puppies." Donovan followed him to the whelping pen where Figgy watched their approach with cautious interest. "Yes. They were born while Zara and I were in America."

Henry bent over the whelping box to get a closer look. Figgy wagged her tail in greeting, and the puppies stumbled around on the pile of blankets, craning their tiny necks in search of the new visitor. They were due to open their eyes any day now. Donovan fully intended to be the first person they saw.

"Cute little devils. And they look as though they'll make good show prospects." Henry aimed a searching gaze over the puppies, no doubt evaluating them through the eyes of a novice dog-show judge. Even though the pups were little, they could still be examined for the obvious things, like level toplines. Henry's judging status was still provisional, but with Donovan's guidance he was making great progress.

"Thank you." Donovan lifted one of the quartet of pups— a male with an unbroken expanse of chestnut across his back that promised a beautiful blanket coat—and handed him to Henry. "I think they're rather lovely myself."

While Henry let the pup burrow into his polo shirt, Donovan gathered Pudding in the palms of his hands. Her freckles were still there. It wasn't as if they would, or could, disappear. Still, every time he looked at her, Donovan half expected them to be gone. He'd never bred a Cavalier with freckles. The fortuitous timing made him marvel at the tiny ginger markings all the more.

"Do you have buyers for them already?" Henry sank back into the wing chair with the puppy curled into a ball on his lap.

"There's a list." It was extensive, necessitating the creation of a spreadsheet to keep track of the buyers who wanted a Chadwicke Cavalier. "There's always a list. I'm keeping one for myself, though."

"You know Helena would give her eyeteeth for one of these puppies. Her birthday's coming up. Maybe I should reserve one for her. Is there room on your list for your oldest friend?" Henry looked at Donovan, his expression open and trusting. Donovan had seen that expression many times over the years and come to love its bearer like a brother.

If the puppy had been for Henry, Donovan would have handed one over, no questions asked. Forget about waiting lists, contracts and payment, he would have gladly *given* Henry a puppy. Particularly since Henry was becoming more and more involved with showing dogs. He'd already gained provisional credentials for judging all of the toy breeds and a few terriers, as well. Donovan was mentoring him when his schedule allowed, teaching him all he could about the finer points of conformation. Tomorrow they were scheduled to judge together at a show in Mayfair.

Nevertheless, Helena owning one of his puppies was out of the question. He didn't need a puppy tying them together for the next ten or fifteen years.

Plus, Helena knew all about the puppies and had seen them a week ago. Didn't the fact that she'd failed to mention them to Henry speak volumes about her true interest in Donovan's dogs?

It wasn't his dogs Helena was after.

Donovan sighed, returned Pudding to the whelping pen and sat down behind his desk. "I'm not so sure that's a good idea."

"Oh?" Henry laughed as the puppy on his lap began to crawl. "Sure it is. She'd adore one of these little buggers. And she could use a dog of her own. You know she's volunteered to show one of your aunt's dogs at the upcoming Ashwyn show?"

"What?" Donovan gaped at Henry, but his gaze was immediately drawn like a magnet to the window behind his head. "No, I know nothing of the..."

Behind Henry's head, the door to the Barrows' house swung open, revealing Elizabeth in a white T-shirt and soft-looking jeans with a rip in the knee as she led Bliss and Sue Barrow's quartet of Border terriers down the sidewalk. Her hair flowed wildly about her face in a riot of loose curls. Even from this distance, Donovan could appreciate her wonderfully disheveled state. She looked as he imagined she would after slipping something on upon climbing out of bed.

His bed, perhaps?

Donovan clenched his fists. He would never get another moment's peace if those curtains remained open.

"Donovan?" Henry peered at him, his mouth quirked into a smirk. Of the two of them, Henry was the one with his head in the clouds most often. Clearly he was amused by their sudden role reversal. "You were saying?"

"Hmm?" Donovan sat straighter in his chair and forced himself to focus on his friend.

"About Helena?" Henry snickered. "You were going to tell me something about her showing your aunt Constance's dog."

"She can't show my aunt's dog. I'm judging at that show. It wouldn't be appropriate for me to judge a family member's dog, particularly one that came from my breeding lines. You know what a violation of ethics that would be."

"Well, she's doing it. The dog's already been entered. I tried to talk to her, but she would have none of it." Henry shrugged. "You know how Helena is. Relax, it's a dog show. It's all for fun, right?"

Having Helena Robson in his ring? Fun?

Hardly.

Henry continued, "Seriously, though. She's very interested in showing. It's all she talks about. She's coming along to the show tomorrow. I'd be named brother of the year if I presented her with one of your puppies. Think about it, mate. Please."

Donovan could no longer hold his tongue. He had to put a stop to this before things got out of control. "Henry, I'm not in love with your sister."

Henry blinked and stared wordlessly for a moment. Then, in his usual jovial manner, he let out a loud laugh. "I thought we were talking about puppies."

"We were. But I'm concerned Helena is only interested in dogs as a way to get to me. You know she has a thing for me." Donovan leveled his gaze at Henry. Surely he'd noticed the flirtation, the innuendos. Helena was his sister, but Henry wasn't blind. "The feeling is not mutual. I need you to know that."

"Right. I know." He waved his hand, as if a force like Helena could be done away with by a flick of the wrist. "So she has a crush? People don't choose these things, you know... romance, love. It chooses them."

It chooses them.

Bollocks.

Donovan couldn't speak for Henry or Helena. But only one person was in control of Donovan Darcy's destiny, and that person was Donovan Darcy himself.

"Well, just so we're clear." Donovan returned Figgy's puppy to the pen and watched as the little wriggling forms inched their way toward their mum in search of milk. Watching the sweet family in action was almost enough to take the edge off his frustration.

At least until his gaze was drawn once again toward the window.

And a flicker of doubt passed through him, as real as the Aston Martin parked at the curb outside.

People don't choose these things...romance, love.

It chooses them.

8

The dog show in Mayfair, Elizabeth's first in the U.K., was being held in the ballroom of a luxury hotel. From the moment she stepped through the door—held open by a uniformed doorman—Elizabeth was keenly aware this hotel was no Holiday Inn.

"Oh, my." Jenna's gaze swept over the enormous chandeliers hanging from the lobby's ceiling, dripping with strands of twinkling crystals. "Now, this is much more like it. Why aren't your shows back home held in places like this?"

"Some of them are." Elizabeth scooped Bliss into her arms and gave her a peck of a kiss on her head. "I just can't afford the entry fees for those shows."

"That's a shame." Jenna shook her head. "I might tag along more often if all your shows were like this."

"It's nice enough," Sue said as she sidled up next to them with a Border terrier tethered to each of her wrists. "But wait until you see the show site next weekend. That one's really something."

Jenna shot a smile over her shoulder as she led them across

the shiny marble floor, following the signs leading to the ballroom. "Count me in."

"Wonders never cease," Elizabeth muttered under her breath.

The ballroom was equally as grand as the lobby, perhaps even more so. Crimson carpet stretched out for miles and, surprisingly, wasn't covered in protective plastic. Elizabeth found this odd for a dog-show site.

Perhaps British show dogs have better manners than their American counterparts.

Within minutes she spotted a pointer lifting its leg and unleashing a flood of urine on a nearby silk-swathed table.

Then again, maybe not.

The pointer's handler shook his head in frustration, and a gloved assistant scurried to clean up the mess. The dog yawned, clearly bored by the entire scene.

"Is that a dog butler?" Jenna asked under her breath, nodding toward the gloved man, now on his hands and knees in dangerously close proximity to the pointer's back end.

Elizabeth smirked. "No way. There can't be such a thing, even in England."

"Said the dog nanny." Jenna gave her a firm nudge with her elbow.

Point taken.

"Come with me, girls. We'll get the dogs situated in the grooming area and then check in with the ring steward." Sue glided past the pointer, his handler and his butler, and led them toward the far end of the ballroom.

As with any other dog show, the grooming area consisted of a maze of tables, chairs and blow-dryers powerful enough to blow the fur off the biggest of standard poodles. After three trips to Sue's car to retrieve various crates and other equipment, Elizabeth had arranged a nice, quiet corner among all the chaos for their dogs. Even with Jenna's help, the sheer amount of *stuff* required to show four dogs was overwhelming. It was a far cry from showing only Bliss. But Elizabeth loved it—the dogs, the buzz of excitement in the air. All of it. And the fact that she was doing what she loved in England, of all places, made the experience even sweeter.

Then Jenna leaned in and whispered in her ear, "Look, your boyfriend's here."

Every nerve ending Elizabeth possessed went on high alert, pricked with irritation. The fact that she knew exactly who Jenna was referring to only irritated her further.

She ventured a glance ringside. Sure enough, Donovan Darcy stood beside the partitions separating the rings from the staging area—partitions consisting of red velvet ropes, with sumptuous gold tassels. No passé white lattice here.

He looked quite noble beneath the glittering kaleidoscope of light filtering down from the grand chandelier hanging from the ballroom's ceiling, as if he were the center of the galaxy, decorated with stardust. The finely tailored suit he wore certainly didn't hurt. Elizabeth had never seen a man look so good in a dinner jacket, and she'd seen her fair share. The entire effect was rather dazzling. Too dazzling, actually.

Elizabeth averted her gaze and aimed it instead at Sue. "What's he doing here? Please tell me he's not our judge."

"He's not." Sue shook her head. "Mr. Henry Robson is our judge today, but he's only provisional. That probably explains Mr. Darcy's presence."

"Provisional? What does that mean?" Jenna's eyes were still glued in Mr. Darcy's direction.

Elizabeth wished she would look somewhere else. *Any-*

where else. "It means he's a novice judge, still learning the ropes. And would you please stop staring before he sees you?"

"Too late. He just looked over here." Jenna bit her lip and shrugged apologetically. Not apologetically enough for Elizabeth's taste, however.

How does this keep happening? Considering she didn't give a damn about Donovan Darcy, Elizabeth got caught ogling him an awful lot. She breathed out a sigh. *Ogling* was a dreadfully strong word. She wasn't sure such a word applied, necessarily.

She allowed herself another quick glimpse in his direction. The corner of his most-sexy mouth hitched into a lethal grin as he looked straight back at her.

God, those eyes. Brooding, dark and dangerous.

Elizabeth's stomach fluttered, and she looked away as quickly as she could manage. Maybe *ogling* wasn't too strong a word, after all. What could she say? The man was ogle-worthy.

Jenna smirked. "Well, if that wasn't a look, I don't know what is. He has the hots for you, Lizzy."

Elizabeth rolled her eyes, but even as she did, she couldn't help but wonder why her heart was beating so hard all of a sudden. And why was she so warm? The ballroom felt unbearably hot. "You're delusional. He can't help but look that way. It's in his genes."

Jenna and Sue exchanged amused glances.

"You're in England now, dear," Sue said. "Mr. Darcy may be many things, but above all, he's an Englishman. Whether you like it or not, you're going to cross paths with him. Often. You're both dog fanciers. I suppose you could say it's your destiny."

Destined to hobnob with the likes of Donovan Darcy? The notion turned Elizabeth's still-fluttering stomach.

"My destiny?" She laughed, but it sounded all wrong. Phony. Forced. "I doubt that."

Donovan looked at Elizabeth Scott standing across the ballroom and drank in the sight of her.

He'd wondered if she would be here today. He'd both hoped for her presence and dreaded it in equal measure. Although standing there under the twinkling lights of the ballroom, with his gaze stubbornly lingering on the seductive curve of her hips, any dread he'd experienced fell away at once.

She glanced in his direction.

He smiled.

She frowned and looked away.

A hot spike of awareness speared Donovan straight through his chest. Unable to look elsewhere, he continued to watch Elizabeth. By all appearances, she was flustered. Donovan found himself wondering if she had any idea how positively ravishing he found her. He doubted it.

"Donovan."

He was barely conscious of a gentle tug on the sleeve of his dinner jacket.

"Donovan."

He cleared his throat, looked down and found Zara peering up at him.

"Sorry," he muttered, adjusting his tie simply to have something to occupy his unsteady hands.

"Is that who I think it is over there?" Zara nodded in Elizabeth's direction.

Donovan cast a cursory glance toward the grooming area. "I'm not sure I know who you're referring to."

"Elizabeth Scott. From America." Zara crossed her arms. "I know you see her. You were just looking straight at her."

Donovan cupped his sister by the elbow and steered her in the opposite direction, narrowly avoiding a collision with a bloodhound slinging drool from his jowls every which way.

"Where are we going?" Zara went along willingly enough, but her countenance was quickly morphing into what Donovan recognized as a classic teen pout. In fact, Donovan had become intimately acquainted with that expression over the past few years.

He pulled her to a stop near the entrance to the judge's hospitality area, where he assumed they were safely out of sight of Elizabeth.

Donovan released Zara's elbow.

She huffed out a sigh in that dramatic fashion teen girls had perfected over the centuries. "What is with you? Why are you hiding from Miss Scott?"

It was difficult to fathom how Elizabeth had mistaken his little sister for his lover. Especially now. She was a child. Did Elizabeth Scott really think so little of him? Was that the kind of man she took him to be?

Then again, she'd seemed unusually rattled by the whole misunderstanding. If Donovan didn't know better, he'd have sworn she'd been jealous.

"I'm not *hiding* from Elizabeth." Saying her first name sent a thrill through him. It was ridiculous, he knew. He wouldn't have admitted it to anyone to save his life. But he was powerless to stop it. Zara's eyebrows lifted in surprise at his use of that first name, so he crossed his arms and tried to look as parental as possible. "From Miss Scott."

Zara rolled her eyes. "I'm just teasing you. Quit brooding."

"Brooding?" He frowned. "I don't brood."

"Yes, you do. You're a world-class brooder."

"That's not a word." Donovan glanced at his Cartier. It was a quarter past eight. He needed to be at Henry's side in the ring in less than fifteen minutes. "Can I trust you to stay out of trouble while I mentor Henry this morning?"

"You still haven't answered my question. That was Elizabeth Scott, wasn't it?" She grinned, clearly enjoying herself.

The way Donovan saw it, there was no way to avoid her line of questioning. Once Zara got started with something, she was like a dog with a bone. Relentless.

"Yes, it was," he said.

"She's really here? In London?" Zara's face grew a fraction paler.

He peered at her, wondering what the sudden change was all about. "South Kensington, actually. For some reason, I thought this news would have delighted you."

"It would. I mean, it does. But…"

"But?"

"What about Helena?" She glanced over her shoulder as if she expected Helena Robson to pop out of nowhere at the sound of her name.

As much as Donovan hated to think about it, Helena likely was lurking around in the crowd. And Helena might, in fact, be a problem. Wasn't she always?

He could handle it. He managed one of the largest fortunes in the United Kingdom. Surely he could deal with one jealous female. "Don't worry about Helena. You're blowing the entire thing out of proportion, anyway. Miss Scott and I hardly know each other. There's nothing going on between us."

"Are you sure about that?" Zara's skepticism was written all over her face.

Donovan debated how to answer that question. Other than

fielding her complaints about Helena Robson, discussing the women in his life wasn't something he typically did with his little sister. She'd grown up without the luxury of a normal family home. Being raised by her bachelor brother already wasn't the ideal scenario. Talking about his romantic conquests didn't seem like the best way to create a stable environment for a teenage girl.

But Elizabeth Scott hardly qualified as a conquest, romantic or otherwise.

"Absolutely. Miss Scott and I are acquaintances. It's certainly not as though we're getting married." Donovan laughed off the notion. Because it was absurd, really. Preposterous. "Now go find a seat and stay out of trouble."

She gave him a final, significant look that made him wonder if he indeed had more to worry about than he thought.

"Goodbye, Zara." He nodded toward the rows of chairs lined up ringside.

"Later."

Once Zara was gone, Donovan stopped by the superintendent's table and picked up a purple ribbon identifying him as a judge. He pinned it to his lapel and headed toward the ring.

Technically, Henry was the judge in charge this morning. Donovan was there simply to observe and point Henry in the proper direction in the event he had trouble. There were nearly thirty breeds in the Terrier Group alone, the first group up. And each breed was judged against its own very specific breed standard. It was quite a bit of information for a novice judge to remember. With a year or so of experience, Henry would be a pro. Until then, Donovan was happy to serve as his adviser.

"At last." Henry grinned as Donovan crossed into the ring. "I was beginning to wonder what had become of you."

"Did you really think I'd be late?"

"No." Henry laughed. "I suppose I'm just not accustomed to beating you to the punch."

He had a point. For as long as Donovan and Henry had been friends—the better part of a lifetime—Donovan had been the responsible one. Now here he was strolling into the ring with mere seconds to spare, facing a ready-and-waiting Henry. And hadn't it been just the other day that Henry had caught him daydreaming? Donovan was forced to take stock of what was becoming of his carefully ordered life.

The answer was as obvious as the famed dreadlocks on a puli's show coat, but Donovan stubbornly refused to believe any change in his behavior had anything to do with Elizabeth Scott. Even so, he had immense trouble concentrating on what was going on in the ring as Henry plowed his way through breed after breed of terriers.

His gaze kept sweeping over the dogs and handlers waiting ringside, searching for just a glimpse of Elizabeth or one of those scruffy Border terriers she cared for. It was a problem. Donovan even somehow managed to let Henry award a first-place ribbon to a dog he was certain had recently made an illegal visit to a beauty salon. The last time he'd seen that same Scottish terrier, it had been a dusty-gray color. Now the thing was as black as a raven. Coats didn't change color like that overnight.

When at last Elizabeth stepped into the ring with one of Sue Barrow's Border terriers at the end of a show lead, Donovan wasn't sure whether to be relieved or irritated. His mood tipped toward the irritated end of the spectrum, with a dash of arousal thrown into the mix...which only made him more irritated.

She was last in the ring, behind Sue Barrow and three

other handlers with Borders. The five of them dropped to their knees to stack their dogs, and Donovan couldn't help but feel somewhat vindicated. It was nice to see Elizabeth there on her knees, seeing as she'd driven him to that position metaphorically in the few weeks since he'd first met her. Donovan wasn't accustomed to things taking him by surprise, least of all things like emotions, feelings...desires. He found it unsettling. And most unwelcome.

Henry clasped his hands behind his back and traveled down the row of terriers. Donovan watched from the other side of the ring, until Henry neared Elizabeth. Then he pushed away from the grooming table he'd been leaning against and joined Henry.

His presence had no visible effect on Elizabeth. Her soft brown eyes remained glued on her terrier. Henry, on the other hand, aimed a questioning glance at Donovan, no doubt wondering what had possessed him to join the action.

Donovan stood his ground, although he really had no idea what he was doing. He supposed he simply wanted to get close to Elizabeth. If doing so rattled her cage, all the better.

Henry furrowed his brow and turned his attention back to the exhibitors. "Very nice. Can I have you go around together, please? And then the first dog up on the table."

Donovan approached the table alongside Henry and remained mostly silent while his friend examined one dog after another. He commented once or twice on mundane things like coat condition or quality of bone, simply to justify his presence at Henry's elbow.

Until Elizabeth's turn.

"Exhibitor number five, good morning." Henry smiled politely, as he'd greeted all the other exhibitors.

"Good morning." Elizabeth looked directly at Henry and Henry alone, returning the smile.

Was Donovan mistaken, or was there a slight tremor in her voice? Not too obvious…barely discernible, in fact. But enough to tell him she was nervous. About the show? Or about being in his presence? Her stubborn determination in avoiding his gaze told him it was the latter.

This insight brought with it a shot of pure pleasure, along with the temptation to toy with Miss Scott.

"Mr. Robson, I believe the exhibitor has a name and it's not number five."

That earned him a look. Finally.

Elizabeth pinned him with an icy glare surely meant to douse the fire of attraction burning low in his belly. Its effect was entirely the opposite.

"Right…" Henry glanced back and forth between Donovan and Elizabeth. "Perhaps you'd like to share?"

"Henry, may I present Miss Elizabeth Scott?" Donovan waved a hand toward her. "Miss Scott, Mr. Henry Robson."

"Pleased to meet you, Miss Scott." Henry gave Elizabeth a slight bow.

Her face glowed bright red. "Yes, of course, Mr. Robson."

"Very well, then. Shall I look at your dog now?" Henry slid his gaze from Elizabeth to Donovan. Questions shone in his eyes.

Donovan cleared his throat.

"Perhaps you'd like to go over the dog, Mr. Darcy?" Henry asked, clearly amused.

"That's quite all right. You do the honors, Mr. Robson." Donovan crossed his arms. "I'm sure you're well acquainted with the breed standard for the Border terrier."

"Of course." Henry ran a hand up and down the dog's spine. Donovan was 75 percent certain it was the one named Rose.

"Her back should be lithe and supple," he said, fixing his gaze once again on Elizabeth.

Her cheeks, already quite crimson, darkened a few shades. Henry cleared his throat. "Yes, it should."

For the first time all morning, Donovan found he was quite enjoying himself. "Her body should be capable of being spanned by a man's hands."

Henry released a quiet cough, and Elizabeth grew instantly still. Donovan waited for her to react, but she kept her composure. He couldn't see how. He'd just about caused himself to lose it.

Her body should be capable of being spanned by a man's hands.

He swallowed, flexed his own hands—slowly, torturously—before clasping them behind his back.

Henry resumed his examination of Rose, moving over the dog's withers, back and hips before stepping in front and checking her expression.

Donovan found he just couldn't resist. "She should possess dark eyes full of fire and intelligence."

Elizabeth's own dark eyes fluttered directly toward him. "Mr. Darcy, I don't know what you think you're doing, but..."

"I beg your pardon, Miss Scott." Donovan shrugged, feigning innocence. "I'm simply quoting from the Border terrier's breed standard. Do you have a problem with that?"

He'd never before realized the breed standards were so laced with innuendo. Who in God's name had written them? Clearly someone who'd been tortured by thoughts of a woman he couldn't have...one who was indifferent to his presence.

Or so Donovan gathered.

"You haven't answered my question, Miss Scott." He winked, and she narrowed her eyes.

She looked positively murderous. "Of course I don't have a problem with your recitation of the breed standard. I wait with bated breath for you to get to the part about the dog's hindquarters."

Henry coughed loudly into his hand. Several times.

"The hindquarters? Of course." Donovan turned toward Henry, waited a beat for him to regain his composure. "What does the standard say about a Border's hindquarters, exactly? My memory fails me at the moment."

Henry pinched the bridge of his nose and muttered, "I believe the standard says, 'The dog should possess long, nicely molded thighs with muscular and racy hindquarters.'"

"Ah, yes." Donovan nodded and grinned with the utmost satisfaction. He'd been perfectly willing to forgo that particular area. Miss Scott had only herself to blame. "Racy."

Elizabeth laughed—an incredulous, spirited laugh, but a laugh nonetheless. "Racy? Really?"

"Really." Donovan bit back a smile. It required superhuman effort to keep a straight face at this point. "And we mustn't forget the terrier temperament...hard as nails, full of fire, yet sweet and affectionate at home. Game for anything."

Elizabeth rolled her eyes. "You wish."

"I'm not entirely sure, but I've a feeling we've ceased talking about dogs altogether." Henry shook his head. Donovan had a lot of explaining to do later, he supposed. "And since this *is* a dog show, can I please see your dog on the down-and-back, Miss Scott?"

"Gladly, Mr. Robson." She smiled sweetly at Henry as she scooped Rose off the table.

His mood now on the upswing, Donovan stood by and

enjoyed the view as Henry finished the terrier judging. Elizabeth and Rose were awarded Best of Breed, which seemed fair given what Donovan had put her through. Sue Barrow and her dog won Reserve Winner. The other handlers left the ring empty-handed, no doubt wondering what they'd just witnessed.

And for the rest of the day, Henry went about his business without asking Donovan for a single piece of advice.

9

Elizabeth may not have understood half of what had gone on in the breed ring, but she was extremely clear about one important fact—dog shows in Britain had better loot than in the U.S. Her Best of Breed win came with not only a rosette the size of a dinner plate, but she was also the recipient of a gorgeous satin sash, which Henry Robson had placed over her head as though she were a contestant in a beauty pageant. Elizabeth was ridiculously thrilled with it, even though technically she'd won it on the merits of Sue's dog instead of hers. Still, it was a rather dramatic entrance to the world of dog shows in the U.K. And Elizabeth naturally had to wonder if Best in Show came with a tiara.

Of course, the dog show had nearly become a sideshow, thanks to one very naughty Donovan Darcy.

At first, Elizabeth had been convinced he was outright flirting with her. She'd even begun to wonder if Jenna had been right—was Donovan actually attracted to her? Then all that outlandish talk about racy hindquarters and fiery temperaments had come about, and she'd realized what he was doing. He was vexing her, getting her back for accusing him of sleeping with his sister. She was sure of it…almost.

"Congratulations." Jenna wrapped her in a hug, then pulled back to admire Elizabeth's sash. "Wow, that's really something. You look like a beauty queen."

Jenna ran her fingertips over the smooth satin draped across Elizabeth's chest and sighed. As little girls, they'd never missed a Miss America pageant. They'd sat glued to the TV year after year, wearing homemade sashes crafted from toilet paper, listening to their mother critique the contestants' evening gowns. Elizabeth wondered if her sister was revisiting those memories, as well.

"Yes, congratulations, dear." Sue fussed with Elizabeth's sash, plucking invisible tufts of dog hair from it.

"Thank you, but let's not forget I won with *your* dog." Elizabeth looked down at Rose, who chose that moment to stretch her mouth wide open in a yawn. Clearly the novelty of Best of Breed wins, sashes and ribbons was lost on her.

"True. And I'll show her in Group later." Sue attached Elizabeth's rosette to her sash and pulled it straight. "But you can keep these if you like."

"Really? I'd love that." Bliss had yet to win something so glitzy. So far, her biggest award had been a set of Tupperware bowls she won at a small show in the Bronx. Practical, yes. Glamorous, not exactly.

"Of course. You earned them—you got Rose all groomed and ready and you showed her to perfection. And now she's another step closer to becoming a Champion." Sue gazed lovingly at Rose before turning her eyes back on Elizabeth. "You gave me a fright for a while there, though. What on earth took so long for Mr. Robson to go over Rose on the table? I thought something awful had happened, like he'd found a disqualifying fault."

"Oh, that." Elizabeth's neck grew warm. She shrugged, and her sash shifted. "That was nothing."

Jenna lifted a suspicious brow. Elizabeth steeled herself, ready for the inevitable third degree from her older sister. Luckily, Henry Robson joined their threesome before Jenna could launch her attack.

"Excuse me," he said, his gaze snagging on Jenna. He blinked a few times before turning to Elizabeth. "Miss Scott?"

"Yes?"

"Congratulations on your win." He smiled and gestured toward her rosette.

"Thank *you*. You're the one who chose us, after all." Elizabeth wasn't about to utter a word about Donovan. She was doing her best to forget he'd even been in the ring with them.

"I wanted to apologize on behalf of my colleague, Mr. Darcy." Henry winced. Elizabeth wondered what part of the conversation he was revisiting. She had dibs on the "racy hindquarters" comment. "He's ordinarily rather quiet."

Sue and Jenna raised their eyebrows in unison. Elizabeth saw that Jenna's gaze was still fixed unwaveringly on Henry.

"No need to apologize. Mr. Darcy never seems to hold his tongue in my presence. I believe I'm growing quite accustomed to it."

Henry's expression changed to one of amusement. "Is that so? How very out of character for Donovan."

Elizabeth had to suppress a snort of laughter. Were they speaking of the same Mr. Darcy? "I believe he was simply mocking me about a, um, misunderstanding we had recently. And as he pointed out, he was simply reciting the breed standard. It was nothing. Nothing at all."

Why did she keep saying that? The more she said it was nothing, the more it began to feel like *something*. Why was that? And why had the breed standard sounded so suggestive coming from Donovan? Would she have so readily seen the sensual overtones in it if someone else had been delivering those same statements?

Elizabeth bit her lip. She didn't even want to ponder that last question.

"Lizzy." Jenna cleared her throat louder than necessary.

Elizabeth's gaze bounced from Jenna to Henry, then back to Jenna. The two of them were watching one another with what looked like ardent curiosity.

"Ahem," she said. "Mr. Robson, I believe you know Sue Barrow. And this is my sister, Jenna Scott."

Henry greeted Sue with a polite handshake before turning to Jenna. "It's a pleasure to meet both of you."

Her hand still clasped in Henry's, Jenna dipped her head in a move so uncharacteristically demure, Elizabeth could only look on in wonder. "Lovely to meet you, too."

She was practically starry-eyed, as if she'd just been introduced to Daniel Craig himself.

"The pleasure is all mine." Henry gave Jenna a warm smile.

He was attractive, in a disheveled, boyish sort of way. No doubt about it. But his wholesome good looks didn't come close to approaching Donovan Darcy's level of scorching hotness. And he didn't have that confident, masculine air about him that Donovan possessed, the one that made Elizabeth all too aware of her femininity when she was in his presence.

Elizabeth blinked.

Since when had Donovan become the standard by which all other men were judged?

"Will I be seeing you later in my ring, Jenna?" Henry

asked, *still* holding her hand in what was beginning to look like the world's longest handshake.

"Oh, no. I'm just here to cheer for my sister and Sue." Jenna smiled amiably, as if she *lived* for being a dog-show spectator. It was one of the oddest things Elizabeth had ever seen.

She narrowed her gaze at Jenna. *Who are you, and what have you done with my sister?*

"Well, that's a pity." Henry shook his head. "We'll have to meet again some other time, I suppose."

"That would be lovely."

Henry angled his head toward her. "Tomorrow evening, perhaps?"

Elizabeth's jaw fell open. Jenna had been on British soil for all of twenty-four hours and here she was scheduling a date with a London aristocrat. And she seemed perfectly comfortable doing so, as if she jetted all over the world and flirted with handsome foreigners all the time.

How was it possible?

She was beginning to wonder if they were actually related when a tall blonde woman nudged her way next to Henry. "Henry, here you are. I've been looking for you everywhere. Have you seen Donovan? I'm bored stiff."

Jenna's dreamy-eyed demeanor took an immediate hit, especially when the strange woman draped herself over Henry's arm. She looked vaguely familiar to Elizabeth. Then again, considering she was thin as a whippet, dressed to the nines and a shade or two tanner than what could be considered natural, she resembled the majority of women on the Upper West Side of Manhattan.

Henry tore his gaze from Jenna with obvious reluctance. "Helena, this is Sue Barrow, Elizabeth Scott and her sister Jenna. Ladies, this is Helena Robson, my sister."

The relief on Jenna's face bordered on comical. Elizabeth stifled a laugh. It made her feel oddly better to know that she wasn't the only one running around making crazy assumptions about siblings.

"Pleased to meet you," Elizabeth said, giving Rose's lead a gentle tug. The Border terrier had reached her quivering nose toward Helena, anxious for a sniff. Something told Elizabeth that Henry's sister wasn't the type to tolerate dog drool.

"Elizabeth Scott?" For a split second, Helena's eyes narrowed. Then, just as quickly, they widened again. Her eyelashes were thick and long—too lavish to be natural. They reminded Elizabeth of the photos many of the brides from Scott Bridal carried around and wanted to emulate.

Real Housewives eyelashes, her mother called them.

Why anyone would wear fake eyelashes and high heels to a dog show was a mystery to Elizabeth. "Nice to meet you, Helena. Are you an exhibitor?"

She didn't need to ask. There was no way this woman could run around the ring in those shoes. But she was at a loss as to what else to say.

"Oh, no." Helena shot a proprietary look in the direction of the ring, where Donovan had returned and was chatting with one of the other judges. "I'm a friend—a special friend, you might say—of one of the judges. Donovan Darcy."

"Helena," Henry muttered, shaking his head.

Elizabeth's grip tightened on Rose's leash. Something about the tone of Helena's voice rubbed her the wrong way. She pasted on a smile. "Oh. I see."

Helena reached a perfectly manicured hand toward Elizabeth's rosette. "Best of Breed. Congratulations."

She wanted to take a step backward, away from that outstretched hand, but didn't think she could manage without stepping on a Border terrier toe. "Thank you."

"He certainly seems to fancy you." Helena cast another glance toward Donovan, who now stood watching them from the ring.

He had to be a good fifteen feet away, but even from this distance Elizabeth could see the storm clouds gathering in his eyes.

She wondered what that was all about. "You're mistaken. It's the dog he fancies."

"If you say so." Helena's lips curved into a smile that in no way reached her eyes behind those crazy lashes. "It was lovely meeting you, Elizabeth."

"You, too," Elizabeth said, wishing with all her might she could get the phrase *special friend* out of her head. Donovan could have all the friends he wanted, special or otherwise. Why should she care?

"Good day, ladies." Henry turned to Elizabeth. "I suppose I'll see you later in the Terrier Group ring?"

"Oh, no. Sue will be showing Rose in Group." *Thank God.*

"Very well, then." Henry nodded, cast a prolonged glance at Jenna and headed back toward the ring with his sister in tow.

Sue frowned in their absence. "Am I the only one who found that whole conversation rather odd?"

"Absolutely not," Elizabeth said. "Henry seems nice, but that sister of his is a piece of work."

"You mean Mr. Darcy's *special friend?*" Jenna rolled her eyes. "She's jealous. I've seen her type a thousand times before— bitter bridesmaid."

Bitter bridesmaid—a term they'd coined years ago at Scott Bridal to describe catty, unpleasant women who accompanied their friends to the shop, then systematically went about criticizing every bridal decision they made. Elizabeth wasn't sure the term altogether applied to Helena Robson, but it was funny nonetheless.

"Bitter bridesmaid." She echoed Jenna's sentiment with a smile.

"Judging is about to resume. Don't you need to get Bliss brushed out, Elizabeth?" Sue asked as they headed back toward the grooming area.

"Yes. God willing, Henry Robson isn't judging Cavaliers this afternoon." He'd given her a big win, but Elizabeth didn't think she could take another round in the ring with him if Donovan would be present.

"He's not, dear."

"It's not Donovan, either, is it?" That would be even worse.

Sue sank into one of the chairs at their setup. Violet flat-footed straight from the ballroom floor into Sue's lap. "No, dear. It's Mrs. Smith-Crowley. She's been a fixture in the dog fancy in London for at least sixty years. Blind in one eye, half-blind in the other and a little on the senile side, I'm afraid."

Jenna tilted her head. "How on earth can she judge the dogs if she can't see?"

Mrs. Smith-Crowley could have been unable to tell the difference between a dog and a cat, for all Elizabeth cared…so long as she didn't have anything to do with Donovan Darcy.

Elizabeth slid her gaze to Sue as she guided Rose into her crate. "This Mrs. Smith-Crowley isn't provisional, is she? No mentor in the ring?"

"I should say not." Sue laughed. "She's been judging dogs since long before you were born."

"Good. She sounds positively delightful," Elizabeth said.

And she meant it from the bottom of her heart.

★ ★ ★

"Jenna, please tell me we don't have to stay long." Elizabeth jammed a twenty-pound note into the machine and retrieved two pink passes for the tube from the silver dish below. "You know how I feel about these things."

"Jeez Louise, settle down. We're not even there yet. We're staying an hour. Two, tops. I have a date with Henry later. Besides, I hung out with you all day yesterday at that dog show. You can suffer through an hour or two at a bridal fair with me." Jenna followed Elizabeth toward the waiting train, weaving through the throng of Londoners headed home from work.

Elizabeth couldn't help but envy them. She'd done nothing but unpack dog-show paraphernalia and trim terrier toenails all day and would have loved the simple luxury of curling up with a pint of ice cream in front of bad reality television. Even bad *British* reality television—they loved Gordon Ramsay with such a passion over here that sometimes it seemed as if he were on every BBC channel—sounded more appealing than attending the Temperley Bridal Market with Jenna.

But Jenna being Jenna had convinced her to come along. Even though the thought of all those wedding dresses was enough to make Elizabeth want to hurl. She'd worn head-to-toe black out of protest.

Jenna eyed her up and down as the train doors closed and a polite British voice told passengers to mind the gap. "You look like you're headed to a funeral."

Elizabeth snorted. "I'd almost rather go to a funeral than a wedding."

"It's not a wedding. It's a bridal fair." Jenna gave the seat beside her a pat. "We'll have fun. Free champagne, beautiful dresses. What's there to be so worked up about?"

The romance of it all, for one thing.

It was difficult to grow up in the bridal business, among all those Bridezillas and over-the-top wedding plans, and not become at least a tad bit cynical about the whole thing. She had no idea how Jenna managed to remain such a romantic.

And then there was the whole Markham encounter—the final nail in the coffin for Elizabeth.

Her interest in romance was already at an all-time low. And the odd encounters with Donovan Darcy weren't helping matters. She was more confused than anything, and somehow spending the evening amid all those yards of tulle and lace seemed like the last thing she needed.

Too late, she thought as she and Jenna stepped into the posh gallery in Chelsea where the Bridal Market was being held. It was like being slapped in the face by Cupid. They'd hardly crossed the threshold and already a waiter was thrusting pink champagne at them, offered up in saucer-style glasses with baby's breath wound around the stems. Elizabeth almost spilled hers as a model wearing a bridal gown nearly as wide as it was long bumped her from behind.

She took a sip to prevent it sloshing over the rim. It was sweet. Sickeningly so.

"Come on, the runway show is toward the back and that's what I really want to see." Jenna pulled her forward.

Elizabeth took a deep breath and allowed herself to be dragged through the mass of giddy brides-to-be. She cast a longing glance at the chocolate fountain in the center of the room. It wasn't exactly that pint of Ben & Jerry's she craved, but it would do in a pinch.

"I have seats reserved in the front row." Jenna steered them toward two white folding chairs festooned with swags of pink roses and placards that read Scott Bridal.

Elizabeth sank into hers and sent up a silent yet desperate prayer that everything with the Barclay School would be resolved. If she lost her job permanently, this was exactly the sort of life she had in store when she returned to the States. Except, in addition to all the baby's breath, she'd have her mother to deal with.

And if she did end up being ousted from the privileged world of the Barclay School, the thought of once again zipping wealthy socialites into twenty-thousand-dollar dresses was difficult to stomach.

She took another gulp of the sweet champagne.

Beside her, Jenna gazed up at the first model gliding down the runway, wearing a slinky ivory gown with a polka-dot tulle overlay. "Oh, look at that. Gorgeous."

Elizabeth gave an absent nod of agreement and glanced at the two empty chairs on her opposite side. Would anyone notice if she lay across them in the fetal position?

Probably, she figured. *Too bad.*

Just as she was about to turn her attention back to the runway, a woman approached the front row…a woman with an unmistakable whippetlike quality about her.

"Oh, no." Elizabeth grabbed Jenna's arm. "Look who's coming this way. Helena Robson."

Jenna's head whipped from the direction of the runway. She craned her neck and peered above Elizabeth's head. "You're kidding. Is Henry with her?"

"I doubt it. This is a bridal fair. Remember?" Elizabeth muttered, hoping in desperation that Helena would move right past them and sit somewhere else. *Anywhere* else.

But of course, she didn't. She sat right down in the chair next to Elizabeth, close enough to touch. Certainly close enough for Elizabeth to choke on the cloud of her flowery perfume.

Balenciaga Paris, if Elizabeth had to venture a guess. A favorite scent of blushing brides everywhere.

Elizabeth coughed and kept her gaze glued to the runway where a satin gown in fire-engine red was drawing shocked gasps from the crowd.

Red wedding gowns actually weren't all that shocking. In some countries, they were even traditional. And of course they were often favored by brides who longed to make a dramatic entrance. The fact that Elizabeth knew these things made her long for a trip to the chocolate fountain all the more.

"What do you think, Elizabeth?" Jenna asked. "We need something new in red at Scott Bridal. We've only carried the same small selection for years."

Elizabeth shrugged. "It's nice, I suppose. If you're into that sort of thing." Personally, she wouldn't be caught dead walking down the aisle in head-to-toe crimson. Not that she planned on walking down the aisle. Ever.

"Elizabeth? Elizabeth Scott?" Helena leaned toward her, her eyes widening in apparent recognition. "It *is* you. How very odd running into you here."

Is it really so odd? Elizabeth bristled. *Why shouldn't I be here? I could be engaged as easily as the next girl…if I wanted to be. Which I* don't.

"Helena, hi," Elizabeth said, trying with all her might to give this ridiculous woman the benefit of the doubt. "My family owns a bridal shop in the States."

"I see." Helena's superplump lips curved into a satisfied smile. "That explains it."

And there it was—the look all those Bridezillas had been giving Elizabeth for years. The smug expression of someone looking down on a servant. Seeing it on the face of Donovan's *special friend* made it sting all the more.

"You're visiting us from America, then?" Helena asked, obviously in no hurry to turn her attention back to the runway.

Elizabeth longed for something crazy to make an appearance up there—a glow-in-the-dark dress, perhaps? Anything.

"Yes." Elizabeth nodded, determined to play nice. "I live in New York."

"New York. How wonderful. Terrific shopping." Helena fiddled with a bracelet on her slender wrist. Elizabeth somehow knew Helena's terrific shopping reference didn't include H&M—or any of the other places on her go-to shopping list.

"And you're here on holiday?"

"You could say that. I'm on sabbatical from my teaching job." She mentally kicked herself for bringing up her job in the States. What had she been thinking? The last thing she needed was for wind of the scandal to catch up with her over here. The less said about her job back home, the better.

"You're a teacher?" Helena lifted a perfectly arched brow. "How positively noble of you."

"I wouldn't go that far." Elizabeth shrugged in a way she hoped looked nonchalant. "It's a job."

"And how long is your sabbatical?"

Elizabeth's lips twitched, and it became almost impossible to hold on to any trace of her pasted-on smile. She had to end this conversation, or at the very least steer it away from her job. "A few weeks."

Not that it was any business of Helena Robson's.

Jenna *finally* interrupted, putting Elizabeth out of her misery. "So what brings you to the bridal fair, Helena? Is there a wedding in your future?"

"Oh, yes. Most definitely," Helena purred and aimed a piercing look at Elizabeth.

Elizabeth squirmed in her seat. Had she missed something here? Why all the hostility?

The air suddenly grew so thick the tension could be cut with a knife. Or perhaps with one of the razor-sharp pleats on the ultramodern bridal gown currently being showcased on the runway.

Elizabeth had to get out of there. At once.

"Well, we've got to get going, right, Jenna? I saw a display of bridesmaid dresses way over there that have our names written all over them." Elizabeth stood. "You enjoy yourself."

"What was that?" Jenna whispered as Elizabeth made a beeline for the bridesmaid display. If her route took them past the chocolate fountain, then so be it.

"Sorry. But something about that woman just gives me the creeps."

"Her brother is awfully cute, though. I can't wait to see him later. He seems so nice. Don't you think? I like him." Talking about Henry, Jenna would have sounded like a wistful romantic even if she hadn't been standing in a room full of lace, tulle and roses.

Elizabeth shrugged. "I suppose you've liked many a stupider person."

"Lizzy!" Jenna swatted her with her tiny clutch handbag.

"Ah, bridesmaid dresses." Elizabeth nearly gasped when her gaze fell on a shimmering, floor-length gold Marchesa gown. "This is much more my speed."

"You know what they say. Always a bridesmaid..."

"Never a bride." Elizabeth nodded resolutely and let her fingertips graze the fabric of the lovely gown. It was like liquid gold in her hands. "That's just fine with me."

★ ★ ★

"I told you we'd have fun," Jenna said as they rounded the corner of the darkened cupcake bakery and headed toward the Barrows' townhome. "And you even bought a new dress. I'll pick it up for you tomorrow after they make the alterations."

"I can't say I had fun, exactly." Although the three glasses of champagne she'd downed after her surprise encounter with Helena Robson hadn't hurt. Elizabeth shook her head. "I don't know what got into me. When am I ever going to wear a Marchesa ball gown?"

"Moët & Chandon got into you. And I'm a bad influence, I suppose. But you never know." Jenna winked. "Perhaps you'll find an occasion to wear that gorgeous ball gown somewhere with your charming Englishman."

Elizabeth snorted. "He's not *my* Englishman, and he isn't altogether charming."

"Ouch." A very familiar, very *male* voice came out of the darkness. "Although I've heard worse things said about me, I suppose."

Jenna stopped in her tracks, peering into the shadows as Donovan Darcy emerged with Finneus trailing alongside him. At the sight of him, Elizabeth's stomach performed a rebellious flip. She felt her face flush, fast and hot, and she found herself grateful for the darkness.

"Donovan Darcy." For some odd reason, it was a struggle to keep her voice even. "That's rather presumptuous, don't you think? This is London. We could be talking about any of a whole host of Englishmen."

His eyes blazed. "Well, I heard the annoyance in your tone, so I jumped to the most obvious conclusion."

"Ahem." Jenna frowned and inched her way toward the

Barrows' door. "I need to change for my dinner date. I'll just go inside and leave you two to chat."

The door clicked shut behind her.

Donovan cocked his head and looked at Elizabeth for a long, silent moment. She felt her breath grow shallow, which was ludicrous really. It wasn't as if she had *feelings* for Donovan Darcy. He'd caught her by surprise, that was all. Lurking around in the dark like that...

He took a step closer. "That was your sister, was it not? The one I met before?"

He lifted an eyebrow, and that subtle movement spoke volumes—*before,* as in *before you knew I wasn't sleeping with a teenager.*

"Yes." She nodded. "Jenna. She arrived a few days ago. It was a nice surprise."

"I suppose she'll be keeping you rather busy, sightseeing and all that?"

Yes, immensely busy. I'll hardly have time to breathe, much less think about you, your ridiculously charming accent or the perfect knots in your ties.

Elizabeth swallowed. "Not really. She's here on business."

"Then perhaps you'd allow Finneus and me to accompany you and your charges on a walk tomorrow?" He frowned, as if surprised at the words that had just come from his mouth.

They caught Elizabeth off guard as well, which was the only logical explanation for her response. "I'd like that very much."

"Very well, then." The frown on Donovan's face relaxed and turned into something more resembling a contented grin. "I'll see you tomorrow afternoon."

"Yes, I'll see you then." Elizabeth took a step backward, toward the door.

She needed to get inside before she agreed to something more. The way the moonlight danced on Donovan's handsome features was playing tricks on her, making her vulnerable. Too vulnerable.

"Good night, Elizabeth," he said, her name sounding far too sultry on his lips.

"Good night."

10

"Lizzy, I totally forgot." Jenna slid a fat manila envelope across the breakfast table toward Elizabeth. "I brought you something from home."

"Oh?" Elizabeth paused from spreading a thick layer of orange marmalade on her toast.

"Don't get your hopes up. It's only your mail." Jenna took a sip of her tea. English Breakfast Tea. Not quite as satisfying as coffee for Jenna, if the wistful look on her face was any indication.

"Anything exciting?" Sue asked as she looked up from her newspaper. The *Daily Mail*. It was a bit racier than your average newspaper. So Elizabeth had discovered when she read an article the other day referring to Justin Timberlake as *Trouser Snake*.

"Let's see." Elizabeth slid a butter knife under the envelope's flap.

A familiar assortment of bills fell to the table among an avalanche of catalogs. *PetEdge. In the Company of Dogs. J-B Wholesale Pet Supplies.*

Same old, same old.

Then she saw something that made her heart leap straight

to her throat—a thick cream-colored envelope with a familiar posh insignia.

Her fingers trembling, she slipped it from the stack of bills. Just as she thought, the return address bore the crest of the Barclay School.

Elizabeth stared at it, paralyzed.

The investigation couldn't possibly be concluded already, could it?

She dropped it as if the heavy card stock had burned her fingers. England had become a healthy distraction from the mess at work. Now, faced with a concrete reminder of all that had transpired, she felt sick. The ache that had settled in her chest that fateful afternoon of her meeting with Dr. Thurston—and had all but vanished when she'd crossed the Atlantic—returned with a pang.

"Is something wrong, sis?" Jenna asked, her voice laced with worry.

Elizabeth massaged her breastbone and tried not to feel faint as she stared at the envelope.

"Elizabeth?" Sue eyed her with concern over the top of her paper. "Everything all right, dear? You look like you've seen a ghost."

Grant Markham's image invaded her memory, his lips curled into a haughty sneer.

Not a ghost. More like evil incarnate.

"I'm sure it's nothing." Heart pounding, Elizabeth picked up the envelope again. "I got a letter from work."

"Oh, no. I didn't see that. I'm sorry I didn't warn you." Jenna's face grew pale.

"Work?" Sue frowned. "You mean the school where you've been teaching? Didn't they lay you off? Don't tell me they're trying to snatch you away from me already. You've barely just gotten here."

Sue's words gave Elizabeth the courage to break the envelope's seal. At least she had a job. And a place to live, far nicer than any apartment she could afford in New York. Of course, she couldn't stay in London forever. She wasn't even a British citizen. Wouldn't someone kick her out eventually? If not Sue or Alan, some immigration official?

"I'm sure it's nothing like that," Elizabeth said as she unfolded the contents of the envelope—a single sheet of paper, with the school crest emblazoned at the uppermost edge.

She took a deep breath and forced herself to start at the beginning and read the words one at a time.

Dear Miss Scott,
The board of directors has concluded its investigation into the matter of the allegations concerning your employment as a teacher at the Barclay School.

We feel that it is in the best interest of all parties involved that your temporary suspension be made permanent, effective immediately. As you may recall, since the Barclay School is a private institution of learning, your employment is subject to termination at any time, with or without cause.

As a gesture of our goodwill, a severance check equal to four weeks' pay will be sent to you under separate cover.
Sincerely,
The Board of Directors
The Barclay School

All ten members of the board had signed the bottom of the letter, with Mrs. Grant Markham's swirling signature given top billing. A coincidence? Elizabeth doubted it.

"Lizzy, what is it?" Jenna reached for her free hand and gave it a squeeze.

The gesture barely registered in Elizabeth's consciousness.

She reread the letter. Once, twice, a third time, telling herself it wasn't the end of the world. At least they hadn't actually accused her of extortion.

It was a small consolation.

After all those years of working at Scott Bridal, catering to the upper echelons of society, she thought she'd finally been accepted. She'd felt as though she'd found her place. Sure, she was still in a different league from the families who sent their children to the Barclay School. But she loved those kids. And she thought everyone knew that about her and respected her devotion to the school.

She couldn't have been more wrong.

She wadded the letter into a ball, her hands trembling with fury. Grant Markham had won, just as she'd feared he would. And now, through no fault of her own, she was no longer a teacher.

"I take it that was not good news?" Sue's gaze flitted between Elizabeth and Jenna as she peered over the top of her glasses.

Elizabeth shook her head, her vision growing cloudy with tears. She cleared her throat. The last thing she wanted to do was spill her guts to Sue, no matter how tempting that might be. They'd grown close in the past week and a half, but she was still Elizabeth's boss. "My, um, layoff has become permanent."

Sue folded her newspaper and laid it on the table. "Don't worry about it, dear. You're in Britain now. You have a job and a place to stay right here. We have loads of shows to attend. Rose isn't a Champion yet. And Bliss hasn't won Best in Show." Sue winked.

Of course Bliss hadn't won Best in Show. She hadn't even cracked into the top four of her breed under the half-blind judge at the show in Mayfair.

Sue's kindness only made Elizabeth feel worse for not being 100 percent truthful. She blinked back a fresh wave of tears and pushed away from the table. "I think I need to let this sink in. Do you mind if I go upstairs for a little bit?"

"Lizzy, let me go up with you. I don't need to get to the Bridal Market right away...." Jenna stood to follow, but Elizabeth shook her head.

"No, please. You go on ahead. I'll be fine."

But as she climbed the stairs to her room, the truth began to sink into her bones.

Things were not fine. She didn't see how they ever would be fine again.

England was going to her head. She would be better off once she realized none of this was real. The letter from the Barclay School had given her a heaping dose of reality. She was a disgraced teacher from America. She was no more respected by the wealthy than she'd been when she'd knelt at their feet to pin up the hems of their wedding gowns.

This land of palaces and charming aristocrats was nothing more than a fairy tale. And once the fairy tale was over, Elizabeth would have nowhere to go.

Donovan took an exploratory look up and down Sumner Place, with a sense of worry gnawing at his gut and a bored Finneus winding his leash around his legs.

Elizabeth was late.

He'd been at their meeting place beneath the awning of the

cupcake bakery for nearly half an hour. After twenty minutes had passed, he'd even tucked Finneus under his arm and ventured inside, searching for her among the mob of customers seeking to satisfy their midafternoon sugar cravings. She wasn't there, not that he really expected to find her inside with all her canine charges. Donovan doubted sneaking the Border terriers into a bakery would be an easy task, regardless of their impeccable manners. Even the air smelled of butter and cream. Finneus's nose twitched, and he trained his eyes on a crystal platter of black-currant-and-licorice cakes. Donovan whisked him outside before one went missing.

One of two things was transpiring, he realized. Either something had happened to Elizabeth, or he'd been stood up.

At first, Donovan wasn't sure which prospect he found more alarming. He'd never been stood up before. Not once in his entire life. The very idea was preposterous. What woman in her right mind would stand up Donovan Darcy? He frowned and wondered if this was the sort of thing regular blokes worried about.

But the idea of some sort of harm coming to Elizabeth was worse. Obviously. He'd have to be a complete monster to prefer her to be harmed in some way to her simply choosing not to spend time with him. And he wasn't a monster.

Of course, if anyone was prone to think him monstrous in any way, it was Elizabeth. Fiery Elizabeth, with her propensity to put him in his place with the least bit of provocation.

Fiery Elizabeth, with those ripe, kissable lips and dangerously seductive eyes.

Donovan frowned and glanced left and right, as though passersby were privy to his thoughts. The apparent nonchalance of the people who strode past him, eyes downcast and headed toward the South Kensington tube station, only spiked his frustration.

"This simply will not do," he announced to no one.

He plucked Finneus off the pavement again, tucked the dog under his arm and marched off in the direction of the Barrows' townhome.

Something was wrong. He could sense it. And if it wasn't... well, this would be the first time he'd been left hanging. There was a first time for everything, he supposed, although the idea of it left him with a dull pain in his temples.

He knocked on the door. It swung open, revealing a surprised-looking Sue Barrow. She blinked at him for a few seconds as her eyebrows crept up her forehead. "Mr. Darcy. What a delight. Would you care to come in?"

The dogs—all four Borders plus Bliss—milled about at Sue's feet, but his Elizabeth was nowhere to be seen.

His Elizabeth?

He knew he had no real right to make such a claim, and frankly, he wasn't even sure he wanted the privilege. The woman could be maddening, as present circumstances indicated.

But still, there it was. Right on the very edges of his consciousness—*his* Elizabeth. "I'm actually looking for Elizabeth. Is she home?"

"Come in, come in." Sue Barrow ushered him inside a foyer identical to his own, but Donovan noticed her smile dim somewhat. "Elizabeth is upstairs. She received some news today that upset her. Perhaps you can cheer her up."

Donovan hesitated, torn between bounding up the stairs two at a time and forgetting the whole ordeal and marching back across the street to the safe confines of his office. "I hate to intrude."

"It's no intrusion, I'm sure." Sue leaned toward him and pretended to whisper, although her voice could still be heard as clear as a bell. "Perhaps you can give Elizabeth a little cheer."

Could he? Could he, really? Or would his presence simply make things worse? It could go either way, he supposed. "I'll certainly give it a go."

Sue lit up as though one of her Border terriers had just been named Best in Show at Crufts.

Finneus squirmed in his arms. He'd spotted the other dogs and made no secret of wanting to be let loose with his walking companions.

"Let that naughty fellow down." Sue waved a hand toward Finneus. "Leave him here with us. The rain has stopped, so we've decided to spend the day in the garden."

As soon as the words left Sue's mouth, the Border terriers all turned toward the back of the house. They looked like a retreating regiment as they headed toward what Donovan assumed was the garden. He lowered Finneus to the ground, and after his dog gave Bliss's nose a lick, the two Cavaliers followed after the Borders.

"Off we go." Sue turned to follow the six wagging tails. She shot a parting glance over her shoulder and pointed toward the staircase. "Elizabeth's right up there. All the way to the top."

"Yes, ma'am." Donovan smiled. "And thank you."

She gave him a final wave over her shoulder. "My pleasure, Mr. Darcy."

If Sue Barrow had drawn Donovan a map, he still wouldn't have reached Elizabeth's room any faster. He was embarrassed to admit, even to himself, he'd watched her looking out of that window enough times to have a fairly accurate picture of the whereabouts of her room. It wasn't until he'd reached the top of the stairs and knocked on her closed door that he realized he hadn't even taken the time to unbutton his coat.

He heard a shuffling noise coming from her room and then there she was…in those ripped jeans that made his pulse quicken.

"Donovan?" She appeared disoriented to find him at her door. Then she gasped, and her head whipped around to look at the clock on her nightstand. "Our walk. Oh, my gosh. I'm so sorry. I totally forgot."

Her eyes were shiny with fresh tears, and the tip of her nose was as pink as a rosebud, but she was still as lovely as ever. Her toenails, equally pink, peeked out from the ragged hem of her jeans. Something about those bare feet and her sad smile gave Donovan the sudden urge to scoop her up and pull her into his lap on the edge of the bed.

He busied himself with unbuttoning his overcoat so he wouldn't act on the impulse. "It's okay. I was worried about you, that's all. I hope you don't mind my coming by to check on you."

"Of course not." She sniffed and dabbed at her nose with a wadded-up tissue.

Donovan pulled a handkerchief from his coat pocket and offered it to her. "Here you go."

"Thank you." She reached for it with a tentative hand.

Her hesitation gave birth to a fear that he was soon to be dismissed. Donovan wasn't about to go. "May I come in?"

"Oh." She glanced at the room behind her, her gaze lingering on the bed for a split second. Just long enough for Donovan to notice. "Um, sure."

She fumbled with his handkerchief as he entered her room. He liked the idea of her keeping it. The thought of her having something of his—even something as simple as a mono-grammed handkerchief—appealed to him. He smiled at her.

She smiled back, but the gesture was accompanied by a slight wobble of her chin. "I'm sorry about this afternoon, Donovan. Did you wait long?"

The bed, a grand affair with tall, slender posts and piled with luxurious bedding, loomed behind her. It pained him not to look at it, to imagine Elizabeth wearing nothing but those soft blue bed linens.

He cleared his throat. "Not long. A half hour or so."

"A half hour is a long time." Her eyes grew shiny again. "I'm sorry. I got a letter earlier today...."

Her voice trailed off, and she gestured to the dustbin beside her nightstand, where, apparently, the offensive letter had taken up residence. Its contents may have been relegated to the rubbish, but they obviously still had the power to cause pain.

"A letter?" he asked, deliberately keeping his concern to himself that the letter might be from a boyfriend. He'd never before considered the prospect she was seeing someone.

A collection of bachelors flashed in his mind—bohemian intellectuals who walked around unshaven, with piles of books under their arms; do-gooder sorts with earnest expressions and worn, leather messenger bags slung over their shoulders; lean, muscled athletes who preferred bicycles to the underground.

His fists clenched of their own volition.

"It's from my employer back in the States." She dropped her gaze to the floor. Donovan followed it, but got momentarily distracted by the pink of her toenails. "I've been fired."

"Sacked?" Donovan did his best to hide his inexplicable relief at the fact that there was no boyfriend and no job beckoning her back home. He told himself it didn't really mean anything. He'd simply grown accustomed to having her around. "That's terrible."

She lifted her gaze to his. "Why are you smiling?"

"I'm not smiling," he said as he tried to stop the grin that sprung to his lips.

"Yes, you are."

"No." He struggled, in vain, to frown. "No, I'm not."

"Not everyone is born rich, you know." Elizabeth lifted an angry eyebrow.

He'd offended her. Naturally.

Still, indignation was far better than tears. His smile grew a fraction wider. "Of course not."

"Some of us have to work for a living. But you wouldn't know anything about that, would you?" She hurled his handkerchief at his chest.

So much for her keeping it.

Donovan caught it before it made contact with his face. "You think I don't work?"

She smirked at him. A full-on smirk he should have found infuriating, but for some reason it bordered on adorable. "When was the last time you had a real job?"

"I have a job. And it's most assuredly real." He went to work neatly folding the now-damp handkerchief.

"Truly? And what is it you do, exactly?"

"I manage the Darcy Family Trust," he answered and slipped the handkerchief back into his pocket, safely out of throwing range.

"And what exactly does that entail? Because to me, it sounds like an excuse to sit around and count your money all day." She sniffled.

It was that single, vulnerable sniffle that stopped Donovan

from turning her over his knee and spanking her as though she were a petulant child.

"It's not as easy as it sounds. I seem to have lost count somewhere around two or three million. When I get home, I'll have to start all over again," he answered drily.

She gaped at him. For once, she appeared at a loss for words.

It was an opening. An opening Donovan wasn't about to miss.

"I think it's time," he said.

"Time for what?" She glanced at the clock on the night table again. "Call me crazy, but I'm not sure I feel like taking a walk with you at the moment. Besides, I should probably rescue Sue. She's been looking after the dogs for a while now."

"Sue's fine. She just kidnapped Finneus and absconded with him, too." He crossed his arms and did his best to look serious. "I think it's time I show you."

"Show me what, exactly?" She gave him a wary once-over.

"One of my favorite places in London."

She glanced down at her T-shirt, jeans and bare feet. Her toes wiggled on the blue area rug. "Now? Look at me. I'm a mess. I spent my morning grooming dogs."

"You're perfect." Donovan closed the short distance between them, ignoring the look of alarm that crossed Elizabeth's face.

She watched with obvious wariness as he unwound the cashmere Burberry scarf from the collar of his overcoat. With a gentle hand, he reached for her hair. Her eyes grew wide, and Donovan heard her sharp inhale of breath as he gathered her chestnut waves in one hand and looped the scarf around her neck with the other.

"Now you just need a coat and you're good to go," he said, noting the husky quality of his own voice.

She brushed her cheek against the scarf. "Mmm, soft. Nice."

Yes. Nice.

"You'll come with me, then?" He gave the end of the scarf a tug and tried not to succumb to the impulse to pull her into his arms. No doubt such a maneuver wouldn't have been well received.

"Look at you, Donovan. You're wearing a suit. I can't just pull on a coat and boots and accompany you to some mysterious location."

He pulled at the knot in his tie and loosened it, sliding the strip of silk from around his neck. After unbuttoning the top two buttons of his shirt, he tossed the tie over Elizabeth's shoulder. It landed on her bed. "Is this better?"

"Are you going to keep shedding articles of clothing until I agree to come with you?" She waved her hand toward the tie, dangling seductively from the corner of the enormous bed. "Is that your strategy?"

As strategies went, it was a bloody good one. "Don't put ideas in my head."

She gave him a soulful look. He could still see the sorrow etched in her features, but the shimmer of tears had vanished from her eyes, as had the anger. They were luminous now. A man could lose himself in eyes like those. Perhaps the man in question already had.

Elizabeth swallowed. Donovan could see the rise and fall of it in the slender column of her throat. Something told him she wasn't thinking about the state of her employment at the moment.

"I'll be ready in five minutes," she said.

11

Elizabeth settled into the supple leather passenger seat of Donovan's Aston Martin as he closed her door, jogged to the driver's side and climbed in behind the steering wheel. It was so strange to see him there, sitting to her right. Elizabeth realized that while she'd ridden in the back of a taxicab or two—and the Jaguar, of course—this was her first time in the front seat of a British vehicle. She wondered if she'd ever grow accustomed to it.

Then Donovan started the ignition, and she forgot all about where she was sitting. The engine roared to life, and she felt as though she were in a James Bond movie.

Jenna would positively *die*.

"Are you comfortable?" Donovan smiled at her as he turned off Sumner Place and headed toward the High Street.

"Very much so." She begrudgingly admitted to herself there were indeed inoffensive perks that came with being wealthy. "Where are we going?"

Donovan shook his head, and his lips curved into a mischievous grin. "I'm afraid I can't tell you."

"Still?"

"It's a surprise." He maneuvered the car past the South Kensington tube station. "Don't worry, though. It's not far."

Elizabeth's stomach flipped, which she attributed to the way Donovan's car hugged the road. She'd been fired. Permanently. Romance was the last thing on her mind. Or so she told herself.

"Almost there, in fact." Donovan turned right onto Brompton Road. A wall of slick storefronts flanked the street on either side.

Names like Emporio Armani, Mulberry and L.K.Bennett were spelled out in tasteful block letters on the white molding of the shops. The farther up the street they went, the more impressive the names. It all looked vaguely familiar, like Fifth Avenue in New York, but with a decidedly English flair.

Surely Donovan wasn't taking her shopping in an effort to cheer her up. If he thought buying her things would make her forget about losing her job, he was sorely mistaken. Even worse, it would mean he didn't understand her at all.

But why would he understand someone like her? They were from completely different worlds.

She squeezed her eyes closed. Donovan's money was the last thing she wanted to think about right now. She'd done enough thinking about aristocrats, their outlandish sums of money and all the power it could buy since she'd opened that letter from the Barclay School. Sitting in the ridiculously comfortable sports car, Elizabeth wanted to forget all of it.

She opened her eyes, glanced at Donovan and was hit with the unexpected realization that she wanted the man beside her to *know* her, to really see her in all her damaged glory. And she wanted him to like what he saw. But the stores zipping past them looked exactly like the places Grant Markham's crowd would frequent. It made her feel sick inside.

The lump in Elizabeth's throat—omnipresent since the arrival of her termination letter—grew so thick she could scarcely swallow. *I don't belong here.*

The car slowed as they crossed Hans Road and approached an enormous building that looked more like a castle than a store. By all appearances, it took up an entire square city block.

"Here we are." Donovan winked at her and climbed out from behind the wheel.

He left the engine running and issued a few instructions to a gloved attendant before coming around to open her door. Elizabeth sat, rooted to the spot, as she read the name on the green canopies that ran up and down the full length of the building.

Harrods.

"Elizabeth?" Donovan crouched down so they were at eye level. "Can I help you out of the car?"

She tried to make herself move, but couldn't. "One of your favorite places in London is Harrods?"

"In a way." He was perfectly calm, showing no signs of impatience, as if having to pry a woman out of a car at the Harrods valet was perfectly normal. Then, as if he could sense the root of her apprehension, he added, "We're not here to shop, if that's what you're thinking."

"We're not?" Elizabeth wondered what else people did at Harrods besides shop. Wasn't it a store?

"No." Donovan's gaze turned tender, serious. Elizabeth felt as if he could see straight through to her heart. "Trust me."

She rose from her seat, even though part of her wanted to insist he take her back to the Barrows'. A big part. She didn't know which was more frightening—the prospect of Donovan taking her shopping at London's most celebrated retail establishment or that penetrating gaze of his.

The green awning overhead whipped in the wind. Elizabeth shivered. The sky had grown dark, and a fine mist was beginning to swirl in the fall air.

She looked up just as the exterior of the building lit up in a grand display of twinkling lights. "Wow. Look at all those Christmas lights."

Donovan lifted his gaze. "They do this every evening. It is rather spectacular, isn't it?" He looked back down at her, with the lights reflecting in his eyes, making them sparkle. Or maybe they sparkled all on their own. "In Britain those are called fairy lights."

Fairy lights. She liked the sound of that, as if something magical might happen. Maybe Harrods wouldn't be so awful after all.

"Shall we go in?" He gestured toward the door. "No one will bite. I promise."

"So long as there's no biting..." She let him usher her inside.

The interior looked every bit as much like a castle as the outside. Enormous chandeliers hung from the ceiling, casting rays of light on the most elaborate crown molding Elizabeth had ever seen. The floor was cool marble tile, just like in the Barrows' foyer, with diamond-shaped bits of ebony scattered about.

And everything was oversize, as if an entire city existed inside rather than a single store. She didn't know where to look first.

Fortunately, Donovan appeared to know exactly where he was going.

"This way." He placed his hand near the small of her back and guided her beneath a sign pointing them toward the lift.

They stepped inside the elevator, a complex affair of mirrors and gold leaf with yet another chandelier hanging overhead. The doors closed, trapping them inside, and immediately the atmosphere seemed more intimate.

Elizabeth looked at Donovan for what seemed like a long, electrically charged moment. Did he feel it, too? This restlessness that crept into her veins at his nearness?

He glanced at her mouth, cleared his throat and pressed the button marked with a gold number four.

Elizabeth smiled to herself. So he *did* feel it. Good. That evened the playing field a bit. There was clearly something wrong with both of them. Why would they feel even a flicker of attraction for one another when half the time they barely tolerated one another?

It wasn't attraction, she reasoned. It was nerves, plain and simple. He made her nervous, with his ill temper and brooding, dark looks.

The trouble was, he didn't look quite so brooding at the moment. The mirrors reflected his ridiculously handsome face in all different directions. Elizabeth found it a bit overwhelming.

"What's on the fourth floor?" she managed to squeak.

"You'll see soon enough." He gave her a lopsided smile, the one that always made her weak in the knees. Mirrored back at her five times over, it was a wonder she remained upright.

She hadn't a clue where he was taking her or what awaited them on the mysterious fourth floor, but she had to admit Donovan's surprise outing was helping her frame of mind. Two or three minutes had gone by without her giving any thought to *the letter*. It was a small, but significant, victory.

The elevator doors slid open. Donovan held them open with one hand. "After you."

As she stepped out, the first thing Elizabeth noticed was the relative hush of the fourth floor, as opposed to the swarm of shoppers and tourists on the ground level. The second thing to capture her attention was the smell. The air carried a soothing scent, one she couldn't quite put her finger on.

"Mmm." She inhaled. "It smells wonderful up here. What's that fragrance? Lavender?"

"It's the smell of luxury." Donovan winked at her. "With maybe a bit of wet-dog smell tossed in for good measure."

"Wet-dog smell?"

He waved his hand toward the right with a flourish. "Here we are."

Elizabeth turned past the smooth white walls of the elevator's vestibule to see a grand black-and-white-tile entryway flanked by two enormous Dalmatian statues. The spotted dogs, easily nine feet high, wore rhinestone crowns. They sat up on their giant hind legs. One held a scepter in its paw, and the other held a flag with the Harrods insignia. Above their heads, black script letters spelled out *Harrods Pet Kingdom*.

"Oh, my." Elizabeth stared at the lettering. What could possibly be found in a kingdom for pets? She was almost embarrassed at how giddy she suddenly felt, like a five-year-old about to see Santa for the first time.

Donovan grinned, obviously delighted at her reaction. "I told you to trust me."

"You sure did." She craned her neck to peek past the Dalmatians standing guard and saw a miniature four-poster bed, strikingly similar to the one she slept in at the Barrows', standing on a tall pedestal in the center of the room. Tiny paw prints were scattered on the pink duvet, and a layer of fine tulle netting enveloped the whole display. "Is that a dog bed? You've got to be kidding me."

Donovan laughed. "Follow me. The best part is past the sales area."

They wove through a labyrinth of dog furniture, clothing and accessories the likes of which Elizabeth had never imagined. There was even an area with collars that sparkled with what she assumed were genuine diamonds, judging by the presence of a pair of armed guards whose size rivaled that of the Dalmatians.

"And here it is." Donovan guided her to a wall of windows that overlooked what appeared to be another world entirely. "Harrods Pet Spa."

She'd never seen anything like it, even in the ritzy Upper East Side area of New York, where doggy spas and day cares were a dime a dozen. The area was divided into several sections. On the far left was the gym, where a long-legged Irish setter ran on a treadmill, its fiery copper coat waving in the breeze of a wind machine. Next to the gym was a bathing area, where the sight of rubber duckies floating in the bathwater reduced Elizabeth to a fit of giggles. To the far right, a few dogs were being treated to therapeutic massages.

"What's going on over there?" She pointed to a corgi with something creamy covering its face. The dog was busy trying to lick the mysterious substance off.

Donovan answered matter-of-factly, "The corgi? He's getting a facial."

She wondered briefly if the corgi belonged to the Queen, since the monarch was known to have a passel of them at Buckingham Palace. "A dog facial?"

The dog's tongue appeared to be getting longer by the second with the effort it took to reach his nose. Whatever was in the facial must have tasted delicious.

Donovan nodded. "Blueberry. It's a favorite around here. Lawrence brought Figgy to get one once, and she smelled like a blueberry muffin for nearly a week."

"*Lawrence* brought Figgy?" She gave him a playful poke in the ribs. "Yeah, right."

"That's my story and I'm sticking to it." His voice dropped a notch at her touch. "Besides, there's nothing wrong with a little pampering now and then."

His brown eyes grew dark, smoldering, and Elizabeth felt an immediate urge to touch him again.

What was wrong with her? This was Donovan Darcy standing in front of her. The same man who'd laughed in her face when she'd told him she'd been fired.

"I suppose not." Her throat went dry. They'd gone from laughter to meaningful silence in a heartbeat. "Thank you, Donovan."

"For what?" He took a step closer.

She could feel the heat coming off him, warming her skin. Surprisingly, it was like stepping into the sunshine after a long season of rain. "For bringing me here and for knowing…"

"Knowing?" He was closer now. So close she could see flecks of gold in his eyes and a tiny scar just above the corner of his suddenly quite kissable mouth.

A voice from somewhere inside her mind screamed, *Slow down! Turn and walk away!*

Too late, she thought.

"Knowing just what I needed." Then, standing in the middle of Harrods Pet Spa, she realized she'd gotten exactly what she wished for. Against all odds, Donovan Darcy *saw* her. He understood her. And on a day when she'd lost her last remaining shred of dignity, he'd known exactly what it took to put a smile back on her face.

She fixed her gaze with his and saw a longing in his eyes so palpable she thought she might be able to reach out and touch it. That same longing throbbed with every beat of her pulse, every intake of breath.

The voice in her head warning of impending doom grew quieter, until it became barely more than a whisper.

She reached for Donovan's hand. He released a long, sultry sigh as she intertwined her fingers with his.

They stood for several long moments, hand in hand, until Donovan brushed the hair from her face and whispered, "You're welcome."

Donovan hadn't expected to find himself hand in hand with Elizabeth Scott at Harrods Pet Spa, of all places. He'd brought her here because he knew it couldn't fail to cheer her up. The last thing he anticipated was for her to reach for him.

Not that he was complaining. It was a surprise, that was all. And certainly more pleasant than arguing with her.

Her skin was soft as a rose petal but somehow still hot as fire against his own, which seemed appropriate given Elizabeth's spirited disposition. And those curves of hers, so close he could reach out and touch them...they looked positively delectable. From where he was standing, he could just catch the scent of her hair. He closed his eyes and breathed in its fresh, citrusy fragrance.

She smelled like oranges and fresh lemons, he realized. Sweet, yet with a tangy bite.

Again, appropriate.

He opened his eyes and found the treadmill empty. A pet-spa attendant was pulling shades down over the windows.

Damn.

"I think we're shutting this place down," he said under his breath.

"It looks that way." She gazed up at him, her expression just a touch wistful.

He was wary of moving, certain they stood on some secret hallowed ground where he and Elizabeth weren't liable to engage in another war of words.

Then a thought struck him. Why leave? The Pet Spa might be shutting down, but this was Harrods.

He bent to whisper in her ear, "There's a champagne bar downstairs."

"Of course there is." She raised a knowing eyebrow, dropped his hand and nodded in the direction of a dog bed fashioned to look like a giant blue box from Tiffany's. "In fact, I'll bet there are a *couple* of champagne bars downstairs."

Donovan shrugged. "I believe there are three total."

He missed her touch.

God, what had gotten into him? It had been all of two seconds since he'd touched her, and he was already growing itchy. It was preposterous.

"Three?" She laughed.

Donovan frowned. She'd pulled even farther away. He could no longer smell her hair, which he found particularly vexing.

"Yes, three." He planted his hand in the small of her back and steered her toward the lift before she could protest. "Come along, then."

The lift was agony. The small space between them crackled with electricity, as it had before. This time, however, Donovan found himself questioning why he didn't just pull her into his arms and kiss her. He'd certainly given the prospect a fair amount of consideration. More than once. And now they seemed to have reached a place where it wouldn't seem altogether inappropriate.

If he kissed her now, would he be taking advantage of the situation? Just hours ago Elizabeth had been so upset she'd sequestered herself in her bedroom at the Barrows'. Of all the myriad times he'd imagined tasting Elizabeth Scott's lips—and those times were growing more and more frequent, to be sure—she'd always been clearheaded, fully aware of what she was doing. Certainly a willing participant.

In some of his wilder fantasies, more than willing.

He was overthinking things, something he'd never been prone to do. He was Donovan Darcy, for God's sake. If he wanted to kiss a woman, he simply took her in his arms and did it.

Good God, he had to stop thinking about it. He clenched his teeth and expelled an exasperated groan.

"What's wrong with you?" Elizabeth asked, breaking the silence, which had become more and more tense during their short journey from the fourth floor to the first.

The lift doors opened.

An opportunity wasted.

Donovan had to stop himself from growling in frustration. "Nothing is *wrong* with me."

"You look angry." She shook her head, sending waves of what Donovan now knew was citrus-scented hair cascading over her shoulders. "I must say, you puzzle me exceedingly."

"You find me puzzling? How is that?" he asked as they approached the champagne bar.

"One minute you're charming and the next you're brooding." She rolled her eyes, then turned away from him to smile at the hostess.

The champagne lounge was operated by the French winery Veuve Clicquot. The bar itself was a mod-looking white affair, with orange-and-black accents. It overlooked a mirrored display of various bottles of Veuve. Donovan, however, had something more intimate in mind than sitting on a pair of stiff, albeit stylish, bar stools in plain view of the shopping public.

He handed the hostess a twenty-pound note, and she escorted them to a banquette in a private corner of the lounge area, obscured by a glass partition of alternating orange-and-gray panels.

"Thank you," he said after she placed two drinks menus on the slick white coffee table facing their banquette sofa.

"Je vous en prie, monsieur." She nodded at both him and Elizabeth and returned to her place at the front of the bar.

Elizabeth watched her retreating form and swiveled her gaze back to Donovan. "What was that?"

"French." He wrapped his arm around Elizabeth's waist and guided her to the sofa. He was unprepared for the way a simple touch spurred a craving for her. One touch wasn't sufficient. The feel of her hip against the palm of his hand was enough to drive him to the brink of insanity. "It means 'you're welcome.'"

Elizabeth settled herself on the tangerine sofa and tucked her legs up beside her, giving Donovan an even better view of her skin peeking through the rips in her jeans. "You speak French?"

"Some." He shrugged and sat next to her, suddenly remembering his earlier urge to pull her into his lap. He picked up the menus instead and handed her one of them. "Is that one of the things you find charming about me?"

She slapped her unread menu down on the low, white-lacquered table in front of them. "When did I say I found you charming?"

"Just now," he answered with a self-satisfied grin. "You said one minute I'm charming and the next I'm brooding."

"And your takeaway from that comment was that I find you charming?" She crossed her arms. "Unbelievable."

"Aren't you the same woman who just thanked me for bringing you here?" Donovan opened one of the menus, grateful for the distraction of something cerebral to get his mind off his most out-of-control libido.

He'd never had this problem before. If anything, Donovan Darcy was civilized. Restraint had never been an issue—with either his emotions or his body. Until recently.

"Yes, but for some reason my feelings about you tend to vary widely from one minute to the next."

"I see." He gave her a frosty look before turning his attention to the waiter and ordering fresh strawberries and clotted cream, paired with a bottle of the Veuve Clicquot Rosé. Once the waiter was gone, Donovan turned to her again. "Perhaps you can elaborate."

"You want an example?" She grinned rather dangerously.

"Please. Enlighten me."

"As nice as this outing has been, I still haven't forgotten how you laughed in my face when I told you I'd been fired." Her grin dimmed somewhat, and there was a glimmer of pain in her soft brown eyes.

And for a moment, Donovan felt as though he'd just kicked Bambi. "Don't pay any attention to that. I barely qualify as employed, remember? What could I possibly know about such matters?"

The waiter returned, popped a bottle open and poured a modicum of rosé into Donovan's champagne flute for him to taste. It was difficult to concentrate on the nuances of the champagne with Elizabeth watching his every move. He imagined he could be drinking from Figgy and Finneus's water bowl at the moment and wouldn't have a clue.

"Very good." He returned his glass to the table.

The waiter nodded, filled both their flutes and situated the bottle in an ice bucket custom-built into the table. After he'd left, Donovan handed one of the slender glasses to Elizabeth.

Her gaze followed the trail of pink bubbles rising from the bottom of the champagne flute. She took a sip, closed her eyes and licked her lips. "Delicious."

Unnerved, Donovan nearly drained his glass.

"So, have you ever been fired before?" she asked. "I'm guessing not."

"No, I can't say that I have. Although it's not out of the realm of possibility."

"Why do you say that?" Her lips turned down in a slight frown, a move Donovan was acutely aware of since he couldn't seem to take his eyes off them.

He forced himself to look her into the eyes. "My boss is an ass. Incorrigible, really."

She narrowed her gaze at him. "It's the Darcy Family Trust. Aren't you the boss?"

"Exactly." Donovan plucked a perfect red strawberry off the platter and dipped it in the clotted cream.

"There you go again." She twirled her champagne flute between her fingertips.

"Pardon?"

"There you go again…seeming almost charming." Her eyebrow lifted, and she pinned him with a spirited look.

He scooped a dollop of cream on his fingertip and dabbed it on her nose. "Almost? That's a bloody shame."

Elizabeth's fine eyes turned serious, and she reached out and touched his face, her fingertips barely grazing the underside of his bottom lip. "Did I say *almost?*"

Donovan swallowed, with great difficulty.

If that wasn't an invitation to be kissed, and to be kissed thoroughly, Donovan didn't know what was. Knowing that she wanted it, he had a mind to make her wait for it.

"Let me get this for you." He scooped the cream off her nose and offered it to her.

Without breaking their gaze, she licked his fingertip. At the sight of that tongue…those lips…all thoughts of making her wait flew right out of Donovan's head. In one swift movement, he took the champagne flute from her hand and leaned in, pressing his mouth against hers.

Her lips were sweet, cold from the champagne. She tasted of strawberries and rosé. He groaned in satisfaction as he felt her body shiver in delight and her mouth curve into the subtlest of smiles.

She wrapped her arms around his neck, anchoring herself to him. He pulled her hard against him, and she kissed him back with an intensity that he should have expected, given her feisty demeanor, but still caught him unawares. Donovan had one final thought before his mind and body were completely lost in a heady swirl of pleasure—*At last.*

Her lips were generous, and when they released the softest of sighs, an unprecedented surge of heat shot through Donovan. That sigh carried him away as never before.

He'd become undone.

Untethered.

Unleashed.

12

Upon waking the next morning, Elizabeth found she couldn't breathe.

Or swallow.

The breathing she attributed to the weight of a certain Blenheim ball of fur sitting square in the middle of her chest. Her dry cotton-mouth, on the other hand, couldn't be blamed on Bliss. That was purely her own doing—the result of an excruciating hangover.

However, she wasn't quite sure whether to attribute the condition to the copious amount of champagne she'd consumed the night before or the intoxicating experience of kissing Donovan Darcy.

So much for the oft-proclaimed English Reserve. There had been nothing restrained, nothing understated and certainly nothing bumbling about that first kiss. Or the one that came next. Or the one after that.

She smiled to herself as she drifted down the stairs and strode into the kitchen. Even the steady fall of drizzle outside—on another dog-show day when she'd have to contend with wet coats and muddy paws—couldn't get her down.

The dogs were all groomed and ready to go. There had been such frenzy over the past few days getting everything ready that the calm atmosphere downstairs came somewhat as a shock. Elizabeth found Sue and Jenna, both still clad in their pajamas, enjoying a leisurely breakfast in the dining room.

Jenna sat nibbling on a slice of toast, looking as comfortable as if she'd lived with the Barrows her entire life. "Good morning."

"Hello there, dear," said Sue from behind her newspaper.

"Good morning." Elizabeth slid across from the two of them at the dining table.

She cocked her head and read the headlines from the back of Sue's paper. There'd been a riot somewhere called Ealing. The London Fire Brigade was threatening to strike in seven days, which was particularly notable since that was Bonfire Weekend. And because Sue read the *Daily Mail,* Kim Kardashian's psoriasis also made the front page.

Elizabeth took a slice of warm bread from the toast rack and took a bite off the corner, marveling that the Kardashians were famous on this side of the pond. She still wasn't sure why they were celebrities in America.

Sue folded the paper and peered at Elizabeth over the top of her glasses. "You seem cheerful this morning. I trust you had a delightful time with Mr. Darcy last night?"

Last night.

A variety of lovely sensations vied for attention in Elizabeth's memory. The feel of Donovan's hands as he cupped her face. The rush of sweetness that spilled through her when his lips first touched hers. The warmth of his breath dancing across the most sensitive curve of her neck.

A shiver ran up her spine.

Then she realized something was amiss. "Wait a minute. How do you know anything about last night?"

"I assure you, I wasn't snooping. But it's hard not to notice a fine-looking man like Mr. Darcy carrying an unconscious woman up the stairs of my house." Sue spread a thick layer of marmalade on her toast. Her eyes danced. Clearly she was enjoying this. "It's certainly not something that happens every day around here."

Unconscious?

Donovan was certainly a fine kisser, but from what she remembered, Elizabeth had managed not to faint or anything.

She ticked off a mental inventory of the evening—Donovan appearing at her door, then taking her off to Harrods, the Pet Spa, the champagne bar and all the yummy things that had happened there, followed by the ride home in Donovan's Aston Martin. Her body had been humming with pleasure, but pleasantly relaxed from the champagne and exhausted after all the extreme highs and lows of the previous twelve hours. She remembered yawning and Donovan stroking her hair as he pulled out of the car park at Harrods. The purr of the engine and the warmth of the heated leather seats had been enough for her eyes to drift closed....

Elizabeth groaned. "I fell asleep on the ride home, didn't I?"

"It certainly looked that way." Sue filled teacups for Jenna and Elizabeth. "Unless Mr. Darcy drugged you. Funny, I didn't think to ask him that last night."

"Donovan didn't drug me." *Does kissing me senseless count?*

"I know, dear. I was only teasing. He's so delightful. We had such a nice evening. Alan and I enjoyed him very much.

It's such a pity Jenna was out with Mr. Robson and missed all the fun."

"Yes." Jenna nodded and speared a slice of melon with her fork. "A pity."

Elizabeth drained her teacup. There wasn't any amount of caffeine sufficient to wrap her mind around this. "Let me get this straight. Donovan brought me home, carried me upstairs and then what happened? You all had a little party?"

Sue shook her head. "It wasn't a party. He just stayed for an hour or so and watched *Strictly Come Dancing* with us."

She tried to picture Donovan sitting in the living room watching reality television with the Barrows, likely being the subject of a matchmaking interrogation. It seemed more humorous than mortifying. And now that she thought about it, a little sweet.

"Well, I'm glad you had a nice time." Elizabeth sighed. "I wish I hadn't slept through it."

"It's perfectly understandable. You were probably exhausted from all that making out you two did at Harrods." Jenna dropped a sugar cube into her tea, and her lips twitched into a smirk.

Wait a minute.

Elizabeth was willing to suspend her disbelief long enough to imagine Donovan watching reality TV with the Barrows, but she was certain he wasn't the type to kiss and tell.

She narrowed her gaze at Jenna. "And how exactly do you know about that?"

"I was *so* hoping you'd ask that question." Jenna held her hand out to Sue. "May I borrow your paper?"

"Oh, dear." Sue placed her newspaper in Jenna's open palm.

"We read about it. As did the rest of London, I imagine."

Jenna flicked open the *Daily Mail* with a flourish and spread it out in the center of the breakfast table. "Right here."

"What are you talking about?" Elizabeth rolled her eyes, until she spotted what looked like an uncanny likeness of herself right there, smack-dab in the center of the paper. "Oh, God."

"Don't you mean 'Oh, Mr. Darcy'?" Jenna snickered.

"Let me get a closer look at that." She snatched the paper from Jenna's hands.

It was a photo of her, all right, midkiss with Donovan. And that wasn't the worst of it. Elizabeth was horrified to see that not only had someone photographed the two of them engaged in a serious lip-lock, but they'd managed to do it at a moment when her limbs had turned liquid—molten, really—and were draped over Donovan's in a most provocative manner. She was practically sitting in his lap.

Had things really gone that far? In a public place?

Yes, she realized, her head throbbing with fresh agony. *They had.*

She stared at the photo in disbelief. God, it was mortifying—Donovan looked as though he were feasting on her. "I don't understand. Why is this news?"

Sue cleared her throat. The poor woman looked almost as embarrassed as Elizabeth felt. "It's the Society section, dear. Mr. Darcy is very well-known. What he does is news."

My photo is in a tabloid. How can this be happening?

Elizabeth felt a sudden pang of sympathy for poor Kim Kardashian.

"You haven't seen the caption yet, have you?" Jenna asked.

"There's a caption?"

"I'm afraid so." Sue gnawed on her lip and cast a worried glance back and forth between Jenna and Elizabeth.

So there was a caption. It couldn't be any worse than the photo. Could it?

Elizabeth read the small print out loud. "'Donovan Darcy spent last evening at the Veuve Clicquot bar at Harrods in the company of an unidentified female companion, casting doubt on the rumors of his reported engagement to Helena Robson. See photo below.'"

"Engagement?" The newspaper shook in Elizabeth's hands. *"Engagement?"*

"Rumored engagement." Jenna wagged a finger at her.

"Reported," Elizabeth corrected. "That sounds far more certain than *rumored."*

"Whatever. You know you can't believe everything you read in the papers. Henry hasn't said a word to me about his sister and Donovan."

Sue nodded vigorously. "Honestly, I haven't heard a peep about Mr. Darcy being engaged to be married. And that's the sort of thing that would make headlines around here. Don't pay any attention to it, Elizabeth."

Elizabeth's gaze dropped to the photo below the one of her and Donovan. It was a snapshot of Helena from the fashion show at the Bridal Market. In fact, Elizabeth could see the tip of her own Jimmy Choo knockoff peeking into the frame of the photo. She'd been sitting right next to Helena when the picture was taken.

She studied Helena's image. Blond hair, stick-thin arms and those crazy eyelashes. *Her* Jimmy Choos certainly looked real, but if Elizabeth's instincts were correct, there was plenty fake about this woman.

"Oh, my God, I can't believe this." Elizabeth shook her head. "It says here Helena was at the Bridal Market because she was shopping for a dress for her rumored spring wedding to Donovan."

"*Rumored* wedding." Jenna took the paper from Elizabeth's hands. "I'd like to keep this, if you don't mind. I mean, unless you want to put it in your scrapbook or something."

"Be my guest." Elizabeth took a bite of toast. It was like sandpaper in her mouth. Donovan couldn't be engaged. Especially not to that catty woman. Could he?

Although Helena Robson did seem to be the type of glorified sorority girl who ran in Donovan's circles. He would never have to talk her out of a car at Harrods. High-end stores were likely her natural habitat.

Elizabeth struggled to swallow. "Why in the world do you want it, anyway?"

Jenna folded the paper into a neat square, with a razor-sharp crease splitting Helena Robson in half. "I don't know. Something tells me we'll be seeing Helena again."

With an unsteady hand, Elizabeth returned the remains of her toast to her plate.

Something tells me we'll being seeing Helena again....

Precisely what she was afraid of.

Unlike the dog shows Elizabeth had attended in the States and the one the previous Saturday at the hotel in Mayfair, most shows in England took place outdoors in parks or the parklands of manor homes, estates or even castles. As Sue had explained during the hour-long drive into the country, today's show was being held on the grounds of a grand country home.

In the backseat of Sue's station wagon, or steering-brake, as she called it, Jenna scrunched her nose. "I thought you said we were going to a castle."

Elizabeth shared a smile with Sue. "We only told you that so you'd come with us."

Jenna's head appeared in the space between their head-rests. *"What?"*

"Don't worry, dear. You won't be disappointed," Sue said, just as they got their first glimpse of the stately home on the horizon.

It was magnificent, like something out of an historical production on PBS. Red brick, with thick clusters of ivy crawling up the facade, the home appeared to have no less than four chimneys and row after row of white sash windows. The grounds overflowed with colorful roses in cherry-red and bright pink.

"Wow," Jenna gasped. "This is almost better than a castle."

"This place is stunning." Elizabeth grazed the car window with her fingertips. She almost felt as though she were looking at a mirage. "Who owns this house?"

"This is Ashwyn House. It's been in the Ashwyn family for generations," Sue answered absently as she steered the car in the direction of the car park.

Ashwyn House, Elizabeth mused. *A house with a name.*

Is this the sort of house Donovan owns?

She frowned and tried not to imagine Donovan and Helena Robson chasing a collection of fashionable, perfect children across the spectacular grounds. The perfect couple. The perfect house. The perfect family.

A series of long, rectangular tents came into view. The show grounds, no doubt. Elizabeth was relieved to have something to focus on that would take her mind off the Society page of the *Daily Mail.* The more she'd thought about it, the more it bothered her. Was Donovan engaged or not? And even if he wasn't, what exactly was the nature of his relationship with Helena? Was she his fiancée? His girlfriend? Or just another in a string of "female companions," as the newspaper had so dubiously referred to Elizabeth?

It was humiliating. Humiliating enough to almost make her forget how sweet he'd been the night before—coming to find her and endeavoring to cheer her up—and how the instant his lips had touched hers, she'd been hit with the sensation that it was the consummation of something she'd been craving for the longest time.

Elizabeth felt sick to her stomach as they crossed the finely manicured lawn and headed toward the show tents. At least the morning drizzle had subsided. Sue pointed out a myriad of spectacular features of the estate as they led the dogs across the damp emerald grass, and Jenna oohed and aahed in appreciation. Elizabeth was barely cognizant of her surroundings. Which was why when Sue stopped in her tracks, she nearly stumbled right into her.

"Oh, my." Sue grew pale, and her hand fluttered to her chest. "Goodness."

Whatever had captured her attention seemed anything but good.

Elizabeth followed Sue's gaze to the area ringside, where the other Cavalier King Charles spaniel handlers were busy fussing over dogs propped on grooming tables. At first, Elizabeth didn't see what had Sue so flustered. Then a shrill laugh drew her attention to a familiar sticklike figure.

"I am so not ready for this," she muttered as a fresh wave of nausea washed over her.

Jenna gripped her arm. "Is that...?"

"Helena Robson." Sue gave a grim nod. "And it looks like she'll be showing against you, Elizabeth. That's a Cavalier at the end of her leash."

"You've got to be kidding me. She has a Cavalier?"

"It certainly looks that way." Jenna lowered her voice to a whisper. "But don't worry. Bliss is way cuter. Way."

This did nothing to slow the panicked beating of Elizabeth's heart. On the contrary, Jenna's well-meaning words had the opposite effect. Things must be even worse than she'd thought if Jenna was willing to inject herself into dog-show politics.

"I don't think it's hers. I've never seen her at a show with a dog before." Sue frowned. "And that's a full-grown dog, not a puppy. She must be showing it for someone else."

"Please don't tell me it's Donovan's." Elizabeth couldn't imagine a more awkward scenario.

"No, it can't be Donovan's dog." Sue paused and finally said, "Because he's your judge today."

And just like that, the situation reached new heights of awkwardness.

"He can't be." Elizabeth refused to believe she was about to step into the ring and show under Donovan against his fiancée, rumored or otherwise. She was going to have to start completing the show paperwork herself, or at least begin looking over Sue's shoulder as she filled out the forms. This business of not knowing the judge's identity until she arrived at the show was like walking through a minefield.

"He is. I'm sorry." Sue wound Violet's leash around her hand until her fingers turned white. "I didn't tell you before because I thought it would be a nice surprise."

"Are you surprised?" Jenna asked, tongue firmly planted in cheek.

"To put it mildly," Elizabeth said as she tried to wrap her mind around the state of affairs.

"Oh, look. Henry is here, too." Jenna unconsciously

smoothed down her long, blond hair. Or maybe it wasn't an unconscious gesture, after all. "I think we should go over there and talk to them."

"Oh, dear." Sue's expression grew wary, not unlike Bliss's on bath day. "I'm not sure that's a good idea."

"There's no time." Elizabeth slid her exhibitor number in place beneath the rubber band fastened around her arm. "Our ring time is in less than a minute."

"This is bad." Jenna shook her head, but Elizabeth noticed she kept one eye glued on Henry Robson.

Elizabeth directed her attention to the ring, where, sure enough, Donovan stood in the center. He turned slightly, and Elizabeth caught a glimpse of his tie. Red silk, fashioned in a full Windsor knot. A slow-motion image floated through her mind—Donovan slowly slipping his tie from around his neck and tossing it onto her bed yesterday.

A surge of desire hit her low in the belly. It was most definitely unwelcome, especially in the here and now, but Elizabeth was powerless to stop it.

Until Donovan positioned himself at the entrance to the ring, where Helena Robson stood ready and waiting. Elizabeth stayed ringside and watched Helena rest a perfectly manicured hand on Donovan's lapel. The yearning she'd felt only moments ago withered and died. It was replaced with a sizzling spike of something that felt oddly like jealousy that struck Elizabeth square in the chest.

Unidentified female companion.

God, it was humiliating.

Shame coursed through her, hot and unrelenting, until beads of sweat broke out on her forehead.

She hated feeling this way.

She *wouldn't* feel this way. She simply refused.

Elizabeth turned her back on the ring, squared her shoulders and went to work channeling all that shame, jealousy and embarrassment into something healthy—good, old-fashioned anger.

13

Donovan almost hadn't seen the photograph in the paper. Or the odious mention of his fictitious engagement to Helena.

He didn't make a practice of reading the Society section. The way he saw it, he was forced to mingle with those people enough in real life. He had no desire to spend his free time reading about them in the *Daily Mail*.

Zara had been the one to bring both items to his attention. She'd come tearing into his office clutching the paper to her chest, red-faced with laughter.

"Helena is going to *die* when she sees this, Donovan." His little sister had been beside herself with glee. "Positively die. I swear, this is the best day ever."

Donovan had found it difficult to focus on what she was saying, riveted as he was to the image of himself and Elizabeth Scott swept up in one another. She was all but sitting in his lap, and he looked more than ready to consume her right there in Harrods. He could see his right hand fisted in Elizabeth's mass of chestnut hair, and his left—he squinted— where was his left hand?

Then he'd smiled as he'd recalled precisely where that hand had been and considered it best that its placement hadn't been captured in the photograph.

Donovan had had to look away from the image. He'd been forced to clear his throat and collect himself. It had required a conscious effort to stop himself from becoming aroused right then and there, standing next to his little sister.

So taken with the memory of the previous night, he'd given little to no thought to the whole business of Helena at that ridiculous bridal event.

Judging by the look on Elizabeth's face as she entered the ring at the dog show, however, she'd had plenty of opportunity to reflect on the matter.

She swished past him, sending him a glare that would freeze the devil himself, and lined up directly behind Helena.

Donovan couldn't help but smile as he looked at Elizabeth, dressed in a saucy red dress with sheer, fluttery sleeves and a square neckline that he wished was an inch or two lower. His eyes remained glued on her until all six competitors had lined up in the ring. Only then did he avert his gaze to Helena, the first one up.

He crossed his arms and addressed her as formally as possible. "Miss Robson, please lead the group once around the ring."

She lit up under his attention as if he'd proposed marriage to her, which she'd clearly already hallucinated at some point. Donovan frowned and watched the Cavaliers trot in a circle. The dog at the end of Helena's leash had its tail between its legs. Poor guy. Donovan sympathized with him.

"Can I have the first dog on the table, please?"

Helena led her shy charge to the table in the center of the ring, then bent down to pick up the dog. She made quite a show of bending low enough to afford Donovan a clear view straight down her dress to her pair of what he was sure were artificial breasts.

He did his best to avoid the show within a show and averted his gaze back to Elizabeth. She was watching him. Pleased to have caught her, he sent her an almost imperceptible wink. She responded by rolling her eyes and fixing her attention back on Bliss.

"Ahem." Helena cleared her throat. "I'm ready."

Don't I know it.

"Perhaps I need to remind you this is my ring, Miss Robson." He began working his hands over the dog on the table, purposefully avoiding fixing his gaze with Helena's.

"Of course, darlin'…I mean, Mr. Darcy."

He didn't need to look at her to know she was fluttering her eyelashes. He could feel the wind coming off them, threatening to knock him over.

He made quick work of going over the dog, giving it only a cursory inspection. It made no difference to Donovan what the dog looked like. That Cavalier could have been a perfect example of breed standard and he wouldn't even award it a ribbon, much less Championship points. The dog belonged to his aunt and came from his own breeding stock. Awarding the dog any sort of honor would be unethical.

Helena had been following him and Henry around the show scene long enough to be well aware of such rules, but clearly she'd chosen to ignore them. And now she was about to learn her lesson in the worst way possible.

He stepped away from the table. "Take the dog down and back, please."

Helena led the Cavalier to the corner of the ring and back

again. The dog had its tail up, finally, and showed good reach in its front end. All in all, it had very nice movement.

It should. Donovan shook his head. *I bred the damned thing.*

"Around." He sent Helena on one final lap before striding back to the table.

Bliss was already in position, aligned nicely in a proper show stack. Donovan examined her topline—nice and even—from the side and then approached her from the front.

He reached out his hands and let Bliss sniff them before cradling her muzzle. She really did have a lovely head. And the freckles were growing on him, for one reason or another.

"Elizabeth, you're looking lovely this afternoon," he said under his breath as he checked the cushioning beneath Bliss's eyes. And then, because he simply couldn't resist, he added, "Pretty as a picture, one might say."

That creamy complexion of hers flushed scarlet, nearly as red as the dress that clung to her curves. "Mr. Darcy," she said, rather crisply.

He moved his hands over Bliss's withers and shifted the placement of her left front leg ever so slightly. "So it's back to Mr. Darcy, is it? I suppose you'd like me to call you Miss Scott."

She lifted a furious eyebrow. "It has a better ring to it than 'unidentified female companion,' don't you think?"

Donovan lowered his voice another notch and moved to Bliss's rear, checking the set of her hips and alignment of her stifle. "I feel I should point out that I've never called you that. I'm well aware of your name. You saw to that at our first meeting, did you not?"

"Donovan, please." His name was a plea on her lips.

For a moment, Donovan forgot where he was and what he was doing. He was aware of very little other than the deep brown of her eyes and the curve of her bottom lip, pink as a rose petal.

"Aah, you're calling me Donovan again. So I'm forgiven, then. Although what I was guilty of remains a mystery." He had to stop himself from leaning over the grooming table and kissing her right there, with the aroma of dog and hair spray—technically illegal at shows, but still used in copious amounts—hanging in the air.

"I thought you might see fit to explain what I read in the paper this morning. You've obviously seen it."

"Oh, yes. I saw it. Rather stirring, wasn't it? Did it bring back as many fond memories for you as it did for me?" His gaze dropped to her mouth. Until he remembered he was supposed to be looking at her dog.

Her lips curved into a smile for the briefest of moments. If Donovan had blinked at just the wrong time, he would have missed it entirely. "That's beside the point. Since you obviously aren't going to offer any kind of explanation, I'll ask you point-blank—are you engaged to be married?"

"Did I act like an engaged man last night?" He stroked Bliss's back with one hand and rested the other on the edge of the grooming table. It inched toward Elizabeth's, as if of its own accord.

"A simple yes or no answer would suffice."

He'd drawn out his examination of Bliss nearly as long as he could. The dog only had four legs and a tail. What more could he possibly look at? "Something tells me nothing about this conversation is simple."

"Donovan…" she whispered. A single, exasperated utterance.

He moved his hand a fraction, so the very tips of his fingers brushed against hers. "Why, Miss Scott, that's a lovely shade of green you're wearing."

She looked down at their hands, barely touching, and then back up at him. "My dress isn't green. It's red."

"I wasn't referring to your dress." He sent her a cheeky wink. "You're positively green from head to toe. Miss Scott, I do believe you're jealous."

She inhaled a sharp breath.

"Let me see your dog go down and back, please. I think we've just about covered everything here." He inched away from the table, not wanting to turn his back lest she stab him in it when he wasn't looking.

She picked Bliss up, set her gently on the grass and led her down to the corner and back. Elizabeth didn't so much as glance at Donovan when she returned and stacked Bliss in a final pose for his inspection. He could see the rise and fall of her breath, every irate inhale and exhale, but she kept her eyes glued to her dog.

Oh, yes. She was jealous. Donovan knew a jealous female when he saw one, and right now, Elizabeth Scott was one perfect specimen.

He tried not to smirk, but he simply couldn't help but be pleased at the turn of events. For the first time since setting his sights on Elizabeth, he had the upper hand.

Finally.

Things were as they should be.

"Thank you, Miss Scott," he said, meaning it from the very depths of his soul.

Jealous?

The idea would be laughable if only it weren't true.

Elizabeth wanted nothing more than to exit the ring as

quickly as possible. But Donovan still had four more Cavaliers to examine on the table, and she knew he couldn't very well rush through them since he'd spent so much time going over Bliss.

She offered Bliss a treat and tried not to look at Donovan. This was typically the time in the ring where exhibitors and their dogs could relax.

Ha!

As if that were possible with Helena Robson studiously ignoring her less than three feet away.

Well, Elizabeth wasn't about to stand there as if she were the other woman, especially when Donovan was so convinced she was jealous. She'd show Donovan she didn't care a lick if he was engaged. He didn't need to know how right he was.

Elizabeth took a step closer to Helena. "Hi, there."

Helena looked at her as if she'd sprouted two heads. She arched a carefully sculpted eyebrow and swept Elizabeth up and down with her gaze. Then she sniffed and turned her back.

"Just so you know, there's nothing between Donovan and me," Elizabeth whispered to her back. "We're…"

How was she supposed to finish that sentence? She couldn't very well say they were friends.

"…we're not intimate, if that's what you're thinking."

Way to go. Denial.

Wasn't that exactly the sort of thing people said when they were, in fact, sleeping with each other?

But she and Donovan *weren't* sleeping together.

Yet.

The word dangled in her thoughts, taunting her.

The only indication Helena had even heard her pitiful disavowal was the stiffening of her spine before she tossed her head, nearly giving Elizabeth a mouthful of bleached-blond hair.

"Can I have all the exhibitors go around together, please?" *Thank God. This is almost over.*

Elizabeth nearly plowed into Helena in her haste to lead Bliss around the ring and toward the exit. As Donovan's gaze roamed over the competition, she tried to remind herself he was judging the dogs, not the handlers. Still, her cheeks burned with humiliation. Being in Donovan's ring next to Helena felt just about as demeaning as if they'd been wrestling for his attention in a tub full of Jell-O.

"You'll be our Winner." Donovan pointed to one of the handlers behind Elizabeth. Someone he wasn't currently sleeping with, planning to sleep with or engaged to marry. Or so Elizabeth presumed. "Everyone please stay as you are for final ranking."

Elizabeth lined up behind Helena along the white lattice ring gate and chastised herself for still hoping Bliss would be ranked higher than Helena's dog. What was wrong with her? *Bring on the cherry Jell-O.*

"Miss Robson." Donovan approached Helena, and Elizabeth's heart sank to her ballet flats. "Your dog is excused. As the dog's breeder, I cannot evaluate it. I'm withholding your ribbon this afternoon. You may leave the ring."

Elizabeth had heard rumors about judges withholding ribbons, but she'd never actually seen it happen. The collective gasp that rose up from the crowd assembled ringside told her she wasn't the only one.

But the loudest gasp of all came from Helena Robson herself.

Elizabeth was too shocked to do or say anything. She simply stood quietly, watching the whole episode transpire until Donovan was suddenly beside her instead of Helena.

"Miss Scott," he said with a smile. "You'll be my Reserve Winner today."

Reserve Winner.

Runner-up, just like at the show in New Jersey. Only this time she was in England, the birthplace of her breed.

A lump lodged in her throat. She swallowed around it as Donovan slipped the Reserve Winner's sash over her head and handed her a rather fancy red-and-white-satin rosette. For one brief, shiny moment Elizabeth felt like a beauty queen. Only better, really, because her dog was the beauty. Her sweet, furry best friend.

It wasn't until she exited the ring that Elizabeth became aware of all the stares and whispers. She may have never caught their meaning if she hadn't heard the words *Daily Mail* tossed about among the scattered murmurings.

"Congratulations, dear." Sue wrapped her in a tight hug. "Reserve Winner. You should be so proud of little Bliss."

"I am. Very much so." Elizabeth looked over Sue's shoulder for Jenna and spotted her a few yards away, clearly enraptured by something Henry Robson was saying.

Helena was nowhere to be seen, and for that Elizabeth was grateful. But as other exhibitors continued to gape at her and aim skeptical glances at her Reserve Winner sash, she began to feel less and less like an unidentified female companion. It was becoming altogether clear that her identity was by no means a secret. At least among the dog-show circuit.

"Are you all right, dear?" Sue asked and rested the back of her hand on Elizabeth's forehead. "You look rather flushed all of a sudden."

"I think…" What did she think?

I think people are staring.

I think everyone in this tent reads the Daily Mail.

"I think I need some air." She inhaled a lungful of oxygen. Why was it so difficult to breathe?

"It's rather chaotic in here. We have plenty of time before the Border terriers show. Why don't you let me watch Bliss, and you can go outside and take a minute to catch your breath?" Sue took Bliss's lead from Elizabeth's hand. "It's been an awfully eventful day already, has it not?"

An understatement, to be sure.

"Thank you." Elizabeth blew Bliss a congratulatory kiss and wound her way through the crowd.

Her breath was coming in gasps now, and she was starting to feel a little sick to her stomach. So she slipped inside the smaller white tent marked Hospitality and sent up a prayer of thanks when she found it empty inside.

She sagged against the wall of the tent, closed her eyes and counted backward from ten.

Ten, nine, eight…

"You're only being paranoid," she whispered to herself.

Seven, six, five…

"Of course no one recognizes you from the picture in the paper."

Four, three, two…

"And they certainly don't think that's why Donovan awarded Bliss Reserve Winner."

"Oh, I'm fairly certain that's exactly what they think," another voice whispered, mere inches from her ear.

Her eyes flew open.

"Donovan." And just like that, her breathing grew erratic again, all the counting and deep yoga inhalations rendered a waste. "What are you doing here?"

"I followed you." He reached up and tucked a lock of hair behind her ear. "I saw you run in here looking all tragic, and decided a break from judging was required."

She cast a wistful glance at her pretty sash. "So it's true? You awarded Bliss Reserve Winner because we...because you..."

"Because I want to do this?" His gaze dropped to her waist, and his hands soon followed suit, then slid around to cup her bottom.

Elizabeth's heart skipped a beat as he pulled her hips toward him, so their bodies were pressed firmly against one another. He was warm. Warm, hard and so very, very inviting. A soft sigh escaped her lips.

"That sound." Donovan's mouth hitched into an easy smile. "So sexy."

She struggled to keep her voice even. "But is it true?"

"Of course it's not true. If anything, I went out of my way not to show you favoritism out there." He cocked his head. "But as you well know, people will believe some foolish things."

Elizabeth could feel his heart beating against her own, every bit as frantic as hers. "Like that you're engaged to Helena?"

He leaned his forehead against hers, then his nose, moving slowly until his lips were barely a breath away. God, if he didn't kiss her soon she would self-combust. "Absurd, right? Especially when just last week I was sleeping with my sister."

He raised his brows, no doubt expecting her to laugh. Or become angry with him for bringing up the Zara thing *yet again*.

She did neither of these things.

She ran her hands up his chest, over those wide, imposing shoulders, and fixed them around his neck. "Would you please shut up and kiss me now?"

"It would be my pleasure, Miss Scott."

14

Elizabeth had never been in a hospitality tent before. She hadn't expected it to be quite so...

...hospitable.

Donovan kissed her with such force that she soon forgot whatever it was she'd been saying. She lost herself in the feel of him, strong, manly, commanding, and the taste of him— oh, so delectable. A thrill of pleasure coursed through her at the sureness of his lips and the insistence of his hands as he gripped her hips and pushed her gently against the wall of the tent. It was surprisingly sturdy.

Who knew when she first walked inside that things would end up like *this*?

Elizabeth slipped her hands up the back of his jacket and couldn't stop herself from releasing a long, satisfied sigh as she explored the muscles straining beneath his dress shirt. Donovan chuckled under his breath and dropped his lips to the neckline of her dress, pressing gentle kisses along the top of her breasts.

"I'm assuming this means you aren't engaged to be married." It took all of Elizabeth's concentration to get the words out. Donovan's tongue dancing across her skin was rapidly reducing her to a quivering mess.

He looked up, his eyes so darkened with desire they were nearly black. "Helena is delusional. Do I seem at all interested in her?"

"No. As a matter of fact, you don't." Her voice had dissolved into a breathy whisper.

His well-formed mouth beckoned to her. She reached up and took a little nip at his bottom lip, which drew a serious groan from him.

"Are we really making out in the hospitality tent?" she murmured as he dropped his lips to the curve of her throat. Elizabeth was sure he could feel the boom of her pulse, probably even see it. It was all she could hear. Her blood thundered in her ears, drowning out even the sound of their breath, growing faster and more frantic.

"It looks that way, except in Britain we'd probably call it snogging." Donovan pulled away slightly, just enough for her to see his face.

His lips—God, those lips!—curved into a naughty smile and something blossomed inside her. Something more than attraction. And it scared the life out of her.

She took a deep, slow inhale and tried to steady herself. This was Donovan Darcy. Sure, he was pretty to look at it. Pretty perfect, actually. And yes, he could be rather gentlemanly at times...when he wasn't pounding people into the ground with that glare of his.

But he was the last man on earth Elizabeth wanted to have feelings for. So she wouldn't. Plain and simple.

The last thing Donovan Darcy appeared to need was yet another woman throwing herself at him. "And here I spent all that time trying to convince Helena we don't have an intimate relationship. What a waste."

Donovan's thumb—currently brushing a slow, tantalizing trail along her bottom lip—stopped abruptly.

He aimed a cautious look at her. "A waste indeed. Although why she would believe such a thing is beyond me. Us? In an intimate relationship?"

Elizabeth blinked up at him. "I know. Crazy, right? I mean, it's almost laughable."

Except neither one of them was laughing.

Donovan took his hands off her, straightened and adjusted his tie. The darkening of his eyes took a more sinister turn, less desirous and more provoked.

Still, Elizabeth's skin all but burned under the scrutiny of his gaze. She was playing with fire, and she knew it. Donovan Darcy wasn't the sort of man to be trifled with. But they were just having fun, right? He didn't seriously think they could embark on any sort of *relationship,* did he?

"It would never work. We would end up killing each other," she said.

Elizabeth struggled to catch her breath. Why was she always growing breathless around him? It was beginning to grate on her nerves.

"You're right. It's no secret I find you maddening a great majority of the time." He gave his chin a haughty jerk upward, but his gaze flitted ever so briefly to her cleavage.

To her horror, Elizabeth shuddered. Were her breasts actually heaving? Oh, God, no. "And, as you're well aware, I despise you."

"Oh, I'm aware." He took a step closer to her once more.

Elizabeth had to remind herself to breathe as he gave the fluttery sleeve of her dress a gentle tug and pressed a searing-hot kiss to the bare skin of her shoulder. His lips traveled up the side of her neck, nipping and taunting her. Elizabeth was barely conscious of the weight of his body against hers. Every firm, hard inch of it.

She had a mind to push him away. Or she would have if she'd been capable of forming a coherent thought. As it was, all she could manage to do was whisper, "Everyone in London now knows me as the girl from Donovan Darcy's lap. I really do hate you."

She wasn't altogether sure it was true. Granted, he was an arrogant, haughty aristocrat, but he was also growing on her in some perverse way. Even though on some level she couldn't help but wonder what he was doing, toying with her like this. Was he slumming? Getting his kicks from fooling around with the wrong sort of girl? The idea filled her with equal parts shame and fury. But what she really and truly hated was the effect he had on her. One look of those brooding eyes sent her heart racing. And with a single kiss, he practically had her on her knees begging for more. It was beyond humiliating. And this time she didn't have the luxury of blaming it on the champagne.

"I know," he murmured, cupping her breast through her dress. "You find me disgusting, don't you? I can tell by the way you tremble under my touch."

The man was infuriating.

Or so Elizabeth reminded herself as her hands somehow landed on his backside, pressing him more firmly against her. "You're not quite as good as you think you are."

"That remains to be seen, doesn't it?" He leaned in as if to kiss her.

And Elizabeth was ready for it. So ready. She licked her lips and parted them for him. But just as his mouth was within a hairbreadth from closing in on hers, Donovan paused.

Every nerve ending in Elizabeth's body screamed in protest, and she glanced up at him with pleading eyes. She was too close to the edge of desire to remind him again how much she loathed him.

Donovan's gaze locked with hers, and she instantly felt more exposed than if they'd been undressed and tangled in sheets. "Come away with me next weekend."

Elizabeth blinked. She was having enough trouble focusing with Donovan's body pushed up against hers, but this sudden change in subject threw her completely. "Come away with you?"

"Yes." Donovan nodded, as if the matter was already settled. "To Chadwicke. It's Bonfire Weekend. London will be ablaze with fireworks, and it upsets the dogs. So I retreat to the country and host an annual house party every year. Come with me."

Elizabeth struggled to take it all in. She wasn't even altogether sure what Bonfire Weekend was, other than that it had something to do with someone named Guy Fawkes, but the reason for the holiday was the least of her concerns.

"You want me to go with you to—" she struggled to force the final word out "—Chadwicke?"

Was he joking?

He certainly seemed serious as his lips finally landed on hers, seeking that kiss she'd so wanted only seconds before. Elizabeth's eyes drifted closed, and for the all-too-brief span of Donovan's bone-melting kiss, she very nearly forgot his ridiculous proposition.

"So?" he said, resting his forehead against hers. He seemed cool as a cucumber. As usual.

Was it asking too much for him to look just a fraction as flustered as she felt inside?

"So what?" She shrugged, feigning nonchalance.

The sleeve of her dress slid farther down, just a fraction, but enough to expose the very edge of the cup of her bra. Donovan glanced at her skin peeking through the strip of lace, and the set of his jaw hardened.

He slid her sleeve back in place on her shoulder. "You know what."

"Donovan, I can't go to Chadwicke with you. You know I can't."

He backed away from her, his gaze thunderous. "I know nothing of the sort."

Had he lost his mind? "You don't want me there, among your friends and family."

She wouldn't fit in there any more than she'd fit in at the Barclay School. She was through fooling herself. The thought of accompanying him to his fancy-schmancy estate and making small talk with his wealthy friends and—God forbid—meeting his blue-blooded family was horrifying.

"I do. Otherwise, I wouldn't have issued the invitation."

"I'm not sure I want my photo in the *Daily Mail* again." Elizabeth lifted her chin rebelliously.

She could see it now—pictures of her at Chadwicke, with all those aristocrats. What would the caption say this time?

One of these things is not like the other....

"There won't be any photographers there." The corner of Donovan's mouth lifted in unspoken challenge. "It's my house, remember?"

She threw up her hands. "You find me maddening, and I hate you. What would we do together all weekend?"

He lifted a single, suggestive eyebrow. "I'm sure we'd come up with something."

So this was only about sex? Of course. She really should have known.

Elizabeth's blood boiled with indignation, although she wasn't exactly sure why. She planted the palms of her hands on his impressive chest and pushed. Hard.

He stumbled backward, but quickly gained his footing. Naturally. It seemed Donovan Darcy never lost control for long. He angled his head toward her. "I'm still waiting for an answer."

Elizabeth slipped out from between him and the wall of the tent. She needed space. She needed air. She needed so many things. "No."

He appraised her with an icy glare. "No?"

"That's my answer. No." She smoothed down the front of her dress. Was it her imagination, or did it look all crumpled now?

Great. Just what she needed—to do the walk of shame at a dog show.

Donovan's gaze narrowed, and his perfect nostrils flared. For a flash that Elizabeth couldn't help but enjoy, he looked like an angry bull. Then he pulled himself together. "If you're worried about work, you can bring the Border terriers with you. And of course you'll bring Bliss. Hell, you can bring the Barrows along, too. And Jenna."

He mumbled something else under his breath. Something that sounded suspiciously like *so long as you're there*.

But that couldn't have been it. She was hearing things. Donovan would never say something so...so sweet.

Would he?

"No," she said again, half shouting this time, before she changed her mind.

Remember what happened…just when you thought you belonged, all of it was swept out from under your feet. Don't make that mistake again.

She spun on her heel and stormed out of the tent.

She'd turned him down.

Donovan couldn't quite wrap his mind around it. He'd invited Elizabeth to Chadwicke, and she'd actually said no.

He didn't know whether to be impressed or livid.

He settled on livid. It wasn't so much a decision, though, as a knee-jerk reaction. He strode out of the hospitality tent, frustration and general displeasure propelling his every footstep.

"Mr. Darcy," the ring steward said as he approached. "Are you ready for the…"

"Call the Border terriers into the ring," Donovan snapped, cutting him off. "Now. We're already behind schedule."

Donovan situated himself in the center of the ring as the steward scrambled around like a nervous Chihuahua, gathering the exhibitors together.

Elizabeth stood beside the white lattice entrance, poised to enter the ring. Unlike her fellow exhibitors, she appeared completely unruffled. Composed and confident, as though she hadn't just been with him in the hospitality tent on the verge of doing God knows what.

Donovan inhaled a ragged breath. He knew what they'd been on the verge of doing. He was still trying to steady his breath from the mere thought of it. And yet she'd refused to consider going away with him for the weekend—as if it was perfectly acceptable to shag him, but not to be seen with him.

Dear God, I sound like a woman. What is Elizabeth Scott doing to me?

Donovan's blood boiled.

He crossed his arms and stared at the three Border terriers and their handlers now lined up in the ring. "I'd like to see all the dogs go around together, please."

Two out of the three handlers flinched, Elizabeth the exception. Perhaps he'd barked out his instructions more harshly than he intended. So be it. Frustration—sexual and otherwise—tended to make a man irritable. And he was only human, after all.

He watched the dogs strut around the ring. Keeping his gaze fixed on the Borders rather than Elizabeth's shapely legs was a bit of a struggle, but somehow he managed.

First up was Sue Barrow, with Violet on the end of her show lead, if Donovan's memory served correctly. Sue flashed him a nervous smile as he approached, and a stab of guilt pierced his consciousness. On some level, he knew it was wrong to take his frustration out on someone as nice as Sue Barrow. Just the other night he'd enjoyed her tea and biscuits as they'd watched that silly but somehow still enjoyable dance program.

He forced himself to smile and nod politely when he reached the table, where she'd arranged Violet in a perfect show stack. Border terriers were smart dogs, keen on learning and pleasing their masters. Even so, Donovan was impressed with Sue's quartet of terriers. She'd clearly spent a great deal of time training her dogs. Violet stood solid as a rock as Donovan examined her. Legs straight, back level, eyes focused forward. A true canine professional.

Donovan gave the dog a gentle pat on the rump at the end

of the examination. "Good girl." He switched his focus to Sue Barrow and winked. "Down and back, please."

"Yes, sir. I mean, Mr. Darcy." The older woman blushed like a schoolgirl. "Sir."

Sue lifted Violet from the table and placed her on the ground. Donovan took the moment of downtime to glance over at Elizabeth, who gazed back at him coolly.

He frowned, crossed his arms and turned to watch Violet's down-and-back. The dog strode to the corner and turned with elegantly elongated legs. On the way back, she glanced up at Sue every few paces. Or, more accurately, she glanced at the sizable chunk of cooked liver Sue had clamped between her teeth. Donovan suppressed a shudder. He'd always despised liver, even though it was a staple wherever he went. Being both a Brit and a dog-show judge, he was destined to run in the same circles as liver. It was his livery cross to bear.

Sue and her dog stopped a meter or so in front of Donovan, and Violet struck a regal pose.

"Very nice." Donovan nodded. "All the way around, please, and I'll have the next exhibitor up on the table."

The second Border terrier wasn't even in the running. It possessed none of the grace and substance of either of the Barrow terriers. And Donovan would have bet a good portion of his fortune that someone had colored the dog's nose with a black Sharpie marker. It was too black for nature. And the poor soul looked somewhat dazed. High from the marker fumes, probably.

Donovan gave the unfortunate dog a cursory once-over. He glowered at the handler. "Down and back."

She scooped the dog off the table, nearly smothering it with her giant bosom in the process, and plopped it on the ground. The Border terrier froze for half a second, and his eyes darted toward the ring gates. Donovan almost expected the dog to make a break for it. But the handler, oblivious to what was happening on the other end of the leash, trotted toward the corner, jerking the dog along with her.

Disgusted, Donovan shook his head. He had half a mind to withhold another ribbon, just to punish the inept handler. But the dog didn't possess any disqualifying faults other than the human running alongside it.

Fine. I'll place them last.

Donovan released a resigned sigh.

He ignored the dog's weak stack at the end of the down-and-back and stalked toward the table where Elizabeth waited alongside one of the Barrow terriers.

Rose.

Or maybe it was Daisy.

No, Rose. He was certain.

"Good day, Miss Scott," he said tersely as he examined the set of Rose's teeth.

"Mr. Darcy," she replied, dripping venom with every syllable.

He smirked. "Nice bite."

He released the dog's mouth and checked the set of her shoulders.

"I get it. You're angry. But you really shouldn't take it out on the steward and the other exhibitors." Elizabeth's words were scarcely audible, but they left their mark all the same.

Not that Donovan cared. The Sharpie-wielding second exhibitor didn't deserve anything beyond professional courtesy, and he'd been nice to Sue Barrow. Hadn't he?

"I was civil, especially to Sue."

"Yes, I noticed the wink. Flirt." Elizabeth rolled her eyes.

"Jealous? Again?" he asked as he stepped away from the table.

Elizabeth laughed. Actually laughed right there in the ring.

Donovan's jaw clenched as she breezed past him toward the corner of the ring before he even had a chance to instruct her on the down-and-back. The dog did well, he supposed. In truth, he'd forgotten to watch.

"All the dogs together, please. One lap around," he called as he considered how to rank the terriers.

The black-nosed dog was last. Obviously. But it was a toss-up between the two Barrow dogs. Both of them deserved the win. He couldn't really go wrong placing either of them first. He should award the victory to Sue. They were both her dogs, after all. And it wouldn't hurt to give Elizabeth a little dose of humility, he supposed.

But when the moment came, Donovan pointed directly to Elizabeth. It was as if she were a magnet, drawing him toward her. Again and again.

"Our Winner," he called out, and she beamed. Something inside Donovan thawed.

He awarded the ribbons and sashes in opposite order this time—the third-place dog first, followed by a gracious Sue Barrow thanking him as he handed her a second-place rosette.

Then it was Elizabeth's turn.

Donovan offered her the silky first-place ribbon and slipped the sash over her head, pausing to inhale the citrusy scent of her shampoo. "Congratulations, Miss Scott."

"Thank you, Mr. Darcy." Elizabeth curtsied ever so slightly, but enough for him to get a brief glimpse down the front of her dress. Donovan doubted the move was intentional, but he took advantage of the view nonetheless.

"My pleasure." He lifted an amused brow and kept a firm

hold on the ribbon as she tugged on it, just as he had at that first dog show in New Jersey all those weeks ago.

"You realize this doesn't change anything," she muttered under her breath, her winning smile remaining firmly fixed in place. "I'm still not going to Chadwicke with you next weekend."

"Are you challenging my integrity as a judge, Miss Scott?" Donovan angled his head toward her and released his grip on the ribbon. As Elizabeth pulled it free, he let his fingertips skim the soft skin on the back of her hand. "I'm shocked. Horrified, really," he deadpanned as a telltale cluster of goose bumps broke out on Elizabeth's arm.

She jerked her hand away and a lovely scarlet flush rose to her cheeks. "I'm serious, Donovan. My answer is no."

"So I heard," Donovan said with a smile.

His pleased expression clearly caught her off guard. She narrowed her gaze at him, her fine eyes searching his for an explanation.

And finally Donovan felt the remaining edges of his irritation soften. His smile grew wider, but he didn't explain himself to Elizabeth. Let her wonder, he decided.

She would be at Chadwicke.

Donovan knew exactly how to get her there.

That's right, Miss Scott. There's more than one way to skin a cat.

15

Henry climbed into the passenger seat of Donovan's Aston Martin the next morning wearing the smile of a man with a secret.

"Morning, mate," he said as he folded himself into the leather bucket seat.

"Good morning." Donovan frowned as he pulled the car away from the curb and into London's morning traffic.

He and Henry were headed to the home of Collin Montgomery, undoubtedly one of the most annoying human beings in England, if not the world. Donovan ordinarily made it a practice to avoid the man at all costs, lest he become the target of one of Mr. Montgomery's rambling monologues, the subjects of which ran the gamut from freezing canine semen to his preferred technique for expressing his dogs' anal glands. Donovan had blanched at that last one. In his opinion, there was only one single method for accomplishing such an objectionable chore—paying someone else to do it.

His eccentricities aside, Collin Montgomery was England's foremost breeder of that bastion of the Toy Group, the Pekingese. At first glance, the Pekingese was all coat. Many a dog-show novice had mistaken the breed for a mop rather than a dog. But underneath all that fuzz, a proper Pekingese possessed a broad chest, heavy bone and good rib spring. The only way to discern such qualities amid masses of coat was a pair of skillful, experienced hands. Henry needed to get his hands on as many Pekingese as he could before he would know what he was doing. Thus, this morning's trip to the dark side, as Donovan had come to think of it.

"What are you glowering about this fine morning?" Henry asked in a manner so cheerful it bordered on maddening.

"You'll find out soon enough." Donovan sped away from Henry's flat in posh Knightsbridge and headed toward Belgravia. "This Montgomery fellow is a piece of work."

Henry laughed. "He can't be that bad."

Donovan lifted a brow. "You may change your tune after an hour or so, but at least you'll know a thing or two about the Pekingese."

"Thank you for the help. As you know, I can use it. Those mop dogs never fail to confound me. I'm sure Montgomery is more bearable than you make him out to be. You can be a harsh judge of character. You've said so yourself."

Donovan had no response to this. He simply grinned instead.

"Ah, a smile at last," Henry said. "And here I thought you were upset about that business in the paper."

Donovan's smile faded instantaneously. "And what business would that be?"

Henry fell silent at once.

"Henry?" Donovan prompted.

"It's the *Daily Mail*." Henry sighed. "Again. You mean you haven't seen it?"

"I don't make it a practice to read that rubbish. You know that. The only reason I saw the photo from the champagne bar at Harrods was because of Zara." He wished she didn't love gossip so much. Perhaps it was the sort of thing teenage girls grew out of. He hoped so. Then again, if that was the case, how did the *Daily Mail* stay in business?

"You might want to take a look at this morning's edition. That's all I'm saying." Henry kept his gaze focused out the window, but Donovan could see the pleasure in his eyes, plain as day.

"Might I say you're even more good-humored today than usual. Anything I should know about?"

"It's Jenna." When he said her name, Henry sounded like a lovesick schoolboy. "Jenna Scott."

Donovan had seen his friend this way more than once over the years. When Henry fell in love, he fell quick and hard. On this particular occasion, Donovan welcomed Henry's unrestrained infatuation. He intended to take full advantage of it. "You still fancy her, then."

"Oh, yes. I've seen her every night this week. She's the most beautiful creature I ever beheld."

Donovan cleared his throat. It was time to make his move. "I suppose you'd like to invite her to my little soiree at Chadwicke?" he asked as casually as possible.

"That would be outstanding." Henry grinned from ear to ear. "Upon my honor, I believe I might in be love."

Upon my honor indeed. Donovan fought an eye roll.

"Seriously, Darcy. I think she might be the one."

"Very well, then. Invite her to Chadwicke. Perhaps the weekend will culminate in a marriage proposal." Donovan smirked at the idea.

"Don't laugh," Henry admonished as Donovan pulled up

in front of Collin Montgomery's home. "You never know about these things."

Donovan killed the ignition. "Do me a favor, mate."

"Anything," Henry said as he unfastened his seat belt. "Name it."

"Make sure Jenna brings Elizabeth with her to Chadwicke."

Henry's brow furrowed. "I would have thought you'd invited her yourself by now."

Invited her? Yes.

And subsequently been shot down in flames.

The turn of events still rubbed him entirely the wrong way. And to add insult to injury, Henry was romancing Elizabeth's sister all over the city. "I'd prefer Jenna to see to it that she comes. Can we just leave it at that?"

"Of course." Henry shook his head, clearly baffled. Then again, it didn't take much to baffle Henry. "Although, from what I saw in the *Daily Mail,* you should have no trouble getting her there yourself," he muttered as he climbed out of the car.

"Excuse me?" Donovan asked over the top of the Aston Martin.

Henry simply buttoned his coat and shook his head. "Oh, no. I'm not telling you. You're not interested in that sort of rubbish, remember?"

Before Donovan could pound on the roof of the car and demand an explanation, Collin Montgomery paraded his way down the walk, with a trail of puffball Pekingese dogs bobbing along behind him. "Gentlemen! You've arrived. Splendid."

Henry shot Donovan a glance.

Donovan had to stifle a laugh. "Montgomery. Good day—

may I introduce my longtime friend Henry Robson? As I mentioned when I phoned last week, Henry is a provisional judge and would like a lesson in Pekingese conformation."

"Fabulous!" Montgomery clapped his hands. Several enormous rings, all sporting clusters of diamonds—or, more likely, stones resembling diamonds—glittered in the morning sunshine. "Follow me, boys. Pekingese Palace awaits."

"Pekingese Palace?" Henry muttered as they followed Montgomery up the steps toward a Victorian-era row house painted fire-engine red. "Is this guy for real, or are you pulling my leg?"

"Oh, he's real all right. But he knows his stuff."

Once inside the foyer, Montgomery closed the door behind them. Donovan gazed at the surroundings and squinted. Every available surface was littered with some sort of figurine or sculpture paying homage to Montgomery's breed, such as little Pekingese faces crafted from marble, crystal and cut glass. Donovan was struck with a memory of someone once telling him that Montgomery even owned bedroom slippers that resembled a pair of show-groomed Pekingese dogs. He hoped to God it wasn't true. Or if it was, that he would never bear witness to the rumor's authenticity.

"And how are you, Mr. Darcy?" Montgomery gushed. "And your lovely aunt Constance? What a wonderful woman, your aunt."

He may have said more, most likely did. But on the ornate round table in the center of the foyer, among the dog figurines and half buried beneath the latest copy of *Show Dog Quarterly,* was today's edition of the *Daily Mail.*

Donovan eyed the newspaper and nodded absently at whatever Montgomery was saying. He'd made up his mind he wasn't going to look at it. He didn't give a damn what the

Society page had to say about him, even though Henry had clearly found it amusing.

But faced with the black-and-white evidence, his resistance wavered. Perhaps it was another tantalizing photo of Miss Scott and himself. He decided that maybe he should give it a gander, if for no other reason than to enjoy a most pleasant memory.

He dragged his gaze from the newsprint and focused once again on the present company.

It appeared he hadn't missed much. Montgomery was droning on and on. And on.

"…my wife will be dreadfully sorry she missed your visit. She would be so thrilled to meet you. Mr. Donovan Darcy and his handsome friend, here in our humble home."

Donovan glanced at a gilt-framed mirror that would have been more at home in Cleopatra's bedroom than in a London townhome. The home was hardly humble. But the real revelation was that Montgomery was married.

Henry lifted his brows and blinked a few times.

Donovan tilted his head. "Pardon?"

After a prolonged glance at Henry, Montgomery replied, "My wife—Charlotte—she's tied up this morning. I'm sure she would have loved to meet you."

Donovan was forced to let out a cough. He'd always assumed Montgomery was gay. He supposed he ought to have learned by now not to judge a book by its cover, no matter how flamboyant that cover might happen to be.

Montgomery, married?

The poor woman.

"We're sorry to have missed her, as well." Ever the diplomat, Henry filled the awkward silence. "Shall we get started with my Pekingese lesson, then?"

"Of course, of course. Follow me, boys." With a flick of his wrist, Montgomery waved them down the hall.

After making way for the trio of waddling balls of hair that were Montgomery's dogs, Henry fell in step behind him.

"I've got a few matters to attend to. Commence with your lesson," Donovan called out after them. "I'll be back shortly."

Henry cast a desperate glance over his shoulder before disappearing down the pink marble hallway.

Donovan shook his head. Pink marble. Pekingese figurines. The legendary bedroom slippers.

Whoever she is, Charlotte Montgomery must be one tolerant woman.

Once alone in the entryway, Donovan slipped the *Daily Mail* out from under the dog-show magazine. He flipped through it, searching for the Society page. There was no mistaking it once he found it. His eyes widened as he took in the enormous typeface.

Dog Show...Or Snog Show? Donovan Darcy and his mystery woman engage in a bit of extracurricular fun at the Ashwyn Dog Show over the weekend.

Snog show? Really?

Donovan shook his head. It was somewhat clever, he reluctantly admitted to himself. Then he let his gaze wander to the accompanying photo. Once again, one of their photographers had caught him and Elizabeth in a compromising position. This time, in the hospitality tent at the dog show. The black-and-white image was a bit grainy—shot with a long lens, no doubt—but it had clearly captured the moment. Donovan's head was dipped, and he was nuzzling Elizabeth's neck. The look on her face was one of pure ecstasy—eyes closed, generous lips parted.

Donovan stared at it, transfixed, as a ripple of pure lust made its way through him.

He slammed the newspaper shut and buried it once again beneath the magazine. What was becoming of him? A simple photo of himself and Elizabeth could awaken feelings he'd never before had trouble keeping tightly under wraps. It was problematic, to say the least. Deeply troubling. Disconcerting, really.

Even so, he couldn't quite help the smile that crept to his lips. A smile that had nothing whatsoever to do with Montgomery and his doggy slippers.

Elizabeth wound the quartet of leashes around her hands and led the Border terriers—along with Bliss, of course— to the corner. Today of all days, she needed to walk. To get outside, breathe some fresh air and exercise. Actually, she felt more like strangling somebody. But since Donovan Darcy wasn't within strangling distance, a walk would have to suffice.

Snog show.

She couldn't get the ridiculous words out of her head. What was wrong with the British press? She'd never seen anything so childish. So immature. So *humiliating.*

How was it possible that she'd been in London for a matter of weeks and her picture had been in the paper not once, but *twice?* And they weren't just ordinary photos. They were private. Intimate.

The whole ordeal was inconceivable. The entire city of London probably thought she was a slut...all because she'd kissed Donovan Darcy a few times.

She blamed him completely. On some level, she knew it wasn't entirely fair to hold him responsible. But if he wasn't Donovan Darcy, mega-millionaire, none of this would have happened.

Elizabeth exhaled a frustrated breath and pushed a stray curl back up into her ponytail. *If he were here right now, I'd tell him exactly what I think of this mess.*

In all truth, she'd probably edit her thoughts just a tad. He didn't need to know that seeing her image splashed all over the tabloids—*twice!*—had birthed a very profound, very real fear that one day she would open the *Daily Mail* and find the ugly Markham mess revealed for all the world to see. What if they discovered she'd been suspended from her job in the States because she'd been suspected of extortion? The prospect made her sick with worry.

Exactly how long would it take for the tabloids to uncover the true identity of Donovan Darcy's "mystery woman"?

A wave of nausea hit Elizabeth as she passed the cupcake bakery. She was forced to stop at one of their cute little café tables and sit for a minute. The dogs milled about at her feet, tangling her legs in a spiderweb of leashes.

Elizabeth's gaze darted to and fro, looking for photographers who might be lurking in the bushes or disguising themselves as innocent cupcake diners. She saw nothing. Then again, she hadn't seen anything out of the ordinary at Harrods or the snog show.

Dog show!

She took a deep breath and told herself she was being paranoid. No one was interested in a woman walking a pack of dogs. There weren't throngs of photographers following her around. She wasn't a princess. Or a movie star. If they were tailing anyone, it was Donovan.

Elizabeth quit looking for imaginary paparazzi lurking in the shadows and went to work untangling the leashes from around her legs. She was sitting, head bent, ballet flat dangling from the big toe of her right foot as she tried to extricate herself from the tangle of twenty-six feet of leather, when another set of fingers slid up her thigh.

"It looks like you could use a hand there."

Elizabeth's heart leaped to her throat at the sound of Donovan's voice. And damned if an intoxicating shiver didn't snake through her as his fingertips made contact with her flesh.

She swatted his hand away. "Not helping. I'm not sure if you noticed, but it's my ankles that are bound together. Not my thighs."

Donovan shrugged. His languorous gaze roamed from her feet, up her legs and lingered at the hem of her day dress. "Pity."

Elizabeth stepped out of the leashes before he could offer more assistance and rose to look him in the eye. "What are you doing here?"

"Finneus and I are out for an afternoon walk." He glanced down at the Cavalier, wagging in ecstasy upon greeting the other dogs.

"In a suit?" Elizabeth snorted.

Looking impeccable as always, he smoothed down his tie. A silk tie…as though he were on his way to meet the Queen rather than out for a walk. "Sorry if I look a bit formal. Believe it or not, I've been working. At my job."

He winked.

She gave her eyes a hearty roll and made every effort to ignore the knot at his collar, perfectly crafted, of course. A half Windsor this time. An assertive man's knot, according to her mother and the stylists at Scott Bridal.

God, she was in trouble. Couldn't he have worn a Small knot or a Four-in-Hand? Would it have been too much to ask to feel at least a little in control of things?

Donovan's brown eyes searched hers. "You're looking at my tie as if you'd like to lynch me with it."

Heat rose to her cheeks. "You look quite handsome, actually."

She could see the pleasure creep into his gaze, along with a hint of suspicion. "A compliment. Where has my spirited Miss Scott gone?"

"Still here." She raised her hand. "Don't worry. I'm sure I'll say something to offend you before long. That is, if history is any indication."

"Something to look forward to, then." He winked and the tingling sensation returned, dancing across Elizabeth's skin and leaving a trail of goose bumps in its wake.

Yep, trouble. Most definitely.

A teenage couple ambled past with their arms around one another's waists. The way they gazed at each other—with naive adoration—made Elizabeth look away. She couldn't remember what it felt like to be that innocent, that trusting. She took a cautious step away from Donovan.

He frowned at the empty space between them. "I'd thought we might walk together. I have a place I'd like to show you."

"I don't think that's such a wise idea."

Donovan's jaw tensed, and his sharp eyes narrowed. "You were right. It's been all of two minutes and I'm offended."

"I guess you haven't seen today's paper," Elizabeth hissed.

"Actually, I have." Donovan lifted a brow. "What in God's name does that have to do with walking my dog?"

"Everything." She took another protective step away from him. She could already feel her body betraying her, leaning toward Donovan as if caught in some invisible, all-powerful force. "It has everything to do with it. I have no desire to see myself in the *Daily Mail* again tomorrow, throwing myself at you. I can't imagine what's next…a photo of me half-undressed, with your hands all over me?"

"Now, that would certainly be a picture worth seeing." The corners of Donovan's lips turned up most provocatively.

"You think this is funny?" Elizabeth's voice rose louder than she intended. The dogs looked at her, alarm written all over their sweet faces. She took a calming breath. "You might find all this media attention amusing, but I don't. Not a bit."

"Don't let it get to you. Trust me. After a while, it becomes easy to ignore." He reached out to stroke her arm.

"No touching," she said evenly.

Donovan's hand stilled. He looked at her with an expression somewhere between irritation and disbelief. "Excuse me?"

"I told you—I'm not going to see myself in the paper tomorrow in another compromising position. So, we can walk together if you like, but no touching."

"We'll see about that." Donovan's voice carried an edge, but he stayed out of arm's reach and motioned for her to step in front of him. "Shall we?"

"I'm serious. No touching." Elizabeth began walking.

The dogs trotted out in front—Violet, Hyacinth, Daisy, Rose and Bliss, joined by an excited Finneus. As they rounded the corner and headed toward the park, Elizabeth was conscious of little else but Donovan seething alongside her.

16

They fell into a silence more comfortable than not, even though Elizabeth remained acutely aware of Donovan walking beside her. His presence wasn't exactly easy to forget. Elizabeth commented once or twice on the weather and her pleasure that the nighttime drizzle had disappeared with the rising sun. Donovan responded with barely a nod of his head.

They passed through Hyde Park Gate and headed west toward the Gardens, walking for some time without saying a word. Elizabeth began to contemplate the possibility that the entire walk would pass without them ever having a real conversation. The idea had its appeal, since half the time whatever came out of his mouth infuriated her.

Then she realized he'd probably prefer her to keep her mouth shut. And she had the sudden urge to talk all the more.

"Donovan," she said, tossing him a glance. "I said touching was off-limits, not talking. It's your turn to say something now. I commented on the weather. Now you should say something about the color of the fall leaves, perhaps. Or the way the dogs seem to be enjoying themselves."

"Do you talk by rule, then, when you're walking the dogs?" He smiled. As handsome as he was on any given occasion, he looked infinitely more appealing when he smiled.

Elizabeth swallowed and looked away. "Sometimes."

"Very well. I'll oblige and say whatever you wish me to say." He pointed an elegant finger to a cluster of trees so heavy with crimson leaves, they blocked out the sun. "The fall leaves are lovely this afternoon. How's that?"

"It'll do." She started to giggle, but the laughter caught in her throat as a stately redbrick compound came into view, surrounded by a dramatic black iron fence. The gates to the fence were topped with gilt embellishments that glowed like molten gold in the afternoon sun. All around the mansion were finely manicured gardens, row after row of boxed hedges and flowering plants that bloomed despite the bite in the air.

It was all so beautiful it took Elizabeth's breath away. "Where are we?"

The corner of Donovan's mouth hitched up in a satisfied grin. Clearly he was pleased at her reaction. "This is Kensington Palace."

"My first palace," she breathed, trying to take it all in. To the right was a path flanked on either side with perfect oval topiaries, like the ones in front of Donovan's house on Sumner Place. Only these were oversize, at least twenty feet tall. Stately conical giants that made her feel like Alice stepping gingerly into Wonderland. "We don't have palaces and castles back home."

"We have our fair share over here. But this one's always been a personal favorite. Queen Victoria spent her childhood here, you know."

Elizabeth narrowed her gaze at him, wondering if he could

possibly know what she was thinking. She suspected he did. "Does that mean what I think it means?"

He nodded. "Yes. Dash, her famed Cavalier King Charles spaniel, lived here, as well."

She shook her head in disbelief. With anyone else, she probably would have been embarrassed about how excited she was to be standing here—in the exact spot where Dash and a young Victoria once lived. But she figured if anyone understood, it would be another Cavalier devotee. Someone who felt the same way she did. Someone like Donovan.

She fixed her gaze on his. He looked back at her, and a startling rush of warmth filled her chest. "Thank you for bringing me here. This is quite an unexpected surprise."

"Consider it a peace offering for that business in the paper," he said. He made no move to touch her, but his gaze drifted to her lips.

Elizabeth swallowed hard and reminded herself to stand her ground.

She turned her back to him, heart pounding. She wouldn't, couldn't, end up on the pages of the *Daily Mail* again. She could just see the headlines now: *Donovan Darcy's Mystery Woman Identified as Disgraced Teacher from America!*

Wouldn't Helena Robson just love that?

"Come with me," Donovan whispered and placed his hand against the small of her back, the heat from his body searing through the wispy fabric of her dress.

Elizabeth scooted forward.

Donovan practically growled, "So we're sticking to that no-touching rule?"

"Absolutely. If you can't abide by a simple rule…" She lifted her chin but couldn't bring herself to look him in the eye.

Dangerous as it would be to give in, she didn't quite trust

herself to follow through with the plan. He'd caught her off guard by bringing her to Kensington Palace. Not only was it an atypically sweet gesture, but it suggested he knew her in a way that didn't seem possible given their vast differences.

Donovan exhaled a sharp breath. "Of course I can abide. I give my word not to lay a finger on you. Follow me, then."

With his spine ramrod straight and shoulders tensely squared, he led her down a path, through the shadows of the colossal topiaries, to a smaller building. "This is the Orangery, built by Queen Anne in the early 1700s. Now it's a restaurant, famous for having the best tea and orange cake in England."

The Orangery. Its name had a lovely ring to it, a sweet simplicity that belied its splendor. It was a smaller, yet equally lovely, version of the palace.

Elizabeth glanced at the six dogs standing beside her and Donovan. As well behaved as they were at the moment— exhaustion-induced, no doubt—she knew they'd never be welcome inside the Orangery, Bliss's and Finneus's resemblance to Dash notwithstanding. "Too bad we can't go in."

Donovan's lips curved into a knowing smile. "I thought you might say that. So I've arranged a little something special."

No sooner had the words left his mouth than a waiter, neatly dressed in black and white, with a tea towel slung over his arm, came bustling toward them from the Orangery's front door.

"Mr. Darcy," he said, nodding at Donovan. "Your table is right this way."

Your table? Elizabeth mouthed as they followed the waiter.

Donovan winked one of his deadly winks. It settled in the depths of Elizabeth's stomach with a jolt of electricity.

The waiter led them to a lone outdoor table. It was situated directly in front of the Orangery, with a perfect view of the palace and its maze of hedges and rosebushes.

A crystal cake plate sat in the center of the table, with two enormous slices of orange cake balanced on it. The icing was at least an inch thick and Elizabeth could smell the mouth-watering combination of butter, sugar and tart oranges before she even sat down.

And if the finery of the accompanying white china and miniature orange-tree centerpiece weren't enough, two large silver bowls sat on the ground in the shade of the table. Water for the dogs. He'd thought of everything.

It was the sort of grand, over-the-top gesture that only a wealthy man could pull off. A man of certain distinction. Elizabeth should have been disgusted. Or, at the very least, uncomfortable. If she'd been on the outside looking in on this scenario, she would have described it to Jenna with a heavy dose of cynicism and a roll of her eyes.

But try as she might, she couldn't muster an ounce of indignation. Quite the opposite. She found herself touched by Donovan's thoughtfulness.

Bewildered, but touched.

Maybe she wasn't quite as jaded as she'd thought.

Donovan watched Elizabeth's eyes drift closed as she took a bite of orange cake.

"Heavenly." She sighed.

Heavenly indeed, he thought. Although those thoughts didn't necessarily refer to the cake.

Donovan was beginning to feel the danger of paying Elizabeth Scott too much attention. She attracted him more than he liked. He'd spent a great deal of effort trying to convince himself it was merely physical. That being the case, he had no idea why he'd brought her here, to the Orangery. She ought to have seen it, being a Cavalier fancier like himself. It seemed a shame for her to miss it. That was all. Someone needed to bring her here, and it may as well have been him.

She opened her eyes. They were the softest brown with hints of amber, like fine, aged brandy. "This is delicious."

"I'm glad you like it."

Donovan looked down at his own plate and noticed it was empty, save for a crumb here and there. That was odd. He didn't remember eating a thing. Then again, he'd been so caught up in watching Elizabeth's fork sliding between her lush, pillowy lips, he'd just about taken leave of his senses.

"I can see why this is one of your favorite places in London." She smiled and licked a bit of frosting from the corner of her mouth.

Donovan had to look away. He averted his gaze to the Cavaliers stretched out in the sun, their little rib cages rising and falling in a lazy rhythm. Her ridiculous no-touching rule was driving him mad. He couldn't fathom why. He'd spent the better part of thirty-five years not touching Elizabeth Scott, and suddenly it was all he could think about.

Touching her.

Tasting her.

He cleared his throat. Those things would come soon enough. At Chadwicke.

He smiled, thinking of how smug she'd looked when she'd turned down his invitation. And now…issuing the no-touching mandate. If she only knew.

"You look almost happy. I hardly recognize you. Perhaps it's the atmosphere." Elizabeth waved toward the palace rising from its garden, sumptuous and green. "It really is lovely."

If Donovan wasn't mistaken, Elizabeth Scott was enjoying

herself. In *his* company, no less. This pleased him far more than it should have. "Just one of the surprises I have up my sleeve. Perhaps I'll surprise you next when you're least expecting it."

Like when you turn up at my country estate.

Elizabeth angled her head toward him. "You've already turned out to be a bit of a surprise."

"I have, have I? You mean since you found out I'm not sleeping with my sister, nor am I engaged to Helena Robson?" He lifted a brow and resituated the napkin in his lap. "You seem to have a keen interest in my romantic affairs."

A frown tipped those tempting lips of hers. "Don't flatter yourself."

He smoothed down his tie. "I'm merely pointing out that you're running out of things to find objectionable concerning me."

A look of incredulity crossed her delicate features. "Hardly."

Donovan raised a curious eyebrow.

Elizabeth clearly took the gesture as an invitation to share her thoughts on the matter. "For starters, there's the media's inexplicable fascination with you."

"As I told you earlier, the media is of no consequence. I'll not allow a bloke with a camera to run my life."

Elizabeth dropped her glance to her lap. "We can't all afford that luxury."

"And?"

"And what?" Her gaze flitted back to him, making his head reel. Donovan marveled once again at the power those eyes of hers seemed to have over him.

"You cited the media, *for starters.* Surely there's more." He leaned toward her and caught a whiff of fresh soap and oranges, a combination he'd never found particularly alluring. Until now. "Elizabeth, why don't you tell me the truth? You've certainly never minced words before."

"It's your money. You really are obscenely wealthy, aren't you?" She turned up her nose in disgust.

"My money?" An incredulous laugh escaped him. It didn't take a maths wiz to add up the number of women he'd encountered who were repelled by his wealth. Zero.

"Yes." She watched him coolly, waiting.

He supposed he should have seen this coming, given all her talk at Harrods about him not having to work for a living. He'd chalked it up as a reaction to her being sacked, not an aversion to wealth itself.

He lifted a brow. "I see. You're a snob, then."

Her mouth dropped open, giving Donovan an unobstructed view of her pink tongue. When they got to Chadwicke, he aimed to make her use that tongue for good rather than evil.

"*You're* calling *me* a snob?" she snapped. "That's ridiculous."

"Ridiculous? Really? You object to me and my job and make assumptions about my character based solely on my wealth." He shrugged, rather enjoying the way her creamy complexion was growing rosier by the second. "Yes. You, Elizabeth Scott, are a snob. You just admitted as much yourself."

"I admitted no such thing." She tossed her napkin, wadded into a tight, frustrated ball, on the table. "I merely said I had a problem with your pile of money, which is preposterously huge by all accounts."

"Snobbery in its purest form. I was born rich, through no fault of my own. Your attitude is no different than if I had a problem with you simply because you were born…" He paused, choosing his next words carefully. He wanted to make a point, not provoke her to such an extent that she stabbed him with her fork. "...beautiful."

She blinked, speechless.

"Were you expecting me to say something else?" Donovan smiled.

"In all honestly, I've no idea what's going to come out of your mouth from one moment to the next." She aimed a pointed look at him, but Donovan could see the trace of a smile on her lips. "I'll have you know I've never been accused of snobbery before."

"As I've never before been accused of romancing my little sister. You, my dear Elizabeth, are even worse than our friends at the *Daily Mail*."

Her smile grew a bit wider. "They're not my friends. And I'm not *yours*."

In the midst of her protestation, all Donovan could think about was that photo from the paper. And the way Elizabeth had looked, lips parted, head thrown back, clearly in the throes of passion.

He leaned forward, loving the way her cheeks grew pinker the closer he got. "Keep telling yourself that. We both know better."

She narrowed her lovely eyes at him.

Donovan ignored her glare and stared purposely at her mouth. "As I told you, I'm a man of my word. Which is the only thing keeping me from reaching across the table right now and kissing you within an inch of your life."

He watched her struggle to catch her breath.

Satisfied—for the time being—Donovan leaned back in his chair.

The waiter returned with more hot water for Elizabeth's tea. As he poured, Elizabeth fixed her gaze on Donovan's and licked her lips. Slowly. Provocatively. Until Donovan began to squirm in his seat.

"Enjoying yourself?" Donovan asked, struggling to keep his ever-present composure.

"I think I am," she said as the waiter disappeared. Finally.

Rules be damned, Donovan was struck with the sudden urge to reach across the table and graze the tips of her fingers with his own. The way her fingertips drummed on the white tablecloth seemed to beckon his touch.

Wary of an annoyed woman armed with a fork, and not altogether ready to admit either to himself or to Elizabeth that he was incapable of keeping his hands off her, Donovan fastened them firmly in his lap. "Shall I give it all away, then?"

She tilted her head. "Give what away?"

"My money, of course." How had she put it, exactly? "The whole 'preposterously huge' pile of it? Since you find it so objectionable."

"That won't be necessary." She laughed. The sound of it—unexpected, charming—hit him like a punch in the gut.

Donovan's self-control wavered. He slid his hand across the tablecloth and met her fingers with the barest of touches.

As always, her skin was warm, soft. She kept her hand perfectly still and tilted her head, as though studying him. In her eyes, Donovan saw a hint of something more than just physical attraction.

He'd known it was there all along. He'd felt it himself. More than once…with that first touch, first kiss. If he was honest with himself, it had been there the instant he'd laid eyes on Elizabeth Scott. From that very day, the sight of her had become almost painful for him. Her presence carved out an ache deep inside him. An ache he'd never felt before—the ache of possibility.

What are you doing, Donovan? This is a bad idea. The worst. She despises everything you represent. And she drives you to the brink of insanity.

The mood spoiled by a heaping dose of reality, he withdrew his hand.

And as they waited for the check, they sat with their fingertips little more than a whisper apart, the air swirling with the fresh scent of ripe oranges and unwanted affection.

17

"So, who exactly is Guy Fawkes?" Jenna frowned into her teacup, obviously not adjusting well to the change from coffee. "Some historical Englishman with a penchant for burning things?"

"Why the sudden interest in Guy Fawkes?" Elizabeth held Rose in place on the grooming table and peered intently at the dog's face. She'd been trying for a good hour to get Rose's wiry moustache perfectly even. Jenna's presence wasn't exactly helping matters. "And you know there's a Starbucks only two blocks away, right across from the tube station. Make two sharp rights out the front door and you can't miss it."

Jenna sank cross-legged onto one of the garden chairs, obviously choosing to ignore the siren call of her beloved lattes. "I know. I just thought I'd stick around here for a while so we can chat."

Elizabeth slid a pair of grooming scissors out of her pocket and took the tiniest snip possible from the left side of Rose's fuzzy beard. "There. Finally. I think her face is even now. How does she look?"

"Exactly the same as she looked when you started." Jenna took a sip of her tea, scrunched her face and abandoned the teacup on the garden café table.

"Gee, thanks."

Jenna shrugged. "Come on, you know I can never tell what in the world goes on at those shows. The dogs all look beautiful. But I swear, last weekend I saw someone putting an honest-to-God wig on a poodle."

"Really?" Elizabeth slid the scissors back into the pocket of her grooming smock. "That's cheating. Hairpieces are against the rules."

"You're beginning to scare me a little." Jenna frowned. "I tell you I saw a dog wearing a wig, and you're worried about cheating. It was a *dog with a wig*. Seriously. This dog-show stuff is not normal."

Elizabeth let out a little laugh, but also decided right then and there not to tell Jenna about Sue's friend who had a toy fox terrier with a new set of braces on its teeth.

"So, back to Guy Fawkes. Who is this guy? And why does London go up in flames every year because of him?" Jenna eyed her teacup and pushed it a fraction farther away with a nudge of her pointer finger.

"It doesn't go up in flames, exactly." Finally satisfied with the state of Rose's goatee, she switched her attention to the dog's eyebrows. "I think it's more of a fireworks kind of thing."

"But didn't you say they sometimes burn this Guy guy in effigy?" Jenna yawned.

"Guy guy?" Elizabeth quirked a brow. "Cute."

"Thank you."

"From what I understand, he was part of something called the Gunpowder Plot, back in 1605. He was caught red-handed with a load of gunpowder trying to blow up the House of Lords. Now the day he was caught is a big national holiday. And that holiday is this coming weekend. They call it Bonfire Weekend." Elizabeth hoped she didn't ask for more details. She was having enough trouble keeping it straight herself. Sue had given her a brief rundown, but she'd still felt compelled to consult Wikipedia. "But really, why the sudden interest?"

"Well, since we're going to Chadwicke to celebrate this dubious holiday, I sort of wanted to know what it was all about."

The silver metal comb Elizabeth had been using to tackle Rose's eyebrows clattered to the floor. It made such a racket when it landed on the garden's interlocking brick that Rose hopped off the grooming table and darted behind a nearby rosebush.

If Elizabeth didn't wrestle her back onto the table soon, Rose was liable to get dirty. Not that Elizabeth could give much thought to a show coat caked with garden peat moss at the moment. She was far too busy marveling at Jenna's casual mention of Donovan's country estate.

How did Jenna know about Donovan's big holiday weekend at Chadwicke? And what had she meant when she'd said "we're going to Chadwicke"?

Who was this *we?*

Elizabeth stomach churned. *No. Please, no.* "What are you talking about?"

"Donovan's party this weekend." She shrugged, as if going away to a big mansion and doing something ridiculous like playing lawn tennis was an ordinary weekend occurrence. "Henry is going. He invited me and practically ordered me to bring you along."

Rose was rolling on her back now. Getting really down

and dirty in the rich, dark soil. Elizabeth hardly noticed. "And what did you say?"

"I said yes, of course. I like Henry. What else would I do?"

"Oh, I don't know." Elizabeth's voice grew shrill. She sounded like one of the Bridezillas at Scott Bridal who threw a fit if she broke a fingernail. "Ask me if I wanted to go, for one thing."

"Calm down. I don't understand why you're upset. I assumed Donovan had already invited you. I mean, you were all over the newspaper last week with your tongues down each other's throats."

Jenna snickered.

Elizabeth glared.

Jenna snickered with greater enthusiasm.

"He did invite me," Elizabeth said.

"Then what's the problem?"

"I told him no."

"What?" Jenna heaved out a sigh. "Good grief, why? You know, this cat-and-mouse game you two have going on is getting old."

"Donovan Darcy isn't exactly the sort to play games, in case you haven't noticed." Although what he was doing pursuing her was a mystery. He couldn't possibly be seriously interested in her. She swallowed and allowed herself to consider the possibility just long enough for a shiver to run up her spine. Then she pushed the idea away.

"Then what's going on with you two?"

"I honestly don't know." It was baffling, to say the least. Every time she made up her mind about Donovan, he did something that surprised her—something sweet. Visiting the Pet Spa at Harrods and sharing orange cake on the grounds of Kensington Palace were probably the best memories she'd have of London when she left.

And then there was the matter of the kissing. God, he was good at it. Too good, really. A man didn't become an expert kisser like that without a lot of practice. She had trouble remembering this important fact, however, when his mouth was on hers.

"He makes me nervous," Elizabeth said, realizing this admission was the only thing she was 100 percent sure of when it came to Donovan.

"Don't be nervous. You're going. I already said you were." Jenna gave her *the look*…the older-sister *do as I say* look she used rarely but with great authority when she chose to wield it. "You'll go away with Mr. Darcy. The two of you will set someone on fire. What's there to be nervous about?"

Nothing…

Everything.

Elizabeth huffed out a sigh. "First off, we won't be setting anyone on fire. In some places on Bonfire Night, Guy Fawkes is burned in effigy—straw dolls, that sort of thing. The actual man has been dead since the early 1600s. Setting him on fire now might be overkill."

"I see your point. Why don't we ever burn anyone in effigy in America?" Jenna scrunched her brow. "We don't, do we?"

"Not that I know of. Who would we burn?" Elizabeth remembered a bonfire way back when she was in high school where they'd burned a stuffed version of the opposing team's mascot. It never completely caught fire. In the end it was just a smoldering mess. A bit anticlimactic.

"Good question." Jenna's eyes lit up. "I could think of a few ex-boyfriends I wouldn't mind burning in effigy. Couldn't you?"

For a moment, Elizabeth was distracted by the image of a straw doll with Grant Markham's face engulfed in flames. She had to admit the idea wasn't without appeal. Like a cleansing of sorts.

She shook her head and reminded herself she had more important things to think about. Such as how Donovan had somehow managed to get her to Chadwicke, even after she'd point-blank refused his invitation.

He'd surprised her again, damn it.

"There's only one man I'd like to burn in effigy at the moment," she said absently.

Things with Donovan were about to heat up, and not in the way she was sure he had in mind.

Donovan felt the indignation rolling off Elizabeth in waves as she sat in the front seat of his Range Rover. And to be honest, he was perplexed by it. Her annoyance seemed rather extreme, even for Elizabeth.

As he pulled the vehicle onto the M40 and headed toward Derbyshire, he couldn't help but wonder if the silent treatment she seemed to be giving him would last the duration of the ride to the country. As many times as he'd pondered the fantasy of a noiseless Elizabeth Scott, one who didn't blurt out every thought that crossed her obstinate mind—like telling him how much she despised him even while his hands were on her breasts, for instance—the reality wasn't quite what he'd hoped for.

It was unnerving, really.

And Donovan had a mind to end it.

"You look as though I'm escorting you to the gallows rather than a weekend in the country," he said, still looking straight ahead.

Even so, he could easily see the exaggerated roll of her eyes in his peripheral vision.

Another minute of uncomfortable silence followed. Then, finally, Elizabeth spoke. "I'll bet you're pleased with yourself."

"As a whole, yes." Donovan nodded and slid his gaze toward her.

That creamy complexion of hers flushed a bit, which made him smile. Good. If she grew agitated enough, she'd never be able to hold her tongue all afternoon. And, as astonished as Donovan himself was to realize it, he preferred an angry Elizabeth Scott to a quiet one.

"Is there some reason I should be especially pleased with myself on this particular day?" He pretended to give it the utmost consideration. "It's been a productive morning, but I don't recall winning the Nobel Peace Prize or anything else spectacular."

She aimed a sweet smile at him. Too sweet. "They don't typically award the Nobel Peace Prize to millionaires, do they?"

Billionaire.

Donovan had to bite his tongue to stop himself from correcting her. "We can't all be Mother Teresa now, can we? What would be the fun in that?"

"Mother Teresa?" Beside him, Elizabeth all but snorted with laughter. "I assure you, you're in no danger of encroaching on Mother Teresa's legacy."

She let out another throaty laugh. Bliss swiveled her head back and forth between the two of them, as if she wanted in on the joke.

It wasn't *that* funny. Wasn't this weekend's polo match aimed at raising money for charity? And hadn't Donovan written a six-figure check to St. Catherine's Hospice just this morning? Not that he would ever share that information with Elizabeth. If she was determined to see the very worst in him, so be it. He doubted she would be impressed anyway, regardless of the size of the donation. Somehow he sensed she was the type who thought anyone was capable of writing a check. No doubt she believed real charity involved getting one's hands dirty.

He frowned and briefly considered the possibility that such a point of view may indeed be accurate.

"Quit brooding, Donovan. I didn't mean to step on your aristocratic toes." She nudged him with one of her slender shoulders.

It wasn't exactly the physical contact he'd been hoping for. But it was something.

"I don't brood," he said, brooding with the utmost intensity.

"As I said before, you ought to be pleased with yourself." She'd moved back to her side of the front seat and resumed stroking the fur on Bliss's back.

Donovan found himself growing spellbound by the rhythmic movement of her graceful fingers and forced himself to refocus. On the road…where he should have been looking in the first place. "Why is that again?"

"You really have to ask?" She huffed out a breath, and the rise and fall of her breasts in his periphery threatened to steal Donovan's attention from the road once again. He'd had his hands on those breasts. And he intended to again. Soon. "You invited me to Chadwicke for Bonfire Weekend, and I said no. And yet here I sit."

"Is that what's got you so riled up?" Donovan shook his head. "You were serious about all that?"

"Of course I was serious."

He grinned and made no effort to hide it. She was right—he *was* rather pleased with himself and the turn of events. Convincing Henry to invite Jenna had been a genius move. More desperate than he cared to admit, but genius nonetheless. "Like you said, here you sit."

"Only because Henry invited Jenna, and she insisted I come along. You may have fooled Henry. And Jenna, for that matter. But you're not fooling me. I know you're behind all this." Elizabeth gestured to the space between them.

Donovan caught her hand, midair, in his, even as she jumped in surprise. But she made no move to jerk away from him, a fact that delighted Donovan.

He turned her hand and inhaled the sweet, faint scent of the delicate skin on the inside of her wrist. She smelled fantastic, wonderfully female. Almost floral. Of lavender, perhaps.

Then he pressed his lips to that exact spot and covered it with a languid, openmouthed kiss.

Elizabeth sighed, and her arm went limp in his hand. Donovan smiled to himself and took another leisurely taste of her exquisite skin before weaving his fingers through hers and settling their interlocked hands on the seat between them.

"And if I am indeed behind this weekend's turn of events, is that so horrible? Does wanting to take you away on a holiday make me the living embodiment of evil?" He grazed her knuckles with the pad of his thumb. "Because you know what they say…"

Elizabeth licked her lips before asking, "What do they say? Do tell."

She was flustered now, and they both knew it. And oh, yes, Donovan was even more pleased with himself than before.

"All's fair in love and war," he said and gave her hand a squeeze.

She slipped her hand from his and returned it to her lap, just out of his reach. "And which one is this? Love or war?"

Thrown, Donovan paused for a beat.

Love or war? That was the question, wasn't it?

"War, obviously," he answered, returning his free hand to the steering wheel and tightening his grip.

Because he couldn't be falling in love with Elizabeth Scott. To do so would be the epitome of bad judgment. She'd drive him mad before they ever made it to the altar. That was, if he ever managed to convince her to consider a trip to the altar to begin with, an idea that seemed nigh on impossible. She'd already made it clear she would have preferred to walk the plank than go away with him to Chadwicke for a simple holiday.

He wasn't in love with her. It was out of the question.

Then why did you go to such pains to get her to accompany you this weekend?

"Obviously," Elizabeth echoed, her voice crisp and tinged with irritation.

Or was that disappointment? Donovan couldn't be sure.

And once again, they fell into silence. Miles passed and the English countryside whizzed by without either of them uttering a syllable. This time, Donovan found he was grateful for the reprieve.

Elizabeth ran her fingertips over the car window, surprised at its coolness as she regarded the rolling green hills, dotted with the occasional cluster of cottony-white sheep spread as far as the eye could see. Every so often a country home rose from the emerald peaks, some grander than others. But all of them were quite large and, despite their size, exuded a sense of welcome that Elizabeth hadn't expected. Most were redbrick mansions with ribbons of smoke curling from their chimneys, promising the sanctuary of crackling fires in the hearth.

She'd begun to convince herself that perhaps Chadwicke wouldn't be quite so awful, as Donovan turned onto a curving road that hugged a picturesque village on one side and a vast stone wall on the other.

Finneus rose to his feet in the backseat. His tail thumped a joyful beat against the leather, and he let out a yip.

Donovan eyed him in the rearview mirror. "You might have let me tell her, you little scamp."

"Tell me?" Elizabeth tightened her grip on Bliss in case she had a mind to join Finneus's little party and leap over the seat. "Tell me what?"

The car slowed, and Donovan guided it with expert precision through a tiny break in the stone wall.

"We're here," he said and nodded toward the wide expanse of green before them.

Elizabeth turned in the direction of his nod and found she was in no way prepared for the sight that greeted her. A lake glistened sapphire-blue in the sunlight and flowed beneath a long, arched bridge that looked as though it had sprung up from another time—one when gentlemen wearing waistcoats roamed the countryside on horseback and ladies in flowing gowns strolled beneath the shade of parasols. A horse-drawn carriage would have been more in keeping with the scenery than Donovan's Range Rover. Elizabeth gulped and resisted the urge to say something ridiculous like *You have a bridge...and a lake,* because beyond the glittering water stood the house.

Wide and imposing, it stretched from one side of the horizon clear to the other. Rather than being box-shaped like the other country homes they'd passed along the way, it featured a tall portico in the center flanked by turrets. Instead of red brick, it was crafted of great masses of stone. It looked far more like a mysterious Baroque castle than any house Elizabeth had ever seen.

Surrounding it was an undulating parkland of hills, gardens and trees. All of it so lush and green that it almost didn't seem real, as though Donovan had driven them through that hole in the stone wall and into some hidden utopia.

Overwhelmed almost to the point of dizziness, she tore her gaze from the spectacle before her and turned to Donovan.

Who are you, Donovan Darcy? And why do you want me here with you?

His lips curved into the barest of smiles. "Welcome to Chadwicke," he whispered and pulled the car to a stop in the grand circular drive.

She was sure he didn't mean for the announcement to sound ominous. There was certainly nothing menacing or threatening about his voice or expression. On the contrary, the look in his eyes bordered on tender. And for a moment, Elizabeth was reminded that this man—the one who'd manipulated her into coming along on this trip she'd dreaded with every fiber of her being—was the same man who'd taken her to the Orangery and Harrods Pet Spa, who'd fed her strawberries and French champagne and kissed her silly until she'd forgotten all about *the letter.*

Tenderness aside, just the word *Chadwicke* filled her with anxiety, as if those two syllables, when strung together, were the most terrifying in all of the English language.

She looked away from Donovan and back toward the house.

House. *Ha!* The word *kingdom* would have been more appropriate. Elizabeth would have felt more at home at Versailles. Not that she'd ever been to France, mind you. But she'd seen photos. And its splendor looked as though it was about on par with Donovan's family home.

No wonder the man acted as though the universe was something he could buy and sell. Growing up in a place like this would no doubt give one an air of superiority.

Well, well, this explains a lot, she thought and let out a little laugh.

Donovan smiled, clearly mistaking her giggle for a sign of approval. Pride was written all over his chiseled face. Even more so than usual. Elizabeth found it slightly nauseating. And, to her complete and utter horror, a bit sexy, as well.

He opened her car door for her and peered inside. "Shall we?"

She swallowed and willed her feet to move and carry her out of the Range Rover. They didn't.

Donovan sighed. "Again? I seem to find myself talking you out of cars with alarming frequency."

Elizabeth said nothing.

The frustration in Donovan's expression ebbed and was replaced by that look again. The one that made her feel as though warm honey was running through her veins.

Tender. Most definitely.

"It's just a house," he said in a way that almost made her believe it was true.

"Okay." She hauled herself up out of her seat, setting Bliss on the ground before she stood.

Donovan opened the cargo door, and Finneus hopped down, greeting Bliss with a wag of his tail.

"What about Figgy and the puppies?" Elizabeth moved to help Donovan unload the brood just in time to see a man dressed neatly in a black coat approaching the tailgate.

Another butler.

Great.

If Donovan found it necessary to employ Lawrence to run things at his London home, how many butlers did he have at his beck and call here? Ten? Twenty? She didn't even want to know.

"Thank you, Patrick." Donovan nodded at the butler, then turned his attention back toward Elizabeth. "All taken care of. And Patrick will see to it that our luggage is put away."

"Oh." Elizabeth gave Patrick a little wave. She hadn't the foggiest idea if this was proper protocol, but the man deserved some kind of acknowledgment. "Thank you."

"Miss Scott." Patrick smiled. "Welcome to Chadwicke."

"Th-thank you," she said and wondered how many more people had to welcome her before she would actually feel comfortable here.

Donovan escorted her to the door, threading his hand through hers along the way. An effort to prevent her from escaping, no doubt. Although where she would run off to was a mystery. She had a feeling he owned every blade of grass, every curve of hillside in view. Even the sunshine seemed to have the name Darcy emblazoned on it, as it sparkled more brightly and more golden than she'd ever seen it in London.

"I suppose I'm about to meet your family." Elizabeth pasted on a smile, even as she imagined a group of people resembling the board of directors of the Barclay School sitting around Chadwicke's hearth. "Your parents? Are they here?"

Donovan's jaw tensed. "My family, yes. But not my parents. They passed away when I was twenty-one. Car accident."

They paused on the threshold, Elizabeth wishing she'd asked about his parents earlier. During the ride, perhaps. Why hadn't she, anyway?

That was right. She'd been angry. She'd refused to talk to him.

Regret, with a dash of guilt, pricked her consciousness. "I'm sorry, Donovan."

"It was a long time ago" was all he said in response.

He flung the door open. The sound of voices echoing off the paneled walls as she and Donovan stepped inside surprised her. Other than the Range Rover, there hadn't been a single car in the drive. Elizabeth had assumed she and Donovan had been the first members of the house party to arrive.

This wasn't the case, obviously, as they joined a group of a dozen or so people sitting in a room off to the right of the entryway. The parlor, Elizabeth supposed. The walls were a deep, rich red, and the floor was covered with huge area rugs. A cluster of burgundy leather sofas sat facing a great marble fireplace, where a fire roared, giving the room a certain coziness despite its enormity.

All heads swiveled in their direction as they entered. The Cavaliers trotted, largely unnoticed, to the hearth and plopped down in front of the fire. Elizabeth couldn't help but envy them. Still, she breathed an audible sigh of relief when she spotted Henry and Jenna among the group.

Jenna rose from her seat and gathered her in a hug.

"Can you believe this place?" she whispered in Elizabeth's ear and pulled away, grinning.

By all appearances, she was having the time of her life.

How does she do it? Elizabeth wondered. Jenna always saw the best in everything—every situation, every person she came across. Elizabeth wished she could be that way. Not so...so *jaded*.

Of course, there had been a time when she hadn't been quite so jaded. Before Grant Markham.

"Donovan." An older woman rose from the seat closest to the fire. "You've arrived. At last."

"Aunt Constance." Donovan strode over to her and gave her a polite kiss on the cheek.

Elizabeth found this a bit odd. And somewhat sad, once she considered it for a moment. This was Donovan's aunt, after all. What was left of his family. And her greeting held all the warmth of the Queen of England welcoming one of her loyal subjects.

As messed up and dysfunctional as the Scott family could be, Elizabeth had always felt loved. Loved to the brink of being smothered, perhaps, but loved nonetheless. And she was always scooped up in a tight hug whenever she made a trip home.

"Aunt Constance, I'd like you to meet Elizabeth." Donovan wrapped an arm around her shoulders. "Elizabeth Scott."

Elizabeth suppressed the very real urge to curtsy. "Hello."

The older woman turned sharp eyes on her. "Good afternoon, Elizabeth. Welcome to Chadwicke."

Her tone was anything but welcoming. And she was wearing a suit that resembled something the First Lady might wear. Or a mother of the bride.

No, not wedding thoughts again. Please, no.

Elizabeth squirmed, wishing she'd chosen something other than jeans and a sweater for herself. Then again, Donovan was wearing the same thing. Perhaps Aunt Constance was the one who needed to reevaluate.

"Elizabeth and Jenna are sisters," Donovan explained to his aunt as Elizabeth spotted Zara eagerly making her way toward them from across the room.

"Donovan!" Zara launched herself at him.

He let Elizabeth go as he embraced his sister.

Now, this is more like it. Real affection. The thought had barely registered in her consciousness when Zara—finished with Donovan, apparently—threw her arms around her.

"Oh." Thrown off balance for a moment, Elizabeth hugged the girl back.

"I'm so glad you're here," Zara whispered in her ear. "It means a lot to my brother. He's never brought a woman here, you know."

No. She hadn't known. Not at all.

In fact, the revelation threw her a bit. She glanced at Donovan, but his expression revealed nothing. In fact, the earlier tenderness she'd found there had vanished. He was back to his usual, detached self.

Elizabeth was caught up in a whirlwind of introductions. Once she was flanked on either side by Jenna and Henry, she finally began to relax. Until Helena pushed her way between them with a roll of her eyes and a distinct sway to her hips.

At least Donovan had had the forethought to mention Helena would be in attendance. And to Elizabeth's relief, he'd even indicated Helena would be bringing a date. Although Elizabeth didn't see a date by her side.

She wore stilettos—again—and a tight pencil skirt that Elizabeth would have had difficulty walking in even if she were on the most level of surfaces, much less tromping through the country.

"It's wonderful to see you again, Elizabeth." She extended her hand for a limp shake. "I'm Helena, Henry's sister. We met at the dog show last weekend. Perhaps you remember?"

Oh, she remembered all right. But they'd first met at the Bridal Market. And the other show at the hotel ballroom. How interesting that Helena had conveniently forgotten.

"Of course. It's nice to see you again."

"Helena." A frown tugged at the corners of Donovan's mouth. "I thought you were bringing a guest."

"Yes." Her cool gray eyes, framed once again by those ridiculous, overdone lashes, never left Elizabeth's. It was unsettling. "He's from out of town. I'm afraid he won't be here until the ball."

"Brilliant. I look forward to meeting him." Donovan planted his hand in the small of Elizabeth's back. "I think I'll show Elizabeth to her room now. I'm sure she wants to get settled."

Settled. That sounded like a fabulous idea.

Though as Donovan ushered her out of the room and she felt at least one pair of disapproving eyes boring into her back, she wondered if such a thing were even possible.

18

Donovan breathed a sigh of relief as he steered Elizabeth toward the hall leading to the wing that housed his living quarters. The introductions had gone as well as could have been expected. Helena had behaved herself. And Aunt Constance had been…well…Aunt Constance. In the event of trouble, at least Jenna was there. Surely her sister's presence would prevent her from fleeing. And Henry and Zara had welcomed Elizabeth with open arms. So all in all, things were looking good.

Except for the fact that Donovan still wasn't altogether sure why it had become so important to him to have her around. He just knew that it had. And as Elizabeth herself had pointed out, he was a man accustomed to getting what he wanted.

And here she was. Right where she belonged, as far as Donovan was concerned.

He glanced at her walking beside him, close enough that he could reach out and touch her if he so desired.

He desired.

Very much.

"Donovan, why haven't you told me about your parents before?" Elizabeth asked, concern shimmering in those fine eyes of hers.

Her concern was sweet, he supposed. It was also somewhat of a libido killer.

"It's not something I talk about often." Donovan's teeth clenched involuntarily as they rounded the corner to his wing of the main house.

"Oh?" she prompted, clearly expecting him to go on.

He kept his gaze fixed on the long hallway stretching before them and said nothing.

A sound escaped her, which Donovan recognized as the universal sigh of a frustrated female.

Fine. Let her be frustrated. He might not have wrapped his mind around why exactly he craved her presence, but he was certain delving into his painful past did not factor into the equation.

"I've no desire to dwell on things that happened over a decade ago." He shrugged, a vague effort at looking nonchalant.

Elizabeth bristled. Visibly. She actually had the nerve to give him a dirty look, as if he'd chosen to lose both his parents and virtually become a father to Zara when he should have been living it up with all the other blokes at university.

Another woman might have tried a more sympathetic approach.

Then again, when had Elizabeth ever acted like any other woman?

Behind her veil of irritation at his reluctance to bear his wounded soul, she still looked uncomfortable as hell. Donovan had no idea what to make of that. Half the female population of England—the single half, as well as a few from the married half, no doubt—would have given their right arm for an invitation to a weekend with him at Chadwicke. Donovan knew this. His aunt Constance did as well, which was why she'd been so concerned when she'd discovered he was bringing Elizabeth along.

Her tirade still rang in his ears.

Who is she, Donovan? An American, for God's sake? What are you thinking? She's trying to trap you into marriage. She's only after your money.

His aunt couldn't have been more mistaken. He'd gone and gotten himself wound up over the one woman who'd have preferred him as a schoolteacher. Or a lorry driver. Anything other than what he was—rich. Elizabeth wasn't at all interested in his money. She'd made that more than clear. And he was certain she wasn't harboring a secret plan to marry him.

He hadn't even taken her to bed yet. Although he aimed to change that.

"I suppose I'm sharing a room with Jenna?" she asked.

Donovan's footsteps slowed. After covering nearly a mile of Chadwicke's wide hallways, they'd at last reached his block of rooms. "Of course not. You've got your own."

"That's really not necessary. Jenna and I can share."

Donovan rolled his eyes. "Elizabeth, do you have any idea how many rooms are in this house?"

"No." She glanced up and down the hallway. "I'm quite sure I don't want to know, either."

From where Donovan stood, he could count at least twenty doors. All en suite rooms, and over half of them vacant on a holiday weekend. And this was only one hallway out of a labyrinth of similar hallways. Donovan had been well into puberty before he could find his way around the house without getting lost.

"Fifty bedrooms," he said, unable to help himself. "Or is it sixty?"

"Now you're just trying to impress me." She looked anything but impressed.

"Hardly." Donovan paused in front of one of the doors. "But say I were...would it be in any way effective?"

"No." She shook her head. "Absolutely not."

He raised his brows.

"Seriously. No." She shook her head, and a wave of fresh citrus scent came wafting from her hair.

Donovan was taken back to that afternoon at the Orangery, a day he revisited often. He wondered if Elizabeth ever thought of it, too.

He looked into her eyes, wide and wary. Despite what she'd said about Chadwicke, she was impressed. Not in a good way, he realized, but rather the intimidating kind of way.

Donovan didn't like seeing that look on her face. Not at all. It didn't belong there, on the face of a woman he'd come to think of as above all the trappings of wealth. And he wondered if it was possible to kiss that look right off of her.

"So, is this me?" She gestured to the door behind her.

"Yes." But he made no move to show her to her quarters. The tour could wait. Donovan was already beginning to regret giving her a room to herself. Sharing with Jenna, however, wasn't what he had in mind.

He wanted her in his room, in his bed.

He took a step closer and planted his hands on the wall behind her, on either side of her shoulders.

He dipped his head, inhaled the sweet scent of her hair and whispered, "It's just a house, Elizabeth."

"Liar," she said. But there was no edge to her voice. And even as she said it, her gaze dropped to his mouth.

Donovan watched her eyes darken with desire, and a slow, satisfied smile came to his lips. Elizabeth Scott was no longer thinking about his house. That much was obvious. And he'd yet to come close to kissing her.

She grimaced, but he could see the thunder of her pulse throbbing at the base of her neck. "This might be the most grossly ostentatious place I've ever seen."

"Ostentatious, is it?" He meant to send a humorous glance over his shoulder at the gilt wall sconce he knew loomed somewhere behind him, but he couldn't seem to take his eyes off the tantalizing dip between her collarbones. "I'm glad you're here, even though you seem to think I forced you into coming."

"You *did* force me into coming." She licked her lips. Every cell in Donovan's body went on high alert, fixated on nothing but the sight of that cherry-red tongue.

"And Chadwicke has never looked quite as exquisite as it does now, with you between its walls," he murmured, half expecting her to laugh at him, even though he was dead serious.

She didn't laugh. Instead, she lifted her chin ever so slightly and took a teasing bite of his lower lip.

And all coherent thought fled from Donovan's head. If he'd thought he was the one in control here, he'd been sadly mistaken. He gave her one long, last look—a final effort to prevent himself from becoming completely undone—before he took her mouth with his.

She rose to meet him, skimming her delicate fingertips over his chest before they wound themselves around his neck. Donovan was vaguely aware of one of them groaning. Him? Her? He couldn't even tell. The kiss was blinding. All encompassing, all consuming.

As he deepened the kiss and leaned his body against the

length of hers, a hot pool of longing swelled deep inside him—so intense it would have bordered on painful, if not for the awareness of where exactly they were. This wasn't the champagne bar at Harrods, and it wasn't a flimsy hospitality tent at a dog show.

This was his home. And right on the other side of the door, no more than a few meters away, was a bed.

He looked up, slightly dazed. Elizabeth practically purred and slipped her hands beneath his shirt, exploring in a way that clouded his vision.

He glanced at the door to his bedroom.

Too far, he thought, not wanting to waste another second. The doorknob to Elizabeth's room was within arm's reach, so he turned it and they both tumbled inside.

It was dark. Donovan couldn't see Elizabeth's face, but he could feel the soft silk of her skin and a warmth that seemed to radiate from her, beckoning him with promises of the kind of joy he didn't even know he'd been longing for.

She laughed—a clear, happy laugh that soothed Donovan without taking the edge off his desire. In the miniscule part of his brain that was still capable of thought, he was somewhat worried about his behavior. He'd had plans to woo Elizabeth, to romance her into bed. He wasn't some randy teenager.

Yet here he was, within minutes of finding himself alone with her, acting as though she was an oasis of sparkling water and he was a man dying of thirst. The bed wasn't even within view, for God's sake.

Where was his usual finesse, that signature Darcy control?

Elizabeth's hands slipped under his shirt again, and he decided control was vastly overrated.

"Where are we, exactly?" she asked in a breathy whisper.

"Your bedroom." He buried a fist in her hair even as he

cursed himself for not inviting her to stay in his room. "It adjoins mine. We can keep the door closed if that poses a problem."

She answered with a nibble to his ear.

"Good answer," he said.

He wanted to see her, to drink in the sight of her eyes darkened with longing and her lips flushed with color from his kisses. He reached behind Elizabeth's head for the light switch.

The room came to life, bathed in light. Elizabeth was such a beautiful sight, captivatingly disheveled, but somewhere in the periphery Donovan saw something.

Something that gave him pause.

He squinted, not at all certain what he was seeing was real. "Is that...?"

"What?" Elizabeth, still slightly out of breath, turned in the direction of his gaze.

Donovan tore his attention from her and fixed it, once again, on her things. Patrick had unpacked for her, as any proper butler would do. Her suitcase was empty, tucked away beneath a large armchair in the corner. The wardrobe cabinet stood with the doors propped open, revealing her clothes hanging neatly inside. And on the open cabinet door hung a garment bag. It was long—designed to protect a gown, no doubt—and white, with swirling gold lettering.

Marchesa Bridal Collection.

Donovan was gobsmacked.

Because the item hanging in her bedroom looked rather like a wedding dress.

Elizabeth glanced at the ridiculously oversize wardrobe cabinet—seriously, where did that thing lead? Narnia?—and her garment bag hanging there in all of its bridal-white innocence.

For a moment, she couldn't figure out why Donovan was staring at it like he was. As though it were poised to leap off the cabinet door and bite him on his very fine ass.

Surely he didn't think...

"What exactly do we have here?" he asked, and his Adam's apple appeared to struggle as it bobbed up and down in his throat.

"It's my gown for the ball." Elizabeth crossed her arms, irritated at how much she wished he would stop asking about her fashion choices and kiss her again.

He didn't honestly suspect she'd dragged a wedding gown to Chadwicke, did he?

He stalked to the wardrobe as if hunting down whatever it was that wealthy Englishmen donning elbow patches and shotguns were always hunting out on the moors, and unzipped the Marchesa bag.

A shimmery, gold floor-length gown peeked through the opening. The one she'd found that day at the Bridal Market in London with Jenna.

One corner of Donovan's mouth curved into an appreciative grin. "Lovely."

Elizabeth suddenly had no interest in his opinion on the dress, however beautiful it was. "Oh, my God, are you serious right now?"

"Of course. It's a very nice dress." He took a few steps toward her, smoldering once again. Apparently, she was the one being stalked now. "It will be my pleasure to take it off you the first chance I get."

He leaned in for a kiss and Elizabeth sidestepped away

from him before she bit him again. Hard enough to draw blood this time.

She crossed her arms while he stumbled. "I can't believe you."

Donovan righted himself. He looked equal parts confused and annoyed. "I beg your pardon."

"You thought that was a wedding dress, didn't you?"

He waved an elegant hand toward the garment bag. "At first glance it looked like one. Surely you agree."

"I suppose that sort of thing happens to you often…women toting around bridal gowns and trying to strong-arm you into marriage?" Elizabeth wasn't altogether sure she wanted an answer to that question. But it was too late. She'd already asked it.

Donovan said nothing. He didn't have to. His wry grin spoke volumes.

"That's more Helena Robson's style, don't you think?" Elizabeth said, remembering her at Bridal Market, acting as though the date had already been set.

It had rubbed Elizabeth entirely the wrong way. And still did, possibly now more than ever. The idea of Donovan thinking she would behave like that, even for a moment, was beyond humiliating.

Donovan laughed, and something inside Elizabeth snapped.

"You can rest easy. Your bachelorhood is safe." To think she'd almost believed she was falling in love with him. *All's fair in* love *and war.* The word had vibrated between them in the Ranger Rover.

The laughter died in Donovan's throat. "Is it, now?"

"Yes." She was trembling, a physical manifestation of her anger. Or was it disappointment? Elizabeth wasn't altogether sure. She balled her hands into fists so Donovan wouldn't see.

"In fact, you are the last man in the world I could ever be prevailed upon to marry."

Something flashed in his eyes. Something indecipherable. "That's convenient, then." His lips curved into a world-class smirk. "Since I don't recall proposing."

His gaze traveled up and down the length of her body, but he made no move to close the gap between them. And despite the ridiculousness of the situation, and the fact that he was without a doubt the most arrogant man she'd ever laid eyes on, Elizabeth found herself growing aroused.

It was shameful, really.

She wanted his hands on her again. It frightened her how much she wanted it.

She told herself all she had to do was go to him, wrap her arms around his neck, and everything would be as it had been only five minutes before. But her feet stubbornly refused to move.

"I should go." Donovan took a step backward. "I need to attend to the details of tomorrow's polo match."

"Oh." Elizabeth forced herself to smile. It required a valiant effort as a rising tide of frustration swelled inside her. "Of course."

"Dinner is at half seven." He sounded uncharacteristically wooden.

"Great, then. I'll be ready." As if she were really ready for any of this.

Donovan angled his head and watched her with a newfound intensity.

He walked toward her, lifted her hand and grazed her knuckles with a kiss. "I'll see you at dinner, then."

The soft brush of his lips against her hand was enough to send a shiver up her spine. Donovan, of course, was reverting to his cool, detached, gentlemanly demeanor. One he'd apparently perfected.

Get a grip on yourself.

He straightened, and Elizabeth hid her trembling hands behind her back. They stood silently, their gazes locked with one another, for a prolonged moment. Donovan seemed torn, as if he couldn't decide whether to stay or go. The air between them crackled with tension, most of it sexual in nature—at least on Elizabeth's end.

She took a tiny step toward him.

With a bittersweet smile, he retreated. Then he was gone—out the door with Finneus trailing on his heels.

19

Elizabeth watched Jenna flop open her suitcase on the immense four-poster bed in her room and frowned. "Your bags aren't unpacked yet?"

"No, of course not. When would I have unpacked?" Jenna pulled out the plastic bag containing her toiletries and marched toward the adjoining bathroom.

The bedroom was huge, although not quite as vast as the one that had been assigned to Elizabeth. That being said, Elizabeth's entire apartment back home in Manhattan would have fit conveniently inside either of the bedrooms.

She wondered if there were really fifty of them or if Donovan had been teasing her. She also wondered why Jenna's bags weren't unpacked when Patrick had meticulously emptied hers and hung all the contents with care. Perhaps that kind of royal treatment was reserved exclusively for Mr. Darcy and his date. If so, what on earth would it be like to be married to the man?

Not that she harbored any desire to be married to him. In

fact, she pitied the woman who would one day bear the name Mrs. Donovan Darcy. Whoever she might be…

"Jenna?" Elizabeth absently toyed with a colossal gold tassel on one of the bed's many throw pillows. "Did you know that Donovan's parents are both dead?"

"Yes, Henry mentioned it," she called from the bathroom. "That's why he's Zara's guardian."

"Zara's guardian? Really?" Elizabeth slipped off her shoes and crawled up and onto the bed. It was so tall she almost needed a step stool.

"Yes." Jenna sauntered back into the room. "Since he was only twenty-one."

"Wow." Elizabeth thought back to what she'd been doing at twenty-one. She'd been in college, getting her teaching degree. There'd been a fair share of parties and reckless behavior, but nothing the average twenty-one-year-old hadn't done a time or two. Twenty-one-year-olds who weren't instant parents, that is. "Zara couldn't have been more than three or four years old back then."

"I know. Can you imagine?" Jenna pulled a pair of jeans from her suitcase and shook out the creases.

No, Elizabeth couldn't.

Granted, Donovan had the financial resources to hire people to help care for Zara. But from the looks of things, he'd genuinely been the person who'd acted as her parent. The affection between them appeared real in every way.

What kind of man takes on the role of parent to a toddler when he's barely an adult himself?

The answer was obvious. *An honorable one.*

It was something to think about, she supposed—this new side of Donovan she'd least expected.

"Lizzy!"

"What?" Elizabeth's head snapped up.

"I've been calling you for a solid minute. Are you deaf?" Jenna's head popped through the doorway to the bathroom. Elizabeth hadn't even been aware she'd left the room again. "Get in here. There's something you've got to see."

She slid off the bed and padded to the bathroom, where she found Jenna standing before a pearl-colored marble vanity.

"You mentioned Donovan." Without averting her gaze in the slightest, Jenna nodded toward the window above the sink. "Speak of the devil."

Elizabeth started to make a crack about him being devil-ish indeed, but her voice caught in her throat when she took in the view.

Jenna's bathroom overlooked a rectangular lap pool, sur-rounded by slate-colored fieldstone. Sunlight glinted off the cool blue water as a manly figure cut through it with pre-cise, stealthy strokes of his arms. He swam with a purpose, as though some invisible force were chasing him, threaten-ing to pull him under.

Jenna cleared her throat and then asked, "That's him, isn't it? It looks as though he's swimming off some serious ten-sion before dinner."

Elizabeth forced out a slow, careful breath. She nodded just as Donovan stopped and pulled himself up and out of the pool in one rapid movement.

Water dripped down his bare chest, which appeared every bit as well built as Elizabeth presumed it would be. More so, in fact. His biceps flexed as he ran one of his hands through his wet hair, sending water droplets in all directions.

Elizabeth's throat tightened, and her gaze traveled down the taut skin of his chiseled abdomen. He was a hard, toned bundle of raw masculinity. And all that water—Elizabeth was surprised she couldn't hear it sizzling from where she stood. She didn't dare look beyond the waistband of his black bathing suit, slung perilously low across his hips.

Well, maybe just a bit.

Oh, dear God.

Jenna sighed. "That is one gorgeous wet man."

From head to toe, he was gloriously perfect.

Every coherent thought Elizabeth had ever possessed seemed to fail her. Her newfound knowledge of Donovan's softer side, combined with the wet, sensual sight before her, was far too much to absorb all at once. After standing for several long moments without saying a word, she somehow managed to collect herself.

"I suppose there's some truth to that," she muttered.

Jenna's only reply was an all-too-knowing smile.

Donovan feigned interest in whatever his aunt Constance was blathering on about and nodded. He'd done a lot of nodding over the course of the past hour. He'd smiled and nodded his way through the bisque, salad and fish course. At present, a slab of lamb was resting on his plate—the main course—and he was still nodding. At what, he had no idea.

Concentrating was a luxury beyond his capability. How could he be expected to absorb a word his aunt was saying when Elizabeth was seated eight chairs away? Elizabeth Scott, who'd made it clear she had no interest whatsoever in marrying him.

It wasn't some grand revelation, of course. He'd known how she felt about him all along. He should have been relieved. Donovan had no interest in marriage.

But suddenly, the prospect of marrying Elizabeth Scott was

occupying a great deal of his thoughts. And he was startled to find the idea had its appeal.

"Donovan?" Aunt Constance frowned. If he didn't start paying closer attention, she was likely to poke him with her steak knife. "Honestly, if I didn't know better, I'd think you haven't heard a word I've uttered all evening."

"I apologize." Donovan tore his gaze from Elizabeth, who was tossing her head back and laughing at something Henry had said, and refocused on his aunt. "I'm a bit distracted this evening."

Distracted. As if one word could encapsulate his emotions.

Distracted didn't begin to describe what he felt. *Intrigued, charmed, captivated*—they were all words that worked. Along with some other choice words, like *unnerved* and *furious.*

He clenched his fists under the tablecloth as he remembered Elizabeth glaring at him.

Your bachelorhood is safe.

You are the last man in the world I could ever be prevailed upon to marry.

What the devil did that mean?

"Donovan, really. What has you so tied in knots tonight?" Aunt Constance narrowed her eyes, as if she were trying to peer inside his head.

Thank God she couldn't. The very idea of a single young lady laughing at the thought of marrying him would have been enough to send his aunt to an early grave. Every eligible woman in the United Kingdom should be delighted at the prospect of calling herself Mrs. Donovan Darcy.

Save one, apparently.

Donovan frowned at his aunt. "I'd prefer Miss Scott be seated next to me in the future." His frown deepened as he realized how pathetic he sounded. What was happening to him? He was coming completely uncorked.

Aunt Constance's steely gaze flitted toward Elizabeth. "It's your house, Donovan. You can sit beside whomever you like. You've just never been interested in such matters before, so I've always taken care of the mundane things like seating arrangements for you."

"I appreciate your help. But this is different." *She's* different.

"Duly noted. I'll speak with the staff and make the proper arrangements."

"Thank you." Donovan ground his teeth as he watched Henry whisper something in Elizabeth's ear.

Then he groaned to himself as he realized he was jealous. Jealous of his closest friend, even though Henry was clearly besotted with Jenna Scott. Donovan was green-eyed simply because Henry was sitting beside the woman he loved.

Donovan almost choked on his lamb and reached for a water goblet.

The woman he *loved*?

Was he in *love* with Elizabeth?

Surely not.

He remembered the crushing weight of her words when she'd told him his bachelorhood was safe. It was that precise moment when reality had hit him like a ton of bricks.

Good God. It was true. He was in love with her.

"I suppose I should get better acquainted with Miss Scott since you seem to be so fond of her." Aunt Constance grimaced, as if the prospect left a bad taste in her mouth. Perhaps it was merely a reaction to the lamb. Donovan thought it was a bit chewy.

"Brilliant." Donovan pushed the lamb around on his plate.

If he was in love with Elizabeth, he supposed his aunt had a point. Although he hoped she wouldn't frighten Elizabeth away.

"I'll make an effort to chat with her at the polo match tomorrow morning." Aunt Constance gave him a wan smile.

Donovan nodded. Again.

He sat through the remainder of the meal in silence. Brooding, as Elizabeth and Zara would have called it. As he could have predicted, his sister watched him from across the table during the dessert course, eyeing him with obvious curiosity.

He was fine. He wasn't brooding. He was simply thinking.

The way he saw it, he had two choices.

The first was by far the more sensible option—he could wait for his feelings to pass. Perhaps he was merely infatuated. Or maybe he was all keyed up because Elizabeth was such a challenge. Would he still fancy himself in love if she didn't find him so abominable?

Yes. His temples throbbed. *Yes, I actually would.*

Which brought him to the second option. When he'd first asked Elizabeth to accompany him to Chadwicke, her answer had been an unequivocal *no.* Yet here she was. Sitting at his dining table, with the light from the gilded candelabras casting sensual shadows across the porcelain column of her neck. God, how he longed to sweep her up and plant a kiss right there where her neck curved into her shoulder. He knew just how sweet that spot tasted.

He cleared his throat and directed his thoughts back to the problem at hand. If he'd managed to get Elizabeth to agree to a weekend at Chadwicke, how much more difficult would it be to persuade her to marry him?

The very idea gave him a headache. He ought to consider an easier prospect. Like climbing Mount Everest. Blindfolded.

There was only one problem—he didn't want to climb Everest. He wanted Elizabeth.

The shuffle of diners pushing away from the table told him dinner was over. At last.

Donovan rose from his seat and headed toward her. She stood beside the table with her chestnut hair tumbling over her shoulders and Henry and Jenna happily glued to her side.

Henry offered Donovan a wide smile as he approached. "Donovan, why have you been hiding Elizabeth? She's delightful."

Donovan slipped his hand around Elizabeth's waist. A very slight, but very real, pang of worry hit him when he realized that one simple gesture caused the pieces of his world to slip back into place. He was in deep. Deeper than he'd ever been before.

It was not a position he reveled in.

So he glanced at Elizabeth and pretended to be taken aback. "Elizabeth? Delightful? Really?"

"I can be delightful when I try," she responded with a saccharine smile.

And then she ground the heel of her stiletto onto the toe of his shoe.

Donovan refused to wince. Instead, he tightened his grip on her waist. "As far as hiding her, I've done no such thing. She's elusive."

"Elusive?" Henry raised his brows.

"Very much so. It's a right miracle she's standing here beside me."

"He exaggerates." Elizabeth rolled her eyes.

Donovan wished it was an exaggeration. "Do I? Because I seem to recall a time not long ago when you said you despised the very sight of me. In fact, I believe it was this morning on the ride here."

"Lizzy, really." Jenna shook her head.

By all appearances, Henry was too shocked to laugh. His mouth dropped open for a few beats before he finally said, "Well, mate. That must have been a blow to the ego. A right switch from all the women throwing themselves at your feet."

"Throwing themselves at your feet?" Elizabeth turned to face him, her expression bemused.

Donovan let his fingertips crawl a little lower, until they rested on the curve of her hip. "Now Henry is the one exaggerating."

"Not really, mate."

"This certainly sounds interesting," Jenna said.

"Henry," Donovan said, his gaze never leaving Elizabeth. "I don't think the lady is interested in hearing stories about women allegedly throwing themselves at me."

"On the contrary. Do tell, Henry." She laughed and leaned into him. Donovan was relieved to see her enjoying herself, even if it was at his expense.

"I'm afraid I can't." Henry shook his head with great solemnity.

"No?" Elizabeth stuck her plump bottom lip out in a mock pout. It took every ounce of self-control Donovan possessed not to bite it right then and there.

He cleared this throat in an effort to get his wits about him. His bedroom was quite a distance away. "It's good to see you have a healthy respect for our friendship, Henry."

"It has nothing to do with our friendship and everything to do with the fact that I'll be on the polo field with you in the morning, and I don't fancy the idea of getting struck in the head with your mallet." Henry winked at Elizabeth, then glanced at his watch. "Donovan, isn't it time for a brandy? Don't tell me you're going to slip away with the lovely Elizabeth and abandon our after-dinner tradition."

Actually, that's exactly what I had in mind.

"You two go ahead. Jenna and I can keep ourselves entertained." Elizabeth slipped from his grasp, prompting Donovan to give serious thought to the whole mallet scenario.

"Join us," he urged.

"No, really. I wouldn't want to spoil your tradition. I don't want to be one of those clingy women who comes between mates."

Elizabeth…clingy? The idea was laughable. So preposterous, in fact, that it in no way made Donovan feel like laughing.

"Besides, we have things to discuss, don't we, Jenna?" Elizabeth's eyes blazed with secrets.

"Oh, yes." Jenna nodded, and her gaze slid to the painted portrait of Donovan hanging over the fireplace at the far end of the dining room.

Me. They're going to talk about me.

Donovan wasn't sure whether this was good or bad. "I see. You two have secret affairs to discuss. Go easy on me."

He winked at Elizabeth, fully expecting a diatribe in return about how self-centered he must be to assume they would be talking about him.

"We can all plague and punish one another." Was it Donovan's imagination, or was that comment infused with less acrimony than he expected? "You and Henry enjoy your brandy."

Donovan slipped his fingers through hers, but she'd already started backing away.

"Good night, Donovan," she said, escaping before he could kiss her.

He watched her as she walked away. For as long as Chadwicke had stood, he'd never seen anyone or anything so utterly inviting between the walls of his dining room.

"Good night," he murmured, a heartbeat too late.

20

"You realize we're standing in a Ralph Lauren ad right now, right?" Elizabeth took in the blanket of green grass before her, almost not believing what she was seeing. A polo field. Donovan's house had a polo field.

Beside her, Jenna sipped a mimosa and smiled as though this were any ordinary Saturday morning. She didn't look a bit intimidated.

How does she do it? Elizabeth mused.

"Try to enjoy yourself, Lizzy. Haven't you ever seen a polo match before? All that athleticism, all those powerful muscles... and I'm not even talking about the horses. I wonder if Donovan and Henry will wear those sexy white pants like Prince Harry does when he plays."

Elizabeth's imagination snagged on the idea of the white pants for a beat, before coming back to her senses. "When have you ever seen a polo match?"

"I haven't exactly." Jenna shrugged. "But I've seen photos. You know...of the royal family, and then there are the perfume ads...Polo, Polo Sport...."

Elizabeth snorted. "I rest my case."

"Are you ladies enjoying yourselves yet?" Henry poked his head between the two of them.

Jenna swiveled to face him. A coquettish grin came to her lips. "Of course we are."

"Is that true?" asked Donovan as he stepped up behind Henry, his piercing gaze glued to Elizabeth.

No, of course she wasn't having fun. This was torture.

She opened her mouth, prepared to tell him just that, but for some odd reason the words wouldn't come. "Um…"

Donovan cocked his head and eyed her with intense curiosity.

Jenna answered for her. "Of course it's true. Everything's lovely, Donovan. Simply lovely."

Donovan's eyes narrowed, but before he could cast any doubt on Jenna's reassurances, his aunt Constance waved and called out to them.

"Donovan, I'm glad you're still here," she said as she made her way toward their little circle.

"Only for a moment, Aunt Constance. Henry and I need to go check on the horses and make sure everything is in order for the match." Donovan's spine stiffened.

Elizabeth thought once again what a shame it was that Donovan's aunt was so formal with him. No wonder he had such a distant, proper air about him all the time.

Maybe he wasn't quite as arrogant as she'd first thought.

Elizabeth blinked. Where had that thought come from? Of course Donovan was arrogant. He was the most prideful man she'd ever met.

"Have you made arrangements for the trophy presentation? Helena has volunteered to do the honors." Aunt Constance waved at Helena Robson, walking toward them with a mimosa in each hand.

Helena seemed to have no trouble maneuvering across the grass in her stilettoes, Elizabeth noted with a stab of envy. She looked as though she were floating.

Donovan slid his gaze toward Elizabeth. There was a challenge in his eyes, one that tickled Elizabeth's insides. "That won't be necessary. I'd like Elizabeth to present the trophy to the winning team."

Super.

She felt totally out of place as it was. The last thing she needed was to draw attention to herself by handing out trophies like she was Kate Middleton or, or...Helena Robson, for heaven's sake. She made a move to protest, but Donovan's aunt cut her off.

"I see." Aunt Constance smiled. It looked a little tense around the edges, but at least it was a smile. "Brilliant. Elizabeth, I do hope you'll keep me company during the match. My nephew speaks so highly of you. I'd be delighted to get acquainted."

Elizabeth smiled back. Woodenly. She'd hoped to spend the morning getting to know Zara, but she couldn't exactly ignore Donovan's aunt, could she? "I'd love to. That would be nice."

"Very well, then." Donovan grinned, his perfect teeth nearly as white as his polo pants. Which, of course, looked even hotter on him than Jenna had predicted. "I'll see you after the match."

He cupped a hand around Elizabeth's elbow and pulled her to the side. He bent low and whispered, his voice sending a hum through her, "And I'll see you when you hand me that silver trophy."

"You're awfully confident." She looked up at him and gave him her best smirk, although she was beginning to feel less and less like smirking around him lately. Odd phenomenon, that.

"Always," he said. "If you care to make it interesting, we could always make a wager. If my team wins, then this afternoon I have you all to myself. Just the two of us."

A rumble of nervousness skittered through Elizabeth. Or was that arousal? "Just the two of us?"

"Just the two of us. You'd be all mine. Or should I say I'd be all yours?" The corner of his lips lifted in a crooked, suggestive grin. "What do you say?"

Visions of him, all wet and intense climbing out of the lap pool, danced in her head. "I say I know better than to bet against you, Donovan Darcy."

"We'll see about that." He leaned forward and gave her a chaste kiss on the cheek.

He winked and strode off toward the stables, leaving her in the company of his aunt, Helena and, thankfully, Jenna. Elizabeth struggled mightily not to stare at his backside clad in those formfitting white pants as he retreated.

She took a steadying breath and turned her attention back to the three women.

"Elizabeth." Helena, oozing charm, drew her name out to at least ten syllables. "Would you care for a mimosa?"

"Thank you." She took a crystal goblet from Helena's finely manicured hand.

"Isn't this a positively gorgeous morning for polo?" Helena batted her ridiculous eyelashes and lifted her mimosa toward her lips. Her arm suddenly stopped, and she gasped. "Oh, how insensitive of me. You've probably never attended a polo match before, have you, Elizabeth and Jenna? I mean, polo isn't exactly commonplace in *New Jersey,* is it?"

Was it Elizabeth's imagination, or did her emphasis on *New Jersey* seem laced with disdain? Like someone all too familiar with those crazy kids on *Jersey Shore?*

"New Jersey?" Donovan's aunt frowned. "I thought Donovan said you were from New York City?"

"I am. I live in Manhattan." For simplicity's sake, she decided to use the present tense. "Although I'm originally from New Jersey. My family still lives there."

"Yes, my mother, sisters and I run a family business there." A glimmer of pride flickered in Jenna's eyes.

"I see." Aunt Constance nodded.

Beside her, Helena smiled sweetly. A little too sweetly. Elizabeth tried to remember when exactly she'd told her she was from New Jersey. For the life of her, she couldn't remember.

"And what do you do, Elizabeth, in New York? Do you work?" Aunt Constance's nose wrinkled a bit, as if she'd gotten a whiff of fruit that had recently gone too soft.

It took a superhuman effort for Elizabeth not to snort with laughter. Did she work? As if she could ever afford to live in Manhattan without gainful employment. She glanced at Helena, with her flawless manicure and *Real Housewives* eyelashes, and wondered if she'd ever worked a day in her life. Somehow, Elizabeth knew she hadn't.

"I teach at a private school there."

Taught. You're not a teacher anymore, remember?

Would she ever grow accustomed to this new state of affairs?

"Elizabeth is a teacher at the Barclay School," Helena said

with a knowing gleam in her eye. "You know the Barclay School, Constance."

"Of course." Aunt Constance nodded absently. "We have friends across the pond who are benefactors there. Excellent school. Excellent indeed."

Elizabeth squeezed her mimosa with such force she was a bit stunned when it didn't shatter in her hand. How did Helena know about the Barclay School? Elizabeth was certain she'd never told her the name of the school where she'd taught. She'd never even mentioned it to Donovan, much less a near stranger.

She aimed a questioning look at Jenna, in case she'd somehow mentioned it to Henry, but Jenna didn't seem to notice. She was staring in Henry's direction. Yet again.

"Did you attend the Barclay School when you were girls?" Aunt Constance asked, suddenly visibly more interested in the conversation.

Jenna shook her head.

Elizabeth said, "No, ma'am. I attended school in New Jersey." God, could they talk about something else? *Anything* else? She would rather have discussed Snooki or The Situation than the Barclay School.

Aunt Constance's face fell. "Private school?"

"No, public." Elizabeth was beginning to feel as though she were on a job interview. And by all appearances, Helena Robson had somehow already procured a copy of her résumé.

She couldn't have been happier when the rumble of horses told her the polo match was at last under way. Elizabeth and Jenna excused themselves and made their way to the edge of the tent, as close as they could get to the polo field. The ground shook beneath Elizabeth's feet as Donovan and seven other players thundered past her. It was all so elegant—the riders in their polished leather boots and the horses with their glistening coats and colorful leg wraps.

What was it Alan had said when Sue had mentioned Elizabeth would be attending a polo match at Chadwicke?

Ah, the game of kings.

The moniker was certainly fitting. And Donovan had never looked more regal than he did at that precise moment. He looked so natural in the saddle, as if he'd been born on horseback.

He shot Elizabeth a dazzling smile as his horse galloped past her. In spite of everything—his maddening sense of entitlement, her disdain and mistrust of all he stood for—when he looked at her like that she couldn't help but feel regal, too. Almost like a princess.

Donovan stood along with his three teammates beside the referee in the center of the field as the announcement was made. His damp hair, fresh from his postgame shower, rippled in the breeze.

"And the winner of the Twelfth Annual Chadwicke Cup Charity Polo Match is our host Donovan Darcy's team, Royal Salute."

An enthusiastic round of applause and a few whoops and hollers followed, most notably from Henry, who slapped Donovan on the back with enough force to fell an elephant. Donovan swallowed a cough and stepped forward to shake the referee's hand.

"Thank you, sir," he said.

The referee replied. Of what exactly he said, Donovan couldn't be certain. He was having trouble focusing on anything but Elizabeth. She stood behind the referee with that lovely chestnut hair whipping in the wind, holding the great silver trophy that was always awarded to the winning team. She looked as though she were having trouble hanging on to the bulky thing. It was rather heavy, as Donovan recalled.

"And here to make the trophy presentation is Miss Elizabeth Scott."

At the mention of Elizabeth's name, Donovan snapped back to attention. The referee stepped aside and made room for her to stand right next to Donovan.

"Congratulations, Mr. Darcy." She held the trophy aloft. It wobbled slightly.

Donovan took it from her and gave her a kiss on either cheek, as was customary. "Thank you, Miss Scott."

She smiled, a welcome sight.

At once, everyone around them burst into applause and celebration. Henry produced a bottle of champagne seemingly from nowhere and commenced spraying anyone within ten feet with foam.

With his free arm, Donovan grabbed Elizabeth around the waist and scooped her off her feet.

"Donovan! What are you doing?" She squealed and clutched at his shirt, holding on for dear life.

As if he would drop her. She seemed to weigh less than the trophy.

"Saving you. Whenever Henry is on the winning team, things tend to get rather messy." He whisked her away from the center of the celebration, handing the trophy off to one of his teammates as he passed, a hulking chap by the name of Alfie who always served as Position Number One. Elizabeth squirmed against him, so he tightened his grip on her waist. "Hold still."

"I will not hold still." She swatted ineffectually at his shoulder. "Donovan, put me down. Put me down right now."

During the match—somewhere among the whack of mallets and his stolen glimpses of Elizabeth standing on the fringes of it all, looking stunningly tragic—a revelation had hit Donovan. Simply put, he'd had enough.

Enough of the witty repartees, the flirtations, the near misses. Enough of this carnal need he had for her that, despite all his efforts to eradicate, refused to go away. Enough of the waiting, the endless waiting.

He wanted her.

Now, while she was his. Before they went back to London and she continued hiding herself away at the Barrows' town-home—just across the street, not more than a stone's throw away, but what felt to Donovan like a world apart.

"I'll do no such thing. We had a deal. If my team was victorious, I'd have you all to myself until the ball tonight. I'm claiming my prize." He carried her toward the main house, eager to slip away before his teammates noticed his absence and tried to drag him back for a victory celebration. The echo of his footsteps on the tile floor was the only sound Donovan heard when he reached the foyer, with Elizabeth still wiggling in his arms. Wiggling aside, he could feel every inch of her frame pressed against his. He wasn't about to let that go without a struggle.

Having her now—*right now*—hadn't been his original intention when he'd suggested the wager. He'd thought they might go on a picnic or saddle up a pair of the gentler horses and take a ride through the forest. He'd had a mind to show her the trees he'd climbed as a boy and the trail where he'd first learned to ride a bicycle.

Such innocent aspirations would have to wait, he'd decided. This restlessness that had taken over him since he'd first set eyes on her could not. Not another bloody minute.

He clenched his teeth in determination as he rounded the corner to the hallway leading to his wing.

Ah, blessed silence.

They were truly alone.

"Put me down, Donovan," she huffed. "I'm not a prize. I'm a human being."

"A woman." He slowed to a stop outside his suite of rooms and slid his hand up her torso, the gray silk of her dress slipping through his fingers like water, and paused just before they reached her breasts. "I'm painfully aware."

Her gaze fixed with his, and he saw fire there. Her brown eyes had gone molten. From anger? Or from something else? Donovan wasn't altogether sure, but he most definitely had a preference.

He'd never forced himself on a woman before, and he wasn't about to do so now. As much as he wanted her, he needed to know she wanted him just as badly.

"Anyway, as I recall, I refused to take that bet." She righteously lifted her chin, but there was a tremor in her voice.

"But I won. Doesn't that count for something?" He set her down gently. Just as he removed his hands from her, he sensed a tremble course through her.

But once free, she stayed right where she was. Only inches away. Close enough for Donovan to become lost in the scent of her. He paused for a long inhale. Her skin was delectable. It carried the fragrance of ripe berries nourished by the summer sun.

Elizabeth's beautiful face filled with color—a soft, rosebud pink. Her sudden bashfulness made Donovan's heart beat with a swift ferocity.

He was aware of little else but that scent, the flow of his blood and the rush of mounting desire sweeping through his body. He was nearly crippled by it. He wanted to touch her… anywhere. Everywhere.

He reached up and stroked the side of her cheek with a tender touch of his fingertips. "You're a difficult woman to sweep off her feet, Elizabeth Scott."

21

You're a difficult woman to sweep off her feet.

Elizabeth forced out a laugh. She heard herself say "I guess you'll just have to try a little harder, then."

But everything inside her seemed to scream something entirely different. *Consider me swept.*

Donovan leaned in to kiss her, his intentions more than apparent in the sultry, determined look in his eyes. In the serious set of his jaw. He hadn't been joking when he'd said he was ready to claim his prize. He'd been dead serious.

She hadn't been teasing, either. She was no man's trophy.

Her hands lifted, poised to push him away. But as his mouth came down on hers, she heard Donovan growl. She'd never heard such a sound pass his lips before. It was so atypical of him—it bespoke of such a lack of self-control—that Elizabeth heard herself groan in response.

Her hands, moments ago ready to shove him backward, splayed over his solid chest and worked themselves down… down…until she was tugging frantically at his shirt, pulling it loose from the waist of his pants.

He tore his mouth from hers long enough to pull his shirt over his head, and Elizabeth had to remind herself to breathe. She tried not to outright stare, but it was oh-so-difficult. His body was beautiful. *He* was beautiful. Every perfect inch of him.

The muscles that his snug-fitting polo uniform had only hinted at were on full display. Up close and personal, this time. He was sun-kissed, lean and powerfully built—surprisingly so, even after the glimpse she'd caught of him through Jenna's window. Elizabeth's first thought was that she'd had no idea just what kind of flawlessness had been hiding under those suits and ties he always wore.

Her second thought was that the sight of him half-undressed had clearly caused her to go mad. Because her fingers were now tugging on Donovan's belt, unbuckling it and pulling it loose.

Donovan leaned into her, planted his elbows on the wall on either side of her head and watched her unbutton his pants, his expression one somewhere between fascination and pure, unadulterated satisfaction. "Are you trying to drive me mad? Because it's working brilliantly."

She was dimly aware of him reaching for the doorknob as she unzipped his fly. What had come over her? She'd never acted this way in her life.

"Elizabeth." His voice was rough. Once again, the thought of him losing his ever-present control sent a tingle up Elizabeth's spine. "Either you come inside this bedroom right now or I'm going to lift you up and carry you in myself."

She laughed and his jaw hardened. True to his word, he wrapped his hands around her waist and scooped her up, moving his hands up her dress and along the backs of her thighs in the process.

His fingers slipped inside her panties, and a riot of sensations skittered through Elizabeth's body, most of them concentrated in the area between her legs and all of them pleasant.

Donovan kicked the door closed behind them, and she wrapped her legs around his waist before he could put her down. His fingers were teasing her, tormenting her, but she somehow managed to speak. "Look at you, sweeping me off my feet again. This is becoming a habit."

"Mmm." It wasn't so much a word as a low groan of gratification.

He carried her to the nearest surface. Elizabeth wasn't even sure what it was. A dresser, maybe? Her gaze was locked with his, and everything in the periphery was becoming hazier with each passing moment. The only thing she was fully aware of was the darkening of his eyes—warm, rich brown with hints of gold. His eyes were strong, almost hypnotic. And they seemed to see inside her, to her core.

She blinked, suddenly dizzy, and tightened her grip on the edge of the dresser or whatever it was.

"Elizabeth." Her name was barely more than a sigh on his lips.

"Donovan." She swallowed, unable to articulate more than that single word.

He cradled her face in his hands and ran the pad of his thumb along her bottom lip. Slowly, gently, until she thought she'd go mad with wanting.

"Kiss me," she whispered, stunned she'd somehow found the ability to string two words together. "Please."

She tilted her face toward his, and he responded with an identical tilt toward hers. Deliberate, slow, as if to prolong her desire. She felt his hardness pressing against her as he leaned into her, felt his breath coming quick in the rise and fall of his chest. And his fingers, once again slipping inside her, making her limp with pleasure.

"Please," she all but whimpered. But the word barely left her mouth before it was swallowed up in his.

The kiss was demanding, urgent, as if they were making up for lost time. Elizabeth's heart pounded, struggling to keep up, until Donovan brushed the hair back from her face. His lips slowed, softened and made a careful trail down the side of her neck.

His hair smelled of soap and cool, clean air, and it tickled her nose. She giggled.

Donovan pulled back to look at her. There was an unmistakable challenge in that look. "You're laughing."

He reached behind her and unzipped her dress, the echo of the zipper slicing though the sexual tension of the dimly lit room like a knife. "Give me five more minutes and you won't be laughing."

Her sleeves slipped off her shoulders, and the silky fabric of the dress pooled around her waist.

Five minutes? Try five seconds, she thought as his hands—and his glorious mouth—made their way toward her breasts. She was helpless. She could do nothing but surrender. With her hands buried in his hair, she released a sigh of pure pleasure. Her eyes drifted closed, and she leaned her head back.

It made contact with something hard. The wall?

"Ouch." She opened her eyes and found Donovan eyeing her with concern.

His hair was adorably rumpled. Bed head. And they hadn't even made it to the bed yet. "Are you okay, love?"

The endearment caught her off guard, but somehow made her glow, from deep in the pit of her stomach to the tingly sensation making its way across her flesh. "I'm fine. More than fine."

Donovan pressed a gentle kiss on each of her shoulders. His lips were velvet soft. And hot. So very hot. "Perhaps we should move to a more comfortable location. There's a bed right over there, after all."

"A bed sounds nice."

He took her hands and ran his thumbs in lazy circles over the insides of her wrists. "Yes, it does."

She was melting. Any minute she would surely dissolve into a puddle on the floor. She slipped her hands free, slid them down the back of his pants, across the smooth skin of his backside, and pushed them the rest of the way down.

Donovan stepped out of them and kissed her again. His lips were hungry, seeking. Patient.

At first.

As soon as their breathing grew quick again, he pulled away. "Come to bed with me," he said on a ragged inhale. "Now."

He wove his fingers through hers and took a step backward. Elizabeth slid off the edge of the dresser as her dress fell in a dainty pile at her feet.

Donovan's eyes flashed, and he took her in his arms, covering her mouth with his as he led her backward toward the bed. Elizabeth ran her fingertips over the length of his body as they went, making her way across his lithe muscles in a glorious exploration. Just when Elizabeth was convinced she couldn't wait any longer, he pushed her gently back onto the covers.

Donovan stood beside the bed and paused, his gaze roaming over every inch of her exposed body, taking its fill. "God, you're beautiful."

Elizabeth felt no self-consciousness or hesitation. On the contrary, her skin felt as though flames were licking across it. Then he moved over her and rested his hands on either side of her head. She was surrounded by him, and still, it wasn't enough. She wanted to touch him, to feel him, to delight in that smooth, hot skin. She held her breath in anticipation as she let her hands skim lightly over his firm chest, roam past his flat stomach and follow the fine line of hair leading to his erection.

Donovan's lips parted as he groaned, and his eyes closed. He lowered his body onto hers. Elizabeth was at once overcome. She felt every inch of him pressing against her. He filled her senses. Even so, her fingers gripped his shoulders, pulling him closer. She wanted more. More of him. She wanted everything.

"Elizabeth." He gave her the gentlest kiss, as though she were made of glass. Then he said her name again, as softly as a sigh. "Elizabeth."

She couldn't get enough of it, the sound of him speaking her name.

Ah-lizabeth.

She wanted him to say it over and over. "Say it again," she murmured.

"Elizabeth," he said. She could feel him smiling against her lips.

"Mmm. Nice."

"Elizabeth, open your eyes."

She obeyed and found him staring down at her with a look so tender it made her heart ache.

"Do you want me?" he asked.

"Yes," she whispered. Her voice was barely louder than

the pounding of her heart. Or was that his? She'd lost track of where her body ended and his began.

"Tell me." His gaze bored into hers.

"I want you, Donovan Darcy. I want all of you."

With one sure push, he was inside her, filling her, reaching every part of her. At last. His every movement, every whisper was a caress that reached into her soul, soothing old wounds and awakening sensations in her she'd never before experienced. And, as she gave herself up to him, Elizabeth Scott had the oddest feeling that she'd finally discovered the place she'd belonged all along.

What now?

The thought wormed its way into Elizabeth's unconsciousness even as she snuggled against Donovan's chest and let her gaze roam down the length of their legs, still tangled together after the entire afternoon in bed.

Donovan kissed the top of her hair and drew her closer. "My God, Elizabeth." He buried his face in the crook of her neck and gave her shoulder a gentle nip.

"I know." She sighed—a sigh of pure and utter contentment. It was outrageous how wonderful she felt. She should have been at least a little embarrassed by the way her body had all but sung under Donovan's careful attention. On the contrary, she was fulfilled to the point of giddiness.

Except for that nagging question.

What now?

A line had been crossed. They'd all but obliterated the line. Multiple times.

"What's gotten into that gorgeous head of yours, love?" Donovan whispered into the crook of her neck. "I can hear the wheels turning."

There was that endearment again. Elizabeth hated it.

That wasn't altogether true. She actually loved it. But she very much hated the way she loved it.

As much as she reveled in how she felt in Donovan's arms, in his bed, the prospect of what would happen once they left his bedroom and stepped out into the real world terrified her.

As wonderful as this was, how could it possibly last?

She swallowed. "Nothing, really."

"Elizabeth." He pulled back and looked at her, his eyes narrowing with concern. "I've just spent the better part of a day making love to you. And now I can feel you slipping away."

Slipping away? It was both the first and last thing she wanted to do.

What had she done? Things were too far gone now. There was no turning back. How would she show under him at dog shows now, knowing what it felt like to have him inside her? Not only inside her, but part of her, under her skin?

And even if she could take it all back, would she?

No, she realized. She couldn't, even if she wanted to.

"I'm not going anywhere," she murmured, willing it to be true, and kissed the corner of his mouth.

"Good," he half groaned. "Because neither am I."

Elizabeth felt herself growing light-headed again, being swept away by another rising tide of desire.

She planted her hand against his chest and pulled back, breathless. "Except the ball starts in less than an hour. I should probably get ready."

"Bloody hell." Donovan's head fell back against the headboard. "I forgot. Do we have to go? I've a mind to skip it altogether."

"As appealing as that sounds, you're the host." She moved to slide off the bed.

"I suppose I am." He caught her by the wrist and drew her back for one last kiss. It was slow, intoxicating, and she felt herself slipping under a spell of longing once again.

"Donovan." She shuddered. "If you don't let me go, your aunt Constance is going to come storming in here in a couple of hours and find us together in this bed."

"All right." He chuckled as he released her. "But I want you right back here, Miss Scott, before the last guest leaves the ballroom."

She held on to that tantalizing thought as she prepared for the ball. After a bubble bath and a minor struggle to tame her hair into a chignon with a minimal amount of tendrils coming loose, she stepped into the glorious Marchesa gown Jenna had convinced her to purchase at the Bridal Market. The corset tied at her lower back with a smooth satin ribbon. She anchored it with a bow, glancing at her reflection in the mirror over her shoulder. Miles of spun-gold chiffon fell over her hips, to just above the floor. She twirled around and her hand fluttered to the delicate rhinestone belt at her waist, and she was hit with a startling realization.

She was actually excited about the ball.

She inhaled a steadying breath. She'd been so busy preparing herself for the worst—to feel like an impostor in a room full of Donovan's peers—that she couldn't even pinpoint the moment when she'd begun to feel the first stirs of anticipation. Surely it had been sometime this afternoon, between kisses and sighs.

She was going to a ball.

With Donovan Darcy.

A soft knock sounded on the door that joined their rooms, followed by the silky smoothness of Donovan's voice. "Elizabeth."

Ah-lizabeth.

A trail of chills made its way up Elizabeth's spine. "Yes?"

"Are you ready, love?"

She swung the door open. "Are you?"

Donovan drew in a sharp inhale as he took in her appearance. "Oh, my."

She smiled, pleased to see him unnerved. As perfectly enticing as Donovan Darcy was when he had his wits about him, he was even more appealing when he was thrown off-kilter.

He reached out and grazed the sweetheart neckline of her gown with his fingertip, then groaned.

Off-kilter.

Most definitely.

"Good God." He shook his head and ushered her toward the hall with his hand in the small of her back. "We need to leave. Now. Before I change my mind."

Elizabeth smiled and fell in step beside him. She couldn't help sneaking sidelong glances in his direction as they headed down one long hallway after another, presumably toward the ballroom. Donovan was perfection in a tuxedo. She really should have expected it, given the fact that he pulled off the whole charming-Englishman thing with such panache. But good grief. In a tuxedo, the effect was mind-blowing. The man made James Bond look like a poseur.

Donovan caught her watching him, and he winked at her.

A surge of something hit her straight in the chest with such force it was almost painful. It was so foreign, it took Elizabeth a moment to put her finger on just what it was. She had to fight back the sting of tears when at last she identified it—happiness.

Against all odds, this—Donovan, the two of them together—made her happy.

"Have I told you how beautiful you look this evening?" he asked as the sound of music drifted into the hallway.

"You mentioned it a time or two." Her voice shook, as did her hands. Was this what happiness did to a person?

He pulled her close and gave her a tender kiss on her temple. She was growing accustomed to the softness of his lips against her skin. At times, she wondered how she'd never missed it before, as if some part of her must have been waiting for him all along.

"Here we are," he whispered as they approached an imposing set of double doors framed by both uniformed butlers and gilded molding.

"More gold," she murmured under her breath.

"Fancy that." And, with a grin, he led her inside the ballroom.

Other than the occasional dog show held in generic East Coast hotel ballrooms, Elizabeth had never set foot in one before. And from the moment the toe of her nude patent-leather stiletto crossed the threshold into the Chadwicke ballroom, she knew with absolute certainty this was no Hilton Garden Inn.

The ceiling was impossibly high and dripped with enormous, tinkling crystal chandeliers as lush and elegant as the multitiered wedding cakes she'd seen in the magazines at Scott Bridal. Crown molding, as white as frosting, surrounded everything in sight. And velvet curtains of the palest blue framed windows that stretched almost from floor to ceiling, showcasing what Donovan called the formal gardens. The name certainly fit. Row upon row of trees had been finely manicured in the shape of giant mushrooms. They were so grand that benches lining a walking path in the shade of the huge trees looked almost like toys.

The scene was so quiet and serene, it almost didn't look real. She'd only been to one place before that had such a dreamy quality about it. The memory of it filled her with warmth.

"It reminds me of the Orangery at Kensington Palace," she murmured, just loud enough for Donovan to hear.

He gave her a knowing smile and curved his hand around her waist. "Perhaps we can go for a walk out there in a bit. After we've greeted the guests, of course. And I've had the chance to dance with you."

"I'd like that." Her heart swelled with anticipation. "I'd like that very much."

"Brilliant."

Elizabeth had been so caught up in the regal surroundings, she'd forgotten all about the dancing. And the guests, who stood clustered in small groups, chatting and plucking delicate hors d'oeuvres and champagne in glasses as fine as spun sugar off the passing trays of smartly dressed waiters. Donovan led her from one group to the next, making small talk and introducing Elizabeth to anyone she hadn't met before.

Through it all, he never took his hands off her, keeping a proprietary hold on her waist or letting his fingertips roam over the exposed skin of her back and shoulders. His hand had just slid up to cup the back of her neck when Helena Robson came into view.

She stood between Henry, Jenna and another gentleman whose back was turned, as he seemed busy talking to one of the waiters. Jenna's eyes lit up as Elizabeth and Donovan approached. Henry waved. Dressed in a red lace gown, so tight that Elizabeth could count every bone in her rib cage, Helena tilted her head and seemed to study the way Donovan's fingertips were playing at the back of Elizabeth's chignon. Elizabeth braced herself for a teeth-baring. Or at least a snide comment or two. But Helena simply smiled sweetly. And, crazily enough, it actually seemed genuine. Elizabeth was only beginning to ponder this when she heard something that chilled her to the bone.

To anyone else's ear, it would have sounded like just another British accent. Upper-crust, refined—not unlike Donovan's in that regard. But to Elizabeth, the difference couldn't have been greater. This was the voice that had whispered in her ear from her worst nightmares, causing her to wake in heart-pounding panic. The voice that had breathed hot against her neck, demanding things from her, as if she owed them simply because she wasn't among society's elite.

The voice that belonged to the man who had ruined her.

She looked at Jenna for a split second, begging for an explanation with her eyes. But Jenna simply shook her head.

Elizabeth's consciousness screamed, *It's him!*

Jenna reached out and touched her arm. "Lizzy, is everything okay?"

The room began to spin as the man standing beside Helena slowly turned around. All the blood drained from Elizabeth's face at the sight of that familiar sneer. Its owner's lip curled with even greater scorn as he took in the sight of Donovan's fingertips playing at the back of Elizabeth's hair.

"Donovan, Elizabeth, allow me to introduce my guest," Helena gushed. She looked as though she had just won the lottery—triumphant, giddy. Clearly, this was the moment she'd been waiting for. She trained her piercing eyes on Elizabeth, giving her a look that left no question as to her motives. "You remember Grant Markham, don't you?"

Jenna coughed on her champagne.

Elizabeth couldn't move, couldn't speak.

This cannot be happening. Not here. Not now. Not when things are finally so perfect.

Markham gave a slight bow and reached for her hand. She was so out of sorts, she could do nothing but watch him take it.

"Elizabeth, what a pleasure to see you again." Markham kept his dark eyes glued to her cleavage as he lifted her hand and, to her horror, lifted it to his lips for a kiss.

22

Donovan watched Elizabeth snatch her hand away from Grant Markham's grasp with such force that her elbow reared back and crashed into his side. The wind was nearly knocked out of him, both literally and figuratively.

"Don't touch me." Her voice was barely audible. Donovan wondered if he was the only one who'd heard it, until she repeated herself loud enough for anyone within a ten-foot radius to get an earful. "Do. Not. Touch. Me."

Donovan had no idea what was going on. He'd known Grant Markham for years. He wouldn't have called him a friend, really. More of an acquaintance who ran in the same circles when he was in England. While Donovan had never found him altogether pleasant, he couldn't imagine what he'd done to elicit such a reaction from Elizabeth.

A stunned silence fell over the group and made its way across the ballroom. Jenna's face grew pale, without an ounce of color in her cheeks. Donovan was vaguely aware of his aunt Constance watching, wide-eyed, from a short distance away.

Henry cleared his throat and chuckled, obviously in an attempt to bring some levity to the moment. "So, I take it you two know each other."

"Oh, yes." Grant Markham set his gaze on Elizabeth in a way that made Donovan's blood boil. It bordered on leering, really. And it didn't sit well. "Elizabeth and I are old friends. Intimate friends, you might say."

Intimate? With Grant Markham?

It wasn't the sort of thing a man liked to hear about the woman he was sleeping with. Ever. But hearing it while the sheets on his bed were still warm from their lovemaking made it sting all the more.

And wasn't Markham *married?*

Rage churned in the pit of Donovan's stomach. He couldn't believe what he was hearing.

Thankfully, the look of disgust on Elizabeth's face told him she couldn't believe it, either.

"That is completely untrue, and you know it," she seethed. Her voice was laced with panic. Her eyes darted to Donovan, as if pleading for help.

He'd never felt so powerless in his life. Not only was he at a loss as to what to do, he didn't have the first clue what he was even up against. Instinct told him to take his fists to Markham and pound him into the ground. A lifetime of good breeding told him to get to the bottom of things first.

He glanced around the ballroom and found every pair of eyes glued to the scene. Why in God's name did everyone love a scandal so much? "I think we should all calm down for a moment," he said.

Elizabeth took a step backward, separating herself from his touch. Donovan could practically hear the wall come crashing down between them. She gave him a look filled with raw pain. "Calm down?"

"Lizzy," Jenna said, her voice pleading.

"Yes, I think that's a wise idea. Don't you, Miss Scott?" Markham's mouth twisted into a salacious smile. The very thought of that mouth touching Elizabeth made Donovan physically ill. "After all, some of us present have secrets. Documented secrets. Secrets that I'm sure you would prefer to remain hidden. I'd be happy to discuss things with you in private, if you wish."

Elizabeth's eyes darted around the group. She looked as panicked as a hunted animal.

Something was most definitely wrong here, and it seemed as though it went far beyond an implied intimate relationship, the idea of which Donovan had quickly come to realize was bollocks.

"I've a nice room just a stone's throw from here." Markham, who'd clearly detected Elizabeth's alarm, took a step toward her, seizing upon it. "Why don't you come with me and we can take up where we left off last time? Or we can stay here and I can share some most interesting things with our host, Mr. Darcy. Choose carefully, Miss Scott."

"Oh, my." Helena smiled into her champagne glass. "This is awkward."

Donovan stepped in front of Elizabeth, placing himself between her and Grant Markham. He leveled his gaze at Markham. It was a struggle to keep his voice even when fury was simmering beneath the surface of his collected exterior. "Elizabeth is not going anywhere with you. Do I make myself clear?"

Markham gave a noncommittal shrug. Beside him, Helena bit her lip. An attempt to look contrite, no doubt. Donovan knew better. This mess had her name written all over it.

"Very well, then." Donovan cleared his throat. "You've upset Miss Scott. I believe an apology is in order."

He turned, expecting to find Elizabeth behind him. But she was gone.

"Bloody hell!" Other than his voice echoing off the tall ceiling, there wasn't a sound to be heard in the ballroom—not so much as a whisper. Since the dancing had yet to start, even the musicians stood silently behind their instruments.

Donovan was well aware of the fact that he was making a spectacle of himself, but he was beyond caring. The damage had already been done.

He spun back around. Markham was shaking his despicable head. "Pity about her running off like that just when things were getting interesting. Although what I find more interesting is that someone of your stature has chosen to get his thrills by toying around with one of the Great Unwashed. She's a bit beneath you, don't you think? Although I can certainly see the appeal."

Helena coughed, choking on a sip of champagne.

Consumed with rage, Donovan nearly overlooked the telltale slip of Helena's carefully arranged composure.

"I would have thought my darling Helena would be more suited to you. What a pity she's otherwise occupied tonight." He reached out and stroked Helena's bare shoulder with a deliberate graze of his fingertips.

Donovan's neck grew hot. He was on the verge of losing it completely, in front of everyone. And he didn't give a damn. He slid his gaze toward Helena, and the guilt-stricken look in her eyes told him all he needed to know.

"You're sleeping with him, aren't you?" Donovan spat. "Is that how you convinced him to come here and embarrass Elizabeth?"

She reached for his lapels, clawing at him in obvious desperation. "But I did it for you. Don't you see? You had to know the truth about her...."

Donovan was so angry, he could barely see straight. But his vision must have been better than he thought, because when he drew his fist back and aimed it at Markham's face, it made contact with startling accuracy. There were a few gasps, and somewhere he heard his aunt Constance wail his name, but mostly the only sound in the ballroom was that of Markham landing with a thud on the polished floor.

Jenna gasped.

"And he's down for the count," Henry muttered. "Good party, mate. The best. Really."

Donovan knew Henry was only trying to defuse the situation, but he was too far gone to stop now. He gave his throbbing hand a good shake, then aimed a murderous look directly at Helena. "As for you..."

"Donovan." She threw up her hands. Champagne sloshed out of her glass and down her arm. She didn't seem to notice. "I know this is all a shock, but you needed to know. Elizabeth is not what she seems. She's not good enough for you."

"Stop. Stop talking right now." He stalked toward her until she was backed up against the nearest wall. Out of respect for Henry, he lowered his voice before speaking again. "I can't believe what you've done to get that man to come here and do your bidding."

The color drained from Helena's face, and she dropped her gaze to her feet.

"Oh, Helena. Really?" Henry shook his head. He didn't appear shocked at his sister's behavior so much as disappointed. And when he spoke, he made no effort to do so in a quiet tone. "You slept with him? You *slept* with him. He's married, Helena. But I'm sure you already know that, not that you care. This obsession you have with Donovan has made you lose your senses. What you've done makes you a whore in the most literal sense. And you think Elizabeth isn't good enough for him?"

She looked past her brother and gave Donovan a final, pleading look.

He couldn't stand the sight of her another minute. "I want you gone. And let's be clear—you are no longer welcome in my home."

He turned back toward the ballroom entrance. All he cared about now was finding Elizabeth and getting to the bottom of this catastrophe.

A hand fell between his shoulder blades. He turned to find Henry behind him.

"She went that way, mate." He pointed his champagne glass toward the exit that led to the garden.

Donovan exhaled an exasperated sigh and searched Henry's face. For what, he wasn't exactly sure. Guidance? Encouragement, maybe? All he found there was the sad awareness that his sister had orchestrated the current state of affairs. Jenna stood with her gaze swiveling back and forth between the two of them, by all accounts stunned into inactivity.

Donovan shook his head.

"Don't worry about me, mate. Go get her." Henry nodded toward the door.

He cut a path through the crowd. All the people who'd yelled and cheered him on to victory on the polo field that morning stood by in silence and watched him go.

Donovan's head swam with nonsensical questions. Why was everyone just standing there? Why wasn't anyone doing anything to help?

He knew he was making little sense, but coherent thoughts were rarely the hallmark of a desperate mind. And his was most definitely desperate.

The jog across the length of the ballroom seemed endless, and he was out of breath when he spun out of the double glass doors into the cool air of the formal gardens. Twilight had fallen. Floodlights shone from the ground, strategically aimed to illuminate the artistic shapes of the trees, but otherwise the garden was bathed in darkness.

Donovan squinted but saw no sign of Elizabeth. Not even a glimpse of the shimmery gold of her dress. At a loss, he headed down the walking path, gambling on the idea that she wouldn't stray onto the lawn with her elegant high heels.

The gamble paid off.

He found her on the farthest bench down the path. She was curled into a ball, with her arms wrapped around her legs. The full skirt of her dress billowed around her, and her bare feet peeked out from its hem. Her shoes lay discarded on the gravel.

Even in her distress, she was lovely. With her bare shoulders caressed by moonlight, she took his breath away.

He took a steadying inhale and came to a stop directly in front of her. The daggers she shot at him with her eyes told him in no uncertain terms he wasn't welcome to sit beside her.

"Elizabeth, we need to talk." His tone was calm, deliberate. A sharp contrast to the riot of emotions going on inside him.

"Are you sure you want to talk to me? You don't want me to *calm down* first?" She waved her arms around, motioning toward the trees that stood as silent witnesses to their exchange. "Or does it even matter anymore, now that there's no one around to hear?"

He angled his head toward her. "You think I was worried about what those people would think?"

"Weren't you? Isn't that why you wanted me to *calm down?*"

"Please stop saying *calm down.*" His temples throbbed. As did his fist.

"Irritating, isn't it?" She shot him an icy stare.

And in that moment, Donovan realized he'd had enough of fighting with Elizabeth Scott. As far as he was concerned, the two of them should have been wrapped in one another's arms out here in the moonlight. Not fighting. He felt as though the wheels of time had been suddenly reversed and they were back to the way it had been in the beginning, when they could barely carry on a civil conversation.

He exhaled a weary sigh and took a step toward her. "Elizabeth, love…"

"Don't call me that." Her eyes filled with unshed tears. "Not now, please."

At that moment, the first threads of panic wound their way into Donovan's chest. He'd assumed that whatever was going on here could be worked out. She would let him sit beside her, and he would hold her hand and convince her to talk to him. He would listen and eventually kiss the tears from her cheeks. And somehow, they would end up falling back in bed together.

He was beginning to question the probability of things playing out that way. "Elizabeth, talk to me. Who is Grant Markham to you?"

She flinched at the sound of his name.

Donovan's hands balled into fists, and the panic he'd only begun to taste blossomed into full-blown rage. "Did he force himself on you?"

"No," she answered, in a voice that was barely audible. "Not that he wouldn't have liked to."

He jammed his hand through his hair and reminded himself to breathe again. He'd rarely seen this side of Elizabeth. She seemed broken, for lack of a better word. And her demeanor was in such contrast to the strong woman he'd come to know that it terrified him to think what had happened to bring it about.

"He's one of the parents from the Barclay School."

"The school in New York that sacked you?" He remembered with perfect clarity the day she'd gotten the letter. She'd been almost catatonic with grief. It had been the only other time he'd seen her like this.

It had also been the day they'd shared their first kiss, so Donovan typically looked back on it with fondness. He supposed he'd allowed himself to forget about the sacking, to some extent.

"Yes." Elizabeth nodded and stared off into the distance. Her eyes glazed over as she spoke, recounting the details. "His son was one of my students. I gave him a failing grade at midterm—a grade he *earned*—and he was suspended from the lacrosse team."

A small surge of relief coursed through Donovan. Perhaps this was all a school-related misunderstanding gone horribly wrong. He nodded and lowered himself onto the bench beside her.

He considered it a small victory when she didn't object, but rather continued telling her story. "At the parent-teacher conference, Mr. Markham tried to talk me into changing his son's grade. I refused, and…"

Her voice trailed off, and she blinked back a fresh wave of tears.

Donovan slid closer to her, his impatience bordering on the breaking point. "And?"

"And he tried to bribe me. When I turned him down he said, and I quote, 'Women like you—the ones who come from nothing—always have a price.' Then he touched me." She covered her face with her hands.

"*What?*" Donovan roared, ready to leap to his feet, march into the ballroom and finish tearing Grant Markham limb from limb. While doing so would no doubt have proven immensely satisfying, he knew there was more to the story, and if he left now, he might never know the full truth.

Still, it pained him to stay put. "Elizabeth, what exactly do you mean he *touched* you? I need you to tell me what happened and I need you to do it now."

He hadn't meant for it to come out quite so harshly. But it was all he could do at the moment to keep his temper in check. He wondered if Markham was still out cold. Donovan half hoped Grant had come around so he could have the pleasure of relieving him of consciousness once again.

Elizabeth turned sharp eyes on Donovan. "He touched my wrist and moved his fingertips up my arm while he stared at my breasts. It wasn't an obvious attempt at a pass, but it was most uncomfortable. Is that what you wanted to know? Are you happy now?"

Not obvious?

Grant Markham's intentions were obvious enough for Donovan to want to kill the man. He'd tried to buy Elizabeth. And when that hadn't worked, he'd tried to intimidate her into submission.

Donovan's blood churned, pulsing angrily in his ears, in his temples and behind his eyes. He bit down hard on his lower lip to keep himself from cursing.

Stay calm.

"*Am I happy? Of course not.*" Donovan paced back and forth before finally coming to rest in front of Elizabeth. He crouched down, gently touched her chin and forced her to look him in the eye. "What else? There's more, isn't there?"

She nodded. "I responded the only way I knew how. I slapped his face."

He let out a laugh that sounded oddly manic, even to his own ears. "Good girl."

"No, Donovan. It wasn't good. It wasn't good at all. I humiliated him. And he retaliated by humiliating me, in turn. He accused me of trying to extort him. He told the board of directors I'd demanded money to change his son's grade, and I was fired." Her voice had an edge to it now, and her eyes sparked with fury.

What she was saying was ludicrous. Beyond ludicrous. It was impossible. "How can that be? Surely no one believed him. How could he prove such an outlandish accusation?"

"He didn't have to. He's rich and powerful and I'm nobody, Donovan. Of course he won. You don't understand," she spat. "But how could you? This is what I've been trying to tell you all along. We have nothing in common, Donovan. You're one of them."

That didn't sit well with him. Not at all.

He stood and glanced toward the house. Even from here, Donovan could see the ball had resumed in his absence. His guests were dancing and having a grand time, and Grant Markham—the man who'd damaged Elizabeth and reduced her to a trembling shell of her former self—was among them.

No wonder, Donovan thought. No wonder it had been so hard to earn her trust. And it was no wonder he'd lost it again, when she'd seen Grant Markham standing in his home, drinking his champagne.

"I'm sorry. I had no idea." He reached for her hand. It lay limp in his own. "I wish I had. Why didn't you tell me any of this before?"

She leveled her gaze at him. "I don't exactly consider it my finest moment."

"I disagree." He gave her hand a squeeze.

"What?"

"You stood up for yourself. You refused to give in." How he wished he could make her see things the way they really were. She was more powerful than she gave herself credit for.

"But now he's here, Donovan. At Chadwicke." Her lips trembled again. The same lips he'd kissed not long ago. "Helena brought him here to humiliate me all over again. She told your aunt Constance things about me at the polo match. I wondered how she knew so much about my life in America. Now I know—she was trying to get rid of me. What kind of person does that?"

Donovan ground his teeth together. "I've dealt with Helena. You have my word on that."

She took her hand back and wrapped her arms around her legs again. Something in her eyes alarmed Donovan, but he told himself not to panic. Now that he had a clearer understanding of things, he could go about fixing them.

"I can't go back in there. What am I supposed to do now?" Elizabeth turned her face toward him. There was a weariness about her he'd never seen before. It made his heart ache.

Donovan ran his fingertips along the side of her face, and with that one touch, he knew. Perhaps he'd known all along. "I think there's only one thing you *can* do."

"What's that?" Her eyes shimmered with uncertainty.

He smiled. "Marry me."

★ ★ ★

She must have heard him wrong. Surely she had. He couldn't possibly have said those two ridiculous words.

She swallowed, barely able to repeat them. Even in her mind.

Marry me.

Marry me?

Was he joking? "Donovan, be serious."

"I'm dead serious."

"No, you're not. You can't be." But he looked serious. And—oh, God, what was he doing?—it looked as if he was going to kneel right in front of her.

Sure enough, he dropped to one knee in the gravel. Panicked, Elizabeth's only coherent thought was that he was going to ruin his tuxedo if he didn't get up. It was a ludicrous thing to be concerned about at a time like this. Elizabeth could only blame it on her mother and Scott Bridal.

He took her hands in his. She tried not to think about how warm and comforting they felt. Or about how agitated Donovan looked all of a sudden, like a man on a mission. "Elizabeth Scott, will you marry me?"

She could only stare at him in wonder. What in the world was he thinking? A hot flush rose to her cheeks, her heart threatened to pound its way right out of her chest, and she finally managed to answer him. "No."

Clearly, her answer caught him by surprise. He paled and seemed to struggle to keep his composure. "Pardon me?"

"No." That time, it came out a bit more forcefully than she'd planned. But really, the whole idea was so absurd. She simply couldn't help it.

Marrying him was out of the question. Marrying Donovan would mean becoming Mrs. Donovan Darcy, mistress of Chadwicke. It would mean marrying into the very upper reaches of British society. Just the thought of it brought on a wave of nausea.

If she'd overstepped her bounds by trying to fit in at the Barclay School, even thinking about marrying Donovan seemed so far-fetched it was inconceivable.

Even if the idea appealed to her.

Just the tiniest bit.

Stop it. You have no business even entertaining his proposal. You're the one who dresses the brides. You always have been. You'll never marry the handsome prince yourself.

Of course she wouldn't. People like Donovan didn't even think she was good enough to educate their children.

"No," she repeated. "I can't marry you."

Donovan winced. He gently released her hands before rising to his feet. "Elizabeth, you must allow me to tell you how ardently I admire and love you."

Unable to hear another word, she cut him off. "Stop. Please."

He crossed his arms and looked down at her with thunderstorms gathering in his eyes.

"I can't marry you, Donovan. The very notion of it is crazy. Look what a mess my presence has created after only one weekend. Your family would be horrified. I can imagine the look on your aunt Constance's face if she ever heard we were engaged." Elizabeth shuddered. Aunt Constance was a handful, even when she was trying to be civil.

Donovan waited a long moment before responding. When at last he did, he'd managed to rein in the temper that still showed in the tightening of his posture. "I'm a grown man. My aunt will not choose whom I marry. If that were the case, I'd have married Helena or one of the dozen or more of her clones years ago. And as for the rest of my family, Zara adores you. Surely you recognize that?"

"Yes, I do, but..."

He'd begun to pace back and forth like a caged animal. He spun on his heel and stopped. "But what?"

Elizabeth suddenly had difficulty swallowing. Why were the reasons so difficult to articulate? Couldn't he see them for himself? "Your peers, Donovan. Your friends. I'm from a completely different world. Good grief, Grant Markham is standing in your ballroom right now."

A vein throbbed in Donovan's temple. "Henry is my closest friend, and he considers you a goddess. Hell, he's half in love with your sister. And if you'd stayed with me long enough back there, you would know that Grant Markham is no longer *standing in my ballroom*. He's flat on his back. It will be a cold day in hell before he or Helena ever set foot in my home again."

At that, something stirred inside Elizabeth. She did her best to ignore it.

"All of this will be a moot point once you're my wife."

Ignoring the *something* suddenly became easier. "What do you mean?"

"I mean that once we're married, people—Aunt Constance, Helena and the like—will leave you alone. It will be too late to keep us apart. You'll be my wife, and that will be the end of it." He stated it so matter-of-factly.

Hearing it put in such a way hurt Elizabeth's heart. Perhaps growing up in the shadow of Scott Bridal had clouded her judgment, but she'd never imagined being proposed to in such a manner. "How romantic. Pardon me while I swoon."

"Romance? Is that what this about? Because I'll romance you to the ends of the earth." His voice bounced off the trees and echoed in the darkness. "For God's sake, we just made love. That meant something to me. And I know it meant something to you, as well."

Elizabeth wiped a tear from her cheek. Funny, she hadn't even realized she'd begun to cry. "This isn't the nineteenth century. Just because we slept together doesn't mean you have to marry me."

"That's not what's going on here, and you know it." He planted himself less than a foot away from her. "Perhaps you didn't hear me earlier, but I said *I love you*. Look, I know things are complicated. I'd be lying if I said they weren't. I've tried talking myself out of these feelings, but those efforts were in vain. I'm in love with you."

Things were *complicated*. If that wasn't the understatement of the century, Elizabeth didn't know what was.

But did he honestly think he was in love with her?

Her heart pounded, as if struggling to accept his words. Her head, on the other hand, refused to even wrap itself around them. "You're not in love with me, Donovan."

He looked at her with a smile of affected incredulity. "Do you propose to tell me how I feel?"

"You're not in love. A man in love doesn't try to convince himself otherwise. You're a man accustomed to getting what he wants. And right now, what you want is me." It was her worst fear, spoken aloud.

Donovan's jaw visibly clenched, but his gaze grew tender. So tender, she almost believed what he was saying, no matter how absurd it sounded. "You're afraid. Don't be. I'm right here, asking you to be my wife."

She could feel the heat coming off his body. It drew her in with an almost primal pull until she began to tremble from head to toe. She closed her eyes and basked in the warmth of him. She was on the verge of giving in. It would be so easy to just say yes.

Yes, I'll marry you.

It lingered there, on the tip of her tongue. She was surprised at how sweet the *yes* tasted, like honey.

But somewhere in her consciousness, she was well aware it was *too* sweet. This…all of it…was too good to be true.

It would never work. We'd kill each other. Or worse, end up hating one another.

Whatever the two of them were feeling wasn't real. It could only be an illusion—just part of the afterglow of really great sex.

And it had unquestionably been great. More than great. Elizabeth had certainly never experienced such passion before. But the best part had been that in the midst of all that heat, there'd been an undeniable tenderness. The things Donovan had whispered in her ear as he'd moved inside her and the way his hands had lovingly caressed every inch of her body were almost enough to make her believe he loved her. She probably *would* have believed it until Markham showed up.

His presence was an ugly reminder of exactly who she was and where she came from. And that place was a world apart from Chadwicke.

She would never belong in a world like Donovan Darcy's.

"You don't love me, Donovan." She swallowed and had to force her next words from her mouth. "You don't love me and I don't love you."

He flinched, as surely as she'd slapped him across the face like she had Grant Markham. "I see."

Elizabeth stared somewhere above his head, unable to meet his gaze.

"Your feelings on the matter are clear. I suppose I should be ashamed of my own since they're obviously not reciprocated. Forgive me for suggesting such a preposterous arrangement."

She simply nodded, turned around and headed back toward the house. Tears were flowing freely down her face now. She was incapable of stopping them. Her only hope was to make it to her room before she completely broke down.

To her great relief, Donovan didn't try to follow her.

But he said her name one last time as she fled. "Elizabeth…"

Ah-lizabeth.

It was almost her undoing.

Almost…

23

"A simple heads-up would have been nice. You disappeared after the ball, and I was worried sick." Jenna plunked her suitcase down on the bed, perilously close to Elizabeth's pillow.

Elizabeth, curled among the blue brocade covers with Bliss and all four Border terriers, lifted her head. The barest hint of sunrise drifted in through the lace curtains of the Barrows' guest room. "Jenna, when did you get back?"

"Just now. Henry brought me." She frowned down at Elizabeth. "Are you still wearing that gown? Look at it! It's going to be ruined."

As far as Elizabeth was concerned, a ruined Marchesa gown was the least of her worries. "It doesn't matter anymore."

Jenna sank down on the bed. "Lizzy, what happened? You ran out of the ballroom, and the next thing I know, the butler tells me you left in a cab."

The cab. Elizabeth barely remembered climbing inside, clutching Bliss and her hastily packed overnight bag. The ride back to London had cost her over two hundred British pounds. She didn't even want to think about how much that was in U.S. dollars. She didn't care. She hadn't for a moment considered sticking around to ride home with Donovan. Not after all that had gone wrong.

"Lizzy, Donovan is a mess. What happened between you two? I can't help you if you don't tell me what happened." Jenna sighed.

She closed her eyes. This part was so difficult to talk about. "Markham was there."

"I know. I saw him." Jenna rested her hand on Elizabeth's arm. "I also saw Donovan pound him into the ground with his own blue-blooded hands."

"Did that really happen?" Elizabeth remembered Donovan mentioning something about Markham being flat on his back in the ballroom, but she wasn't entirely sure how he'd ended up that way. "I wasn't around to see that part."

"Well, it's all over the *Daily Mail*. They even have a piece about Helena being publicly expelled from Chadwicke. Would you like to see it?" Jenna pulled a newspaper from the side pocket of her bag.

"No. Absolutely not." Elizabeth had seen enough of the *Daily Mail* to last a lifetime. "Please tell me I'm not in it this time."

Jenna shook her head. "You're not."

Elizabeth couldn't help but wonder how she'd escaped mention after all that had transpired at Chadwicke. Had it been Donovan's doing? Had he kept her name out of the press, as he'd promised?

"You missed it. Markham crumpling to the ground was something to see. Donovan could have sold tickets." Jenna laughed. "Oh, wait, I forgot. He doesn't need the money, since he's richer than God."

Elizabeth sighed and slumped back into the pillows.

Jenna seized on the gesture at once. "No. Do *not* tell me

that's what this is about. You ran away because Donovan is rich? Seriously? I thought you'd moved past this."

"I did." A lie, if she'd ever uttered one before. "Besides, that's not why I left. I left because Donovan asked me to marry him, and I said no."

Jenna's eyes widened, but all in all, she didn't look quite as surprised as Elizabeth expected she would. That was odd.

"He asked you to marry him? And you said no?" Jenna asked quietly. Calmly. Too calmly, really.

"That's pretty much how it went." Elizabeth fiddled with the rhinestone belt of her ball gown. What was she doing still wearing the thing? She was beginning to feel like some perverse version of Cinderella.

Except she'd left something far more valuable behind than a glass slipper. Elizabeth's chest felt hollow, scraped from the inside out, as though she'd run away from Chadwicke without a sizable piece of her heart.

"Tell me something, Lizzy." Jenna, more appropriately clad in jeans and a fuzzy oatmeal-colored sweater, leaned forward and rested her hands on Elizabeth's shoulders. She looked directly into her eyes. "Do you love him?"

It was the question Elizabeth had been afraid to ask herself since the day Donovan had taken her to Harrods.

Her throat grew dry. Her head pounded. "Yes. I mean, no. I mean, I don't know." She couldn't think. It was all so confusing. "I'm afraid he asked me for all the wrong reasons."

Or maybe she was just afraid, period. Like Donovan had said.

Jenna sighed and squeezed Elizabeth's hand. "I need to tell you something."

Her words, coupled with the serious look on her face, caused Elizabeth to blink and attempt to shake the fog from her head. She tried to focus all her attention on her sister, on the present, but she still felt as though she were only partially there.

Part of her—the best part, possibly—was still back in the garden at Chadwicke. With Donovan.

She blinked and met Jenna's worried gaze. "What is it?"

The question had barely left Elizabeth's mouth when Jenna's lips curved into a bashful smile. "This is the worst timing ever. Please don't be upset, but I just can't keep this a secret from you."

Elizabeth frowned. "Jenna? You're scaring me."

"Don't be scared." Jenna grinned. It was then Elizabeth noticed her sister's blue eyes were positively dancing. In fact, she had a glow about her—a sweet animation to her that made her look more beautiful than Elizabeth had ever seen her. "It's good news."

"Tell me, please." Elizabeth forced a smile. She had a sudden premonition where this was going. But surely she was wrong. It was far too soon, ridiculously too fast...

"Henry and I are engaged," she said.

Apparently it wasn't too fast.

Elizabeth was shocked into silence at the news. Henry and Jenna engaged? How had this happened? She and Donovan had been vexing one another for weeks, drawn to one another, yet both reluctant to admit it. And somehow, in half that amount of time, Jenna and Henry had fallen in love and become engaged. It didn't seem possible.

How could affairs of the heart be so easy for some and at the same time so perplexing for others? Elizabeth found it quite baffling and, if she were truthful, a touch heartbreaking.

"I'm sorry." Jenna bit her lip apologetically and shook her head. "Like I said, the timing is just awful. But I had to tell you."

If ever there was a time to put on a happy face, it was now.

Elizabeth wasn't about to say or do anything to take away her sister's happiness. She beamed as if her life depended on it. "Don't be silly. And don't you dare apologize."

Elizabeth swallowed around the lump in her throat, wanting to say more. But she didn't trust herself to speak.

"I know it seems sudden." Jenna smiled a beatific smile. "But it feels right. It really does."

Elizabeth blinked back a few tears, took a deep breath and gathered herself together. "Of course it does. You're in love. It's wonderful news. I couldn't be happier for you. Honestly."

Jenna's smile wavered. She peered intently at Elizabeth. "You're in love with him. I can tell. You're in love with Donovan Darcy."

This time it wasn't a question.

"It doesn't matter how I feel about him, Jenna." Elizabeth shook her head. She refused to believe she was in love with Donovan. "He doesn't love me."

Jenna blinked. "Wait a minute. He asked you to marry him, but he never told you he loves you?"

"No, he told me," Elizabeth whispered. "But it was too little, too late."

"You want to know if he loves you? If you love him? You want to know if he proposed to you for all the right reasons? Maybe this will give you the answers you're looking for." Jenna slipped her hands into the pocket of her sweater and pulled out an envelope.

Elizabeth's name, written on the outside in Donovan's careful penmanship, taunted her, daring her to open it. She reached for it, then drew her fingers back.

"Go ahead. Take it. He asked me to deliver it to you." Jenna set the envelope on the bed and stood. "I'll let you read it in private."

Elizabeth stared at the envelope for a long moment after Jenna had left the room, both terrified and eager to read its contents. When at last she opened it, the sound of the thick paper tearing was deafening.

She scooped Bliss into her lap and held on to the dog for moral support as she unfolded a single page. It was dated from Chadwicke, at two o'clock in the morning.

My dearest Elizabeth,
You've only been gone from Chadwicke a matter of hours and already the magic that swept over this old estate with your arrival has vanished, leaving me alone with nothing but my thoughts.

I'm sorry I hurt you, Elizabeth. More sorry than I can say. And I apologize for the pain inflicted on you by Helena. I want you to know that I will never allow her to be in a position to hurt you again. And as for Grant Markham...let's just say he's tending to more than a bruised ego.

As much as the actions of Helena and Markham added to your distress, I realize the bulk of the blame for your hasty departure rests squarely on my shoulders.

I went about the proposal entirely the wrong way. What I should have said from the beginning, and what I mean with all my heart, is that I love you. Quite ardently so. Yes, we come from different backgrounds. And yes, the thought of Grant Markham taking anything from you sent my head spinning. But the truth is my head started spinning the moment I first laid eyes on you back in America. I've loved you from the moment I met you.

I won't go on, because you've made your feelings for

me—or rather, lack thereof—more than clear. Do not be alarmed. This is the last you will hear of my affection for you, and I vow never again to repeat the sentiments and offer of marriage which only hours ago were so disgusting to you.

I simply wanted to set the record straight and apologize for proposing an arrangement that obviously pained you to even consider.

—D. Darcy

Elizabeth looked down at the ink-stained pages, but the words were lost behind the veil of her tears.

What have I done?

"Mr. Darcy, sir."

Donovan sat at his desk in his office with his back to the door, ignoring Lawrence. And the window. The sight of the Barrows' townhome was too much for him to bear.

He hadn't laid eyes on Elizabeth since that night over a week ago in the formal gardens. After he'd stormed back into the ballroom to ensure Grant Markham had been sent packing and tell a gaping Aunt Constance to mind her own damned business, he'd returned to his quarters to find her gone. Bliss as well, which had left him with no hope of Elizabeth's return.

"Mr. Darcy?" Lawrence repeated.

"Yes?" he said, to the wall more than to his butler.

"You have a visitor." Lawrence rushed to add, "Mr. Robson, sir."

He needn't have hurried to announce Henry's name. Donovan had all but given up on the notion of Elizabeth coming to him. She'd made her opinion of him abundantly clear when she'd turned down his marriage proposal.

"Send him in," Donovan said absently.

He took a pained breath and steeled himself to face Henry. As much as he cared about his friend, Donovan had gone to great pains to avoid Henry since the announcement of his engagement to one Jenna Scott.

It was a cruel irony—Henry and Jenna had become engaged the night of the ball at Chadwicke. The same night he'd asked Elizabeth to become his wife. Donovan found it most profoundly imbalanced.

He spun his chair around and fixed his gaze on the puppy pen. The four pups were getting so big. Figgy no longer spent all day with them. They were fat, happy and fully weaned. At present, the little scamps were wrestling over a fleece toy shaped like one of London's red city buses—a gift Elizabeth had picked up for them at Harrods Pet Kingdom. Pudding appeared to be on the verge of winning the battle.

The sight of the puppy's sprinkling of freckles gave new life to the ache in Donovan's gut. He averted his eyes just as Henry walked in.

"Blimey." He frowned. Henry rarely frowned, so on the rare occasion he did, it tended to make an impression. "You look like shite."

Donovan scrubbed his hands over his face. "I haven't slept much."

An understatement, to be sure. At Chadwicke, he couldn't even bring himself to go near the bed. It had reminded him too much of Elizabeth. He'd spent a single, sleepless night there before returning to London, where Elizabeth had never been anywhere near his bedroom. As it turned out, it wasn't the sheets, the walls or the furnishings that were haunted by the memory of her. It was his heart. And his heart still refused to rest.

Sometimes Donovan wondered how far he would have to travel to escape the memory of her. Or if such a place even existed.

"Well, your lack of sleep shows." Still frowning, Henry sank in one of the chairs opposite Donovan.

"Thank you," he ground out.

"You're welcome." Henry lifted a brow. "You still haven't heard from her, have you?"

"No, I haven't."

Henry leaned forward, with his elbows on the edge of Donovan's desk. "What exactly happened between the two of you? I can't even pry the details out of my darling fiancée. She just tells me not to worry…that it will sort itself out."

Sort itself out?

Not bloody likely.

If Jenna thought what had transpired between Elizabeth and himself was that simple, she was even more of an optimist than Henry. The two of them were obviously perfect for one another.

Donovan leveled his gaze at Henry. "I wouldn't count on it sorting itself out."

Henry winced. "I feel responsible. My sister did her best to rip the two of you apart with her bare hands. I should have seen it coming, I suppose. I apologize."

"It wasn't your fault." Donovan meant it. To think Henry, or anyone, for that matter, could have controlled Helena even for a minute was laughable.

"I know." Henry smiled, finally. But the grin was gone as quickly as it appeared. "I'm still sorry. I know how you felt about her."

"*Feel*," Donovan snapped.

"I stand corrected." Henry's voice softened. "*Feel*. I know how you feel about her. So, what went wrong?"

Donovan closed his eyes and saw Elizabeth, her bare shoulders caressed by the moonlight, that captivating gown she'd worn fluttering in the night breeze. Then he saw himself dropping to one knee....

He opened his eyes. "I asked her to marry me."

Henry froze for a moment. It was obvious he'd never considered the possibility that he hadn't been the only one to propose recently. He blinked a few times before recovering. "That's quite a surprise. To be honest, I've never thought of you as the marrying type. I am, of course. Always have been." He let out a self-deprecating laugh. "But you?"

Donovan shrugged. "People change."

Because love changes them.

Henry furrowed his brow. "When did this happen?"

"At Chadwicke. The night of the ball." The same day they'd made love, which made it both the best day of Donovan's life and the worst, all at once. Of course, it was also the same night Henry and Jenna had become engaged.

Henry didn't bring up that little coincidence. Thank God. "I imagine that wasn't the best timing, what with Markham showing up."

"So I've learned." The dull pain in Donovan's head, which had become his constant companion of late, throbbed. "Her answer was an unequivocal *no*."

He'd botched it, of course. He'd realized as much even before her fleeing form had disappeared from view. He should have told her he loved her from the very beginning, not the end.

Which was why he'd written the letter. Not that it had helped matters. In it, he'd wielded his love as if it were a weapon. He'd been so proud of his feelings. He'd boasted about his love for her as if it made him superior to her in some way.

It was that very pride that made him act in exactly the way Elizabeth feared.

"You're not giving up." It was a statement, rather than a question. "I've never known Donovan Darcy to give up when he set his mind to something."

"Henry, she doesn't love me."

There was a prolonged moment of silence.

Finally, Henry spoke. "You sure about that?"

Donovan's gut ached. Must they revisit this? "She told me as much."

"And you believe her?"

"Yes." *And no.*

Donovan swallowed.

He considered telling Henry about the letter he'd written in the heated aftermath of the proposal. He thought it best not to mention it, seeing as the fact that Elizabeth had yet to even acknowledge it only added insult to injury.

As if Henry could read his mind, he leveled his gaze at Donovan and said, "I know about the letter."

Donovan ground his teeth together. So this was how it was going to be now that Henry and Jenna were engaged? No secrets? Even worse, were he and Elizabeth destined to have their lives intertwined simply because her sister was marrying his best friend?

Donovan couldn't imagine the agony of standing alongside Elizabeth in a church on Henry and Jenna's wedding day...a day that should have been theirs. The very idea filled him with fresh indignation.

"I suppose the contents of the letter turned up in the *Daily Mail?*" Donovan asked, his voice dripping with sarcasm.

"Relax." Henry held up his hands. "I know nothing about the contents. Jenna simply told me you asked her to carry a letter for Elizabeth back to London."

Donovan lifted a brow. "If you know about the letter, then surely you know I've received no response."

But did he blame her? It wasn't as though he'd repeated his offer of marriage. In fact, he'd gone out of his way to revoke it. Permanently. If memory served, he'd even vowed never to ask her to marry him again.

Henry frowned. "None whatsoever?"

"None." He slammed the diary closed on his desk. The diary was of little use to him now. It was full of meaningless appointments over the course of the following days. Appointments he intended to miss. "It's of no consequence. The matter is over."

"Jenna says—"

Donovan held up a hand. "I've no interest in what Jenna says when Elizabeth herself has already spoken volumes on the subject. She doesn't love me, and she certainly doesn't want to marry me. Case closed. Like I said, it's over."

"Over? Just like that?" Henry didn't believe him. That much was clear.

"Yes." Donovan nodded with great resolution. "Over."

He'd left out the most crucial bit of information. But that was for no one to know but Donovan alone. Part of him wished he could tell Henry the whole truth, but his friend's upcoming marriage to Jenna made such candidness impossible.

By tomorrow Donovan would be gone. Thousands of miles away from Elizabeth Scott.

He was leaving.

On the first plane out of Heathrow.

24

Donovan was gone.

No one had advised Elizabeth that he'd left the city. Not even the *Daily Mail*. Since delivering Donovan's letter, Jenna had kept altogether mum on the subject of Donovan Darcy. The few times Elizabeth had seen Henry, he'd been remarkably quiet and low-key. Elizabeth got the sense the newly engaged couple was tiptoeing around her, afraid to rock the boat any further. If she'd been able to bring herself to talk about Donovan, she would have told them to save the trouble. The boat was beyond rocking. She and Donovan had all but capsized and dropped to the bottom of the ocean.

Jenna and Henry may have been keeping Donovan's sudden disappearance under wraps, but it was far from necessary. She could feel the absence of his presence as if the vacuum he'd left behind resided squarely in the center of her heart rather than in the townhome across the street.

Unless Jenna had spilled the beans, Sue Barrow still had no idea what had transpired during the weekend at Chadwicke and, from all appearances, was afraid to ask, choosing instead to minister to Elizabeth with copious amounts of peppermint tea and biscuits. She was also generous with the amount of time she allowed Elizabeth to groom the Border terriers. Hand stripping the dogs had taken on an almost therapeutic quality, and since returning from the country, Elizabeth had spent hours upon hours with Violet, Hyacinth, Daisy and Rose propped up on their grooming table. Using the upcoming Earl's Court Annual Dog Show as an excuse, she plucked the poor dogs within an inch of their lives.

Jenna's silence on the subject of Donovan had begun the instant she found Elizabeth clutching the letter—that perplexing letter!—and crying into Bliss's fur when she returned from a date with Henry on their first night back in London. For once Jenna seemed hesitant to offer any sisterly advice, which frightened Elizabeth nearly as much as it relieved her. It appeared she wasn't the only one at a loss as to how to respond to the letter.

Elizabeth could think of little else.

She could almost recite the letter by heart. She studied every sentence, and her feelings toward its writer were at times widely different. While he made no secret of the fact that he was indeed very much in love with her, regardless of her feelings for him, Donovan had by no means repeated his offer of marriage. Elizabeth was keenly aware of this fact. She couldn't help but wonder why he was so insistent upon letting her know the validity of his feelings when at the same time assuring her he had no intention of proposing to her again.

He loved her.

She'd almost come to accept it.

He loved her. And he thought she despised him. The end.

Sometimes the pull she felt from the townhome across the street was too much for her to bear. On those nights, Elizabeth would sit in the window seat, waiting for Donovan to appear in the moonlight as he'd done on the night she'd first arrived in London all those weeks ago. On the occasions he did step outside with Finneus weaving around his feet, Elizabeth had watched and waited with her heart in her throat and her breath fogging the window. But Donovan had never looked up. Not once.

And now he was gone.

So when Sue carried in the mail one afternoon and announced a letter had arrived for Elizabeth, she couldn't help the desperate tug of hope she felt that it might possibly be from Donovan. Perhaps he'd written to tell her of his whereabouts. Or maybe he simply missed her. Wherever he was.

"You have a letter, dear," Sue said, aiming an appraising look at Hyacinth up on the grooming table—*again*—as she bustled into the dog room.

"Oh?" Elizabeth's hand shook with anticipation. Or dread, perhaps?

She lowered the grooming scissors before she did irreparable damage to Hyacinth's coat. Their next show was in three short days.

Jenna and Sue exchanged worried glances, leading Elizabeth to believe that Sue did, in fact, know about what had transpired between her and Donovan, the vexing letter included. She tried to muster up at least a morsel of indignation at the thought of Jenna and Sue whispering about her behind her back. But she just didn't have the energy for it.

"Here." Sue held out an envelope.

The envelope indeed looked familiar. But the return address on the thick parchment didn't bear the Darcy name.

Elizabeth looked up at Jenna. "It's from the Barclay School." She lifted her brows in obvious surprise. "Really?"

"Yes." Elizabeth stared at the envelope, confused. "What could they possibly want?"

"You'll never know, dear, unless you open it." Sue gathered Hyacinth in her arms and lifted her off the grooming table. "Come with Mummy. I think you've had enough for one day."

Bliss scrambled up from her nap underneath the grooming table and followed Sue and Hyacinth out the door, likely in hopes of a romp out in the garden. A flicker of guilt washed over Elizabeth. She'd been remiss in walking the poor Cavalier lately, afraid she'd run into Donovan. What would she say? What would *he* say?

She took a deep breath. None of that mattered anymore.

"Lizzy?" Jenna reached out and touched her arm. "Are you going to open it?"

"Oh." Elizabeth ran her thumb over the creamy envelope resting unopened in her hand. "Yes. Yes, of course."

She broke the seal and slid out a single sheet of paper.

Just like last time, she mused. Only now, her movements weren't propelled by fear as they were before. They'd already fired her. Grant Markham had already made good on his promise to exact his revenge. With the utmost effectiveness. What more could he possibly do?

She was perplexed more than anything as she unfolded the letter.

"Read it out loud," Jenna said. "And hurry. The suspense is killing me."

"Okay." Elizabeth cleared her throat. "Here goes…

"Dear Miss Scott,
It has come to our attention that we were remiss in our termination of your employment. After further inves-

tigation, the board of directors has come to the conclusion that you are guilty of no wrongdoing.

Please accept our sincerest apologies for any suffering this matter has caused you. Should you decide to return to the Barclay School, we will find a place for you in the classroom at once.

It is our sincerest hope that you will choose to return at your earliest possible convenience. To that end, please expect a phone call from Dr. Thurston in the coming days with an offer of extended employment and a generous salary increase.

Again, our earnest and heartfelt regret at the manner in which this matter was handled cannot be emphasized.
Sincerely,
The Board of Directors
The Barclay School"

The now-familiar, large swirling signature of Mrs. Grant Markham immediately followed. Elizabeth stared at it, almost unable to believe it was real.

"Oh, my God." Jenna snatched the letter from her hand. *"Oh, my God,"* she repeated, seemingly at a loss for anything else to say.

Elizabeth was rendered speechless. She gripped the arm of the sofa and sank into its cushions, her heart beating wildly as she tried to take it all in.

The Barclay School wanted her back.

They'd admitted right there in black and white that she was innocent.

They'd *apologized.*

It was everything Elizabeth had ever dreamed of, but hadn't once allowed herself to hope for.

"Lizzy!" Jenna squealed, clutching the letter and gathering Elizabeth in a tight hug. "Do you realize what this means?"

Elizabeth shook her head, not sure of anything anymore. The world had been tipped upside down.

"This means you can go home," Jenna whispered, with unshed tears shimmering in her eyes.

Home.

Elizabeth nodded mutely.

"You should come home with me this weekend. We can fly back together." Jenna gave both Elizabeth's hands a squeeze.

A large, emerald-cut engagement ring glittered on Jenna's ring finger. It had appeared there less than a day after the engagement announcement. Elizabeth didn't know if Henry had presented her with the ring when he proposed or if they'd chosen it together.

She was ashamed that she didn't know the details of her sister's engagement. Jenna was her big sister, her closest friend. The two of them should be staying up late, whispering in the dark about all of it—how Henry had asked her, if it had taken her by surprise. She didn't even know if Henry had gone down on one knee, as Donovan had done.

Elizabeth glanced at the ring again, swallowed hard and looked back up at Jenna. "But I can't. The Earl's Court Annual Dog Show is Saturday, and I promised Sue I'd show the Borders. Bliss is entered. I can't miss it."

"Then we'll leave late Saturday night." Jenna beamed. "I'm anxious to get back to the States. I want to tell the family about Henry, but I can't do it over the phone. It's really the sort of thing I need to tell Mom and Dad in person. This is perfect! Can you believe it? You've got your job back. This is such great news. Everything you've wanted for such a long time. Now you can truly put Grant Markham behind you. For good."

Elizabeth stared at her for a moment, still too shocked to absorb it all until she saw a flicker of worry pass through Jenna's gaze. That was all it took to gather herself together, at least enough to respond. "Of course. The best news."

Jenna smiled. "See, everything's going to be okay. You're going home."

Home.

Elizabeth allowed herself to be congratulated and wrapped in another hug. She made every effort to smile, nod and say all the right things.

Home. I'm going home, she told herself with bittersweet conviction.

At last.

But deep inside, she feared she no longer knew where home was anymore.

Plans were made.

Airplane tickets were purchased.

The lease on Elizabeth's old apartment was renegotiated.

Everything was falling into place. She was on the verge of having everything she'd wanted all along.

Then why do I feel as though I've lost everything all over again?

The arrangements had been made with such military-like efficiency on Jenna's part that Elizabeth felt as though her sister were trying to usher her out of the country before the realization could set in that her heart had been broken.

Too late, Elizabeth mused as she exited the Stratford tube station, feeling more like a spy on a secret mission than an out-of-work teacher headed for a job interview. Although, she was no longer technically out of work. Her job at the Barclay

School was ready and waiting for her. And if she boarded the plane in three days as scheduled, her old life would no longer be a distant memory. Once again, she and Bliss would be at home in their tiny Manhattan apartment. London, South Kensington, her shaggy quartet of Border terriers, Hyde Park, Harrods—and most of all, Donovan Darcy—would be part of her past. She could go about her life again and forget that she was once a dog nanny, or that she'd eaten orange cake in the exact spot where Queen Victoria had grown up.

The trouble was, she didn't want to forget. Ever.

The unexpected letter from the Barclay School, along with her imminent departure, had awakened her to a most inconvenient truth—she didn't want to leave London. She felt at home here. More at home than she'd ever felt at Scott Bridal or the Barclay School.

She was well aware of just how crazy that sounded. For weeks now, she'd been fighting against so many conflicting feelings about her surroundings. The gorgeous dog-show grounds at Ashwyn House, Sue and Alan's upscale neighborhood, the Orangery. Even Chadwicke. She'd been prepared to despise all of it, and yet...

She'd come alive here and hadn't even realized it until she'd thrown it all away.

Enough of that.

She may have lost Donovan, but that didn't mean she had to lose England. She would never be mistress of Chadwicke, but that didn't mean she couldn't call herself a Londoner. She just had to find a way to make London hers.

Step one was finding a teaching job. She loved teaching. Sure, the Barrows would probably be happy to let her nanny their Border terriers until their muzzles turned gray with age. But Elizabeth couldn't let her experience with Grant

Markham keep her out of the classroom. Even in London. Hadn't there been enough casualties from that phase of her life?

Even so, she'd kept her first interview for a teaching position in London a secret. She'd deal with trying to explain herself to Sue, Jenna and the rest of her family if and when she got the job. In the meantime, she had a copy of the letter from the Barclay School in the once-controversial Prada handbag. Right next to her résumé.

She looked around at the colorful graffiti that covered most of the surrounding townhomes and smiled. She was far from South Kensington, far from Chadwicke, but she was still in London. And she felt comfortable on these streets, perhaps even more so than when she walked the dogs on the sanitized, well-kept sidewalks of Sumner Place.

The school secretary at the secondary school in Newham appeared far happier to see her than Mrs. Whitestone ever had at the Barclay School. She welcomed Elizabeth with a warm smile and a cup of tea before leading her into the headmaster's office.

The headmaster, a Dr. Grant, seemed far younger than Ed. Good. Perhaps she could avoid giving this one near heart failure. "Ah, Elizabeth Scott. From the prestigious Barclay School in America. We're pleased to have you."

She juggled her teacup in one hand and shook Dr. Grant's huge hand with her other. "Thank you very much."

He waved toward an empty chair on the opposite side of a desk piled high with folders, books and papers. "Have a seat. Please. And tell me how you've come to find yourself on this side of the pond."

Elizabeth swallowed. She'd known this question was coming. She'd even rehearsed a rather vague, nonspecific answer during her ride on the tube. Somehow, though, her carefully planned words were failing her.

"Um." She cleared her throat. "Well, I was given four weeks' leave. One of my students earned a failing grade, which meant he would miss an important sporting event. When I refused to pass him without merit, it caused quite a scandal."

"Not surprising." Dr. Grant shook his head. He didn't look the least bit fazed. Why had she allowed the Markham mess to loom so huge in her mind? If she'd simply told Donovan about it up front, could all the pain and heartbreak have been avoided?

Maybe.

Probably.

Her heart ached with fresh hurt. A month ago, she wouldn't have believed it, but it seemed that Donovan Darcy was far more difficult to forget than Grant Markham. Impossible, in fact. "My position has been reinstated, but I've grown quite fond of London. I have a letter from the school absolving me of any wrongdoing if you'd like to see it." She reached for her handbag.

"Not necessary. Problems like that are all too common in certain circles, I'm afraid. You won't find that kind of trouble here. We have the opposite situation—under-involved parents rather than control freaks. Truancy and the like. I've worked in all sorts of schools, and it's been my experience that everyone has issues—the haves, the have-nots and everyone in between. There's always something. Do you suppose that means we're not all that different after all?" Dr. Grant eyed her from across the cluttered expanse of his desk.

We're not all that different after all.

She'd thought she was so righteously above it all—money,

status, the trappings of wealth. Had Donovan been right when he'd called her a snob? She'd thought the fact that she was poor somehow made her more honorable. But being honorable had nothing to do with a person's bank balance.

Did it?

Elizabeth nodded. "I believe you may be right, sir."

Elizabeth clicked off her cell phone and slid into her chair at the breakfast table on what was scheduled to be her final morning in London. She and Sue were to show the dogs in the afternoon, and by midnight she was to be on a flight bound for the States. By Monday, the Barclay School would expect her back in the classroom.

But she'd just received the phone call she'd been anticipating for two days. Finally. She'd gotten the job in Newham. She was a real Londoner.

"I have news." Elizabeth stirred sugar into her teacup. She was so excited about her announcement that her hands were shaking.

Jenna and Sue looked up from their breakfasts and exchanged glances.

"Oh?" Jenna asked.

"What is it, dear?" Sue's expression was a little too bright. She probably thought Elizabeth's news had something to do with Donovan Darcy.

It was best to put a stop to that assumption right up front. "I was just offered a teaching job here. In London. I'm staying."

"Really? Are you sure that's what you want? I mean, I'm delighted. Of course I want you to stay." Jenna's gaze flitted to her engagement ring. "But are you sure?"

"What about Mr. Darcy? Does he know?" Sue leaned forward. There was that look again. Everything about her countenance rang with unfettered hope.

"Yes, I'm sure. And no, Donovan doesn't know." And then she muttered under her breath, "Not that he would care."

"Nonsense. Of course he'd care." Sue spread her toast with a thick layer of orange marmalade.

Elizabeth suppressed a snort. "I assure you he hasn't lost a moment's thought to what I'm doing these days."

Ever the diplomat, Jenna chimed in. "This is wonderful, Lizzy. I was a bit worried about getting lonely over here by myself."

"By yourself? What about Henry?" Elizabeth winked.

"How do you suppose your family will feel about the two of you moving to England? Won't your mother miss you?" Sue asked.

How would her mother feel about Jenna marrying a well-heeled British barrister? Sue would likely hear their mother's squeals of ecstasy from all the way across the pond.

"I imagine they'll miss us. And I'll need to find someone to take over my job at Scott Bridal. But I'm sure our family will be very excited about the wedding, particularly our mother."

Jenna and Elizabeth exchanged glances. And snickers. If the thought of the wedding itself filled Elizabeth with panic, seeing Donovan…in a church…wearing a tuxedo, so be it. She would simply learn to grin and bear it, for her sister's sake.

"Jenna's right. Our mother will be beside herself with excitement," Elizabeth said.

"That's good to hear. And Mr. Robson is such a fine young man. When your family finally gets a chance to meet him, I'm sure they'll be delighted." Sue flicked open her newspaper and spread it out on the table.

Elizabeth glanced at the *Daily Mail* and frowned. She'd

given up on gossipy newspapers and magazines of late. It might be weeks before she'd even care if Jennifer Aniston was pregnant with triplets. If ever.

"Mr. Robson? You mean Henry?" Jenna winked and sipped from her enormous paper cup from Starbucks. The reappearance of her ubiquitous Starbucks cup was a sure sign Jenna mentally had one foot back in the States already.

"Yes, Henry." Sue made a face, as if she were uncomfortable referring to him by his first name. "Has Henry said anything about Mr. Darcy? I can't help but think he'll return before long."

Not again.

Sue aimed a cautious-looking glance at Elizabeth. "Perhaps you two could get reacquainted?"

Much to Elizabeth's chagrin, the sound of Donovan's name stung. *Get over it. Get over him. You have a brand-new life. Be happy.*

"That's not going to happen," she said a bit more sternly than she intended. "Sorry. But I can't put my life on hold and wait around here for Donovan to return. No one knows where he is, not even Henry. Right, Jenna?"

"Right," Jenna answered quietly. "He doesn't know where Donovan is or when he'll be coming back. Henry is actually quite upset about his mysterious disappearance."

"It *is* rather odd." Sue sighed and went back to turning pages. "Elizabeth, dear, you may not be my dog nanny any longer, but you must stay here. That bedroom is yours for as long as you wish."

Elizabeth reached for one of her hands and squeezed it tightly. "Thank you, but I'm paying rent this time."

Sue acted as though she didn't hear, which seemed strange. Elizabeth had been prepared for an argument where the rent was concerned. But Sue's unwavering gaze was suddenly fixed on her newspaper with great intensity.

"Jenna, tell Henry he no longer needs to worry about Mr. Darcy's whereabouts." Sue paused. "I know where he's been. And I know where he is right now."

"What?" Jenna sat forward in her chair.

Elizabeth's heart leaped to her throat.

She told herself to calm down. Donovan Darcy was no longer any of her concern. In fact, she didn't even want to have this conversation. She would simply push her chair away from the table and walk away.

But her legs refused to move.

"It's right here in the paper." Sue jabbed at the newsprint with her pointer finger. "The Society page."

That damned newspaper.

"Oh, God." Elizabeth's stomach churned. "Who's sitting in his lap this time?"

She tried to prepare herself for the answer. He was Donovan Darcy, after all. The most eligible bachelor in England.

Of course, if she'd said yes that night at Chadwicke, Donovan would no longer be a bachelor. He would be hers.

"Why don't you see for yourself?" Sue turned the paper around and slid it across the table.

Elizabeth couldn't bring herself to look at it, fearing the worst. What if he really was with another woman already? And—*oh, please, please no*—what if it was Helena?

"Look, there's a photo," Jenna said.

Elizabeth took a fleeting glance. There was Donovan, alone, standing in front of a familiar-looking building. She squinted. It couldn't be what it looked like. It just couldn't. But her blood began to thunder in her veins at the possibility.

Breathe, just breathe.

She found she had to concentrate on the simplest tasks of inhaling and exhaling as Jenna read the caption aloud.

"Donovan Darcy in New York earlier this week, where it's been rumored he delivered a check from the Darcy Family Trust to a private school in Manhattan. Mr. Darcy will be back in London today, where in a last-minute substitution, he's scheduled to serve as a judge at the Earl's Court Annual Dog Show."

Stunned silence fell over the kitchen.

The soft panting of the dogs as they sprawled on the cool tile floor was the only thing that could be heard for several long minutes.

Jenna was the first to speak. "I don't believe it. Lizzy, you know what this means, don't you?"

Elizabeth knew exactly what it meant.

The Barclay School had absolved her of any wrongdoing. They'd put it in writing. They'd called and given her an offer that was nearly double her former salary. She'd been given the chance to go home to everything she'd known and loved.

She had the freedom to choose what kind of life she wanted...all because Donovan had bought back her reputation.

"This is crazy." Jenna reread the caption. "Seriously crazy. I wonder how much he donated."

"An enormous sum, I suppose. Mr. Darcy is known for being quite extravagant when it comes to charity." Sue leveled her gaze at Elizabeth.

Extravagant didn't even begin to cover it.

She closed her eyes, and at once she was back at the Orangery, eating that delicious cake, her insides all fluttery as Donovan winked at her. What was it he'd said about his money that day?

Shall I give it all away, then? Since you find it so objectionable.

He'd done more than simply give away a big chunk of his money. He'd gone all the way to New York, written a check for what was certainly a staggering amount and somehow negotiated an arrangement for the Barclay School's board of directors to eat crow and apologize. All for a woman who'd refused him, who'd taken his love and flung it back in his face.

These weren't the actions of the type of man she'd accused him time and again of being. She should have known better, especially after she'd learned that he'd raised Zara after their parents had been killed. Why hadn't she allowed herself to see him as he really was?

Elizabeth was struck with a jolt of humility that hit her right in her core. She grieved for every saucy speech she'd ever given Donovan about his wealth, his arrogance, his entitlement and most especially about how she didn't love him.

But somewhere in that grief and humility, she felt a stir in her soul. A stir of hope. Donovan had a made an extravagant gesture. One that spoke of extravagant love.

Perhaps it wasn't too late, after all.

25

Donovan was drowning in Scottish terriers. They were everywhere. As soon as he finished judging a class of four, five
more marched in right behind them. He wondered, not for
the first time, what had possessed him to agree to this judging
assignment. He'd barely had time to shower and change on
the way in from Heathrow, and his jet lag had reached brutal
proportions. He could barely keep his eyes open.

Then again, that was nothing new. Sleep was elusive these
days. The secret was to just keep moving. Stay as busy as
possible. So long as his mind was occupied, he might have a
remote chance of keeping stray thoughts of Elizabeth Scott
from creeping into it.

Elizabeth.

He assumed she was on her way back to America by now.
He'd seen to it that the damage done by Grant Markham had
been rectified. It was his parting gift to Elizabeth, his way
of making up for all that had gone wrong. Buying her job
back had been easy enough, particularly when he'd shared
Markham's whereabouts Bonfire Weekend with his wife.

And now the Barclay School would soon have a new library. Funded by an anonymous donor, of course. The written apology he'd insisted on had cost him new lab equipment for the science program. Worth every penny.

The slate had been wiped clean.

If only it would have been as easy to undo all the emotional destruction Markham had wrought. Perhaps then he and Elizabeth would have stood a chance.

"Mr. Darcy? Are you ready for the next class, sir?" Mr. Deas, the ring steward, cleared his throat.

Who knew how long he'd been trying to get Donovan's attention? He really needed to get his wits about him.

Donovan nodded and tried to shake off some of the exhaustion as he made his way to the center of the ring.

He turned around and straightened his cuffs as he watched the next group of dogs make their entrances. More Scottish terriers. Good God, this wasn't Scotland. How many of them could there be? He exhaled a tense breath and let his gaze travel down the row of jet-black dogs, one lined up right after another.

Then he was forced to do a double take as he spotted a familiar pair of legs in the background. Legs that most assuredly did not belong to a dog. Scottish terrier or otherwise.

Donovan's breath caught in his throat. He would have recognized those legs anywhere, even before the single afternoon he'd spent caressing them, kissing them, entwining them with his own. Still, he let his gaze linger on the sun-kissed skin of Elizabeth's calves, knees, and what he could see of her thighs beneath the flirty hem of her dress, for a prolonged moment. He was reluctant to let his eyes wander to her face, he realized as his pulse kicked up a notch. He was worried about what he would find there...sadness, anger or, worst of all, indifference?

Finally, he met her gaze.

Amid all the chaos of the show—the barking and howling of the dogs, the constant, steady hum of blow-dryers and clippers, and the fleeing glimpses of paws of all shapes and sizes, trotting alongside sensible shoes zipping from one ring to another—Donovan could sense Elizabeth's breath catch in her throat. Heard it as if she'd been standing directly in front of him. Saw it in the subtle widening of her beautiful eyes. Felt it as keenly as he felt every beat of his own heart, every breath he took himself, as if she were still a part of him.

Because she *was* still a part of him. And very likely always would be.

Before he could process her bittersweet expression, he looked away. He still had a job to do, after all, and he was determined to do it properly. He directed his attention back to the Scottish terriers and sent them around together as he strode back to the middle of the ring for a better view...where he stood and looked right through the dogs. They could have been kangaroos for all the attention he paid them.

Donovan was profoundly aware of Elizabeth watching him from outside the ring, together with Sue, Jenna and Henry. What he didn't know was what Elizabeth was doing there. Or any of them, for that matter. The only one he'd expected he might see today was Sue. Henry's name didn't appear anywhere on the judging schedule. Of course, if he'd shared his plans with Henry before he'd gone to America, perhaps Henry would have done the same.

Donovan cast a questioning glance at Henry, who answered with nothing more than a shrug and a slight smirk.

Wonderful.

Donovan directed his attention back to the waiting Scotties.

"I'd like to see the first dog on the table, please." Donovan waited for the handler to arrange the Scottie in a solid stack, then ran his hands over the dog's back.

Why is Elizabeth here?

The dog was a bit swaybacked, he noted, and congratulated himself on having his wits about him enough to make a fair assessment.

She should be back in America by now.

"Around please, and I'll have the next dog on the table," Donovan said to the Scottie's handler. His external actions were in no way compatible with what was going on in his head.

He made quick work of evaluating the rest of the Scottish terriers. Once his hands were buried in wiry terrier fur, he found he was grateful for the familiar task of grading coat condition, assessing thickness of bone and discerning skeletal structure. There was a comfort to it—the routine, the knowledge that he was in his element. Because the presence of Elizabeth Scott meant that once he stepped outside the ring, he wouldn't be anywhere near his comfort zone.

Her appearance at the show had thrown him. He'd been fully prepared to wait weeks, months, to see her next at Henry and Jenna's wedding. They'd yet to announce the date, but whenever it was, Donovan would have at least had time to ready himself—to prepare for the ache that would hit him like a two-by-four at the sight of her.

Who was he kidding? There was no way to prepare for such an onslaught of feelings. The only way to survive it with his sanity intact was to simply put his nose to the grindstone and get through the day the best he could.

Easier said than done.

He strode over to the judge's table to mark his pick of the Scotties in the book, wishing he could to go to Elizabeth, to speak to her, even for just a moment. Kennel Club rules forbade any interaction between judges and handlers on the day of the show until ring time. And as if seeing her for the first time since his ill-fated proposal wasn't already the epitome of awkwardness, he was actually scheduled to judge Border terriers next.

He should have never taken the assignment. What had he been thinking?

I was thinking she'd be halfway to New York by now.

Donovan recorded the name of the winning Scottish terrier in the book with enough force to drill a hole through the paper with his pen.

Liar.

He clenched his jaw. Somewhere beneath the surface, that was not what he'd been thinking at all. Deep down, deeper than he cared to examine, he supposed he'd hoped for this. Yearned for it...not that anything would come of it.

Donovan distributed the awards to the Scottish terriers with as much fanfare as he could muster before returning to the judge's table. He stood silently, less than twenty meters away from where Elizabeth and Sue stood waiting to show the Border terriers. Elizabeth aimed her dazzling eyes toward him once, and only once, for a split second. Just long enough to make him wonder how the hell he was going to judge her or her dog, as the steward called out, "Border terriers in the ring, please."

Donovan cleared his throat as Elizabeth and Sue lined up, knelt and went to work posing their dogs. He'd seen the schedule and knew there were only two Border terriers entered. Two was a small entry, yet more evidence that had led him to assume Elizabeth wouldn't be making an appearance. So much for assumptions.

Donovan stood with his arms crossed, watching, waiting.

At last Elizabeth looked up. Donovan saw a multitude of emotions in those familiar, fine eyes, along with a dash of determination. She lifted her chin a fraction, and Donovan took the gesture as an unspoken but most definite challenge.

He fixed his jaw and approached her, stopping a few feet in front of the dog at the end of her leash. He glanced at the armband wrapped around Elizabeth's slender biceps. Number eight. The same armband number she'd worn at that first show, back in New Jersey.

Fortuitous, perhaps? Of course not. Since when did Donovan Darcy believe in fate?

"Exhibitor number eight?" He lifted an eyebrow.

"Yes?" Elizabeth's lips quirked into a sly grin, drawing Donovan's attention immediately.

Damn it, he'd missed those lips.

Very much so.

How dare she walk into his ring after all that had transpired, tormenting him so?

"I'd like to see your dog on the table, please." Donovan fumed, extending his arm toward the grooming table in the center of the ring.

This is happening, he surmised.

Whether I like it or not.

Elizabeth fought to steady herself as she walked Rose to the table. She imagined she felt Donovan's gaze from behind, roaming over her hips, her waist, the curve at the nape of her neck...all the places he'd once kissed. Surely she was imagining things. He hadn't looked at all pleased to see her. Surprised maybe, but not pleased.

Elizabeth was beginning to wonder if she'd misinterpreted Donovan's generous donation to the Barclay School. Perhaps he didn't still love her, after all. Maybe he was simply trying to get her out of the country, as far away as possible.

No, that can't be, she told herself, although it was more of a plea than any kind of assurance.

She swallowed around the lump in her throat and steeled herself for Donovan's approach. And suddenly he was right there beside her, and Elizabeth's heart felt as though it would beat right out of her chest. She gripped the edge of the table in an attempt to ground herself, to keep from being swept up in his familiar, delicious scent, the dangerous air he always had about him, his *Donovan*-ness, as she'd come to think of it.

"Good morning, Miss Scott," he said, his gaze glued to Rose's muzzle.

Elizabeth tried to ignore the disappointment that sliced through her. She'd hoped he would continue calling her number eight, that they could have a repeat of their exchange at the show in New Jersey. A fresh start, of sorts.

"Good morning, Mr. Darcy," Elizabeth said, all business, as he checked the texture of Rose's coat. "Welcome home."

No response. Not even a nod.

A chill of panic ran through Elizabeth. Donovan was already making his way to the far end of the table, examining Rose's tail set and the angulation of the stifle. Where was the banter they'd always shared at the table, even before they'd gotten to know one another? What Elizabeth would have given for a saucy recitation of the breed standard right then...

"Do you find her build to your liking?" she asked, heart

thundering in anticipation, and peered up at Donovan through her lashes.

The corner of Donovan's mouth twitched. At last, a crack in his composure. Still, he said nothing.

"What about her hips?" Elizabeth added, looking at him full-on this time. "Too slender, too wide?"

He angled his head, his gaze searching. Elizabeth bit her lip in an effort to keep it from trembling. She felt as if Donovan's penetrating eyes could see straight into her soul, wished they could, so he would know the profound regret she felt about that night at Chadwicke. The night that had begun so perfectly and should have ended so, as well.

If only...

A glimmer of a smile flashed on Donovan's perfect face. "I find her hips to be the perfect size. In fact, I've never before had my hands on such a lovely specimen. Not a single fault, disqualifying or otherwise." He paused, and his jaw clenched. "On the contrary, she seems to be the one who's found fault with me."

He spun on his heel and walked away.

Elizabeth somehow found the wherewithal to lift Rose off the table and execute a suitable down-and-back. She was barely cognizant of what she was doing, had no idea if Rose even bothered to follow along or not. At the end of the down-and-back, she found Donovan was no longer watching. Elizabeth didn't even have a chance to arrange Rose in a final stack. He'd already moved on and was examining Violet on the table, speaking politely to Sue.

Everything was going so horribly wrong.

"Can I have the dogs go round together one more time, please?" Donovan's voice boomed from the center of the ring.

Elizabeth couldn't bring herself to take a step. *What now? Where do I go from here?*

Sue nudged her from behind. "Elizabeth, move. Take a step."

Move. Take a step.

Elizabeth moved out, clicked her tongue and prompted Rose to strut. She moved that dog around the ring like she'd never moved before. A scattering of applause even broke out ringside, right before Donovan pointed at her. "You'll be my Best of Breed today."

Elizabeth slowed Rose to a walk and headed toward the judge's table, dreading this—receiving her ribbon and sash, knowing it meant her time in the ring was coming to an end.

"That's it! You've done it, dear," Sue whispered. "Rose is a Champion now."

"Yes, she is." Elizabeth found it difficult to swallow all of a sudden. Rose was a Champion. She'd accomplished all she'd set out to do in London. Why did the victory feel so hollow?

"Miss Scott, I present you with your Best of Breed rosette and sash." Donovan lifted his hands. The sash was spread over his open palms, and he offered it to her.

Just as Elizabeth reached for it, Donovan gave her a wistful smile, lifted the sash and slipped it over her head.

His every gesture felt like a goodbye. Still, Elizabeth's breath caught in her throat at his sudden nearness. When his fingertips grazed her shoulder, she went weak in the knees. And Sue's words reverberated through her....

Move. Take a step.

She swallowed.

Tell him...just say it...you know about the Barclay School. You know it was him. You know what he did and you love him. You always have.

She licked her lips, drawing his gaze to her mouth. "Donovan, I have to tell you something. I…"

Donovan leaned toward her, and she imagined she could see hope burning in his eyes. "Yes, Miss Scott?"

"I…"

"Excuse me. Mr. Darcy? Miss Scott?" Mr. Deas stepped beside them. The ring steward shuffled from one foot to the other, and his Adam's apple rose and fell, struggling against the collar of his shirt. "I'm sorry to interrupt, but the show secretary would like a word with you both at once."

Elizabeth blinked. "Now?"

"Yes, he indicated it was rather urgent." Mr. Deas shot Donovan a nervous glance. "Sir."

"Well, then. We shall see what he wants." Donovan took a step backward. And all the hope and possibility Elizabeth had felt only moments before withered away.

She passed Rose's leash to Sue and fell in step behind Mr. Deas. They exited the ring in single-file order—Mr. Deas, Elizabeth, then Donovan. Jenna and Henry sent them worried glances as they passed, and a hum rose up from the crowd.

For a moment, she was back in Manhattan, about to follow Mrs. Whitestone into the school principal's office. She didn't know what the show secretary could possibly want with her and Donovan, but she had a definite feeling this was not good. Not good at all.

"I know the way. We certainly don't need an escort," Donovan snapped as he stepped up beside her.

Mr. Deas trembled like a frightened puppy. "Simply following orders, sir."

"I'm not about to be led around like a dog on a leash. Come along, Elizabeth." Donovan planted his hand in the small of her back and hastened their steps until the ring steward was left in their wake.

"What do you suppose this is about?" Elizabeth asked.

"I've a feeling. Don't worry. As out of character as it will be for you, try not to say anything. Just let me do all the talking, okay?" Donovan looked down at her, and for an instant, things felt like they had before.

Elizabeth nodded. She wished she could stop time, keep things exactly as they were. "I still need to tell you…"

"Here we are." Donovan gave her a tight smile as they approached the show secretary's table. He bent down and whispered, "Remember. No talking."

"Ah, Mr. Darcy. Miss Scott." The show secretary—a Mr. Akins, according to the Kennel Club name tag attached to his lapel—sat with his hands folded in front of him. A classic headmaster pose, if Elizabeth had ever seen one.

Clearly, she and Donovan were in big trouble.

Donovan smoothed down the front of his jacket and adjusted his cuff links. Cool and composed, as always. Elizabeth couldn't fathom how he did it. "You've got three seconds to explain what this is about. I'm supposed to be judging Jack Russell terriers at the moment."

"Mr. Darcy." Mr. Akins flinched. Evidently he hadn't expected Donovan to go on the offensive. "Sir, it has come to our attention that you and Miss Scott here are involved in an intimate relationship. As I'm sure you're aware, such a conflict of interest is a violation of the ethics rules of the Kennel Club."

Oh, no.

"Actually, that's not necessarily true…." Elizabeth stammered.

Donovan turned razor-sharp eyes on her.

She closed her mouth. For once.

Donovan dragged his attention back to Akins. "First off, the nature of my relationship with Elizabeth Scott is none of your concern."

"I'm afraid the *Daily Mail* has made it *their* concern. And that makes it hard for *me* to ignore." Mr. Akins slid his gaze to Elizabeth and back to Donovan.

Elizabeth's cheeks burned with heat. She knew all those ridiculous pictures of her and Donovan would come back to haunt her. She just knew it.

Akins adjusted his green blazer that sported the Kennel Club logo stitched neatly beside the left lapel, a move no doubt designed to remind Donovan that as show secretary, he had the backing of the entire club behind him. "Since the nature of your relationship with Miss Scott is—"

"Enough." Donovan's voiced echoed off the walls of the show arena. "Mr. Akins, since you seem to possess *intimate* knowledge of the Kennel Club's regulations surrounding judging and ethics at Championship shows, I can only assume you are familiar with the rules outlined in Section F.1., number 30 of the current guide to show regulations."

Elizabeth furrowed her brow as Akins's face went blank.

"Perhaps you need a reminder?" Donovan raised his brows and waited.

"Perhaps, sir."

"F.1., number 30 is the section of regulations that pertains to emergency judging situations. Do you have any idea what they might say?"

Akins swiveled his head toward Elizabeth and then back to Donovan. "I suppose I could venture a guess."

"I suppose you could. But just in case, let me spell it out

for you. In an emergency judging situation, the customary rules no longer apply. In other words, Miss Scott could have waltzed into my ring and shown a dog I bred myself and there would have been no conflict of interest." Donovan inched closer to Elizabeth. She could feel the heat coming off him, and she wanted so badly to bask in that heat.

Elizabeth had never been the type to yearn for a man to rescue her from her troubles. She'd always been independent, fought her own battles. But she couldn't help but watch, feeling equally fascinated and comforted, as Donovan had transformed into a crusader. Defending her, defending himself, defending *them*.

It was rather stirring.

"Mr. Akins, now do you understand why I'm upset by the implication there's been any wrongdoing here?" Donovan crossed his arms.

"Certainly, sir. I apologize to both you and Miss Scott." The show secretary stood and bowed at Elizabeth.

She was about to wave a hand at Mr. Akins and tell him not to worry about the misunderstanding when Donovan spoke again. This time, something in his tone gave her pause.

"All that being said, I'll save you the trouble and embarrassment you seem to be worried about, Akins." Donovan glanced at Elizabeth, and her insides went inexplicably frosty. "I hereby withdraw from judging the remainder of the day."

Wait…what?

"Henry Robson is in attendance, and I'm sure he would be glad to step in. Good day," Donovan said, bowing to Mr. Akins and then to Elizabeth.

Her heart stalled to a stop.

And before she could take it all in, he was gone.

★ ★ ★

Morning turned into afternoon, and Elizabeth stumbled through all of it as if in a daze. Since the Border terrier judging was complete, and Sue opted to show Rose in the Terrier Group ring as she always did, Elizabeth's duties as a dog nanny were officially over. All that remained for her to do before she went back to her life as a teacher was to show Bliss. As soon as she stepped into the ring one last time, it would all be over.

And she wouldn't see Donovan again until Henry and Jenna's wedding.

If he bothered to attend.

Clearly, he wished never to see her again. He'd disappeared after the confrontation with the show secretary, and Elizabeth hadn't laid eyes on him since. Granted, she hadn't had time to search the show grounds for him. But he'd withdrawn from judging. Didn't that speak volumes?

Why hadn't she told him how she felt the moment she had the chance? Why had she wasted what little time she'd had with him flirting, dancing around what she really wanted to say? It had all happened so fast. Her head was spinning.

So it was with a heavy heart that she stepped into the Cavalier ring.

"Good luck, Lizzy," Jenna whispered. "Go get 'em."

"Yes, best of luck." Sue nodded. "Bliss looks beautiful, dear. I think you really have a chance this time."

Elizabeth glanced at Bliss, then at the other Cavaliers lining up behind her. Of course she thought Bliss was the prettiest dog in the ring, but that was always her opinion, regardless of what the other Cavaliers looked like. Bliss could have been shaved bald, and Elizabeth still would have thought she deserved the top prize. In the dog-show world, the only thing that mattered was the judge's opinion. In this case, that judge was a Mrs. Pitt. And she was quite...*rotund*. To such an extent that she maneuvered around the ring via electric scooter instead of the power of her own legs.

Elizabeth was relieved the schedule had been changed—yet again—and Henry would not be her judge. It was all starting to feel so incestuous. More than anything, she didn't want to get called in front of the show secretary again. Certainly not without Donovan there to come to her defense. So the idea of Mrs. Pitt—in all her motorized glory—judging Cavaliers was simply delightful to Elizabeth.

She didn't realize just how delightful it would be until Mrs. Pitt slipped the Best of Breed sash over Elizabeth's head, followed an hour later by the Group First sash.

"Oh, my gosh. I don't believe it. This can't be happening." Elizabeth drifted out of the Group ring, into the waiting arms of Jenna and Sue. "Did Bliss just win the Toy Group?"

"She certainly did." Sue pulled back and smiled wider than Elizabeth had ever seen her smile before. She looked even happier about Bliss's victory in the Group ring than she did about Rose's new Championship status. "And now you get to compete for Best in Show! You could win, dear. Fancy that?"

"You're going to win." Jenna nodded. "I can just feel it. So many of those other dogs were frightened by the judge's scooter. But Bliss wasn't fazed a bit. You've got it in the bag. This is so exciting."

In any other circumstance, Elizabeth would have asked Jenna when she'd started to care so much about dog shows, but she didn't have it in her to tease her sister. The day had been filled with such highs and lows, she thought she might lose her bearings altogether. And she still had to show Bliss in the Best in Show ring!

She barely had a minute to run a comb through Bliss's Blenheim coat before ring time. For what seemed like the umpteenth time since she'd woken up that morning, Elizabeth wished she could slow the hands of the clock. She wanted the opportunity to savor the moment. Instead, she bustled to the ring with Sue calling out a steady stream of advice along the way.

"Line up last, dear. Let all those big dogs get in front of you so they don't pile up behind you as you go around the ring together."

"Yes, ma'am."

"And don't rush Bliss. Just let her find her stride."

"Okay." Elizabeth's stomach fluttered with the beat of butterfly wings.

"And most of all, have fun." Sue gave her a final hug and pushed her through the ring gates.

Fun.

Elizabeth shook her head. She'd forgotten that was why she did all of this in the first place—to have fun. How had she managed to lose sight of that?

Right here, right now, she was in the Best in Show ring with her dog. Opportunities such as this rarely came along. Most handlers could only dream of competing for Best in Show. And Elizabeth had certainly fantasized about it happening, more than once. And now those dreams were coming true. She was going to enjoy every second of it.

Her only regret was that Donovan wasn't there to see her compete.

One dog from each Group—the best of the best—strutted around the ring as the announcer called its breed name. First came the Gundog, then the representative of the Hound

Group, followed by Working, Pastoral, Utility and Terrier. And then at last, the Toy Group.

"And from the Toy Group, we have the Cavalier King Charles spaniel," a voice boomed from the loudspeaker.

This was her cue.

"Ready, Bliss?" Elizabeth smiled down at her dog and then stepped into the spotlight.

A rush of applause filled her ears as she led Bliss around the ring. The cheers of the crowd welled up inside her, carried her and her beloved Cavalier while they posed on the plush green carpet, went through the examination on the table and ran around in what seemed like endless circles behind the other dogs—all of them bigger, all of them flashier and certainly all of them more experienced at showing than Bliss.

But in the end, none of that mattered. Because when it was time for the announcement of Best in Show, Mrs. Pitt sat in her scooter and pointed her judicious finger directly at Elizabeth.

"What?" Elizabeth had to fight mightily to remain upright. She trembled from head to toe and would have thought she'd only imagined the outcome if not for Jenna and Sue jumping up and down and cheering just beyond the ring gates.

She glanced at Henry, who stood at Mrs. Pitt's side. He winked at her and then, and only then, did it really sink in.

Best in Show.

Tears pricked the corners of Elizabeth's eyes. She scooped Bliss into her arms, accepted the congratulations of the other handlers and waited to be awarded her rosette.

She hoped Henry would be the one to slip the sash over her head. He was soon to be family, after all. It seemed more personal than accepting the award from one of the other judges, none of whom she really knew.

They approached her as a group—Mrs. Pitt wheeling down the center of the ring, flanked by Henry and the judges from the Hound, Pastoral, Working and Utility Groups.

"Congratulations." Mrs. Pitt smiled. Her smile faltered when it became apparent she didn't know Elizabeth's name. "A very nice win, um, exhibitor number eight."

And suddenly, Donovan stepped out from behind the group of judges. "I believe her name is Miss Scott, not number eight."

Elizabeth's body reacted to his presence before her brain could process that he was actually there, standing in the Best in Show ring. Her pulse boomed so loudly that she was certain he could hear it. She clutched her chest, as if to keep her heart from leaping out of her throat. "Mr. Darcy."

He smiled down at her, a poignant smile that seemed to say exactly what she was feeling inside. *Oh, how I've missed you.* "I was hoping you'd allow me to do the honors. That is, if you don't mind?"

Elizabeth shook her head. "I don't mind at all. In fact, I love the idea."

As I love you.

Donovan turned to Mrs. Pitt, who handed him the Best in Show sash.

"Why don't we allow Mr. Darcy and Miss Scott a moment of privacy?" Henry said and guided the rest of the judges toward the ring gates as if he himself were a herding member of the Pastoral Group.

One of the judges yelped as they left the ring. Elizabeth thought perhaps Mrs. Pitt had run over his foot. She wasn't entirely certain.

Donovan stepped closer to her, until he was scarcely a whisper away.

Elizabeth gazed up at him, convinced more than ever she was living in a dream. "What are you doing here? I thought you'd gone."

"Leave? And miss this?" He winked. "Not likely. I withdrew from judging because I didn't want to cause you any further scandal. I know how you loathe that sort of thing. Our experience with the *Daily Mail* wasn't for naught. But I've been here all along. You said there was something you wanted to share with me, so where would I go?"

"Oh," she murmured, blinking back tears.

"But first things first. I'm pleased to award you Best in Show." Donovan's voice was rough, clogged with emotion. It seemed to scrape Elizabeth's insides as he slipped the shiny sash over her head.

A single tear slipped down her cheek. As Donovan reached up and wiped it away with a swipe of his thumb, the thought occurred to her that she would gladly let him wipe away all her tears from this day forward.

She returned Bliss to the floor and ran her fingertips over the words *Best in Show* emblazoned across the sash in purple satin letters. As exciting as it was, Elizabeth no longer wanted to discuss the show. She had more important things to say. Things that could no longer wait.

"I know it was you, Donovan." Elizabeth rested a hand on his chest. That simple contact sent her head reeling. "You're the one who got my job at the Barclay School reinstated. It was in the *Daily Mail*."

Donovan's lips curved into a wistful grin. "Bloody newspaper. That donation was supposed to be anonymous."

"You've given me everything—my reputation, my future." Tears were flowing freely now down her face. "You've given me my life back."

He tilted his head, reaching out to tuck a lock of her hair behind her ear, before cupping her cheek. His earnest expression held her spellbound. "I suppose I have."

She leaned into his hand as he swept her tears away. "The trouble is, Donovan, I don't want that life anymore. My life is here now. In England. I've accepted a teaching job here, in London."

His lips curved into a smile. Its genuineness made her heart soar. "Is that so?"

"Yes. I'll be teaching English at a secondary school in Newham."

"Newham?" His eyebrows shot to his hairline. "That's a far cry from the Barclay School."

"Do you have a problem with that?" *Please, no. Haven't we moved beyond such matters?*

"Not at all. The school in Newham is actually a pet project of mine. The Darcy Family Trust supports many of their programs." He crossed his arms. "Surprised?"

She wasn't sure if she'd ever loved him as much as she did right at that moment. "No, actually. I'm not. Pleased, yes. Surprised, not so much. I've misjudged you before. I won't be making that mistake ever again. I love you, Donovan. I've loved you all along."

"Miss Scott, am I to assume you've had a change in heart? Because my wishes are unchanged, but one word from you will silence me on this subject forever." He smiled at her again, and suddenly she no longer felt like crying. In fact, she had the overwhelming feeling that everything in her world had slipped into place.

"You...silent? Not for long, I'd wager," Elizabeth whispered, her voice breaking. "Ask me again, Donovan. Please."

And then, right there in the Best in Show ring, Donovan

Darcy dropped down onto one knee. With dog hair clinging to his trousers and a collection of stunned members of the British dog fancy as his witnesses, he asked Elizabeth Scott to become his wife. Again.

This time, she said yes.

★ ★ ★ ★ ★